I0665739

ON THE OTHER SIDE
of the
GOLDEN GATE

BY
RA LYNN LONEWALKER

Who keeps a diary?

I don't know the statistics of who or what percentage of us keeps a diary, but I know firsthand how exciting it can be to read a diary. Writing, whether it's a movie script, a novel, an interview, sports commentary, or poetry, is done with intent. The intent to be published and to entertain. Yet when readers hold a diary in their hand, they hold something that was written privately, something intended for a very small audience. A diary can be interpreted as a therapeutic release in written form. It's a private world not usually meant for the world outside.

A diary can be where the diarist writes privately and without discretion to fight their fears or discover why they feel shame. It can be where they express anger and frustration. A diary is a world unto itself that doesn't have the same rules or judgments we get from our secular world. The diary can serve as a catharsis, a confessional. It's a brainstorm on paper, a place for the irrational to meet the rational. It's an honest place that has no fear of the critic or the censor.

When we read a diary, we aren't peeking over the shoulder of the diarist. We are entering the inner psyche where we can excavate the buried heart. Here in the deep mind are the spontaneous thoughts and emotions that find their expressions without the clumsiness of searching for the perfect descriptions. What we read in a diary is the first-hand description of moments as they happened, or maybe written shortly after. The writing is usually the most genuine report from the perspective of the diarist.

The intimacy of a diary is seen in a series of vivid personal experiences that reveal extraordinary people in their everyday interactions. When we read a diary, the ordinary becomes special because of the differences between the diarist's life and our own. We are different in, among other things, time, circumstance, encounters, genetics, geography, and experiences. It's our differences that make us interesting. Sometimes we find bound diaries that were never intended to be published. They fascinate us.

I suggest that a diary is the account of a person who may have questions we never think to ask, or maybe it's a scribbled account of the diarist's fears, which we may not understand because the diarist lived in another time. Suppose you find a diary written by an elderly wife who lived in Nagasaki, Japan, and when you read the last line, *I am afraid of the bombs they are going to drop*, you already know that an atom bomb landed on Nagasaki August 9, 1945. That would be a dramatic last line in any diary, but we know she was directly under the falling atomic bomb. Her diary somehow survived what she couldn't survive, and her story gives us insight into an extraordinary moment before an atomic weapon changed the world we live in.

What you are about to read is a fictitious diary written by a woman who has survived breast cancer and is dealing with life after being disfigured by the treatment and surgery. Although Hope is a fictional character, much of her story is true. She tells her story as she lives her every-day life. Her diary offers us a glimpse into how it is to be human and live in fear and what it is to make mistakes. We also see forgiveness, both given and received. Her aim is to explore the idea that the most important thing about living is loving and validating your love.

Enjoy Hope's diary.

Dedicated to Sara, Mike, and Pam

THEIR SOULS MAY HAVE MOVED ON FROM THE PHYSICAL, YET THEY HAVE LEFT ME WITH MANY BLESSINGS.

ON THE OTHER SIDE
of the
GOLDEN GATE

M y skin is generously shaded with colors, but mostly it's soft brown. Some people have called me a light-skinned black woman, but I don't see myself as black or white. I don't see race in myself. I just see me. I'm a blend of my parents: a white mother and a black father. Although they contributed to my appearance, I never knew them at all.

When I stand in front of the mirror, what I see are my imperfections. Some small, almost undetectable birthmarks, some wrinkles and veins that decline to stay deep under my brown skin. But it's a large, particular scar that bothers me. It has left me looking unbalanced. I have two arms, two legs, two eyes, two lips, two nostrils, two ears, two butt cheeks. But I have only one breast.

They made me a prosthetic so I look balanced when I'm wearing clothing. I can almost show my cleavage, it looks so natural. But I know it isn't natural. I used to be proud of my body. It was fit. I wore it well. I felt secure inside it. But now when I go out in public, I know I should feel normal since no one is pointing at me, but I'm very aware of my missing breast. My body is disfigured.

I should be over this. It's been eight years and the threat is gone. The cancer shouldn't come back. Is it ever really gone, though? I'm paranoid that one day I will get the news that my enemy has returned. I've had dreams lately that freak me out, dreams of an illness so bad there is no treatment, no remission, no escape.

I can read my body like a book. There's the smiling scar from when Conrad was born and the stretch marks from my other two kids. There's the scar under my eye from my childhood, when my friends and I were having a dirt clod fight and Becky, my best friend, landed a good one that split my cheek wide open. How did we ever stay friends? It seemed like she was trying to kill me.

Becky became my best friend after the car accident, the one that killed both of my parents and sent me to live with my grandparents. That was in the days before MADD and strict laws regarding drinking and driving. My parents were on their way to get me when a drunken man drove his car into them, head-on. He was so drunk his body went limp when the cars collided. He only suffered bruised ribs, a concussion, and a broken wrist. But the impact was so awful that my parents had a closed casket funeral. My granddad had to go to the morgue and identify the bodies. He told me that that moment changed his life. He said my mother, his daughter, was recognizable only by the pattern on her dress and the wedding ring on her finger.

I take care of my skin; I like how unique it is. I've lived in this town most all my life. It's a small town with mainly white folks, and I have never been aware of any difference in color. No one treats me any different because of my skin. This small town is my home. I love it here. In the past, I had good offers to leave it, but when it came down to it, I couldn't. I love it that much.

But I was writing about my scars, wasn't I?

I don't see taking care of my skin as a chore. I see it as a ritual. When I'm spreading lotion on my body, I also rub it over my scar. I feel it. I've become intimate with it. It doesn't hurt, but sometimes I feel a strange almost tickling sensation under it, like the nerves that were cut are confused and don't know what to stimulate. I can feel the nerves firing, but then they surface in another part of my body, not where I'm touching it.

It's different from the paresthesia that is associated with the nerve damage by the chemo. That's more like a slight burn, or sometimes a severe itch. My scar is different. It's the scar that has made me ugly and at times unwanted by my husband Colt.

Colt is a good man. He's a fantastic father to our children. He's a great husband. Or was. But ever since the mastectomy, he avoids intimacy and if he has to touch me he does ever so gently that I barely know I've been touched. Is it me? Or is it that he's found someone else to give his affections to?

AUGUST 11TH

There had better be a real good reason why Colt isn't home by now. It's damn late or very early in the morning, depending on how one looks at it, and I've been up for hours worrying about him. Maybe the band wrecked that old bus of theirs and they had to spend the night at the hospital. Maybe every one of their cell phones has lost its charge and he has no way of calling home.

God help him if he's out cheating on me!

If he's fooling around with some whore he stumbled across while I've been home alone in this bed, he's got something coming to him when he does get home.

I suppose she's young and cute with two perky boobs and a tight ass. She probably looks at him with wanting eyes, young eyes, or worse, seductive eyes.

How can I blame her? He's damn good to look at, especially when he's on stage. And that voice of his…. It's just my bad luck (or Colt's good luck) that I'd get old and ugly and he'd stay young looking and handsome. I see the girls looking him over when we go out. I used to be proud that he got those hungry looks. Now that I'm fifty, I'm afraid of those looks. I'm afraid of girls looking at him.

What should I use to the knock the shit out of him with when he gets home? I don't want to kill him. Hell, I love him too much for that. I just want something heavy in my hand when he makes his excuses. Once I see the lie in his eyes, I'm going to swing and BOOM! I'll knock the lie right out of that deceitful mouth.

Like I said, there had better be a damn good reason why he didn't come home, or tonight I'll be down on my knees begging God to forgive me for the beating I gave him.

AUGUST 12TH

Well, Colt came home this morning and tried to feed me some bullshit story about his sister being sick. Hell, that woman's been sick all her life! He's never needed to spend the night with her before.

What bothers me is how *concerned* he looked when he told me the story. The other thing is, I checked my voice mail. He'd left me three messages and sent two texts saying his sister needed him. That damn cell phone sits at the bottom of my purse. I never hear it ring.

I listened to Colt tell me his story. I pushed my suspicions aside and played along.

The thing is, Colt is my Achilles' heel. I've always loved cowboys, a man with harden muscles from working with cattle and the land. Not the city dude in boots and a hat, not an imitation but the real deal in faded jeans.

I remember when we first began dating. I was so naive in the ways of cowboys. But not men in general. I'd had my share of men before I found Colt, but Colt was my first and last real cowboy. He lived on his parents' ranch and mileage was accumulating on my Mazda RX-7 because I visited there so often. But I didn't mind. How could I resist a man that rode a horse named Mr. Personality? Little did I know that I was being carefully extracted from the independence I was so proud of.

My grandparents had passed away a year apart. I was young and filled with romantic ideas, but I was also lonely and still grieving. My granddad left me their house and some money. I sold the house, hoping to rid myself of the pain that lingered from their deaths, and bought a loft in the middle of town down by Washington Park.

I remember it too well. Winter was coming on, and the threat of being alone was starting to overwhelm me, so I spent more time up at the ranch. I'm sure Colt and his family thought a ranch was the last place a black, hippie girl wanted to be, but I did. In fact, I was there so often that his dad, Garrett, asked me if I had moved in without him knowing it. I was there so often that his mom, Tammy Jo, became someone I would gladly call my friend. She told me she was thankful for me because I seemed to tame the wildness in her son. If I did tame him a little, it came naturally. I didn't put any effort into it. Back in those days I remember how, after I spent the night there, I would get up to get dressed and Colt would pull me back down on the bed and then he'd spend the next two hours putting another smile on my face.

I had been out of college only a year. I thought I knew things. I thought I was smart. Well, he taught me things that made my degree seem worthless. He has a degree in veterinary science, so he's book smart. But his real knowledge comes from nature and the animals he works with. He'd gone into the Marines to get the G.I. Bill for school, and when I met him he'd been out of college for two years. He'd decided to help his father on the ranch. On the weekends, he played in his band. That is where Colt really shines. On stage.

I'm not an aggressive person, and before I met Colt, I always detested hunters, guns, and anything I saw as destructive. But Colt spoke about going to places like Alaska, Colorado, Wyoming, and Montana to hunt eatable animals. Caribou. Musk ox. Elk. Deer. Dall sheep.

"Have you ever shot an animal?" he asked me one time.

"No," I said. "No, I haven't." I wanted to tell him I didn't like hunting or hunters; but I already knew that I was in love with him, so I acted interested. I didn't want to put him off.

"Do you want to go hunting with me sometime?"

"That's something for men to do, isn't it? I've got no business killing an animal."

"I can see your perspective," he said. "I won't hunt anything I don't eat, and I eat it because it's the healthiest food available."

At first I didn't like the taste of his wild animals, but after a while eating them in every meal, it grew on me. I'd work in the kitchen with Tammy Jo using elk burger, venison steaks, or Dall roast to make a meal with, and the meat was always complemented with corn, carrots, potatoes and even eggplant that she grew in her own garden. I doubt she even had a thought that her garden was filled with organic produce, but that's exactly what she grew. I'd always wanted to be an organic farmer, and working with Tammy Jo taught me a great deal about gardening, canning, and storing the harvested vegetables. It didn't take me long to enjoy what Colt's mother put on the table.

Colt and his family were pure country, not just cowboy boots, western clothes, and pickup trucks. I knew I'd met the real deal, a fading breed of folks who've been replaced by modern conveniences. I'm from the city, and I won't argue that I have a city attitude, but I appreciate Colt and his family for the lifestyle they're living. Sometimes I feel guilty for taking Colt off the ranch. We live in town now. That's because the reality for me is that if I'm raising a family, we need health insurance, a steady income, good schools, and (I hate to admit it) all the other modern conveniences. I guess I need to be fair, though. Little did Colt know he was being extracted from the life he loved.

Oh, crap, I got off track again. Colt and his family opened their home to me and I spent my first Christmas since my grandparents passed away with a warm, comfortable family. I was aware how important it was for me to have someone like Colt in my life. More important was having that feeling of family. I didn't just want it; I *needed* it.

I also hate to admit it, but I was a suspicious girlfriend. After losing my grandparents I realized that just because I loved someone that didn't mean they would be a permanent part of my life. I felt vulnerable and when he got a phone call and I wasn't sure who he was talking to, I interrogated him. "Who was that?" I'd say, and then I looked in his eyes for glimmers of deceit. Or if I hadn't seen him for a day or so and he came and gave me a big kiss and a hug I used the kiss and hug as an opportunity to sniff him for the smell of another woman. I was afraid of some beautiful ranch woman who knew how to hunt and was strong in ways I wasn't. I was afraid he'd found someone who could love him better than I could.

He never knew I didn't trust him. But can anyone blame me? He was a dream right out of a romance novel. I was sure every girl who ever saw him wanted to be with him. When his band played, I'd hear the women in the bathroom talking about him. Some women can be very explicit. All my jealousy and suspicions were pushed away, however, on the second Christmas. That's when he proposed to me.

August 13th

I met with my financial advisor today to discuss my retirement and investments. Afterward, I drove to Washington Park and took a few minutes to stroll and think. As I walked in the park, I thought about the future and what I would do in my retirement years. I don't think I can handle too much leisure. Maybe I could expand our garden. I love working with the dirt and watching the growth of everything in the garden. It gives me peace. I give each and every thing growing there a name. Every plant is a friend of mine.

Gardening gives me a sense of peace. My mother-in-law taught me it was fine to love gardening, it was all right to individualize the plants. I love her big garden. I remember how Tammy Jo helped me during my bout with breast cancer. Gardening became my therapy.

At first, the cancer wasn't a moment of high drama like we see in movies, where the star is overwhelmed by illness and the doctor comes running into the exam room, yelling at the nurse to do several things to save the patient's life. Cancer is sneaky. It creeps up quietly, achingly, it can be slow and elusive and subtle. I was fighting symptoms thinking they were the illness. But the symptoms weren't the main event. They were only transformations of a deeper problem that twisted itself up in my right breast. The deeper problem that manifested and would have to be excavated out of my body had created fear, grief, and stress that had no boundaries.

During my war with cancer, our insurance company determined it was a *preexisting condition* and wouldn't cover it. How can they do things like that? Colt and I went through colossal financial difficulties, including threats of losing our home, repossession of our vehicles, and liquidation of most of our assets. It was a very dark time for us on so many levels. So, today as I walked I was thankful I still had my retirement fund and could discuss it with my advisor. I was thankful to be healthy enough to walk around on a hot summer's day.

Thank you, God, for remission! I don't necessarily believe in God, but isn't that who we are supposed to thank in times like this? Maybe I just don't know who God is.

I thought about the blessing of remission while I was walking in the park. I didn't want to squander my retirement years doing mundane crap. It was strange. It was as if my walking only made me think about my remission more and that led me to want more than the life I'm living now. Things have changed. I don't know if it's Colt, the kids, or me. I don't know, but what I do know is that something's changed at home. And work...well, work is shit. It's full of politics and cliques. I'm so tired of all that.

While I was walking, drifting along in my thoughts of gratitude for life, I was suddenly besieged by a craving for a Mountain Dew. It's funny, but during my treatment phase I started craving Mountain Dew. To this day, I've never lost it. There are a couple hot dog venders in Washington Park, but only one of them sells the nectar I was in search of. I found him, bought my soda, popped the top, and took a long drink. The fizzy liquid quenched my dry throat. Ahh, relief.

I sipped the rest as I walked. The sky was as bright and blue as it should be on good summer days. Soon I felt moved to pray. When I pray, I pray to my granddad. He's the closest person to God I ever knew. In fact, in my mind he was even better than God, and that's why I pray to him.

If I had one wish that could come true, it would be that I was young again and with my granddad. He made the world a simple, loving place to live in. He wasn't ever afraid of anything, and he knew the answer to my every question or doubt. To be honest, the older I get, the more I need his courage. The world isn't simple anymore. Since the cancer, I've lived every day in fear. Just once, I would like to feel in control of my life. I feel like the things that are the most important to me are the smallest part of my life. Like gardening. It's important to me but I never seem to have time for it.

I have a small garden, but I still miss going out to the ranch and helping Tammy Jo. I've been so busy these last few years that the things I used to do, the things I like to do, have been put off for other "more important" things. Maybe when I retire I'll have time to keep a big garden. I feel sad, though. By the time I'll be able to retire, Tammy Jo will probably have passed. Time is my enemy.

AUGUST 14TH

In order for me to be any good in the office, I have to put myself in a state of fantasy. I have to almost hypnotize myself by daydreaming about retirement and a better life. If I don't pause from my fantasy of retirement, my fingers get stiff and don't function on the keyboard. It's as if when I'm lost in my daydream, my body goes into some kind of autopilot and does work in a timelier manner.

I had to write something by hand today, and I was embarrassed by my penmanship. It was so inelegant. I remember when I was young. In college, I was proud of my handwriting. I got pleasure out of watching my hand form the letters, like the capital B with its curls and swirls, and the little f that adds so much personality to the letters in a sentence. I had a way of innovating my handwriting that people took notice of, but today it only looked wiggly. It looked like the handwriting of an old woman.

I don't dislike the mechanical, non-human part of my job. I like the routine nature of my work—data entry—and all the thousands of entries that I input every day to generate a temporary balance and assure the management team that everything is in order. This doesn't tire me. What it does is give me time to think about other things. It allows my mind to dream.

Sometimes I feel like I'm two different people. One is the person that knows the work in the office like a machine, the woman who is completely a master of the ins and outs of her job and is always confident, professional, and efficient.

But the other me is a dreamy and enthusiastic woman who is full of frustrated passion. I'm a sad woman who longs for more from her unsophisticated life. I'm an absent-minded woman who has no concern for how much data she's processed or if the account is balanced. A woman that dreams of romance, excitement - who longs to be understood.

The insufferable part of my job isn't the routine. It's the latest dilemma, the unexpected urgent demand that comes down from the constantly shifting management team. The director comes down and demands a special task get immediate attention. I cringe when I hear the words "Can you do me a favor?" because they always have some complicated surprise hidden behind them. There are also those times when my supervisor tells me, "The management staff would like your team to gather the data for Account X." Concealed under the casual request is the real demand that screams *URGENT*. Like an audit of an account over the past five years. Or the forecast of an account ten years into the future. Since the request is more than routine everything within me stops, and the two people that live inside me have to work together. The daydreaming comes to an end. I can no longer think about my best interests, I have to shift and think about what is good for the company. Why should I care about the approximate profit from one of our accounts in the third quarter of the fiscal year two years ago?

...

I had a dream last night that's been bothering me all day. I relived the death of my granddad. There he was, dying in his bed, with his doctor standing there. He was a practical man, my granddad. Even when he was dying, his attitude was that he'd better get on with it because any delay would keep folks from getting their chores done. In my dream, I looked at the doctor, and he said, "Your granddad has lost his voice. He can't speak for himself." I could see that. Granddad was in pain, his breathing was shallow. And then he forced a breath past his vocal cords. He made some coarse, rough sound. But he wouldn't say any words. He was only crying out because of the pain.

Then the doctor put a syringe in my hand. "The law says I can't do it, Hope, but you can," he whispered after he'd look around to make sure no one could hear. "You're his closest relative, so it will be considered an honorable act. Just put this in his IV tube and he'll be dead. Give him the relief he's asking for."

"No," I almost shouted. "No, I can't do that. I love him." I held onto Granddad's hand and cried, "I love you so much I can't do this, I just can't."

The doctor said, "It's an act of love. You can do this. It's an act of mercy."

I knew my granddad wanted me to do it. I knew if he could have done it himself, he would have already done it. I looked around the hospital room. As the inflatable hospital bed moved him, it groaned as much as he was groaning. The feeding pump hummed at a low frequency, the oxygen mask hissed, the alarm on the IV pump kept beeping. Granddad's hands were tied to the sides of the bed so he wouldn't try to harm himself. His face was pale, paler than usual, and he had dark rings under his blue eyes. His gray hair looked waxy.

That dream was so real, I could even smell the antiseptic used to clean the floor. As I studied my granddad, the words *quality of life* danced through my mind. I wanted my granddad to be alive. Selfishly, I wanted him with me forever...but not tied to a bed, unable to talk or feed himself. Then the words *death with dignity* surged through my mind. And I grabbed the syringe out of the doctor's hand and stuck it in the IV line, killing the one man I loved more than anyone else in the world.

"Thank you," the doctor said. "You know, he was my best friend. I just couldn't stand for him to suffer any longer."

And then I looked at my granddad and he smiled at me, and a sense of peace came over me. It was a strange dream. Part of it was true. My granddad hadn't been able to speak. He'd been restrained at the end. But his death really came in the form of a severe stroke. No one injected anything into his IV line, and the doctor was a stranger to him, definitely not his best friend.

I wonder about dreams. Why do we have them? Are they some kind of communication? From who?

AUGUST 18ᵀᴴ

I had dinner with my family tonight. One by one, all three of my children have come home. They each have their own reasons, but whatever the happenstances are that brought them back to me, they're all back at home. Maybe it's the mother in me, but I love having my family under the same roof.

Colt had a gig at the Country Club and was in a hurry, but I've enjoyed sitting with my family and sharing a meal. Colt had dinner cooked when I got home, so all I had to do was sit down and eat it. He's a great cook. I swear he could make a good meal out of boiling water and a rock. And not only can he cook, but he also has great skill at time management. He's able to go set up for the gig, come home and make a wonderful dinner by six o'clock, and then make it back to the club for the sound check by eight. But tonight something was wrong with the PA, so he needed to get there early. I didn't like the unsettled feeling I had when he rushed out the door, but I tried to put it out of my mind.

When I looked at my kids I noticed that none of them resemble me. That bothers me. In the first place, they see life as work and money. That's all that is important and everything in life is so very serious. I almost see them without joy. They have a go at life different from me when I was their age. Maybe I'm wrong here, but their attitudes seem so different compared to Colt's or mine. Where do they get that?

Colt Jr. is the eldest—we call him Junior. Out of my three children, Junior is the least sociable. I'm not sure, but he seems angry with me, though maybe I'm wrong. But he seems irritated all the time. I'm not sure who he's pissed at, he just looks like an angry or hateful young man. I don't like his anger, but I think he respects me. I'm not sure....

Conrad, the middle child, is perhaps the family's special one. I love all three of them, of course, but Conrad and I have a deeper connection, some kind of bond on a different frequency than I have with the other two. Many times, he'll call or pop in and say, "I could feel you needed me for something. What is it?" And he'd be right. At that very moment, I'd be thinking I needed Conrad to help me with this or that. He seems more thoughtful, more sensitive to the world around him. I don't know what it is, but recently it's become apparent that a barrier exists between Junior and Conrad. I wish I knew what it was. Or at least what brought it on.

Cleo is my youngest, my little girl. She's only twenty-one. She and I have something in common: in this household, we are the only two women. In some ways, she's very much like me. She enjoys her privacy and is unwilling to share her most difficult problems with anyone, even me.

She and I differ on some things. Like she has it in her head that our house is in constant disorder, that our diets are out of control, that our dirty clothes are never taken care of the way she would like them taken care of. She'll learn, though. When she has her own family, she'll learn that it's damn hard to keep a house in order, have an ideal organic diet, she'll find out that it's almost impossible to keep up with the laundry.

Lately she's been very moody. I think her approach to life borders on hysteria, though she knows how to collect herself when she gets upset, especially when it comes to her brothers. I admire her ability to leave a fight before it actually starts. I usually start a fight, then leave when the fight is all out of me.

I think the kids really love each other, even though the kind of love between them carries its usual quota of shared annoyance. But like I said, they don't resemble me. Not even physically. Junior looks a lot like Colt, Cleo has his eyes, and Conrad inherited his mouth and cute butt.

I wonder if Colt sees anything of me in the kids?

AUGUST 19TH

It's four a.m., and I suddenly feel intolerably empty. I woke up and felt the bed. Colt didn't come home again last night. I cried. I hate to cry!

I'm sick and tired of the way things are in my home! I've checked my cell phone. He called to let me know that, since he was playing a gig near where his sister lives, he would stay the night with her again. I'm drained. I've done a self-inventory. I don't have any love for him anymore. I wonder if he'll be surprised that I don't love him anymore. Or is that what he has wanted all along? If it didn't hurt so damn bad, I would hate him. Well, I'm sure I'll get around to hating him soon enough.

AUGUST 20TH

I can't believe the weight of emptiness that followed me to work. At 2:30 this afternoon, I felt awful, both physically and mentally. I told my boss that I had to go to the bank to arrange some money for a family emergency. That was a lie. I couldn't endure one minute more in my cubicle, staring at the wall. Since we're no longer allowed to have personal pictures in our cubicles, I noticed how empty the wall looked. It kept reminding me how empty I felt.

I don't know what would have happened if I'd stayed and looked at that blank wall any longer. It's possible that I would have screamed or freaked out completely. On my way to the bank, I convinced myself that I needed to get a grasp on reality or more panic attacks would come. Then I would be humiliated because I wasn't in control of myself.

I have to face it. All the signs are right there in front of me. Colt's not coming home. He is spending his nights somewhere else. I know our marriage is over. There's been no big fight, no fuss. Sure, I slammed some doors, but no one was around to hear them. My marriage unraveled while I wasn't looking, when I wasn't expecting it to. That's what I told myself as I walked to the bank.

At the teller's window, I began the process of separating my money from his (meaning I setup my own account and that my paycheck goes to via direct deposit.). Then I went back to the office and phoned my financial advisor. Since I'm losing more money every quarter in investments, I threatened him that I might as well liquidate that money to my savings account. Of course my advisor wants to discuss it. Sure, my money makes him money, even when I'm losing it. We left my investments as they are for now, but he is supposed to come back to me with a new strategy. We'll see. I don't trust him.

I'd like to cash it all in, even though I'm not sure what I'd do with the money. I'd like to do something rash, something uncalculated. Well, I'll think on it. But whatever I do I'd like to see some happiness.

I've lost my sense of home. My house doesn't welcome me anymore. The rooms seem average. They don't have that warm feeling they used to have. I want to do some deep cleaning, but I'm afraid if I clean too much, the house will feel completely empty, void of any love. Is that crazy? To be afraid of cleaning?

Depression has attached itself to me since my bout with cancer. I take antidepressants daily and I have anti-anxiety pills for the bad days. Have I survived cancer only to fail in life?

I wasn't very productive at work today. I spent most of my time surfing the Net. I did the *what are the celebrities up to* thing, but their lives are so ridiculous and pathetic, that got boring very quickly. Then I searched for a first edition of *Vingt mille lieues sous les mers* (that's *Twenty Thousand Leagues Under the Sea*). I collect old books and don't mind spending a large sum of the money I've earned to buy one of my favorites.

Jules Verne. Where did that man come from? I mean, when I read *Twenty Thousand Leagues Under the Sea*, I try to put myself in his shoes, to go back to 1869, that's when he wrote it, and I can't believe that his imagination was so accurate. Who dreams up an atomic powered submarine eighty-three years before the technology was available? People go crazy over the Bible and its power, but the power of Verne's vision really got my attention. And he's only one example of man's ability to see into the future. People who claim that Nostradamus was *the* modern prophet have never read Verne, or they'd think he was the most modern. I wonder why the seers seem to come from France. Is there something in the water there?

After searching for a first edition (which I didn't find), I wrote an email to my best friend Becky. She moved to Spokane several years ago when her husband Dale got transferred, but then they got a divorce and she stayed in Spokane for some reason. I wasn't real specific in my note, but I complained to her that I wasn't happy and I wanted some changes in my life. To my surprise, she responded instantly.

Hey girl, your timing is perfect, she wrote. *It's a New Moon, and a New Moon means good Mojo, man! Here's what you need to do. Take some time today, reflect, gather your thoughts and know exactly what you want to attract in your life. One of the main preparations for the New Moon is getting your shit straight and knowing what you want. Make it clear. Make your intentions clear!*

She went on to describe the ritual I should follow for the New Moon and my desires. When I read her email, it gave me a boost. Becky can do that when no one else can. I promised her I'd do her hippie-witchy ritual tonight and that I would commit to getting my life straightened out.

So...tonight I smudged my room with sage, hid the pictures of my children and Colt in my dresser, and wrote my wishes down on a piece of notebook paper. Then I lit two candles and set them on my dresser. As instructed, I filled my bathtub with hot water and added a handful of sea salt. I sat in the salt water and let my mind wander freely until I felt grounded. Then came the crazy part. Becky told me to get up on my roof and pray with my best intentions. So there I was, standing on the roof of my house in the nude, eyes closed with arms stretched out, freezing my ass off in hopes of restoring my home.

Wouldn't you just know it. Colt had to take Sahchi (our Akita) out for her nightly relief just then. He looked up and saw me on the rooftop and saw me in my pose and prayer. What, he wondered, was the cause of his wife's craziness?

"Don't jump, Babe," he called up to me. "Things aren't that bad. Besides, we don't want the coroner to come out here and see you in your birthday suit when you hit the ground."

I opened one eye and looked down at him. He was laughing at me. That's what I get for praying, I get a laughing husband. Becky is going to hear about this.

<h2>August 22nd</h2>

I woke up this morning and cried. I was sleeping on one edge of the bed, and Colt was on the opposite edge, and it felt like there were miles between us. I cried because I felt alone in the world, I felt alone in my own bed! I shouldn't feel alone in my bed when my husband is in it with me. Why do I feel so lonely?

The little girl that lives inside me wanted her granddad there so she could talk to him. Maybe that's why I cried, maybe it's because I'm an adult who doesn't know what she's doing in her life. No, I think I cried because I realized my marriage is too far gone. Maybe my subconscious knows what my conscious mind doesn't want to admit, and so it's my subconscious that was crying.

By the time Colt woke up, I had collected myself and wiped away the tears and blown my nose. He seemed fine. He didn't even seem to notice the distance between us in our bed. "Good morning, Babe." He gave me a kiss.

But I wasn't feeling like his "babe." I didn't feel like his partner or his friend. He didn't have much time to notice my attitude because I was in a rush to get to the office. I sprinted through the shower and down the stairs, collected my things, and was out the door before Colt had time to say another word. Did I rush because I was late or because I didn't want to think about the space growing between us?

At work, as usual, I fantasized about retiring and having the freedom to do what I like with my time. It's like when I graduated from the university. I felt a huge sense of freedom. I relished that freedom. I read the books I wanted to read. I researched things I was interested in. Sometimes I did nothing. Sometimes I just relaxed. Ahh, freedom.

I don't think I will continue this diary when I retire. That's because I've promised myself that I'm going to be too busy being happy. The last thing I want to do in my retirement is abandon myself to a lazy life. I refuse to surrender to the geriatric drowsiness I've seen in other people. People get lazy and live on their couches, and their brains, muscles, and energy start getting ready to die.

Not me. I need no training for death.

In my valuable leisure time, I want to be as adventurous as I was when I was young. I also want to be inwardly adventurous. I want to discover myself, discover the real Hope, the person that exists beyond the everyday Hope. You know, the one that's above going to work every day, schlepping through life and only existing to accomplish the next task. It is my hope that I get the luxury of meeting myself. It's my hope that I will be happy to live with her for the last years of my life.

It seems strange to be thinking of retirement. I have many years to go before that's even possible, but that's where my mind takes me. When I left the office for lunch, I wasn't feeling well. I don't know what's the matter, but I feel flu-ish, or maybe it's my period. Whatever it is, I feel nauseated with terrible pain down there, combined with feeling like I have gallon of loose fluid sloshing around in places like my neck. Anyway, I felt like crap, so I left the office for lunch and went for a walk. It was such a beautiful day.

And while I was walking in the park again, something reminded me of a day, years ago, when I was walking the kids to school. Conrad, with his little hand in mine was talking to me, chatting rapidly. He had a good vocabulary for his age, and the imagination to go with it. I loved to hear his ideas and his observations of the world. Everything was new and exciting for him, and his excitement radiated out to me. Junior and Cleo always seemed to be unaware that I was there.

On this particular day, when we got near the school, Conrad gave my hand a squeeze and adjusted his voice to make it sound older, more mature. He was five at the time. He looked up at me and said, "Mom, you know how much I love you, but I'm older now. I go to school with the older kids and I think it's time I walked to school on my own."

I was at a loss. What could I say? I guess he wasn't expecting me to say anything, though, because he wasn't asking me. He was telling me he didn't need me for safety anymore. I always loved walking to school with my favorite child. I never once thought there would be a day when I wouldn't be there. It was our routine. So I had the hardest time letting go of his little hand that day.

Of course after Conrad delivered his proclamation, his older brother, Junior, thought it over and joined in. "Yeah, Mom. We're all big kids now. We don't want everyone to see us being walked to school by our mommy, who gives us each a kiss. Big kids don't do that."

And then Cleo considered what was going on and, being a freethinker even at age four, she had her own opinion. "Mommy, will you walk me to school?" She wasn't in school yet, but she always enjoyed our walk for the boys. "I don't care what the other kids think," she said. "I always like having you with me." Sweet Cleo. She's my girl.

That was the day I knew that on every day after, my boys would be taking steps toward autonomy. They wouldn't want me to be involved in their lives. They were heading for their independence. And now I see my children living back at home, but still not wanting me to be involved in their lives. They rush in and out of my house in fear that I might stop them for a moment to see how their day is going.

Am I really that bad?

When I got back to work, I still didn't feel well.

AUGUST 24TH

It's Friday. Tonight Colt is playing down at the Sour Mash Saloon. It's a good gig because he draws a large crowd and it's consistently packed. Which means it brings in some good money. But my worst fear is someone standing in that crowd. She's Colt's side salad, the young woman he's been seeing. He denies it, but I'm sure of it.

He told me last night that he loves me, and only me. "You're the love of my life," he said. "I would never do anything to damage our love."

I told him I wanted a divorce anyway. I don't believe a word his mouth says. She's real. No man is true to his woman. Don't all men crave sex from younger, better-looking women?

"Why would I have another woman?" he asked me. "You're the only girl I want to be with."

"Because I'm old and ugly!" I shouted at him.

"You think I think you're ugly?"

"Yes," I said. "I became ugly eight years ago when they removed my breast. If I was ever a pretty woman, she got up and walked out the door of that surgery suite. Now I'm scarred and ugly. I'm less of a woman. You obviously need more than who I am today."

"Oh, Babe—" even today I go weak in the knees when he calls me Babe "—don't say that! I'm sorry if you feel that way. You're not ugly. You're beautiful."

"Colt, you've stopped touching me. Before the cancer, you used to make love to me, you would take me with your firm hands, you would spend hours with me, and we would share our love. But now? Now when we make love, it's done in three minutes and your hands barely touch me."

He looked away from me and winced as though I had

burned him. "I'm sorry. I can see what you're saying. Babe, all I can do is apologize. It's just that since your cancer, when I saw you so weak and fragile...well, I guess I've been thinking you never gained your strength back. When we make love, it's not like it used to be. I'm afraid I'm hurting you."

I've never looked at it that way before! He sees me as fragile, something precious. Something breakable.

But that doesn't change anything. He hasn't explained the nights he doesn't come home. I went to the bathroom, shut the door, locked it, lit some candles, and drew a bath. Maybe he wasn't done talking, but I was. After my bath, I let him know I wouldn't be sharing my bed with him any longer.

Colt has moved into the guest room for now.

August 26th

I wish they made a pill that would cure the way I feel. A pill that would make these feelings go away in a matter of minutes. A pill that would make me forget all about this heartache. That would get him out of mind. A strong pill that would take away the physical pain, too. Oh, how my periods frustrate me!

I don't drink or do drugs, but last night I didn't want to feel anything at all, so I ran out to the liquor store and bought me a bottle of Jack Daniels. I got the idea from a movie I'd been watching. I had to look in the phone book for the location of a liquor store. When I got home, I locked myself in my room and I poured me a glass...and instantly remembered why I don't like to drink alcohol. It tastes worst than medicine. But being the fool that I am, I sat home alone, drinking glass after glass. Stupid!

I could still feel the loneliness, the emptiness, the fear. Like a complete dumb-ass, I drank the whiskey, thinking it would help me. I was so drunk I don't know if Colt came home last night or not. I woke up in a disgusting state. I had puked in my bed and then rolled around in my own puke all night. Dumb!

This pain will have to find another way to fix itself. That damn booze isn't for me. Christ, I hope I never sleep in my puke again. I'm an idiot!

I don't think there is anything more pathetic than what I turned into. I was curled up in the dark, wrapped up in my fear and drinking nasty whiskey. I'm certain there are better ways to manage this. Maybe marriage counseling?

Even aside from the booze and my problems with Colt, I just don't feel right. It's like I have the flu or some kind of bug. I've had a low-grade fever for the past week now, and I feel achy, too. I usually blame this on my period, but to be honest I don't think that's what it is. Whatever it is, it's making me bitchy, and I don't like being bitchy. If this continues, even though I hate to go, I'll go see the doctor.

It's Sunday night now. It's quiet here. The kids haven't been home all weekend. I have no idea where they go or what they're up to these days. I only know they don't do whatever it is they do together. And Colt is gone, I don't know where nor do I care. He was here earlier, but I let him know I didn't want anything to do with him. I've stayed in my room most of the day. Colt loaded up Sahchi in his truck. They probably went to the ranch.

August 27th

Today I ate lunch alone near the cathedral. When I walked down Mulberry Street feeling ill (still hung over. Did I say I was a dumb-ass? Well, I am!), I passed a gentleman dressed in a suit that dated back to the forties. He was dressed the way I remember seeing my granddad dressed on special occasions, like when he went to church. I couldn't keep from looking at this gentleman. He was conspicuous, yet I didn't see anyone else paying him any mind. Well, he noticed me looking at him and gave me a nod. I must have nodded back or looked back at him, because he stopped and, after some hesitation, turned and came toward me.

His face was strange, though not strange in the negative sense. He looked familiar, though I was certain I'd never seen him before. His face reminded me of someone I had known in times past. He offered me his hand, as a gentleman would, and I shook it as I apologized and confessed that he looked familiar but I wasn't quite sure who he was.

The look he gave me was oddly comforting. The feeling I got from his hand was warm and reassuring. "I don't think we have met," he said, "but you seem familiar to me, too. I couldn't let the moment go by without at least saying a common hello."

I held his hand in mine for longer than would have been normal for a simple handshake. But I swear it was like holding my granddad's hand. I didn't want to let go. Finally I said, "I'm Hope. And you are?"

"My name is Mr. Goldsole."

"Mr. Goldsole. Wow, so formal. No first name?" I asked.

"Hope," he said, "I'm an old man who is old-fashioned in his approach to the world. Please forgive me if I only offer you my last name. You have a sweet face, a pretty face, and as an old man I want to leave this world with a good memory of me, so I don't let things pass me by. If I feel the urge to say something to some stranger, I don't hold back. I tell them and let them do what they want."

I smiled at him. "Well, thank you! I've been feeling very ugly these days. Your compliment has definitely lifted my spirits."

"Oh, have your spirits been down lately?"

I hesitated before answering. After all, this man was a perfect stranger, and yet there was something about him that I was comfortable with. "I guess you could say I've been out of sorts lately," I finally said.

He fell into step beside me under a clear, soothing, blue sky.

"Let me understand this," he said as we walked. "You said you've been feeling ugly and out of sorts. It seems to me that you may have been facing the wrong way."

"I'm not sure I understand what you mean."

"You've been facing the wrong way," he repeated. "You need to allow your soul to turn around and take a good look at things from another direction. Facing inward. You are not ugly."

"Yeah," I said, "but I feel that way sometimes. It's nice of you to compliment me."

We stopped and he turned to face me. "Maybe you feel ugly because you're looking for validation from others. But what others say about you means very little if your soul doesn't agree. Try this. When you have some time—*alone*—close your eyes and visualize your soul. Look at yourself and your soul. Become acquainted with yourself and your soul. Imagine your soul what it looks like. Is it bright? Dim? Is it full of energy or is it mellow? Then think of your physical being, and after you've had some time to consider these things, then ask yourself if you're ugly." He smiled at me, "You should have a good relationship with your soul."

"My soul?" I didn't know what to say for a minute. "That's pretty complex for two people meeting for the first time."

I felt very uncomfortable talking about my soul with him...or anyone else. It wasn't that Mr. Goldsole made me uncomfortable. I realized that it was me being uncomfortable with my own spiritual identification that was the real issue. I'd never looked at my soul before. I've always been told that everyone has one, and I guess I just took it for granted that my soul belongs to God. But then, I don't even believe in God...so where does that leave my soul. Do I have a soul? Should I put up a sticky note on the refrigerator that says something like:

Note to self, take your soul out for lunch. Get to know

it, build a relationship with it.

This old man was making me curious about souls. I wanted to know if I even had one to believe in.

"How do I know if I have soul?" I asked him.

"That's a good question," he said. "But only you can answer it. As I said, the next time you're alone, get to know your soul. If it's in you, you will discover it. It only takes your wanting to get to know your soul. That's the first step."

I didn't say anything more, nor did he. We just walked together through Washington Park. The cathedral sits on the edge of the park furthest away from my office building, so it's a nice long walk. The further we walked together, the more familiar he seemed to me. I noticed his brown leather shoes. They were well worn, cracked in places but filled in with polish, just like my granddad used to do with his good shoes. My grandparents weren't wealthy. They took care of what they had, and those dress shoes served Granddad for over thirty years, right up to the day he passed away. In fact, he was buried in those shoes. And in his outdated suit. I could have bought him a new suit to be buried in, but if I know my granddad, he would have frowned at that. "I'm comfortable in this suit," he would have said. "Why do I need a new one?" So I buried him in the suit he was comfortable in.

When Mr. Goldsole and I got back to my office building, he shook my hand again and wished me a good day. As I watched him walk away, I honestly felt my vitality increase. Is that the right word, *vitality*? Well, anyway, I felt my life energy rise out of depression. Thank you, Mr. Goldsole!

And tonight I lay in my bed with my eyes closed, ready to try his little experiment. I was disappointed, though. There I was, eyes closed, emptying my mind with the intention of meeting my soul and saying, "Hello, I'm Hope. It's so nice to meet you." But nothing happened. After an hour, I gave up. There wasn't anyone or anything talking to me. Am I soulless? Crap, I hope not! I'm not sure what it means to have a soul, but I want one.

AUGUST 28ᵀᴴ

I hardly ever spend any time with my children. Our schedules don't often mesh, and our plans or interests are less than compatible. Is it simply the distance between our generations that separates us? Or could I be doing something that impedes communication?

Tonight we had dinner together. It's been a while since our last so-called family meal, so I jokingly asked what special event it was we were celebrating. Was God intervening in the ways of our world so that our family could be together? My joke just echoed through the dining room. Cleo looked at me and smiled, as if to say she understood that my intentions were good. But that was all.

I sat there, looking around the table as I ate, observing the few interruptions in our almost unyielding silence.

Junior said the spaghetti sauce was too bland.

"You have a salt shaker less than four inches from your hand," Cleo told him. "Pick it up and use it. Only an idiot would just sit there and complain!"

Yes, the spaghetti sauce was as bland as my mood was when I made it. It needed something, salt, maybe, but why did he feel the need to point it out?

A few minutes later, Conrad remarked that the weather was going to be windy tomorrow. He didn't tell anyone specifically, he just spoke to the table.

Junior was texting someone by then. I find it so rude when a person texts during dinner. I told him so. Junior put his phone down, but his manner didn't change. It was as if he had gone on texting. He was boorish and pissy.

One thing we all noticed was that Colt wasn't there. Cleo told me he was with his sister, but that attempt at conversation went nowhere. His sister Nina has been ill for a very long time, I know that. She was institutionalized when she was a little girl. Has anything changed? I doubt it.

Then I told my story of meeting Mr. Goldsole, trying to make it as impressive to them as it was to me.

But Junior just asked, "You shook hands with an old guy in an old suit?" and laughed at me. "Really mom, you touched him? I bet he's homeless and dirty, and you gave him your hand. You might want to go down to the nearest clinic and get a tetanus shot or something."

I frowned at him, but he looked away. Did I raise him to be that way?

Earlier today I went to my GP, and she drew some blood and did the usual exam. Then I gave her my list of complaints, and she told me I was "clinically depressed." How is that different from just being depressed? Hell, I knew I was depressed! "Demands at the office that are impossible to satisfy," I told her. "Bills at home that are more than my income plus a divorce equal depression. It's that simple." I already have pills for depression and anxiety.

"I can write a different prescription for stronger meds if you like," the doctor said.

"No, thank you," I said. "I don't want a chemical lobotomy. The meds I have are strong enough."

"Hope," she said, "I'm worried about you. Your blood pressure's up, you're complaining of headaches and body aches, and I've confirmed your fever. I think you're overstressed. You need to *do* something."

"Yeah, you're right. I am pretty stressed out. But what can I do?"

"Get control over the stress factors," she said. "You know what would be a good idea? You need to do something for yourself. Find something that's fun, that you like to do, and do it." She gave me a cheery smile.

I shook my head. "I'm in such a routine, I don't even know what I'd like to do. I'll have to give that some thought."

"You do that." She made a note on my chart. "Take some private time for yourself. Find a quiet place. Close your eyes and imagine what it is that would make you happy."

"I heard something like that just the other day," I told her.

"Take some time to introduce myself to my soul." When I said it, it sounded like a question.

She nodded. "Yes. Reintroduce yourself to yourself. Find that love you had for yourself and express it. Take yourself out and have some fun." She scribbled on my chart again, then patted my leg. "I'm going to run some tests. It's all routine, nothing to worry about, but I want to see you for a follow-up after the results come back."

I walked out of her office feeling a little puzzled. Two people had given me the same advice. *Get to know me.* It's just coincidence, but it's intriguing.

AUGUST 29TH

Sometimes I like to ride my bicycle to work. This morning was a beautiful summer morning, but even on my bike, the commute was no different than any other day. Just a typical morning. What makes every morning the same is that I see myself sharing the road with unsmiling people in their cars headed to their jobs. Like we're all living out a life sentence, and our office, work site, or whatever our place of employment is, it's a big prison. Every morning, it's a dreadful march to a dreadful place we all would rather not go to. I'm sure there are a few people that love the commute and their place of employment, but only a few.

I stopped with the traffic at a red light at a crowded intersection, balancing myself with one foot on the pedal and the other extended so my toe touched the pavement. In that moment I looked around. Cars surrounded me, and in those cars were solo drivers with mournful faces. The drivers looked like me, as if they were two separate people. One side of them was sad, reluctant to get to work, fearful of losing their freedom for the next eight to ten hours. And looking at them, I felt sorry that I couldn't release them from their burdens.

But as soon as the light turned green, their other side came alive. The drivers stomped on their gas pedals, unleashing their aggression, and I had to move quickly because cyclists are not appreciated on the road. But, you know, I think that's what I like about commuting on my bike. It's exciting to race through the tight spaces in the traffic, gambling my two wheels against their four. Getting hit by a car is always a real possibility, so I always look the drivers straight in the eye to make sure they see me.

It was plenty hot this morning. Sweat trickled down my sides and gathered at my waistband. I don't wear the typical cyclist clothes. I figure I'm not a sponsored racer, I don't see a sporting activity as a fashion competition, so why should I look like I'm in a race by wearing racing jerseys and spandex shorts with no pockets? I wear what's comfortable. I wear men's cargo shorts and my Georgia O'Keeffe "Ram's Head White Hollyhock" T-shirt. I love men's cargo shorts. They have great pockets. I found some cargo shorts for women, but when I tried to put my hand in the pockets, they were too damn small, and some of the pockets were stitched shut! Who designs clothes for women, anyway? I'm a utilitarian. If it isn't functional, I don't want it. In my backpack are a water bladder and my professional clothes. Lucky for me, we have a locker room where I work, so I can shower and change.

But, like I said, the light turned green and traffic bolted forward and the sound of all the acceleration echoed off the walls of the buildings around us. I pedaled wildly to make it across to the left-turn lane. Of course I can't outrun cars, but I can get where I need to be if people see me and are respectful. Today, though, I almost got run over because some shit-kicker in his lifted pickup didn't want me to get in front of him. He revved his engine and pushed ahead, then shouted something rude at me and cut me off. Jerk! After that, as I was making my left turn, a lady who seemed more interested in texting on her cell than driving pulled right in front of me without even turning her head to see if anyone was coming. I had to leap onto the sidewalk to avoid being hit. She had no idea I was even there. Ditz!

And while all of this was going on, I became acutely aware of Mr. Goldsole and my GP telling me to get in touch with me, my inner me. My soul. As I pedaled, I became aware of how much I enjoyed using my own energy to travel. It was putting effort into a laborious task that could be easily escaped if I drove the car, but I believe I was learning about my soul as I pedaled to work. My senses were keen. I saw so much more in the city—the people in their cars on their way to work, the birds in the trees, the school buses hauling kids to school, the litter everywhere, the flowers in full bloom. It was amazing how much more attentive I am to my surroundings when I'm on my bicycle. I believe my soul loves the exercise, the feeling of being outdoors, having the freedom to choose my route to work, loving the sensation of flying.

I took a deep breath in and let it out slowly. I felt time standing still for a moment, like I was transcending to a higher frequency of perception. The moment froze, my sensory perception became stronger, the dread of going to work slipped away. I turned my face upward toward the sun, let my mind go with the impression, closed my eyes and let my projected reality fall and allowed the experience to happen....

"Hello, Soul," I said. I said it out loud.

I felt a giggle somewhere down deep inside of me. A giggle that said *Isn't this fun?*

"I'm enjoying it," I said. And right then I knew like I have never known before, I knew with the utmost certainty that my soul was awakening. "It's so good to know you exist," I said.

The moment was over and the traffic was all around me. My legs were pushing fast and hard. The traffic moved as if nothing had happened. But for me something had happened. And was still happening.

Sure enough, in another dimension, one that is measured near to me yet is on a wavelength parallel to me, *my soul does exist.* Above the exhaust fumes, away from the layers of noise and heat was something spiritual and evident. When I inhaled, I tasted something different from the fumes, something more like the taste of stardust, if a person can taste what heaven is made of. As I pedaled past the modern office buildings, I imagined them as prisons that were expecting their prisoners to arrive before nine o'clock. I passed the banking, insurance, investment, construction, and government institutions, all waiting for their employees to arrive and make them money. *Profit.*

My soul opened my mind and allowed, new thoughts, new perspectives to flow into my conscience. The buildings rushed by as I made my way, yet, I became aware of the corporate mentality buzzing through the city's skyscrapers, where the people went in to serve a nonhuman entity. I could see that the individual, the human being, had dreams, but individual dreams were not as big or strong as the corporations' drive to gain profit and power. So the people put their dreams in the back of their minds so they could do the work that earned them a paycheck.

I wasn't excluded from this ritual. I, too, had work to perform, and my work was data entry.

Data.

It's the most significant kind of currency that our modern world uses.

Data.

It's what allows every computer to function, makes the Internet operate.

Data.

It translates into information that provides proof as to the strength of every company. Strengths and weaknesses are listed as assets and liabilities.

I pushed my legs faster feeling the burn that one gets from strenuous exercise. (I love to feel that burn. It's a good feeling to me.) The more I pushed the more I felt my soul communicating with me, working my mind to see life differently. She wanted me to see life from a different point of view.

I could visualize spreadsheets that had assets and liabilities charted out. Among the data were the employees, humans, people, listed in the columns. It hadn't dawned on me before that an employee was nothing more than piece of equipment in the eyes of the corporate machine. A person is a device that once they are considered obsolete they are laid off.

As I rode on toward work my mind was processing the information my soul was passing on quickly. I would contemplate a thought and another was rapidly taking its place. It was cool. I like that my brain is able to work so fast.

My soul brought forward memories from the past. I remembered that when I had cancer and needed time off, I was scrutinized, my position was analyzed, and they threatened to let me go. I was made to understand that my illness became a liability for the company. Back when I was diagnosed, I held an entirely different position in the company. I made quite a bit more money than I do today. When I was home, recovering, my position was analyzed and deemed unnecessary. I was so sick and I'd lost my hair from the chemo and radiation. Colt and I had to go to HR to try to save my job. The lady in HR looked right at me and said, "Please don't take this personally, it's not you, it's the position, it's no longer viable, times are hard and we need to cut back." And just like that, I was laid off.

Colt and I retained a lawyer and fought the company. It took time and money because we also had the medical bills staring at us, but we won (sort of) and I was able to get a position I could go back to between my treatments. And I was allowed to keep my sick time and vacation time. I needed all of it to get through. But I felt so betrayed! I never understood why all the people I had worked with for so many years and called my friends had become so cold when I was diagnosed with cancer. Today, my soul made it a point for me to realize that it's because of data, capitalism, and the corporate mentality. When it comes to making a profit and projecting power, a company simply can't recognize that a human being can be ill. A corporate device shouldn't get ill, break down or need anything that might cost the company anything.

We had some very hard times then. Colt and I did all we could to keep from losing our house and filing bankruptcy. Don't take it personally, my ass!

As I pedaled along the streets, my soul communicated to me through my mind. She spoke to me about how companies use data to not only profit from human effort but to also control human beings. And I began to understand the expense companies put into protecting data. They have expensive firewalls, fancy passwords, fireproofed rooms with one-of-a-kind locks, security personnel with guns.

Data.

I smiled into the wind. I could feel my soul! I felt my mind opening up to the possibility of its—of *her* existence and the clarity she offered. I curled my back and rotated my right knee out to make a quick right turn onto Cherry Street. It's an older, narrower road with less traffic. My sense of freedom increased as I left the heavy traffic behind. With each thrust of my leg on the pedal, I felt like I was breaking an encrypted code showing what my human purpose is on this earth. I knew I needed to plan my escape from the soulless corporate world. It would take planning, serious planning, to mine out enough money to live on. I understood from her words in my head that if I approached my escape with a chant invoking something higher than my self for help, I could do it.

I arrived at work. After I locked my bike up, showered, and donned my professional clothes I asked myself, *Is my soul nothing more than my active imagination? Is she an extension of a fantasy?*

I rushed from my cubicle to a meeting with the director to greet some new employees. Their faces were young, glistening with fear and excitement. They kept looking around the office but tried not to be seen looking. They also looked envious of those of us who have been employed for a long time. I was kind of listening in the meeting, but I couldn't help my mind from wondering. *It was thinking about something higher* than my self. What did that mean? God? Whatever it was, I sensed on a soul level that I did indeed need help with my life from something higher than me.

The director was droning on and on about our mission, and how every employee gives a hundred and ten percent. All the typical bullshit lies that are fed to every new hire. Then the director appointed the new hires to their assigned departments. I was given two guys and one girl.

Now I've got six employees under my supervision. For the first time in a long time, my department is at full strength. That's a good thing. I hope the newbies work out. We sure can use their help.

The new men don't look bad. Besides the two assigned to me, there's a handsome guy in his thirties down the hall. But he's wearing a wedding ring. One of the guys assigned to me is young and has a face with little strength. It's a delicate face, and he has a look that's shifty when he smiles. The other guy is a nice-looking young man and at least gives me his full attention when I'm talking to him. He seems to understand what I've explained.

My three new employees are James, Devin, and Kelly. Along with my employees came a new urgent assignment. To my surprise, the director took me aside after the meeting and explained that my team was being assigned to gather the records of a specific client. Back-2-Back Videogames was paying the company I work for a very large sum of money to bundle the data we had acquired over the years regarding their competitor, Bio-Sport. Warning flags went up. Back-2-Back Videogames isn't our customer. They are an outsider requesting data on their competitor.

I've come to understand that the videogame industry is very competitive. I also understand that what my team was being asked to do was, to say the least, unethical. Bio-Sport had been our client for twelve years. Back-2-Back has high hopes that with our data they will gain the edge. Our task was deemed both urgent and secret. The director instructed me to get my team up to speed quickly but keep them in the dark as to why they're doing this work. Once the data is bundled, Back-2-Back Videogames' CEO and analysts will have a day in our conference room to review it and make partial, untraceable copies. After that, the company I work for will collect some huge amount of money with more than six zeros. Then we will reshelf the data and maintain our relationship with Bio-Sport.

I felt sick. This is corporate espionage. My team is doing the dirty work. To be fair, most of the financial reports are available to the public, but Bio-Sport is one of our dependable clients. Blythe (one of my employees) has been their financial specialist this whole time. We should have their best interest at heart. It's my understanding that the CEO of Back-2-Back worked our director over pretty hard and kept increasing the offer until our director couldn't resist.

Money and power.

Soul and mind.

AUGUST 30ᵀᴴ

B rent, our director, called us managers into his office today. For over an hour, he lectured us about the low efficiency of the staff. He said that the board of directors had sent him a nastygram about the company. Evidently, the company as a whole isn't doing very well, and in this economic climate we need to be "mindful of our performance."

"I'll be watching everything you do more closely," he concluded. "No one should be as slow as a tortoise." Can you believe he actually said tortoise? We had to listen to him bitch, moan, whine, and demand. To be honest, I quit listening after the word tortoise fell out of his crooked mouth.

What did he say about my team? Oh, yeah, *low performing*. We were the *low performing team*. I wanted to yell some profanities and tell him that *all of my people work*, not just the experienced ones, but the new ones, too. We come in every morning and go at it and everyone is pulling their weight. Sure, I've seen Mary surfing the Web from time to time, but she does it discreetly and not until after her work is done. And, yes, Raj takes advantage of his trips to other departments and takes an extra ten minutes for himself to get a Coke from the pop machine. I understand we have scheduled breaks for that, but if Raj needs ten-minutes to himself to be efficient the rest of the day, by God, I'll look the other way. And then there's Blythe, who goes to the toilet every morning at exactly 10:35. When he waddles off, he has the sports page under his arm, and we don't see him again until ten after eleven. But his work is always up to par, and during the hours when the pressure is on, my team works enthusiastically and as a team to accomplish the goal. I am confident that each of them is an expert. I know things are not only done, but they're done the right way. We rarely have to go back and do something over again.

I know very well who the director's outburst was aimed at: the team in a completely different area from my team, and over there, they're known to do poor work. But why did the director call all of us into the meeting? Why put blame on us? What I also know is that he didn't want to single out the manager of that area because she's sleeping with his son. He's not a bad looking guy, that son of the director.

. . .

I had a real conversation with Cleo after dinner tonight. We were alone, I was getting comfortable with a good book - *The*

Good Earth, by Pearl Buck – and she was fidgeting with her smart phone. Out of nowhere, she held her phone up in the air in one hand. She looked lost in thought. Even a bit sad. I watched her over the top of my book for a few minutes, then asked her what she was thinking about.

My words awakened her. She gave me a dismal glance and, unable to contain herself, she hid her head in her hands. When my child cries, first I feel helplessness, then I feel awkward. This time, I followed an impulse that came to me. I got up, went over to her, and began to pat her hair. I didn't say anything at first. Nothing needed to be said.

Little by little she relaxed and the weeping went away. She dropped her hands, and I used one of our cloth napkins to wipe her eyes. At that moment, she didn't look like a woman of twenty-one, but like my little girl who, years before, had broken her doll and cried.

"Why are you sad?" I asked her.

"I don't know."

I wasn't too surprised by her answer. Sometimes I feel miserable for no discernible reason. But against my own intuition not to push for an answer, I said, "Surely there's something wrong. It's not like you to cry for no reason."

That's when she unloaded, talking at full speed. "I have the feeling I'm getting older and older but I'm not accomplishing anything. Nothing is happening in my life. I feel that nothingness down to the very core of me. I look at Junior and at Conrad, and I'm sure they feel the same way. We're adults living at home. We've all got jobs, but there never seems to be enough money to break out and live on our own." She took a deep breath and looked straight at me. "Mom," she said, "I look at you and I think how much I don't want to reach fifty and be like you. Ever since you got sick—got cancer – you've resigned yourself to being dull and boring. You've lost your energy. That's horrible. I know you're not the dull person you've become."

Now my own tears began. What could I do? I told her that she was right. I have lost my energy for living. That awful fear when I was diagnosed with cancer took away my playful side. Life instantly became serious, and that feeling of seriousness has never left me.

I also told her I was proud of her for recognizing the change in me and not wanting to be like me. I could feel the crying of my own heart as I remembered how things were ten years ago, before the cancer. I held her tight. She's grown up, and I'm not sure when, if ever, I'll be able to hold her again like this. As my kids have grown, the less they like my embrace.

Finally she smiled at me. "Mom, you're the greatest! I thought you would be mad at me. Thank you for understanding and not getting defensive." She flung her arms around my neck just like she did when she was young. "I love you, Mommy, I really do, and I want to see you happy again."

"I'll work on that..." I promised her, but more, I promised myself. She's still my little girl. I loved our moment together, even if the basis of our conversation hurt me. I'll be honest. I don't like knowing that I'm boring.

Well, anyway, Cleo and I were in the kitchen. It's not a traditional kitchen. It has the usual cabinets and appliances, but it's also large enough to accommodate a whole dinner party. The kitchen and dining room are basically one big room, where the cabinets end there is a bit of space then there are bookshelves and window seats that wrap around two walls and our table sits there with chairs on the outer places. The dining area is a nice place to sit and read. We were sitting on one of the window seats, and her embrace was something I needed.

Colt and I were lucky when we found this house. It was an expensive, custom home built in 1922 for a wealthy family. But when we bought it in 1988, the market was down and I felt like we sort of stole it. I had the money from selling my townhouse, and Colt had money he'd saved, so together we had more than the down payment. That brought our payments to a very affordable level. We almost had the mortgage paid off when I was diagnosed with cancer. That's when we had to refinance to pay the bills. That really sucked. It's a nice big home, and each kid has his or her own room, plus there's a guest room (Colt's room for now), a hobby room that has somehow evolved into a storage room, a family room, and a breezeway to the garage that is a nice place to have breakfast because the windows face east and welcomes the sun. My favorite room is the master bedroom. That's where I retreated to after my conversation with my daughter.

There is a large wardrobe mirror in my room. Cleo's words still stung my heart. I stood in front of the mirror, nude, where every night before bedtime I habitually rub vitamin E oil on my scar. I probably don't need to continue doing that, but it was recommended after the surgery so the scar tissue would not harden up unevenly. Vitamin E is supposed to keep the skin supple and fade the discoloration of the scar and make it look closer to normal skin. The scar tissue feels funny when I touch it. My finger feels tissue that is thicker and harder than the rest of my chest. The doctors told me that rubbing the scar also helps my circulation. Scar tissue has less blood flowing to it, and that's another reason it's different.

When I rub it, the area where my breast used to be feels the pressure, but the sensation is distorted. It's a mixture of tingling, ticklishness, and tenderness. At times, my scar itches, but scratching it doesn't help. I could scratch at it all day and the itching persists. The cure I discovered is a good slap. It seems to confuse the nerves that were cut, and in their confusion they stop itching.

The scar tissue isn't very flexible. A few years ago, when I gained a bunch of weight, the scar didn't move. But the tissue around it puffed up. There is nothing that made me feel more ugly. I suppose it's in our culture to see big-breasted, thin women as normal. With only one breast and an odd looking scar accentuated by fat tissue, I felt like the ugliest person in the world.

Thankfully, I've lost the weight and now continue to lose weight, even though I've not dieted in a long time. (I'm not complaining!) Looking at the scar, I know it represents healing, just like the one on my stomach, that thin smiley face from my C-section that represents the birth of a healthy child. Physical scars are as permanent as the mental ones, I suppose. Good or bad, the scars exist, and I must search for the good in them.

Tonight, while I was rubbing the vitamin E oil on my scar, I looked at it. That made me upset because it reminded me how the cancer changed me. Like Cleo said, I am a changed woman. My happiness seems to be gone, drained away by the malignancy. Somehow, when they cut into to me and removed my breast, they also removed the playful part of my personality.

Knowing that hurts.

AUGUST 31ST

Colt came to me after he loaded the small bus for his gig tonight. He wanted to know if I was over being mad at him and if he could move back to our room.

"Hell, no," I said. "I've made an appointment with my lawyer."

He looked at me like a deer in the headlights. "You mean you really do want a divorce? This isn't just a bad mood?"

I didn't say much, other than to confirm my intention to divorce him.

He frowned and looked at the floor. "Well, Babe, if that's what you want…."

"It is," I repeated. "And until we get it all worked out, the guest room is all yours."

I felt like I had power over him for the first time, but not too far away from that feeling of power were the pangs of guilt. Especially when he looked away from me. I thought I saw him tear up.

"What have I done so wrong that's gotten us to this point?" he asked.

I didn't answer him, but I wanted to yell and scream, *Go to that hussy of a girlfriend you've been spending time with and ask her!* But I didn't. He should know my mind. It's obvious what's going on. How dare he spend time with another woman, most likely a younger woman, holding her while I'm at home holding on to nothing, nothing but emptiness! I hate this lonely feeling.

I ran up to my room. I wanted my grandparents. I wanted to climb up on one of their laps and hide from the world like I used to. I remember when I was little. If I was hurting, I'd cry myself to sleep in my grandmother's arms. I was comforted by the sound of her voice, rich and resonating from deep inside her coming up through her bosom, where my ear rested. She used to sing while rocking me in her arms. It was a spiritual song, "Where the Soul Never Dies." I longed to hear that song tonight.

But tonight, when Colt drove off, my emptiness expanded and I swear I was in the abyss. It's a warm summer night tonight, but I felt cold. I drew a hot bath and climbed in. The fear I feel is incapacitating me to the point that I just want to sit and cry. I want to feel like I belong to something more than work. I don't feel like I belong to my family, to Colt, or anyone else. Okay, I admit it: I gave myself a pity party. I invited my heartache and insecurity, and my inadequacy along with my foolishness. We were all there. We had a grand ole time.

In the hot bath, somewhere in between the tears, my soul whispered in my ear and I discovered something. Knowing it really scares me. I'm ashamed of it now, but what she told me was true. I say things to hurt Colt. I forget who he is. When this divorce is final, I will have lost not only my husband but the best friend I ever had. How do I overcome that? Even worse, I've discovered that I resent him. I really hate it that he's healthy, normal, and secure in life. Not that I want bad things to happen to him! But why did I have to be the one who got cancer? Why is it me who is disfigured? And old and ugly? I mean, it's not fair that he's as handsome as ever. He hasn't even lost any hair. Aren't men supposed to go bald when they're, like, forty? What the hell? He's got nice, thick hair, and I think he's been healthier after he turned fifty than he was in his twenties.

"No wonder he's got another woman," I told my soul. "God favors him! My life gets shitty, and his gets better and better." Was my soul listening? "And the kids are my proof. They think he's the best dad ever. They think I'm their depressed, unhappy mother."

I don't like knowing I resent Colt. It's not his fault I got cancer. He was so supportive when I was going through treatment. He did all the housework, the laundry, the cooking, plus he did his job. He even quit the band for a long time, until I was stable and in remission. No wonder God favors him. He's a saint! The man can do no wrong! I swear the man shits and flowers come out. How can he be so perfect? I suppose he feels entitled to another woman because he had to put up with me being sick and old and ugly.

That's the other thing I discovered sitting in the hot bath water talking to myself. (To my soul?) I feel like I failed him. When we got married, I looked at us as the perfect team, not only husband and wife, but best friends, too. Now I feel like

I didn't hold up my end. I let him down. I'm not a complete woman anymore. Maybe I can't satisfy him. So now he's gone off and found a way to get his gratification. At fifty, I wanted more than this. I envisioned my life being completely different. I saw Colt and me growing old together, playing with our grandkids, and me being equal to him.

I'm beginning to hate Friday nights. There's never anything fun or exciting for me to do.

SEPTEMBER 2ND

Colt came home early in the morning. I heard my bedroom door open. He undressed and climbed into bed with me.

"What do you think you're doing?" I asked him.

"Shush," he said. "Don't say a word. I'm tired, and I just want to go to sleep. I want to sleep feeling you next to me. When we wake up, you can beat the hell out of me, rant and yell later, but not now. Just let me lay here next to you and sleep."

I was tired, too, so I surrendered and went back to sleep.

I had a dream that I was young and in school with Becky. We must've been in the eighth grade. We were in general science class, and the teacher was teaching basic human anatomy. Becky and I were lab partners. When the teacher told one of us to make a fist, Becky made a fist.

"Now put your fist against the chest of your lab partner," the teacher said. "Like this." And the teacher placed her fist against the left side of her chest. "This is where your heart is. It's about the size of a fist."

I looked down at Becky's fist. Becky laughed. She always laughed. "How can my fist be the size of my heart?" she asked. "It's too small. There's no room for God, no room for my love for Jim Morrison, my feelings, or all the passions I have"

"My heart must be smaller than your fist," I said. "Because I don't believe in God."

"Girls," the teacher said, "there is no talking when I'm talking."

"But Hope doesn't believe in God," Becky said.

Everyone in the class stopped what they were doing and starred at me. The teacher got a nasty look on her face. "Hope," she said, "it's time for you to go home. Go home and think about what you said in my class."

Becky walked me to the door. I couldn't believe that my best friend was angry with me, but she was. "It's time for you to go home," she said.

"Why are you mad at me?" I asked her.

"Oh," she said, "I'm not mad at you. I'm mad because you've got to go home and I want you here with me. It's so hard for me to let you go, but you have to go."

In my dream, I walked home feeling sad, hoping my grandmother would help me understand. When I walked into the house, she wasn't surprised to see me at all. She was picking nutmeats out of their shells and putting the edible kernels in a Mason jar.

"I got sent home from school today because I don't believe in God," I told her. "Are you mad at me now, too?"

"Of course not," she said. "How can I be mad at you?

I'm almost done here. You can help me with the sewing in a minute."

The thing I remember most about my grandmother was that she was always doing something with her hands. I don't think I ever saw her when she wasn't darning or pickling vegetables or rolling dough or doing any number of things with her hands.

When she was ready, she fetched the sewing kit. I sat down next to her, and we began sewing hems, she on a tablecloth and me on the worn cuff of my granddad's work pants. Our arms touched as we moved, and I loved the contrast between her very pale white skin and my light brown skin. There was something indescribable about how her skin complimented mine.

"Well," she said, licking the thread so she could poke it through the eye of her needle, "let me tell you a secret about God. God is different for everyone. He approaches us in a way we're comfortable with. He'd be useless if his approach put fear into us, don't you think?"

In my dream, I thought about that for a minute. "That makes sense. But does he even exist? I've never seen him, heard him, or felt him."

"Oh, he exists if you search him out," she said. "He may not even be a *he*. He might be a *she*, if that makes you feel comfortable. Child, God is something for you to learn. No one can teach you about God. That's between you and God."

"What about church?" I asked. "They teach a person about God. Should I go to church?"

"Church? Some people go to church. They find God there, sure enough. Some people find God in other places, but I think you can find God if you ask God to find you. Like when you were little and I lost you in the grocery store. Remember?"

I nodded.

"You asked someone to help you," she said, "and they called me over the loud speaker, and I found you. Same way with God. Call out and ask him to find you."

We sat there next to each other in my dream, stitching, and I could feel the warmth from her body, and it felt good. But then she took the sewing out of my hand. "You have to prepare for your journey, child." And she walked me to the door. My eyes widened, because in my grandparents' yard stood a beautiful white flying horse. Pegasus.

"Go, child," my grandmother said. "Fly up to heaven. Get close to your heart's desire. Remember that God isn't down on the ground. You must look up toward the stars to find God."

In my dream, the Pegasus was big. He had to have been almost eighteen hands tall, so it was a struggle for me to get mounted. But with my grandmother's help, I was able to get myself situated.

"Go on, be safe," she said, "but live a good life. Your granddad and I will be right here waiting for you."

Even in a dream, the sensation of flight is thrilling. The Pegasus soared up high toward the sun. I could see the earth down below. I could see the people and traffic moving in the city. I could also feel a presence. God. I don't understand it, exactly, but there was something greater than me at work while I was in flight.

Well, after that dream this morning, the sun's rays shining through my window I just lay still, feeling the warmth of sun. Then I felt Colt's arm on my shoulder. I didn't want to disturb the moment, so I didn't move. Somewhere in that sunlight, I could still feel the warmth of my grandmother. She was a large woman, big around and well-endowed. In my eyes, she was the most beautiful woman in the world. She was wise in the ways of nature. I suppose that's no surprise, her living in an agricultural town all her life. There were many women like her, but none exactly like her.

After the state university put a campus in their town and several corporations moved in, the women of my grandmother's caliber dwindled. Women like me got degrees and became professional women, and the sewing circles, quilting bees, and harvest gatherings became things of the past. I'm living in a modern era. It makes me sad to think my grandparents' era is now known as "the old times" or "back in the day." Those phrases seem to add distance between them and me.

I'll admit it. It was nice to wake up next to Colt. But I'm not confused. I don't forgive him, nor will I forget that he's got another woman. But I wasn't feeling strong enough to argue, so I just wiggled out from under his arm and let him sleep.

Today is Sunday. My favorite day. I've always considered Sunday my day to do whatever I like. This morning, I made a decision. I'm heading out for an adventure. Even though I didn't feel very good, I got on my bike and rode the twelve miles out to the graveyard where my grandparents are buried. It's been years since I went out alone to see them. I've been several times with the family, like on Memorial Day, but today I wanted to be alone with them.

I doubt their spirits are still hanging around the graveyard. If their spirits are anywhere, I'm sure they'd be at the home they lived in for fifty-eight years. But for some reason, I felt it necessary to go to their graves.

I grabbed some GORP - granola, oats, raisins, peanuts all mixed together, plus my own mixture of cashews, sunflower seeds, raisins, dates, shredded coconut, and dark chocolate. You've got to have chocolate. That's what puts the GO in GORP! I shoved that pouch in one of my cargo pockets and filled my water bladder with ice water. On the bike, I have a pair of water bottle cages and I use the bottom one for my bottle of Mountain Dew. No bike ride is complete without a bottle of Mountain Dew! I think I've discovered what calls my soul forward or what wakens her from her slumber…it's cycling, dark chocolate, and Mountain Dew.

Sunday is the perfect day for pedaling. Hardly any traffic, so I can fly. I pedaled hard and fast, feeling just like I felt in my dream on the back of the Pegasus. At every red light, I pulled the bottle of cold Dew up to my mouth and slammed a few gulps. Then the light turned green and off I went again. In my mind, there was no city, no streets, no houses, no cars or trucks. There was only the wind on my face. And my soul. I felt connected to my soul and to that spiritual frequency again. They seemed to be urging me on and I pedaled with a smile on my face.

At the graveyard, I dismounted and walked my bike to the twin gravesite. I sat on the grass. "Hello," I said aloud. "I know it's been a while since I've been out here. Sorry about that. I wanted to come out today and thank you, Grandmother, for visiting me last night. The dream made me lonesome for you, so I thought I would just come on over and tell you these things in person."

If I have ever known true love, it's with my grandparents. And even though it's been over twenty-five years since they've passed, I still feel their absence every day.

"Thank you for loving me when I was growing up," I said. "I can't remember if I ever you told you that before, but, really, thank you. If living life has an expression, your expression was love. I felt it every day you were alive, you expressed so much of it, I can still feel it. I felt it last night. Sometimes I feel so alone in this world, and I wish you were here for me to hug. Oh, what I'd give if I could have one more day with you. I yearn to feel your arms around me, to hear the sounds of your voices, to smell the baking bread. If only...."

When I was little, grandmother never bought bread from the store. She made every loaf we ever ate. I miss the smell of fresh, home-baked bread.

My grandparents were so much in love with each other that it felt good just to be around them. They were the definition of balance. What she lacked, he made up for, and what he lacked, she found a way to complete.

I was still feeling flu-ish, eating the GORP wasn't helping me. I decided I should go and get something more substantial. "I'll be around for another visit soon," I said. I walked my bike back to the road, but before I mounted it, I turned around.

"Grandmother, I want you to know I heard you last night. I will call out to God. Hopefully, he or she will find me."

I wasn't flying so much on the way back home, but I still enjoyed the ride. I stopped at the Snake River Grill over on Birch Street. They have what they call their bitterroot salad. It's yummy, but the name is deceiving. It's named after the Bitterroot Mountains of Montana. It doesn't have bitterroot in the ingredients. Actual bitterroot was used for medicinal purposes, for ailments of the heart. That's what Granddad told me when I was young. The salad has dried cranberries, bleu cheese crumbles, aged white cheddar, smoked salmon, asparagus tips, sliced avocado, tomato, lettuce, and a house-made honey-mustard dressing that is made with coarse-ground mustard that really brings out all the flavors.

This was lunch, and it was delicious. I took my time riding home. The world seemed so rich and vibrant that I wanted to take it all in. I pedaled over twenty-two miles today. That's pretty good for me.

Colt was playing with Sahchi in the back yard when I got home. I was hesitant, but I wandered back to talk to him. He looked at me and threw the tennis ball that Sahchi had slobbered all over in my direction.

"I'm not picking that nasty thing up," I said.

"Get it Sahchi! Get it!" he said, and our dog pounced on the ball and carried it back to him. He looked at me. "Since when are you afraid to get a little dirty?"

I gave him a hard look. "What did you think you were doing this morning, getting in bed with me?"

"Oh." He stood there, holding that dripping, dirty ball in his hands. "I was wondering when you were going to chew my ass about that. It was nothing. I just wanted to sleep next to you. So sue me."

I shook my head. "Don't let it happen again."

"Hope, when are you going to stop this? I love you."

"Love? Shit! You should've thought about that before you found yourself a little girlfriend."

"Goddammit!" he practically shouted. "I don't have a girlfriend! Will you please stop this? Nina's been getting worse, and it looks like I'm the only one who can calm her down. I sing to her. That seems to help. I'm going there tonight. How about you come with me? You can see for yourself."

But I just turned and walked away. I didn't want to hear his lies anymore. I'd had a wonderful day. Why spoil it with lies and heartache? I heard him drop the dog's ball on the ground. He just stood there. With every step I took, I felt something deep inside me at work. Colt has always had a mysterious way with people and animals. Is it possible he's been telling me the truth?

As I walked up the stairs to my room, my soul called up a memory. It was years ago, when I went with Colt on a hunt for Dall sheep. They live in the Alaskan range. It was September, too, a beautiful time of the year, but that part of Alaska is probably the most rugged place on earth, at least the most rugged terrain I've ever encountered. When we got there, the other men in our hunting party actually made fun of Colt.

They laughed at him for bringing me along. They weren't used to seeing a woman up there, much less a light-skinned black woman.

"This is no place for women," they said.

And what did Colt say? "I'll bet any one of you that Hope will tackle this place better than you big, strong men." He looked at me. "Isn't that right, Babe?"

"You betcha!"

Then those mighty he-men laughed at him for bringing an old lever-action .300 Savage rifle.

"I'm sure that gun's good in the lower forty-eight," one of them said, "but it has no place in Alaska. Too small."

They talked tough, but they, too, were from the lower forty-eight. They wanted to make Colt and me think they were locals, but only one of them was actually from Alaska.

"Since when has killing an animal changed?" Colt asked. "Those canons you guys are carrying are fancy, but killing is still killing, no matter what your weapon is. I learned that in the Marines. This gun is capable of killing any critter, even the most dangerous ones...the ones that walk on two legs."

He wasn't popular the first week up there, but during the second week our party accidentally disturbed a mother bear with her almost grown cubs. I don't know if she was a grizzly or not, but she was damn huge. Meeting her with her cubs wasn't a good thing. That bear stood up on her hind legs, and I swear she was over ten feet tall. She stood up tall and sniffed the air. Her cubs imitated their mother and stood up sniffing, too. They looked to be seven feet tall on their hind legs. Were we scared? You betcha. Me and every one of the mighty he-men hunters. But what do men do when they are scared? They pull out something elongated with a hole at the end of it. Am I right or am I right?

So as the men chambered rounds and shouldered their rifles, ready to blast the hell out of every living thing in sight, Colt walked right in front of them. I don't remember or didn't hear what he said to the mama bear, but he said something, and he said it loud. His words blew away in the wind. Whatever he said, she heard him, thought, and she and her cubs went down on four legs. Then she collected her cubs and ran them in the direction of some thick berry bushes.

Even the guide was dumbfounded. "You either have no fear," he finally said, "or you're the dumbest city slicker to ever come up here."

But I knew better. Colt has a way of communicating with animals. I don't think he even understands the totality of his ability, but at the end of the hunt, the only one who bagged a ram was Colt. The others had their chances, but even with their expensive, high tech rifles, they all missed their shots.

When he was butchering his harvest, Colt said, "Look at this meat. It's beautiful! You can't get this in any store that I know of."

There is no doubt that that meat made one of the best meals I've ever eaten. We didn't use marinade because Colt said it would only cover up the natural taste of the Dall. We just sliced up palm-sized pieces, poked a stick through them, and roasted them over the campfire. It was wonderful.

I love Alaska. I'm not a woman that condones hunting. I'm an advocate for nature, wild animals, and protecting the wilderness. But living with Colt, I've learned the best way to take care of a human body is through eating natural game meat. No chemicals, no antibiotics, no growth hormones—nothing but natural food. And I've watched Colt hunt. He's a different man in the wilderness. I've seen men use a hunting trip for an excuse to drink and get tough and brave, be belligerent. They start shooting at harmless squirrels, birds, and what they refer to as pests, just so they can kill something. Colt won't admit it, but it's a religious experience for him. I've observed him closely and I noticed early on that he prays before the hunt. And he prays again after he's bagged his quarry. He prays over his game. He is very aware of the animal's soul. I have always liked that about him. Colt was the most popular guy in camp after he spoke to the mama bear and after we ate that sheep. Whatever God put into making Colt's soul, he put in the right combination of ingredients for animal and human alike.

It is entirely possible he has found a way to help Nina that most of us wouldn't understand. But I can't make excuses for him. He's been sleeping with another woman and using Nina as cover for his rendezvous.

SEPTEMBER 3RD

It's good to have an intelligent, charming, and energetic employee. I tested Devin today. First, I explained how to perform a task above his level and gave him an assignment. I expected it to be a total mess, but when I came to check on him, he said, "Look, *Ma'am*, I'm finished. I think I understood it well enough, but will you check the work to make certain I did it correctly?"

I had asked Blythe to work with him and look over the work. He reported that Devin had done the task perfectly. I was impressed! However, one thing bothered me, that word *Ma'am*. It makes me feel old.

Afterward, I sat Devin down in my cubicle. I do that with every new employee after their first week on the job. I like to offer them an opportunity to discuss their opinion regarding the new job. I also like to hear any suggestions as to how we might improve. I like to make sure my employees are happy. I don't want to have them resign over something simple that I could have fixed the first week. If they're having trouble understanding what's expected of them, I want them to see me as a resource for help.

Anyway, I kept catching little glances from him…. I'm not sure, but I think he was looking at my legs. (I was in a skirt today.) He was fidgety and nervous. I think my position as his boss intimidates him. Poor newbie! I didn't have the heart to yell at him for calling me Ma'am, but I'm too damn young to be called that. Although I did tell him to feel free to call me Hope, and during our conversation he called me by my given name. But when he said my name, he blinked. He's not especially attractive, but he was so cute with his nervous blink when he said my name that it made me giggle.

Mid-afternoon, I was summoned to Brent's office. He's the director of the company and he's putting pressure on me to make certain no one knows that my team is distilling data for Back-2-Back.

"Hope," he said, "I can't impress upon you enough how to keep this project under tight control. I'm relying on you to work your team in such a way that they see no connection between Back-2-Back and Bio-Sport."

His mouth kept moving, but I quit listening. I felt queasy, my head was pounding, and my heart felt like it was racing. *What the hell is wrong with me?* Normally, I don't look forward to a doctor's appointment, but I wanted some answers, so I'm glad I have my follow-up appointment tomorrow.

Anyway, Brent just kept rambling on about the importance of the assignment and the weight of my assignment, the weight he was placing on my shoulders. Blah blah blah. But I couldn't care less. He's lucky I didn't just puke on his shoes. It was hard to get through the rest of the day. When I got home, I went straight up to my room, closed the door, and read until now. Its 8:30, and I'm going to sleep. I still feel like crap.

SEPTEMBER 4TH

I left work early so I could go see my doctor.

"I'm sure it's nothing to be concerned about," she told me, "but your white count is on the high end of normal."

"But why do I feel so out of sorts?" I asked her. "It's like I have the flu all the time."

"I'm not sure," she said. "An elevated white count, fever, and other symptoms are indicative of an infection. Just to be safe, I'm going to prescribe an antibiotic and more blood work. You'll probably have to fast for the next blood draw, but I'm not sure. Here's the phone number. Call the lab and ask them about prep. Do you take any supplemental vitamins?"

"Not really," I said. "I eat healthy and I exercise, so I didn't think I needed supplements."

She looked at my chart again and said, "I think it'll be a good idea for us, on your next follow-up, to have a talk about menopause and hormone replacement therapy."

Menopause? Really? Now I *really* feel old and ugly.

After my nice little chat with the doctor, I went to get groceries. Pulling into the parking lot, I saw someone that looked a little familiar. I wasn't certain at first, but, sure enough, it was Mr. Goldsole. He didn't see me right off, but when I went up to him, he turned, and when he saw me his smile grew so big.

"How are you doing, little Hope?" he asked.

"I'm well."

"Would you mind if I accompany you? It appears we have a common chore."

"Mind it? I'd love some company!"

He is such a lovely man. I wish I could describe how I feel when I see him. He walked through the aisles of the grocery store with me, chatting about this and that, and I felt the warmth of family surrounding me. I swear it! It wasn't anything specific he said or did, but just having him standing next to me...I don't know, but there's just something about him, something familiar, something special. I hope I see him again.

I think it's likely, since we shop at the same store. Anyway, I hope I do get another chance to see him.

When I got home, Conrad and Junior were shouting at each other in the kitchen. Junior was saying something about Conrad's friend (girlfriend? Does Conrad have a new girl?), but they stopped yelling as soon as they realized I was home, then they tried to act like nothing was going on. But Conrad's jaw was obviously tense, and Junior's eyes were narrowed and focused on Conrad.

"What now?" I asked them. "What's going on between you two?"

Conrad shrugged his shoulders, and Junior said, "None of your business."

Now I was pissed off. I was in a great mood after meeting Mr. Goldsole again, but it's amazing how someone can drag you into their bad mood.

Somehow I kept from slapping Junior across the face. His face is so stiff, I don't think anything will ever soften it. None of my business? Hah! I went to the refrigerator and started putting away the groceries. I felt defeated and embarrassed and humiliated to be yelled at by my own child. It just isn't possible that my son just talked to me that way. But I was a fool. I didn't say anything. I just popped a can of Mountain Dew and took a sip.

A second later, I heard a yell coming from the other room. It was Colt storming into the kitchen. "Since when do you boys think you can speak to your mother that way?" he shouted at them. He waited for an answer, but both boys looked away. "You're not big enough yet to challenge me." He looked squarely at Junior, then at Conrad. They both hung their heads. "I'll take you to task the next time I hear either of you use that tone of voice at your mother. Apologize to her." He waited, and when neither of them moved, he yelled, "NOW!"

"I'm sorry," Conrad said. "Junior and I are just working something out. We didn't mean to bring you into it."

Damn. When Colt came to my defense, I remembered all the reasons why I fell in love with him. Even at fifty-five, he's so strong, there are few men who would step up and challenge him. My temples hurt, and I closed my eyes for a second. When I looked again, Colt had a hold of Junior's arm.

"You need to show her some respect. Apologize!"

Junior pulled away. "Why do you care?" he asked. "You two don't even sleep in the same room any more. Why should you care what I say to her? You don't love her anymore."

That was it. I knew I had to intervene when I saw the change in Colt's face. When he's angry to the point of rage, it's obvious in his eyes, his face, even his posture. Nothing but disaster ever follows that. I put myself between them.

"What are you doing?" Junior asked.

"You idiot," I said, "I'm saving your life! Your father is a good man, but he's not above killing one of his sons, and I'm not above covering up the crime!"

Colt turned away so he wouldn't show the terrible laugh he was holding in. After that, Junior apologized, but only half-heartedly. It wasn't quite what I wanted, but it was enough.

Colt left the kitchen, as did the boys, but all of them went in different directions, and then I was alone again. I held in my laughter, but also the tears. I love that man, I do, but because of the other woman, what we had is gone, and that makes me so sad. The change that has infected both of us is now apparent to our kids. They're spiteful because of us.

We had dinner as a family, well, excluding Junior. He didn't come back after he stormed off. I wonder what's going on with him. Well, dinner was quiet, with a few pleasant requests to pass the salt or can I have some more of that, but nothing that added up to a conversation. Cleo was off in her own world. I don't think she'd even heard the argument between her brothers or her father yelling. Poor child. She's off in her own world so much.

Later, Colt and I said goodnight to each other and went to our separate rooms. I wanted to believe things were like they used to be and call him up to my room, but that would be wrong. I'm the first one to recognize the change between us. There is no reason to confuse things.

SEPTEMBER 6TH

I've lost a good amount of weight! I'm so happy. I'm just not that hungry anymore. When I do eat, though, I eat healthy. The only thing that I suppose isn't that good for me is Mountain Dew or a chocolate bar now and then. Maybe I should stop drinking the Dew.... Yeah. Right!

Anyway, after work I went out and got my hair done and bought me a new dress and shoes. No special occasion. I just wanted to feel pretty again. I felt good in the dress, and my prosthesis wasn't noticeable, even with the low cut. It's time for me to feel good about myself again.

SEPTEMBER 7TH

This morning, the other new guy, James, tried to confess something to me. I don't know what it is about my face that seems to invite the strays to come and confide in me. Several of my coworkers have done this. They look at me, they smile at me, some go as far as to start sobbing, and then they open their hearts. Honestly, most of their problems don't interest me. It amazes me, the shameless way that some people want to talk about their secrets.

First thing this morning, I had just sat down in my cube and was listening to the thirteen voicemails that were waiting for me, when James waltzed in like he knew me, like I was his friend. He plopped down in the other chair.

"I don't think anyone here likes me," he said. Then he paused and looked at me, I assume, waiting for me to say something. To feel sorry for him?

"Pleased to meet you, Mr. Pity," I said. "I'm a cancer survivor," I said with a gesture intended to counter his unwanted drama. My surviving cancer moved his emotions less than his lack of popularity. But I felt it was necessary to speak before the dikes of his conscience broke and I found myself up to my neck in intimate details of his life.

He tapped his thin finger on my desk (which annoyed me) and the multiple bracelets he wore jangled and made more noise. "Oh, never mind," he said after a minute, and he left my cubicle.

Damn right, never mind! I thought. A newbie that had the gall to come into my cubical, throw himself down, and expect me to comfort him is getting nothing from me. I don't mind his effeminate approach, but I do mind unwanted drama.

I sat there and stared at the wall for a few minutes. It was ugly. That drab Bella-Dura industrial fabric lacks any human embellishment. It's like being surrounded by concrete. There were no funny cartoons of Garfield and Odie, no family photos, nothing but a single bookshelf with corporate manuals in black binders all lined up. I felt my soul crying for release from this prison.

I turned and looked out the window across the room. It was beautiful outside. I didn't want to be at work. In fact, this was the last place I wanted to be. I wanted to leave, go out and climb on my bike and ride around town. I wanted to pedal through town, stop and have lunch somewhere fun. I wanted to smile because the sun and wind were on my face. That's what I wanted to do. But what I had was a bleak little cubicle that gave me some semi-privacy among all the other cubes in the huge common area of the third floor.

I remember when I loved my job, when I really enjoyed coming to work. But something's changed now, either within me or within the company. Or maybe both. If I'm honest, it's not that some*thing* has changed but more that some *things*— plural things—have changed. There was a time when the break room had refreshments, free of charge. That was back when we were encouraged to use the break room. Now the tables have been put away and the serving dishes are getting dusty in the storage room. We used to be a friendly bunch. This place was modeled on the software companies in Silicon Valley, with modified work hours, daycare for the parents with children, and work attire was something comfortable. We had the latitude to post pictures of our friends and families on our walls. My cubicle didn't seem small back then. Some passerby would see a picture, stop, and chat about it for a moment, and in that moment a friendship was born. There wasn't as much micro management back then. People put in more hours off the clock because they felt their work meant something back then.

It seems to me like when the country went off to war in 2003, our corporate world sprouted a military mentality. We started to feel the grip of management around our necks, and then the memos started piling up, dictating the dehumanization of our work areas. The work hours became strictly nine to five, and the daycare was closed due to cost cutting. Work attire was no longer casual, and anyone that wore anything that was comfortable was deemed a "liberal," as though thinking with an unregimented mind was some kind of criminal activity.

Then came the employee badges. An I.D. card of sorts, but magnetically integrated into the newly installed timekeeper that tracks not only the time of arrival and departure of all employees, but it also tracks our movements. Now management is able to see who leaves their work area and for how long.

It's all automatic, and only two people can make any adjustments to the system. This can be problematic. For example, when I'm working on the "secret Back-2-Back project," I have to use a spare office to keep it secret. While I'm in the spare office, the timekeeper clocks me out of my work area, meaning I don't get paid for the hours I'm not where I'm officially assigned to be. I have to get Brent to get the tech guy (whose title is longer than I am tall) to adjust my time so I get paid properly. It's a bunch of micromanaging crap. I'm human. Not some damn robot that interfaces with the corporate computer system.

The other day, I was called into Brent's office because the timekeeper had tracked Blythe to the men's room at 10:35 and he didn't resurface until seven after 11:00.

"What was Blythe doing for thirty-two minutes in the men's room?" Brent asked. I think he was actually angry with me.

I looked him square in the eyes and said, "I'm not sure, but I think that's a pretty good indication of a stuck turd, don't you?"

"That's not funny," he said. "We need to keep our teams productive. He's not productive if he's in the men's room. You need to take him down to HR and sign a reprimand."

"What? Are you serious?"

"Look at this timesheet. Every day, he's off to the men's room at 10:35, and he spends at minimum ten minutes in there."

At first, I didn't know what to say. Then, "Oh, come on. Is it really my job to manage a man's bowel activity? Does anyone stand outside the men's room when you're doing your business and time you?"

He got mad, but I was madder. This interconnected system tracking all of our activities pisses me off. I'm certain my soul had control of my mouth in that meeting. She's been pointing out to me how the company is inhuman and I am a human being, and a human being has needs that a non-human entity can't recognize. My soul is right. I should have left work and gone riding today, but I stayed there because I've been conditioned to stay.

I took my brown-bag lunch to the cathedral. I went with the intention to call to God to come find me, but then I got embarrassed and came out again. Well, I got embarrassed, not because of my intention, but because when I went in, it was dim and my eyes hadn't adjusted to the low light, and I banged my knee hard on the edge of a pew. I'm such a klutz! I ran right into the corner of the pew in full stride. It hurt so bad I yelled out, "God-damn-it!" Well, the people sitting in the pews and praying weren't too happy that I was there after they heard that, so I covered my face with my hands and practically ran out the door.

Good job, Hope, yelling profanities in the house of God. I'm sure you got his or her attention.

Before going back to the office, I wrote Becky a quick email on my smart phone to let her know that being naked and praying under the moon was another embarrassing situation. She wrote back and explained that I'd misunderstood her. I was to bathe, but then get dressed and then go out and pray. She said she couldn't stop laughing at my email.

How did I get that wrong?

I suppose I envisioned praying in the nude, but in my vision there wasn't anyone else around. I was all alone.

*Notes to self.
Don't swear in
church. Be well
dressed for prayer.*

SEPTEMBER 9TH

Sunday is always a relief. Sometimes I like to stay in my room until late, at least nine or so. It's my time. I'm not obligated to anyone, and that's a wonderfully freeing feeling. But this morning I woke up to the hurting in my lower abdomen. I couldn't go back to sleep. Lately I've been feeling ill, but this morning it's the pain. I've been thinking it's pre-menopause, but who knows what this throbbing is? The pain finally subsided in the afternoon, and I was able to go out. I wanted to treat myself to lunch, so I pedaled out to the Good Eats Café over on Oak Street. I like it there because they have a nice patio in front.

I got a table near the street and ordered my favorite, a BLT with sweet-potato fries. I love those sweet-potato fries dipped in honey mustard. Of course I had the Dew, too. I swear it makes any meal better. After I ordered, I watched people walking up and down the street. I am guilty, I admit it. I watched the men going by. Today I was paying particular attention to what attracted me to them. I figure if I'm going to be single again, I want to see what's on the market.

In the space of an hour, I counted thirty-five men that I'd consider making love to based only on physical appearance. I took inventory. I wrote the results on my napkin. Of two, I liked their face; of four, their height and hair; of eight, their arms and chests; of fifteen, the way their asses filled their pants, jeans, shorts, etc. It was a grand victory for the asses. I guess the results are in. I'm a girl that goes for a cute butt.

I'm blessed with a shapely derrière myself. When someone asks me what my favorite body part is, that's it. (Have I ever really been asked that question? I don't know for sure.) If I'd had butt cheek cancer, and the surgeon had had to remove it and left my ass lopsided, I wouldn't have recovered from the surgery. I'm certain of that. That's another reason I like to pedal my bike so hard, it works the *gluteus maximus* and keeps my fifty-year-old ass muscle in shape.

Isn't it funny how I can see different parts of my body as independent from my whole body? Why do I do that? I mean, like, my ass, when I look at it, I only see it and nothing else. When I put on weight, I don't look in the mirror and say damn I'm getting fat. I look at my ass and it looks HUGE and it's the only thing I see. Then I cuss it.

My ass is part of my Southern region. It shares territory down there with my vagina, but the two have very different personalities. The vagina is where my desires live. It contributed to the lives of my children. My butt is my pillowy throne where my attractiveness is founded. Colt once told me that my butt hypnotized him when we were first dating. I didn't understand why, I had two breasts back then, and I used to wear low-cut shirts, hoping to bring him in. But he told me what he liked so much about my butt is that it was covered. It was mysterious.

However, I think most men really prefer breasts. Two nipples poking through a shirt will have the majority of the men in a public place turning their heads. I must believe this because when it's going to be cold out, sometimes I put a special button in my bra over my prosthesis so when my natural nipple pokes up, both breasts match.

I remember one time I did that and Colt was walking with me and he looked and looked again. He never said a word, but I knew he was staring. He looked like a pervert staring at my boobs, but he wasn't looking because he was attracted. He was staring because he was amazed at the thought of my prosthesis having a working nipple.

After lunch today I decided to ride around and enjoy the day. It won't be much longer before winter is here and I won't be able to ride.

SEPTEMBER 10TH

Sometimes I am plagued by insomnia.

I heard Junior come in at midnight, Conrad, thirty minutes later, and Cleo an hour after that. None of them were quiet about it. I heard the boys and their vulgar talk as they were digging around in the kitchen in search of something to eat. I think Junior was a little drunk. It sure sounded like he was stumbling around. Conrad, who never drinks, was swearing at him, and when Cleo came in, I heard Junior yell something to her from his room. She told him to mind his own business. After all that, the house was silent again.

Then this morning, when Cleo and I were alone, I told her I didn't like her staying out that late. She wasn't disrespectful to me, though I'd expected her to talk back. I know she's grown up, but it is the duty of a parent to be protective. There are two things I'm sure of with my daughter. We love each other, and she's not doing anything abnormal for her age.

I'm beginning to rethink this menopause business. I feel so depressed. Sometimes, I feel like I'm pushing my family away. Instead of sounding concerned about Cleo, I think I came off sounding bitchy. Is it my hormones running wild?

It started today even before I saw Cleo. It started when I woke up this morning. I didn't want my sleep to be over. I hated the fact that it was morning. More importantly, I didn't want to be me waking up alone in my bed. I didn't want to be me going to work, to my job. Mondays suck, but this morning really sucked because I was so depressed that nothing in the world seemed good. I don't think I smiled once today. Is that even possible? Surely I smiled at someone today, perhaps when they greeted me...well, I can't remember.

And I felt queasy at work again. There was acid sloshing around in my stomach. My hair was a wreck, and I know I looked a fright. I didn't care. Doing any kind of work made the pressure behind my eyes get worse, and the pounding caused me to take eight ibuprofens, way over the recommended dose.

Will life ever get better? I want to get to a point in my life where everything is good at the same time. I want my children to want to share time with me. At the same time, I want the perfect husband who sees me as the most attractive woman in the world and gives me the affection I desire. I want to have money so I don't have to work for a living. I'm not saying I want to be rich, just have enough to pay the bills with some left over to enjoy my life. Can I squeeze all of this happiness out of my retirement days?

SEPTEMBER 12TH

I'm such a fool. I wanted to feel pretty, so I put on my red dress. Actually, getting dressed today became a ceremony of sorts. I put on new, lace panties. I bought them specifically to be arousing, something that would turn a man's head. Then I put on the garters and stockings and finally the dress and heels. Then—the diamond necklace and matching earrings Colt gave me for our anniversary. I stood in front of the mirror for a while, admiring my reflection. I turned my music up loud and danced around my room.

Is that foolish?

I hate to think so. I really enjoyed myself. I was free to make a fool of myself and I wanted to feel that freedom.

I thought I was home alone, but when I went down to the kitchen to get something to drink, Colt was standing in the hallway.

"I've never seen that dress before," he said. He gave me a big smile. "You look really good."

I didn't say anything I just walked past him and into the kitchen.

He kept talking. "Babe, things have been strange between us. Now this new look you've got has me thinking...you're drifting further away from me."

I didn't want to get into a huge discussion or argument with him, so I just started back up the stairs.

But he kept going. "I never thought I'd see the day when we weren't in love." He said that loud enough to make sure I heard him. "Babe, what's happened to us?"

I went up without saying a word. I swear it wasn't because I was being mean, but because I just couldn't speak. I didn't know what to say. Before I closed my door I heard what else he said.

"Hope, my sister isn't doing very good these days. Things here aren't, well...I guess I'll be spending more time with her."

I slammed the door shut. I knew what that meant. It hurt so much to picture him wrapped up in another woman's arms. He was going to be spending more time with his little whore, that's what he meant. Using Nina as an excuse.

SEPTEMBER 13TH

I worked all afternoon with Devin. We were still distilling data for Back-2-Back, which is the most tedious kind of task in the world. We strained our eyes from staring at the LED monitors and extracting specific numbers, but Devin kept at it patiently. I'm so accustomed to this kind of work that I actually prefer it to more complex, challenging tasks.

And I felt noticeably better today. When Devin was going down the column and reading integers to me so I could insert them into the proper columns, I found myself looking at his arms, his chest, his mouth and cheeks, his hair. He continued giving me numbers. I either entered them or checked them off on the spreadsheet. Suddenly I felt something strange. I raised my eyes in the middle of a number—he was looking at my legs again. I knew for sure he was looking at my legs. When I smiled at him, he nearly died of embarrassment. Poor boy! He doesn't know that I'm a serious, professional, woman and would never, absolutely never, start anything with one of my employees. But he's cute. And I'm flattered.

I got called into Brent's office after lunch. "Back-2-Back needs to speak with you," he said, "so I set up a conference call in the vacant office. It's more private than your cube."

As if he had to explain why! I know damn well there's no privacy in my cube. I took the call. The men I talked to at Back-2-Back make me nervous. There was so much testosterone flowing through their language. They were saying things like "assassinating the competition," "taking out the investors" of the competition, "it's kill or be killed in this industry," "I'm going to drive a stake into the heart of their company," and my favorite, "I'm going to eat their young!" Who talks like that? I felt like I was being prepared for a preemptive strike in some war in the Middle East. And that Back-2-Back had endowed me with a penis, which they see as a lethal weapon. And I'm on a top-secret mission.

They asked me if I had sent any emails to anyone regarding the project, or had I been cc'd anything from Bio-Sport. This kind of posturing went on and on, like they were trying to impress me with all their tough talk. I know what my job is, but evidently they didn't understand the details and were a little insecure about that fact. I reassured them and reassured them again. I think these businessmen must be as young as Conrad, who is twenty-three, and they're in control of a multibillion-dollar company that they're treating like one of their video games. Well, I could be mistaken, but all that war talk made me uncomfortable. I don't normally go around telling people that I'm gong to kill the competition or assassinate the boss and eat his young. I wanted to say, "Now, boys, if you can't talk nice, we will have to take a time-out." But I didn't. These guys have enough money to run a small country. Their fantasies about the act of simple data mining as assassination make me shudder. What if one of these guys wants to bring his video game to life? He has the money to arm eager young kids. I don't want to think about that.

Toward the end of the conference call, they asked me what kind of bonus I was going to get for doing this project. "Bonus?" I said. "No bonus here. It's my job. I'm expected to do it. In fact, I heard some rumors around the office about cuts to wages, so I'll be lucky if the next time we speak I'm making what I'm making today."

"Hope," one of the men at Back-2-Back said, "believe me. When you have completed this project, we will send you a handsome bonus. Discreetly. To your home. You can keep it all." There was a suggestive pause here. "Or you can share it with whoever provides you assistance. But to reiterate—the confidentiality of our relationship will also have a bearing on your bonus." He didn't identify himself, but I knew he was in charge. The big guy. He sounded older than the other guys. I could be completely wrong, though, because I'm only going by the sounds of their voices. His was deeper.

The conference call lasted an hour and ten minutes, but it seemed longer. I was bored after the first ten minutes so my eyes began to wander. The vacant office is next to Brent's office and I could see his receptionist banging away at her keyboard. Her reddish hair looks expensive, so do her clothes, and she gets what she pays for. She always looks good. She's one of those girls who spend too much time primping. Brent had installed—at her request, I'm sure—a large mirror across from her desk. I swear, she'll type for five minutes, then she'll look at the mirror on the wall and reapply her lipstick, type some more, then check her makeup again, type another few lines, then check her hair. She doesn't sit in a cubicle, so the mirror looks like it's just part of the office décor. But I know why it's there.

A little later, thanks to that mirror, I could also see Brent's son and his girlfriend in the throes of passion. Brent was out of his office, as usual, and the two kids thought no one could see them. Thanks to the mirror, I did see them. The things that go on in the office!

When my conference call ended, I walked back to my cubicle, shaking my head in disgust at both the conference call and the reflected fornication. I don't like what is happening at work. My company is evolving into something much different than what it used to be. My mind was saying,

You need an exit plan. This place is becoming acidic with negativity. Your boss is in bed with some bad

*people in charge of this project. His son's office affair
is symbolic of what's leading the company. You can see
the effect that bad judgment can have on you.*

I know that bundling the data for Back-2-Back is only part
of the mission to destroy Bio-Sport. And I'm part of it. I'm a
helping hand in destroying a company whose employees will
be affected. The humanity in me can imagine the hardships
inflicted when the company is destroyed. The unemployment.
Frustration. Unpaid bills. I've been there, done that. I'm sure
there is a big-enough market for Back-2-Back and Bio-Sport
both to survive in this world. Neither has to kill the other.

I don't like how this makes me feel mentally and soulfully.
Am I allowing my work to command my behavior?

SEPTEMBER 14TH

My car was in the shop today, so I had to take the bus to
work. I don't find it fun, riding the bus. And then I had
to stay a little late for the Back-2-Back project. I had to report
some corrections in private to Brent. All that secrecy always
makes me feel like I'm doing something illegal. The time it took
for Brent and me to have that little, secret conference made me
have to run for the bus as it was pulling away. It stopped for me,
and I got on, but when I found a seat, I thought I was going to
pass out from dizziness. I was getting settled in the seat and my
bare arm touched the arm of the man sitting next to me. He was
wearing short sleeves, too. That gave me an odd feeling. I wasn't
sure if it came from him or me or both of us. I pulled out my

iPad and opened the book I've been reading (Bram Stoker's *Dracula*). He was reading a paperback mystery. I finally caught my breath, but I still felt light-headed.

The man next to me moved his arm several times, but I noticed that he moved with conscious effort not to separate our bare arms. I looked out the window, then, trying not to be obvious, glanced over at him again. The bus turned onto Ash Street, and all at once my purse toppled over, and a second later it looked like a yard sale on the floor of the bus. After the man helped me gather up all the crap that had spilled out, I told him thank you.

As we came to the next stop, Pine Street, he picked up his briefcase, stood up, and asked my permission to get by.

"Oh, I'm getting off here, too," I said, yielding to an impulse I have never had before.

He stepped off the bus and began walking, and within four or five steps, I overtook him. He acted like he didn't notice as we walked side by side for a block. I was amazed when we continued down the second block, then the third. What in the hell was I doing? I was thinking hard about this, when, without breaking his stride, he began speaking.

"I don't think that was your stop."

"Uh…." Oops! Busted! Was I that obvious?

"Are you teasing me?" he asked.

"No, I'm not teasing you."

"Stalking me?"

"No."

"What about that wedding ring you're wearing?"

"I thought it complimented yours very nicely." Who was this person talking out of my mouth?

"I'd like to give you a chance to change your mind."

We walked two more blocks without saying a word. He looked me up and down, and I looked him up and down. The tension between us was apparent. So was the attraction. The wooden heels of my shoes clicked on the sidewalk. We seemed to be walking faster.

"I see that you haven't changed your mind," he said.

"Let's just say I'm curious."

"Curious?"

"Yes. I'm curious about that little spark I felt when your arm touched mine on the bus."

He smiled. He had a nice smile. "I thought I was the only one who felt that tingle."

"Nope. I felt it, too."

We came to a stop in front of a comfortable home on Willow Street. There was a small fence around the front yard. He opened the gate and held it open, like gentlemen do for ladies. I walked past him to the front door. He pushed his key into the lock, somehow in a sexy way. Is it even possible to make the unlocking of a door seem sexy? He held the door open and gestured, and I walked into his home. I felt just a little bit like an invader. The house had a nice scent suggestive of lavender and sandalwood. I excused myself and ran to his bathroom, where I stood trembling, looking in the mirror. I was both excited and terrified.

What happened next? Well....

Am I ashamed?

Maybe a little.

Am I glad?

Yes! It put a smile on my face. I've been needing something to smile about.

So I relaxed, and when I walked out of the bathroom, he took my hand and led me to the bedroom. I closed my eyes and walked beside him, one foot in front of the other. My mind was full of right and wrong. I felt desperate with the need to feel attractive and to have my attractiveness validated by this man I'd met on the bus.

I must confess that this was the first time I've ever let a man conquer me with just the touch of an arm. It was also the first time, once we were in the bedroom, that a man undressed me so fast. I was worried about being nude. In the low light, I could see his eyes flutter when my prosthesis came off with my bra. But it was only a splinter of time. He looked at my prosthesis, looked at me with a question on his face.

"It's okay," I said, shrugging my shoulders. "I've had a mastectomy. Nothing more, nothing less."

His eyes surveyed the rest of me, and then he was out of his clothes just as fast.

He had a body to be proud of. He was muscular, rugged, but he also seemed like he was wound-up so tight that he needed some release before he burst into flame. When I touched him, every one of his muscles seemed to be flexed. He was rigid with stress. For an instant, I was afraid he might get violent, but that was only for a second. He was kind and courteous. I felt like he was giving himself to me, not taking anything from me.

He laid me on the bed, gently caressing my skin and looking in my eyes. Looking into his eyes I could sense that he was carrying some mysterious form of anger against someone. Not me. Not a stranger, but someone he cared about. He had superb control over himself, and his approach to me was soft and polite. But that isn't at all what I wanted. I wanted someone who took me with his strength, who imposed his desire for me onto me. I encouraged him to release his anger, to take it out on me. I could feel a change in him, his raw tension, his exposed nerves. Whatever frustrated him, he vented it into me.

I felt vulnerable. But vulnerability was quickly erased by the aggressive, shameless way in which he released his desires. He kissed me passionately. If what we were doing was wrong, we were doing the wrong thing right because it sure felt good. I needed to have passionate kisses on my body. I needed to feel attractive to a man. He did that for me. He gave me full enjoyment. And he was a gentleman. No foul language. He actually used the word love. Well, what we were doing wasn't love. I knew that, but it sounded real nice in a whisper in my ear. It wasn't my best, but I think I left him satisfied, too.

Afterward, he used the bathroom and left me to examine the bedroom. I saw pictures of him and his wife together. Pictures of them in cool places like Mount Kilimanjaro (how did I know that? It was written on the picture frame.), also Machu Picchu, even Mount Wellington in Tasmania. They seemed to be adventurists and large on life, and I envied her. But also

I felt a tinge of resentment, the same kind of resentment that I carried toward Colt. She was healthy. She had two breasts. She had good things in life that I didn't have. She probably had parents that were alive, a mother she could go to for advice for when her world fell apart. My resentment burned a little, but I pushed it to the back of my mind.

Leaving was a little awkward. How should I say goodbye to a one-night stand, knowing I wouldn't see him again? He walked me to the door and stopped me before I opened it. He pulled me in tight, hugging me. A good long kiss goodbye. And then I walked home.

We didn't exchange names, phone numbers, or anything personal. I've always been told that men do nothing but think about sex. Perhaps that's true, but my mind was pretty full of sexual thoughts, too. Is that wrong?

I can tell that fall is near. I could smell it in the air on my walk home. It was also getting chilly after sunset. I strolled along, smiling from ear to ear, feeling the shakiness that comes after making love. I was in no hurry. Colt was playing tonight, the kids were probably out, so all that was waiting for me was an empty house.

The man I had left behind was also alone in an empty home. I wonder if that's why he was so accepting of our passionate encounter. Was his loneliness, his need to feel attractive, equal to mine? I have pictures of happy times, too, pictures of Colt and me, of the kids and me doing fun things, smiling in all those photos. Had that one-night stand occurred in my bedroom, the man would have seen framed photos very much like his, though with Alaskan mountains instead of African. What makes two people reach for one another like we did? We were strangers. We should have been more cautious. Sport-fucking is not something I do or have done in the past. Why did I act on that impulse today? Why did I get off the bus and follow him?

Well, there's also something about the risk we took that made the sex more attractive. Combined with a rush of adrenaline, our sex was a high that no drug would have given me. Yes, that high followed me all the way home. I'm still feeling it as I write this. I like the high, but, well, I'm not addicted to it. I know that for certain I won't try to find the man again. I will not try to reenact what happened tonight.

For the first time in a long time, I felt like I was worth spending time with. I felt important. I was the focal point of someone's attention. It was an adventure. Despite what my children think of me, I see myself as an adventurous person. They think I'm dull and boring, but maybe I'm a privately adventurous kind of person. Like some comic-book caped crusader who has all of the adventure possible, but has a cover identity that everyone sees as lackluster.

I'm not saying I'm going to go to bed with every man who touches my arm. I'm saying maybe I will bungee jump from a helicopter next week, but not tell a soul I did it. There's an adventurous person inside me. I think that's where my soul lives. She seems to come alive when I'm having fun. I wonder if she was there tonight. I wonder if she approves of what I did. Or is she disappointed in me?

Honestly, I don't know how to feel. Part of me feels like I was wrong for several reasons. He's married and I'm married. Those are two big reasons not to act on impulse like that. Yet even if it was wrong, I'm a woman that has needs, and tonight some of those needs were met. There's just no getting around it. I feel better.

SEPTEMBER 15TH

I woke up this morning aware of the little girl that lives inside me. She brought up memories of Granddad and how he always loved me, protected me, and praised me. Granddad was my hero. He could do no wrong in my eyes. If I got hurt, he swooped me up in his arms, and the pain instantly stopped. If I did my homework and still only got a C on it, he told me that I'd done a good job, but next time I should let him help with my assignments. It rarely happened, but if anyone said I was different because I had brown skin and my grandparents' skin was as white as snow, he was always quick to protect me.

I lay in bed for a while this morning, still in a kind of dream state, thinking about that little girl and how I had been with my grandparents and how I am today as an adult without them. I took time to honor them and my happy memories. They made me smile.

After my shower, I went out to the garden and spent some time with my growing friends. I cleaned up the litter the wind had blown in and tended to each and every plant friend. They are my friends. I've given them names. I chat with them, and

I'm not the only one that does that, either. Colt knows their names. He spends as much time as I do with them. I love it in the garden. It's like group therapy as I chat and in my mind hear answers, comments, suggestions, and even advice. It's all my imagination, perhaps, but I don't worry about where those soothing voices come from. I'm just happy they exist.

The garden was a good distraction because I still wasn't certain about how I felt about last night. I don't have any regrets...or do I? I feel so confused. My grandparents surely didn't raise me to be an adulterer. I wonder what they would say to me if they were here? But why should I feel any guilt as Colt and I are getting a divorce? I just didn't think I would have any opportunity to have sex before the divorce or even before one of us moved out. I feel like my encounter with the man on Willow Street has a deeper, unseen meaning, like it was suppose to happen. I don't feel like a bad person, but at the same time I don't feel that I've done the right thing, either. It's all very mystifying. I think the best way to deal with it is just to put it out of my head.

SEPTEMBER 17TH

Work is really pissing me off. Thanks to Brent and Back-2-Back, I had to stay at the office until eight o'clock this evening. Brent called me into his office today and demanded that I come up with an SYD (that's the sum of the year's depreciation) for the year 2004 in the Bio-Sport's R&D department and weigh it against a projected depreciation for this year. He said I had to have this done by tomorrow morning. What crap! It was a task for three or four people, not just one. Devin, being the nice guy that he is, offered to stay and help, but I took pity on him and sent him home.

Because we changed systems in 2008, our data prior to 2008 has to be mined, extracted, and manually entered. It's crazy. It shouldn't be this way, but the company I work for—actually, mainly Brent—listened to a consultant and purchased the system before realizing it didn't interface with our old system. I don't know who hired the consulting firm, but they had no idea what we really do and they never asked any of us who work (hands-on) with the system if the change in systems would impact us. They could have at least sent out some surveys to get a feel for what the people who work here think. We, the actual work force, have had some great cost-saving suggestions, but no one ever wants to listen to us. So now we suffer with an antiquated system that is incapable of working with this quirky new system.

Anyway, James and Kelly called out numbers, and I searched the spreadsheet for their counterparts. By six-thirty, my back was in spasms all the way up to my shoulders. By seven-thirty, I had become accustomed to the pain and just kept on working. When we finished, I took James and Kelly to the pub on Ash Street and bought them each a drink. I think they were a little pissed at me because I let Devin go home and asked them to stay. But all seemed to be well when we parted.

I had to walk through Washington Park on my way back to where my car was parked. It was moonless and dark. The distant streetlights outside the park made the park seem all the more dark. But I wasn't afraid of the dark. Actually I felt the opposite. The sky was cloudless and the stars were bright, brilliant, enticing. I couldn't keep from looking at them.

"Aren't they beautiful?"

The voice coming out of the darkness startled me.

I turned and saw who it was. "Mr. Goldsole! You surprised me."

"I'm sorry," he said. "I didn't mean to. How have you been, Hope?"

"I'm all right," I said. "I had to work late. I'm enjoying the stars, though. Now I'm on my way back to my car."

"Do you still feel ugly?" He fell into step beside me.

"Um, at times, yes, but I'm doing better. I took your advice. I introduced myself to my soul."

"How did that work for you?"

"It's strange. It wasn't where I thought I'd find it."

"Where did you find your soul?"

"While I was cycling. Isn't that funny? It turns out that I connect to it when I'm doing something fun. I heard something, I felt something specific deep within me, so I pedaled faster, and I giggled. I heard my soul giggle. It felt great."

"Your soul doesn't come *to* you," he said. "It is always *with* you. It's just that you are able to recognize it better when you're having fun. The more you identify with it, the more easily you'll be able to recognize it."

Mr. Goldsole was dressed in the same suit I had seen him wearing before, which suddenly made me wonder if he had any other clothes to wear. The strange thing about him is the overwhelming feeling of comfort that I'm pulled into. He has a positive gravity that holds me in his orbit. I feel safe with him, like I'm safe in an ugly world. When he's talking, there is no place I'd rather be. I want to hear him, see him, and feel his energy. It's uncanny how he reminds so much of Granddad.

"So," I asked him, "you think I should communicate with it often?"

"Do you remember in school when the teachers told you there is no such thing as a stupid question?"

"Yes…yeah. That was common, even when I was in college."

"Well, Hope, this isn't one of those times. That *is* a stupid question."

I was taken aback. "Did you just tell me I asked you a stupid question?"

"Yep."

I couldn't believe my ears, but then he started laughing at me, so I couldn't help it. I had to laugh too.

"Your soul is important," he said when we stopped laughing. "Why wouldn't you want to communicate with it as often as possible?"

"Uhh, because people will think I'm nuts for talking to myself. Isn't this like being schizophrenic?"

This time he just gave me a sad smile. "That's an example of where we go wrong as humans. We let other people tell us what is normal. It's in our nature to have conversations within ourselves. With our souls. Somewhere in our so-called progress, we threw away what feels natural and replaced it with what is to be called normal. I say it's 'normal' to have a conversation with my soul. When my soul and I communicate, I am then able to live a more fulfilled life. My soul and I live both in this corporeal world and on the spiritual plane, too. Each and every person has this same ability."

"But if we all have this ability, why is it so strange to me? Why does it seem supernatural?"

"Because it has become normal to ignore our spiritual side," he said. "When you remember school or you review your life at work, do you ever remember hearing anyone giving you an assignment regarding your soul?"

"Are you kidding me? No. Especially not at work! They don't even want me to be human, let alone have a soul."

He nodded. "That is exactly right. The soul is problematic for systems that want to be in charge of the individual. People who rule these systems, such as churches, governments, and schools, want to tell you that you can't communicate with your soul. That's how they try to control you. The people who want to control other people can't allow those other people to gain any spiritual ground by learning from their souls, so they tell you to doubt your abilities. They say the soul isn't normal. Because they're in a position of influence, they manipulate the masses, and then it's easy for individuals to doubt what is happening in their own soul."

Now I nodded, too. "When I'm here with you," I told him, "the idea of the soul makes sense to me. I feel comfortable with the idea of my soul being with me all the time. But when you're not here, doubt takes over. I think it's all in my imagination."

"*Faith*, Hope. You need to discover faith. *Live in faith or live in fear.* That's an adage someone taught me a long time ago. I believe it applies very well to life. Don't you like the sound of it? Say it out loud. It has a ring to it."

"Live in faith or live in fear." It did have a nice soothing sound. "But faith in what?" I had to ask. "In God?"

"Why don't you start small," he said. "Work on having faith in yourself first. Then have faith in your soul. After that, have faith in something greater."

"I'm sorry, but I don't have that faith. Nor do I think I will ever have a strong, unshakable belief in myself."

"Is that what faith is to you?" he asked me.

"That's what I remember the meaning of faith is."

"Hope, do you trust yourself? Do you have confidence in yourself? That's all faith asks of you in regard to yourself."

"Well, *sometimes* I have confidence in myself. But more often I feel like life has control over me. It robs me of my confidence."

He nodded again. "Yes, I suspected that when you told me you felt ugly. When I look at you, I see a stunning woman. It's hard for me to see anything ugly about you. But for you, it's a reality. So start there. Start with confidence. Believe in yourself. Trust in yourself. Then you'll find the foundation of faith."

"I guess I was over-thinking faith," I said after a minute. "If it's as simple as trusting myself, I can do that."

We had reached a corner. "This is where I leave you, Hope, I take Mulberry Street. But before I leave, say it again for me."

"Live in faith or live in fear."

"That's right. No more fear for you, Hope, I want you to live in happiness. Good night."

I watched him walk down the dark street and, like that, he was gone.

I found my parked car. I was still feeling good about myself. I always feel good when I see Mr. Goldsole. I hope I see him again.

SEPTEMBER 18TH

I got some bad news today. I had a doctor's appointment before going to the lawyer. Something's amiss. My white count is increasing. Since I've had breast cancer, the doctor is concerned. So I've had some more tests, and now it's the waiting game for the results. The doctor said it's probably nothing, but I can't seem to get it off my mind. It sure makes it hard to sleep.

However, besides the white count, she confirmed that some of the other symptoms are most certainly due to menopause. In our next visit, she wants to discuss hormone replacement therapy. My depression and sadness, my feelings of unattractiveness and longing for family have been confirmed to be caused by hormonal imbalance. I'm not sure if I feel better or worse knowing that. It takes time to digest information I get from doctors and nurses.

I have "white coat syndrome" in a bad way - ever since, and probably before, I was diagnosed with breast cancer, I've been anxious around doctors and nurses. I have horrible panic attacks before and after all my appointments. It got so bad that I went into therapy. One condition of therapy is this diary. When I told my shrink that I thought she had done all she could do for me and I wanted to stop therapy, she suggested I write in a diary frequently. That way I can monitor my moods, and if I feel like I'm having a bad day, I can incorporate the mental tools she taught me. That's why I write this. It helps me.

SEPTEMBER 21ˢᵀ

I took my lunch to the cathedral again today. The wind was blowing so hard, it was tricky to get there, but I was determined. I wanted to talk to my soul and to God. I need to do something. This bit about my white count, the fevers, the aches, and so on have me worried. Aren't we supposed to turn to God when we're worried or in need? Anyway, I figured there had been enough time since my last visit to the cathedral that anyone who was there wouldn't remember me as the one who started swearing at God.

What if I had taken church more seriously at a younger age? Frankly, I don't know if I even believe in a god. At times I imagine God exists, but if I had more faith I wouldn't be so bothered by doubts. In reality, the information that he (if God is even a *he*, which I doubt. I would like God to be a woman. I like the thought of that.) has made available to me regarding faith doesn't seem sufficient enough to guarantee his existence. And within the walls of the house of God, I felt like no one's home, like I'm alone with my thoughts. And those thoughts frighten me. Feeling alone, I started thinking that I could believe in a god and live my life or I could *not* believe in any god and still live my life. Either way, my life will be lived.

Coming out of the cathedral less satisfied than when I went in, I ran into Mr. Goldsole, who was sitting on the steps. I fell, scraped my knee, and tore my pantyhose. But he was right there. He examined my knee for damage, apologizing all the while. I felt like a little girl with her good ol' granddad fussing over her. That was an awesome feeling. After he was certain I was fine (except for the scraped knee), we sat together on the steps.

"You always seem to pop up, don't you?" I said. I noticed that the gusting wind had calmed down.

"It seems to me," he said, "that we are on the same path at the same time. Nothing more, nothing less. I assure you I'm not stalking you."

I laughed at the thought of him stalking me. "I don't worry about that," I said. "You remind me so much of my granddad, and he was such a good man, that I have no doubts about you."

"If you have time, I'd like for you to tell me about your granddad."

"Well," I said, "What I remember the most about him is that no one ever made me feel as loved or wanted as he did. He gave me everything he could afford to buy for me and did anything he could to make me smile."

And I told Mr. Goldsole how my parents were killed in a car accident when I was young. My grandparents were my closest relatives, so I went to live with them. I remember that day like it was yesterday. I was crying. I couldn't understand why my safe little world had to change. I loved my parents. I couldn't comprehend that death was final. I was certain that my parents would come back to get me.

So there I stood, wearing my yellow sundress and my black, patent-leather Mary Janes, and I was afraid of the future. That's the first time I remember being afraid. I couldn't understand why God would take my parents away from me. What could I have done so wrong that God would leave me standing there at my grandparents' house, all alone?

Their house was small, but they had a bedroom for me. Granddad opened the door of that room, and, oh, you should have seen it. It was as empty, as desolate as I felt inside. I looked in that room and my tears just fell and fell. Granddad squatted down in front of me so he was eye level with me. "When I was your age," he said, "my granddad called me Chief, and that always made me feel special. How about I pass that nickname on to you?"

I sniffled and nodded and agreed.

Don't worry, Chief—" my granddad called me Chief from that day forward and it did make me feel special "—we will fix this room up straightaway. You and I are going to make this the best room ever! What do you say?"

I nodded again, and he told me to change into my jeans. He took me on a trip to the hardware store. We spent a little time choosing colors in the paint section. He told me his idea. That got me excited. "Go on," he said, "get any color you want and we will paint that room just like you want it." He knew how sad I was, so he wanted me to have a cheery room.

When we got home, he opened the cans of paint we'd bought and gave me a washed out soup can to pour my own paint in. Slowly, but methodically he guided me on our painting journey. I loaded my brush with sunflower yellow paint and painted it on the wall. He picked up a roller. We painted that wall yellow, and after it dried I decorated the wall with the names of my parents and my best friends in blue, green, and red on one wall. On the other walls, sky blue, we used stencils that we got from the hardware store to paint pictures of my favorite animals with the green earth at their feet.

Grandmother stood in the doorway, shaking her head and smiling at the same time. It was summertime, and she brought us bacon sandwiches and homemade lemonade. I remember it all.

"When she gets older," Granddad had said to Grandmother, "we'll paint this like a standard room."

"Oh, that won't do," she said. "If this child likes her room like this, then we'll just leave it like it is."

After all four walls were finished, Granddad looked up at the ceiling, "I have something very special in mind for up there," he said. He moved the ladder to the one end of the room and began. I watched him roll out a nice coat of sky blue on the ceiling, and after it dried, he very carefully painted some white puffy clouds, not too many, but enough to make it look like the sky. After that, he painted a big yellow sun that filled part of the two walls that were sky blue and a full corner of the ceiling. When he was finished, we cleaned up our brushes and put the paint away. We returned to the room to examine our work.

"Now," he said, "when it's cold and snowy outside, you can lay here on your bed under a warm and sunny sky."

And it worked, too. In the dead cold of winter, I'd come home from school and lie on my bed and feel warm. I loved that room.

Granddad told me to never be afraid of things in life because there was always a sunny sky in my bedroom. Maybe that's why, in my child's mind, I thought I had no need for God. He had taken my parents from me. But in my room with its eternal sunshine, I found a new god, and this god was more like Santa Claus, and he lived only in my room.

"You know," I told Mr. Goldsole, "while I was growing up, things in life got to me and I broke down and cried. But in that room under that yellow sun, life never seemed quite so bad."

"What a wonderful story that is."

"My grandparents were wonderful parents to me. No one will ever compare to them. They're gone now. I've had to learn to live without them."

"Are things so bad now?"

I shrugged my shoulders. "You know how it is. Girls grow up. We want to have our own family, so we fall in love and get married. But now my home and my family aren't that happy right now, and I long for my grandparents and their home. They're so far away from me, both in distance and time. I understood that I would outlive them, but I always denied it. I took it for granted they'd always be here." I caught my breath. "Now I'm fifty. Adult life isn't as much fun as being a child. I'm not where I thought I'd be when I turned fifty. I married a good man, but somehow I've lost him. My children want to stay as far away from me as they possibly can. I want so much to feel the love I felt when I was a child. My grandparents ruined me."

"What do you mean they 'ruined' you?"

"They taught me true love, the kind that doesn't exist in my reality today. I miss it. I miss them. I wish I had someone who would hold me and tell me everything will be okay. Do I sound childish? Selfish?"

He patted my knee. "No. You're just longing for love. That's part of human nature. We have a need to be loved."

"Yeah. And a need to feel attractive and wanted, too, and those needs have driven me to do things I'm not sure are good." I was thinking of my one-night stand with the married man whose name I never learned. I was just talking, not really thinking about what I was saying.

"What kinds of things have you felt driven to do, Hope?"

I wasn't comfortable discussing this so I quickly changed the subject. "It sure is warm today, isn't it?"

"I understand," said Mr. Goldsole. "I didn't mean to invade your privacy. You know what, Chief? Things in life have a way of working themselves out as they should. I think you'll be all right. I doubt that I'm the person you have in mind to hold you, so I won't even try. However, I can reassure you that everything will work out."

"I appreciate that," I said. "You have a way of soothing my soul. You really do, and I want you to know I appreciate you."

"You're welcome," he said with a smile. "And thank you for the story about your granddad. I take it as a compliment that I remind you of him."

"Do you think I did something that made God take my parents from me?"

"No. Not at all. A god doesn't cause good or bad thing to happen. Circumstances usually influenced by humans are the causes of such things. But a god is there to understand you. A god can help you restore balance in your life."

"How can I find balance in my life? Pray? Confess? What?"

"You have free will, Hope. That is the greatest gift ever given to mankind. Use your free will to choose the path that leads to a balanced life."

"I don't understand. I *choose* to live a balanced life. And that's it?"

He almost laughed. "You choose the path of your life and walk that path in faith."

"Oh, here we go again with *faith*!" I said sarcastically." I won't ask any more questions. Last time, you said I asked a stupid question."

This made him laugh and laugh.

And then, just like that, he had to leave me. I shook his hand and watched him walk down the street. When he turned a corner and I could no longer see him, the wind started gusting again.

I managed to get back to work looking just a little frazzled. When I got to my desk, I was still lost in my thoughts about Mr. Goldsole, faith, free will, and the balance of life. There is something so comforting about that man. I hope I see him again.

SEPTEMBER 22

Colt came to talk to me in our bedroom this afternoon. I looked up and saw him standing at the door. He looked like he thought I was losing my mind. Maybe I have lost my mind. Since it was Saturday, and I didn't have any plans, I felt like being creative. I had gone to the hardware store and bought several cans of paint in bright colors. So there I was, in my favorite jeans, the ones that have holes and shreds hanging off of them, and one of my favorite Georgia O'Keeffe T-shirts, "Pelvis with Moon," painting the bedroom. The sky blue ceiling was drying, and I was working on the big sun in the corner. Colt didn't say anything at first. He just stood there and watched. I was having so much fun, I didn't even notice him at first. I had already painted one of the walls winter mint green, and added the names of my kids in pomegranate red, sunflower yellow, and tangerine orange. I put Colt's name in intuitive purple.

"Hope, what is going on?" he finally asked, quietly, like he was afraid there was a nut running loose in the house.

"I felt like changing the room."

"Boy, I guess so! This is quite a change."

I turned to face him. "You don't like it?"

He came in a couple steps. "Actually, I love it," he said. "The blue sky and sun sure brightens the room. And I like how you wrote out the names of the kids...the writing on the wall compliments the room very nice. You always had good penmanship. I just didn't know you could write with a paintbrush. Oh, and my name, too. I like that. What I'd like to see is *your* name by mine. They'd flow together, make it complete...don't you think?"

"I hadn't thought about it," I said coolly, "but I'm open to suggestions."

He was right, of course. I should put my name on the wall, too. I need to recognize myself, not in a selfish way, but in a self-aware way. I had painted all the names with good quick strokes, and the calligraphy had come out very nicely, if I do say so myself. On the opposite wall, I had written the names of my parents and grandparents. Writing their names made me feel closer to them.

It was early afternoon by now. Colt had played a gig the night before. He looked good in his faded jeans and a black Batman T-shirt. His feet were bare and he hadn't combed his hair. He sat quietly on the floor near the doorjamb and watched me and drank his coffee.

I had so many things in my mind that I wanted to say, but I held it all in. I wanted to tell him about the doctor, the tests, the waiting. But why worry him? I don't want him to take my weakness for forgiveness. I have seen no indication that he has gotten rid of his girlfriend.

But that was earlier today. Now it's almost the middle of the night and everyone else is gone and I'm alone. Colt is playing at the Sundance Skyway over in Fremont tonight. That's over an hour's drive from here. He won't get home until four or later. And the kids? Well, let's see. I haven't seen any of them since Thursday, so who knows what they're doing.

I'm having a good, relaxing night. I drew a bath and soaked for a while. Then I read *The Sky Is Gray*, by Ernest Gaines.

It's one of my favorite stories. When I was in college, Ernest came and gave a talk. It was an open platform and we students were able to ask him questions. I was thrilled to be there and listen to him tell about his life. After the Q&A, to my absolute delight, he read from *The Sky Is Gray*. No one, I mean *no one*, can read one of Ernest's stories better than he can. Well, James Earl Jones could come close. But Earnest and his baritone voice really anchored me to the story. Tomorrow I will reread *"A Long Day in November."*

Now I'm lying here in my room under a sunny sky and thinking about my grandparents. I'm also thinking how much I love that sunny sky on my ceiling. Now when the test results come back, I'll have a place to run to where I'll feel better.

I'm afraid.

SEPTEMBER 24TH

This morning, when I arrived at the parking lot of the company where I work, I saw him. He was stepping off the bus, the man who with the touch of his arm seduced me. I stood there in the parking lot and stared at him. He was walking with a petite, youthful woman who was holding tightly to his arm. I recognized her from the photos in their bedroom. In person and from a distance, she seemed to be happier than she looked in the photos. They stopped at the café on the corner, and I saw her lean affectionately into him.

I was amused that I had led him to cheat on his young, athletic, wife. I never thought I was capable of doing such a thing. Gee, what else am I capable of? I also wondered…what is the true connection between the man going into the café with his wife and the man who undressed me and had me on his bed in record time?

Observing them from a distance stirred something within me, an echo of our intimate passion, perhaps, but I felt something from somewhere within me that tugged at my soul. I watched them and felt a twinge of jealousy poking at my insides. They were laughing. I wanted to laugh, too. She was clinging to him. I wanted someone to cling to, too.

Where is my happiness?

I stood there, watching them and yearning, for so long that I was late for work. Except when I was ill, I haven't been late for work in over ten years. But no one even noticed. The only thing that noticed was the time clock.

Oh, yeah—I got a phone call from the doctor's office. They need me to come in this week, so I made an appointment for Wednesday. I'll go during my lunch hour. Am I going to be plagued with doctor's appointments for the rest of my life?

SEPTEMBER 25ᵀᴴ

We had to stay late for the Back-2-Back project again today. I will be so glad when that damn thing is done! Brent puts pressure on my team, and they're beginning to ask questions about what is so special about the Bio-Sport account. The only two that could stay late with me were Raj and Devin. It was almost 8:30 when Raj approached me in a way he never had before. "Boss," he said, "how much longer will we be here tonight?" I told him at least until nine o'clock unless the work mysteriously gets itself done. Then he lowered his voice so Devin couldn't hear him and confessed that he had a date and he needed to go and meet her. First, I made him suffer a bit by replying that it might be past nine when we finish, then I asked him, "Is she worth the trouble, Raj?"

"Oh, yeah, Boss, she's the bomb! I've never met anyone like her before."

All of my employees know the best way to overcome me is honesty. Of course I let him leave early.

And then I saw a change come over Devin when we were alone. He became more tense than usual. Something about being alone with the boss always seems to make people's nerves get wacky. He wouldn't look me in the eye, and when I asked him to pass me a thumb drive, I noticed his hand was sweaty. Or was it my imagination?

"Am I that fierce?" I asked him. "You don't need to be intimidated."

He laughed. "No," he said, "You're not fierce."

"Don't be afraid of me," I said. "I'm not that bad. Really! Relax."

As we worked, I noticed it again—he was looking at my legs. I had them crossed and my shoe was dangling on my big toe. I caught his eyes following the curve of my calf from my knee to my shoe. Is that just a focal point for his eyes, or is he infatuated with my legs? And if so, what does that mean to have a man stare at my legs? Is it attraction?

After I told him to relax again, he worked more easily, and I think we had fun, at least as much fun as you can have while working overtime. He relaxed, for the most part, except that he started calling me ma'am again. I don't dig being called that. At 9:15, we found a good stopping place in the data. I asked him if I could buy him something to drink at the pub, like I had with the others.

"No, ma'am," he said. "I'm fine. But thank you."

"Devin," I said, "I'm going to say this the best way I can. When you call me ma'am, I feel very uncomfortable. The only ma'am I ever knew was an old, wrinkled, English teacher I once had. Would you mind just calling me Hope?"

"Sure thing. Hope."

My car was the only one in the parking lot, so I turned to him and asked, "Is your wife or girlfriend coming to you pick up?" He looked awkward and confided in me that he had a girlfriend, but they had been arguing for the past few days. He doubted she would be along to pick him up. I offered him a ride and he accepted. In my car, he got his courage up and asked me if I was married. I held up my hand and showed him my wedding ring, but I added, "No one knows at the office yet, but I'm getting divorced."

"I won't say a word to anyone," he said. I think he was struggling with the rapid change of subject and telling me he was sorry about my situation. As if it was his fault. Cute. Then he began to talk about his girlfriend. I didn't pay much attention, but I think he said they have been together for two years, had moved in together earlier this year, and now she was having second thoughts. I really didn't want to invite his personal life into my head, so I was mentally blocking what was coming out of his mouth. He stayed in disclosure mode until we stopped at the corner near his home and he got out of my car.

SEPTEMBER 26TH

I got an email from Becky today. She's bored with Washington and is coming back here in October and wants to catch up with me. That's good news. I have so few friends as close as Becky. At least, she's the only one I can think of that I can talk to about certain subjects without feeling worse.

When Granddad died all those years ago, I was devastated. The only thing that kept me going was the renewed rage I had against God. My aunt Agnes was there and running her mouth nonstop. That woman is unbearable at times! There were also strangers at the funeral, some people I knew by sight, but no one close. Then Becky arrived. She came right up to me and just wrapped me in her arms. Her mom, dad, and one of her brothers came, too. They were like my second family when I was growing up. I don't know what I would have done without them, either back in our childhood days or at Granddad's funeral.

Becky was cool at the funeral. She didn't act like Granddad hadn't died or avoid the subject. She began to talk very naturally about me, about her, and about my grandfather and the positive things he did in life. Her conversation was calming. And having her family there to comfort me was of great significance in my life. The rest of the funeral was bearable after their arrival, and I think we honored my Granddad's memory very well.

It will be good to have Becky back and nearby.

On a darker note, my visit with the doctor wasn't good. They ordered some x-rays, so, nothing definite yet. That means more worry and anxiety. Oh, fun, fun.

However, my doctor took the time to discuss menopause with me. And hormones and how replacement therapy could help. The depression, the anxiety, and the hot flashes might be treated. I need something because I don't feel in control of my body, or of my mind, either. I told her I would think about it.

September 27th

I had a dream last night that has me head over heels. I was in Washington Park, walking on the grass in my nightgown. Suddenly, on the sidewalk in front of a luxurious house, I saw Devin, and he was running toward me. He came to me without hesitation. He was wearing a snappy, dark blue, pinstriped suit. When he got to me, it was instantly nighttime, and he said, "You smell lovely." I didn't resist him. He was clear about what he wanted. He took possession of me.

Then we were lying on the grass in the middle of the park and he lifted off my nightgown. I was afraid he would see I only had one breast. But when I looked, they were both there! I was a whole woman again! I took him inside me, and it was like it was more his spirit than his physical body touching me. His spirit was a part of me. We were joined in a way I have never experienced before. The lovemaking lasted and lasted and lasted, and when I woke up, I was as feeble and exhausted as a newborn child struggling to catch its first breath. I love waking up feeling all a mess with the afterglow of making love.

Well, get this. This morning when Devin came in to work he was wearing the exact same dark blue, pinstriped suit. I about had a heart attack there in my cubicle! "What a snappy looking suit," I said to him. "Devin, you look very dapper this morning."

He looked right at me with panic in his eyes, exactly like a person who is about to march down to HR and file a sexual harassment complaint. And it went from bad to worse when I tried to explain away my comment, and one of the other younger women who was walking by stuck her head in and said, "Dapper? Who says that these days? That's so twenty years ago!"

I suddenly felt degraded. Hell, I felt *obsolete*. Later I noticed Devin walking past my cube with a certain mistrust in his eyes. Just proof that what happens in a dream needs to stay in the dream.

SEPTEMBER 28TH

Tonight as I was rinsing off some dishes before putting them into the dishwasher, I was thinking about my granddad. Ever since Mr. Goldsole asked me about him, I've felt this odd longing. I can't describe it. So many things are running through my mind. Colt and his girlfriend. Granddad. Work. Devin. Doctors and tests.

I just wish Granddad were here so I could talk to him. He'd know what to do. I wasn't as afraid of the world when he was around, but now it seems like I'm always scared. I'm sad, too, but tonight after I took off my wedding ring while I was washing the dishes, I never put it back on. I just left it there on the windowsill above the sink.

What about my life? What should I do?

Tonight I played "Jolene," the song by Dolly Parton. I like the White Stripes rendition better. Even though it's a man singing it, his conviction is painfully familiar. Sitting alone, feeling damn sorry for myself, I played the song over and over. I don't know who the woman is that Colt has been running around with, but I've named her Jolene.

I like to think of myself as a tough, self-sufficient, professional woman. I believe that I worked hard to become self-sufficient so I would be superior, maybe not too much, but at least have the appearance of being strong. The rhythm I have given my life is nothing more than a calculated routine made with the simplest of motives. Spontaneity has never been one of my strengths. At least my family doesn't see me as spontaneous. And now I'm baffled because I was capable of being someone more exciting the other night with that man on the bus. Cleo was right when she said I've become boring. Aside from bike rides, I seem to do all of my daily duties with absolute calculation, making sure there isn't any room for chance.

Is that why Colt went off to find Jolene? Because I'm dull and boring?

When I was single, I had it made. Before I met Colt, before I had three kids, when I had just graduated from college, I took pleasure in knowing all the academic demands and expectations were behind me. I was in a peaceful, enjoyable place in my life. I read books I wanted to read, not the ones assigned in class. I had a place of my own and I could cook myself good meals because I had read some good cookbooks, too. I used to bring home fresh cut flowers and set them on my dining room table because I liked them, because I made the arrangements. I loved my job, I loved my friends. I lived the single life in this comfortable town. There were no drugs, no booze. It was a cool time. Life wasn't full of pressure like it was in college. I was living a life I believed was right.

I was a "mippie." That's the word Becky made up to describe me, a metro hippie, a city-dwelling, organic-living beatnik. I saw life as fresh and vibrant, and I couldn't wait to get into living. I wanted to expand my mind with philosophies from random parts of the world. I wanted to travel to strange places, get lost in the countries where adventure would be waiting around every corner. I was free, far freer than almost anyone I knew. Everyone I knew had family, and their families influenced their decisions. I didn't have any of that. Yet, my freedom had a sobering effect on my grandiose hopes. I looked at my freedom, and sometimes it frightened me. My freedom was large, and being large, it was largely empty. What I really wanted was to feel some kinds of boundaries around me. Not limiting boundaries, but something that held me in the arms of comfort.

Then one night I went out dancing in a club, and there, up on the stage, was the man that would change everything. I mean *everything*. The stage was a strange reality. He stood there, looking just like a star, and I could only see him. I couldn't touch him to see if he was real. His voice, the passion in the words he sang, they brought light into the dark spaces within me. He didn't notice me out there dancing with my friends. No, he didn't see me, but I was sure he was singing just to me, and my heart listened to him.

That old-fashioned country band sounded like home to me. They played the music my granddad always played around the house when I was growing up. Colt is very talented. He can play most instruments, and that night I watched his hands tickle the fiddle the way I wished he would tickle me. Something inside me locked in on him, and whatever it was, it had more strength than any other part of me.

I followed Colt and his band (The Wild Bunch) from one country bar to the next in hopes of getting a chance to talk to him. Oh, how I wanted him to notice that I kept coming to watch him play. I danced with many a drunken asshole to get a chance to meet Colt. It must have been two or three months before he finally noticed me, though. My friends were all getting tired of going to country bars and had abandoned me to my own pursuits. So I went alone, and that night he noticed me and came to me on one of his breaks. We chatted and the connection went deeper. I knew before he ever touched me that I was in love with him.

He altered my dreams. Everything I thought I wanted out of life was gone right then and there, replaced by something new and exciting. He became the man I admired most next to Granddad, who had already passed away by then. I used to sneak off from work for an early lunch. I loved to have lunch with him because he was honest, the one rare guy that brought some kind of magical energy into my life.

I loved the way his eyes followed me when I walked away from him. He lived in a place I could only imagine, some ranch nearby but far away from anything I had ever known. And when he talked about his life, he never named names but referred to everyone as if they were nothing but energy, moving and spinning around in his gravity. And, boy, does Colt have gravity! Once you're in his gravitational pull, you have no way of resisting. And the anchor that holds you in his orbit is his style of lovemaking. Oh, the sex! It was the church where I worshiped.

What changed us?

I blame it on breast cancer, but maybe I'm at fault, too. Maybe I failed somewhere along the way. Love is fun when you're in it. But it hurts when you're on the outside. I didn't think remembering him...us...could be so painful.

Colt, do you think of me when you're with her?

Jolene take good care of him, won't you?

OCTOBER 1ST

Devin has something that attracts me to him. That's evident. But why?

I wish I knew what it was. Today, I was studying him. I wonder what is happening with his girl friend. Are they still a couple, or are they separating? After all, she didn't come to pick him up that night I drove him home. Hell, even when I'm my maddest at Colt, I've never left him stranded. Do they have passionate sex like I dreamed about?

That's the question, isn't it?

OCTOBER 3ᴿᴰ

I went to the doctor today and they did an ultrasound. All of these so-called precautions scare me! At least my remaining breast is fine, although there is a swollen node under my arm. I hate this feeling of always being suspicious of my body. I hate being tested and waiting for the results!

OCTOBER 4ᵀᴴ

Brent brought in a consultant today, and the consultant had to spend time with each of us managers. When he came to my cubicle, he started annoying me. Just his being there annoyed me. No one expected him to be such a nuisance. He started by asking for the figures for an account we no longer represent. "But you have records of the account, don't you?" he asked, looking down his nose at me. He's a funny-looking guy with a shaved upper lip but wiry whiskers on his chin. Of course we have the records, jackass! I didn't say that out loud, of course. After that, casually, as if he wasn't asking for anything at all, he asked for another account's books, and then he sort of demanded that the books be broken down into the lists of subdivisions figuring in the open inventory.

So I spent the day searching databases and running back to the warehouse and pulling hard copies. I trotted out dilapidated books no one had seen in over two decades. Audits! I thought after seven years records didn't matter, but, oh, no, not with this guy. Did I say he was a jackass yet? (Please note the emphasis on the *ass* part.)

He was polite, though. He smiled and begged pardon when he almost stepped on me to get around the stacks of dusty books. He even said thanks a lot from time to time. A jackass nonetheless! He should drop dead from badgering me. In the beginning, I kept my rage inside, answering him with words that barely fit between my teeth, but cussing him under my breath until my head hurt. Afterward, my strong language gave way to another feeling. I began to feel old! I saw the dates in those old books and then I recognized my handwriting. Oh, my God, have I actually worked there for over twenty years? And my penmanship has changed over the years. It looks all crabbed and dried up now. Am I dried up?

I don't know what it's like to be old. I've always thought of myself as young. What is it like to be old? I assumed I would be dried up, carrying the burden of fatigue that rest won't satisfy. I'm afraid of getting old, or should I say *being old*.

This feeling that life is incomplete and that I somehow didn't play my part very well brought tears to my eyes today. I was stubborn, though, and held them back. Instead, I acted like the dust from the books was irritating my eyes. The doctor had mentioned that my hormone levels were out of range. Maybe that's what makes me feel this way. And maybe it's what keeps bringing tears to my eyes and I can't explain why.

I never thought life could make me feel this way. I want to feel secure. I want to feel loved. I want to feel good about living again. Does anyone get that? Do I get that? It's like I'm living life to make sure my kids are taken care of, my husband is happy, but beyond those functions, I'm just a mechanism. I would love to be showered with affection, to have someone, anyone, ask me how my day was or ask what I would like to do for the weekend. Instead, I can forecast my weekend perfectly. I'll be alone.

I will be able to describe how slowly the hands move around the face of my clock. I won't have to worry about the ringing of the phone disturbing me. It rarely rings anymore. Mr. Goldsole told me to live in faith or live in fear. I'm losing faith faster than I'm gaining an understanding of it. And when it's dark and my queen-size bed holds only me, my troubles don't vanish. I can't run or hide from them. Maybe it's insecurity.

I'll make an appointment to see my shrink next week. Or maybe not?

The consultant gathered up all his data (everything revolves around data) and retreated back to wherever he came from. Brent told me he was going to analyze the data and then return with recommendations. However, Brent wasn't honest with him. He never mentioned the deal with Back-2-Back. It's all so top secret.

Tomorrow, which is Friday, I get to go on a field trip. Brent is sending me directly to Back-2-Back to discuss the project and our progress on it. I'm not looking forward to that.

OCTOBER 5TH

Jerome Atwood is the CEO and owner of Back-2-Back. I've never met a man as driven as him. I mean, I've known men and women that are driven, but what drives them? What is the inner mechanism that drives them to achieve? Is it greed? Power? Or (like Brent) are they just overachievers? Well, Jerome is motivated by anger, resentment, and the drive to defeat his competition at any cost. Intimidation is his favorite weapon, but I get the feeling that not too far behind his favorite weapon is the violence he's willing to use to back up his seriously applied pressure.

He's about thirty-six but looks younger. I guess I expected a younger man, maybe in his mid-twenties, a computer geek who's spent ten minutes alone with a woman in his whole life. I suppose I expected an immature man so I could excuse his rough talk as lack of good judgment. I further thought he might be excited to see me, that he'd congratulate me on my progress. I was secretly hoping he'd say he liked my force of character.

Well, that fantasy dissolved the minute I saw him. Meeting Jerome was like this: first, his attitude comes through the door, then his cockiness follows right behind, and finally the so-called human being enters the room. His posture foretells his anger. He seethes so much that I (or anyone else) hesitate to make direct contact with him. I kept my head down, trying to not draw his attention directly to me. I wanted him to stay focused on the project.

"I run my business like one of our video games," he said. "It's warfare, it's battle. I've assembled people I trust around me, people who are willing to take the front line and destroy the enemy. Bio-Sport is my next target." He finally looked right at me. "And you are going to help me bring them down."

He wasn't exaggerating about surrounding himself with like-minded people. His posse is made up of guys that sweat testosterone. They dress like him, too, in designer suits that cost more than I make in several months. They probably think Armani is cheap. They wear Brioni and Kiton bespoke suits. How do I know this? They told me.

When Jerome was out of the room, the conversation went beyond his rage and his tantrums. It's known that when he's in a bad mood, it usually costs someone his or her job. And he doesn't just fire people. They said he likes to humiliate them. They said he's addicted to winning and being the best. He's fit and a great athlete, so he likes to challenge his employees to physical competition. Once someone accepts a challenge, he makes it a company event and no one has to work until the contest is over, and if the employee knows what's what, they let him win. But losing has its downside. I overheard one of the men say that Jerome likes to humiliate the loser unmercifully until he finds a new victim. Actual employees told me these things. I was, to say the least, impressed with Jerome. But not in a good way.

So I got to spend my morning with Jerome. And he was difficult. I hated him immediately. He likes to give the impression that when he dies, wherever God resides in heaven he (God) will have to pack up and move out because Jerome will be taking over. I think he honestly believes that.

He's rich beyond my comprehension. I think the money has messed up his mind.

Back-2-Back's building is an architectural gem that seems a little out of place in our town. At the same time, I understand why companies have been moving and building here. Laws have been passed by our city council to make it attractive to big business. The plan's working. Our little town is expanding and growing, which is good. But do we really need the devil living here?

Jerome's office is over the top. I don't think Napoleon Bonaparte could have competed in grandeur. I was following him (Jerome, not Napoleon) when he opened the door to his executive reception area. It was like something out of a movie. The walls were paneled with some exotic wood and had bright brass ornamentation, and there were twin secretarial desks made of mahogany with gaudy vermeil accents. Behind the desks were typical, young, fashion-model bimbettes that looked like they couldn't type a single word without misspelling it. I couldn't even talk to them without staring at their bought and paid for, collagenized lips that make them look like Mick Jagger. And of course their breast augmentation made them look like Dolly Parton. Or worse. I couldn't help but think that their primary responsibility was giving Jerome blowjobs, which I'm sure he's turned into a competitive sport.

I sat in a small chair across from his enormous desk. I'm sure he intentionally had the chairs made smaller and lower so visitors have to look up at him. Anyway, I sat there and explained the numbers my team had packaged thus far, and he listened and took notes. He was taking notes, not the two bimbettes. All they did was sit at their matching desks and fix their hair and makeup and apply more lipstick. His posse stood with their arms folded in front of them looking quite intimidating. This picture made quite a contrast from the team I work with at my office. My guys are so down to earth, nice, polite and...what's a good word? Ah, yes. Human.

Jerome finally spoke. "Bio-Sport has dug itself into my most valuable segment. Its games are becoming all the rage with the teens and twenty-somethings. I won't have it! " He slammed his fist on his desk.

I looked at him, surprised by his outburst. The thing that really bothered me was his goons didn't even blink.

"We are going to find a weakness and destroy them," he shouted. "We are going to break their back and make them suffer. They'll crawl and beg for mercy until we kill them!"

I was practically freaking out by then. I was waiting for one of the goons to bring in the CEO of Bio-Sport and tie him (if it is a him, I don't know) to a chair. I was sure he had been kidnapped on the way to work this morning. Then I expected them to get out blowtorches or waterboards and torture the poor bastard till he died. I mean it! I was really frightened by the tough talk.

Jerome was still going. "No business, no person will ever get the best of me, I will personally kick the shit out of them, do you believe me?" He actually asked me that.

Oh, yes, I wanted to say, I believe you, there is no doubt in my mind. There is no doubt in my mind, you crazy freak! But I didn't say it out loud.

"I need all the data, every drop of data you can muster," he said as if I had answered him, "and from that data I can squeeze out a weakness. I want your team working on this. This is your only priority. Do you understand?"

I nodded. "My top priority. I get it." I was afraid if I didn't reply the way he wanted me to, he would send his thugs to get me and blowtorch my ass, too. I felt nauseated, and my fever came back in full force. I could feel a migraine coming on. He was ranting so loud and so fast my head was beginning to spin. I wanted to run out of his office.

"Jerome," I managed to say, "my team is the best and we'll get it done." I sounded to myself like I was a team leader of some Special Forces unit. But I didn't want to sound tough. This was a job, for heaven's sake, not some covert Navy SEALS operation.

"Address me as Mr. Atwood," he said. "And I'll send for you when I need you. Don't call me for anything. You will give your messages to Brent and he will contact me. Is that understood?"

I wanted to slap his face and scold him for being so condescending. He was acting like a tough but spoiled brat and I was fed up with it. I squinted at him. "Yep. Got it."

He stood up and towered over me. "Remember, Hope, you will get a handsome bonus for this, but in order to get the bonus you need to do as you're told. And maintain a level of respect. Are we clear?"

"As crystal."

It was about 11:30 when I left Back-2-Back. I was so stressed out I decided to go home instead of heading to the office. It was a nice, warm, fall day. I was going to eat something and then pedal back to work. I might be late, but who was watching the clock for me? Brent was having my time manually entered into the timekeeper, so he only had my word as to when my meeting with Jerome ended.

When I got home, I made me a garbanzo-bean-butter sandwich with honey on bread that I baked Tuesday night. It's a good sandwich, but it makes me fart. That makes me laugh because the funny thing about my office is that none of the guys think women ever fart, so I can always blame it on one of them. Why is it that they think women don't fart? I'm going to ask one of the guys.

After lunch, I changed clothes and jumped on my bike. Chestnut Street was quiet because St. Luke's School was in session, so I took that street. But passing the school at 2:30 when the school lets out is something always to be avoided. As I was pedaling, I was smiling I could feel the connection to my soul. I was alive and happy to be away from the office. Any office. When I turned onto Mulberry and pedaled past Washington Park, I spotted Cleo walking hand in hand with some guy. I didn't do anything to attract their attention, but she saw me anyway. I couldn't believe what happened then. We made eye contact and Cleo took her beau by the arm and swung him in the opposite direction and walked quickly away from me.

Why did she do that?

Do I embarrass her?

It hurt to see my little girl avoiding me. I wasn't going to do anything to make her uncomfortable. I was on my way to work, so I didn't have time for a long chat. I wouldn't have taken up too much of her time. I remember when she was tiny, I used to hold her in my arms and she always looked up at me with a wide smile. Now this.

Note to self: When encountering Cleo out in public, avoid her.

OCTOBER 6TH

I went up to the attic today and pulled down the Halloween decorations. It's that time of year again. I love it. Fall is in the air. Tammy Jo called and we scheduled time to do our harvesting. She helps me with my garden and I help her with hers. Her garden is four times the size of mine, but she still shares her harvest with me. This takes up a few days of the month to do the work, so we make a family thing out of it. But I don't know how to engage in this activity when Colt and I are having problems. I guess I'll just act like nothing is the matter.

The lawyer called me on my cell this afternoon. He said he was wondering why I missed another appointment. I think I'll wait on the divorce until I know more from the doctor. Besides, I said, there's no rush for either of us. The lawyer told me he is going to bill me for missing another appointment. I swear everyone is just looking for money. He didn't ask me if I had a problem that was keeping me from the appointment. He just went straight to why did you miss the appointment, but before I could answer, he had already jumped to the part about billing me. Jerk.

Preparing for Halloween is one my favorite activities. When the kids were young, we had so much fun dressing them up and getting them to parties and of course trick or treating. This year, I think I'll find all the photos I took of the kids in their Halloween costumes from last year all the way back to when they were little, and then I'll post them on our Facebook page. It'll be a hoot, seeing all of those old photos. I hope the kids will get a kick out of it.

OCTOBER 8ᵀᴴ

A funny thing happened today. The phone rang, but when I answered, it was our main switchboard. Reba, our receptionist, said, "You have a call from a current client on line five." I didn't think anything about it. This is routine, it happens several times a day. But this time it was the founder, owner and chairperson of Bio-Sport. It was nearing the end of the third quarter, and she had a standard question. Before I could answer her question, I felt my soul kick me. Hard.

I was compelled to meet the owner. I have always suspected that the owner of Bio-Sport would turn out to be a woman. I told her it was a coincidence that she had called because I needed to go over something in their account, and could she meet with me. She agreed to have lunch with me. I suggested that we meet at the Snake River Grill over on Birch Street.

I quickly gathered up some of the data and made a list of errors and things that needed clarification. I don't know why I did that. I only knew I had to see the CEO in person. I had to see the head of the company that Brent had sold out to Jerome. I got to the restaurant first and secured a table, but she wasn't long behind me. She is tall and big-boned and has fair skin. I think she must be about sixty, whatever sixty is supposed to look like. I would say she was an energetic sixty.

Her hair is gray, short, thick, and beautiful, but I'm not saying she's a beautiful woman. In fact, she's average in appearance, yet it was something about her *way* that drew me to her. She is sophisticated, confident, and has an exceedingly pleasing personality.

"You must be Hope," she said, offering me her hand. "My name is Quintana Adams, but you can call me Quint. Everyone does."

I shook her hand and we both sat down and ordered lunch. While we waited for our food, I spoke about Bio-Sport's expense adjustments as if I had a genuinely inaccurate data. I took out a pencil and made some marks on the papers I'd brought along.

"It's not possible for me to give you exact figures," she said. "I'll have to ask Rebecca in our pseudo-accounting department to contact you."

"That would be fine." I said, "You know, all I ever see are numbers and screens. I hardly ever have a face to go with the account, so it's really nice to have the opportunity to meet with you." I wasn't lying. Data is usually all I ever see. It really was nice to meet her. Then I folded up my notebook and put it away and gave my attention to lunch and chitchat. She opened up to me and talked to me like I was human. She's not at all like Jerome, who thinks he's God.

I learned that Quint is very accomplished. She used to be a schoolteacher, but now she's incorporating teaching strategies into the videogame industry. "I don't want to see impressionable kids only experiencing violence in games," she explained. "My greatest dream is that they gain wisdom from our games that applies to everyday life. I think we are starting to see a trend of kids coming over to our games because they find our games interesting and see their applications in life. You know, with all of the cutbacks in schools and the advancements in technology, kids are looking for alternative ways to learn."

"My children are now out of college," I told her, "but I'm glad to hear this. School is such a different place now. I like your approach to the videogame industry."

"Thank you," she said. "Sometimes I really need to hear that what I am doing is important. When I took over the company, our most popular videogames were nothing but virtual gangs that got points for fighting, killing, and stealing. Do you realize that children from the ages of six to thirteen have witnessed over six million simulated deaths a year?"

"I had no idea—"

"Not only that, but the average child will have participated in over a million of those simulated deaths through virtual murder. The statistics are disturbing! As a society, we look to videogames and movies to raise our children because we're so busy working. It's sad that the companies that make so much money off our children put out products focused on war, crime, darkness, and wickedness. That's why I made a decision that I would do my best to change what I can. I sure don't want my grandchildren playing those kinds of games. But saying no to them isn't the answer, either. Children cooperate best when given options."

Quint quickly became my heroine. She was actually doing something about an issue. Most people, myself included, complain a lot but do very little to make any kind of change come about.

This is what my soul was asking of me. It wanted me to identify with Quint and make a decision myself to do the right thing. And I knew the right thing to do was defend Quint from the evil of Back-2-Back. I'm not sure, but I think I made a friend today in Quint. She seemed to like me and was open to meeting me again as friends. I like that.

*Note to self:
Make arrangements
to have lunch with
Quint again.*

OCTOBER 9TH

I called the doctor's office today. They didn't have much to tell me. They only let me know that they'd sent a prescription for me that I can pickup at the drug store. I'm so sick of waiting to hear the results. How long must this go on?

I'm also tired of being sick. I haven't felt good today at all. I feel like my body is going one way and I'm going the other way. I hope the meds help.

OCTOBER 10TH

It's Junior's birthday today, and in our family tradition, we had dinner together. I think we were jovial and got along well. Colt was his typical self, charming, funny, the great father he has always been. Junior was even cracking some jokes, and he received our embraces without hesitation. Cleo and I prepared the meal, and when you have a good meal, it influences the people eating it. It's not absurd that mac and cheese, grilled burgers on homemade buns, and red velvet cake for dessert make my family happy and more optimistic about life.

God, how I love to eat! It doesn't matter if I'm in grief or in times of joy, I still love to eat. I suppose that I like to eat because of the taste of the food. I don't know why, but my appetite is off lately. I don't eat as much these days.

But enough about that! We ate and had the delightful cake with ice cream and then raised our glasses in toast to Junior's day. At the end of dinner, when Colt, Cleo, and I were clearing the table, Cleo dropped some news on us. She has a serious boyfriend. It's the guy I saw her with in the park.

Conrad was quick with a look at his sister. I wasn't sure what the look meant. Junior asked with genuine interest, "So who's the unlucky guy?" but she didn't answer him.

I was happy about her news, but I wonder why she turned him away from me when I saw them in the park. I didn't mention the park tonight. "When do we get to meet this new wonderful guy?" I asked.

"Ward, his name is Ward," she said "is awful busy with work. I meet with him Mondays, Wednesdays, and weekends at his house. So, it's hard for him to find the time to come over and meet you."

I'm sure I frowned when I heard the words "his house."

"Don't you have enough confidence in me to think I know what I'm doing when I go to his place?" she asked. "Don't you trust me?"

What can I do when any of my kids puts it to me like that? "Of course I trust you."

Junior limited himself to showing that he was still skeptical by sighing loudly. Conrad continued to be silent.

Does he know Ward?

OCTOBER 12ᵀᴴ

Brent called a meeting of the managers today. Juan, one of my colleagues, took advantage of the occasion to bring up some "truths" we don't normally talk about. He is the department head for the executive accounts. I admire his energy. As for me, I'm the low manager in the organization. I don't give two shits about titles, the pecking order of things in the office, or "for the good of the company." That kind of crap. The hierarchy has never attracted me. My secret axiom has always been, "the lower the title, the less the responsibility and expectation." The truth is, I see that a person lives more comfortably without the weight of heavy responsibilities. But Juan is doing the right thing for himself because among the department heads, the only people considered for promotions would be in order of seniority. Juan knows he has nothing to fear from me in competition for promotion. And I'm happy with my little cost-of-living pay raises.

The high point of the meeting was when Juan realized that the next promotion would pass him by and would more than likely go to the woman who is sleeping with Brent's son. It was priceless when Juan shot out, "Brent, would you happen to have a daughter that's available for the department head of the executive accounts to sleep with?" Then he gave his phone number for her to call.

Brent's face turned bright red. He asked Juan to be professional and said that if not, he was looking at a two-week notice.

"I'm not looking to be fired," Juan said. "I'm looking for a promotion, and I understood that is the process at this company."

I was trying, but failing miserably, to hold in my laughter.

Brent looked around the room at us and decided not to fire Juan right then. "Juan," he said, "let's talk after the meeting." I know what that means. Juan's won himself a trip to HR. Juan, you are my hero for today! I admire you on many levels. When I got home, I started gathering my winter clothes, which were stored in the guest room. I rotate my clothes from my walk-in closet to the guest room according to the season. Actually, I should just narrow down my wardrobe and put limits on my shopping. Oh, well, anyway, while I was digging around in the guest room closet, I came to a little box that I hadn't put there. I opened it, and there was a necklace in it. I presume it's for Colt's girlfriend. I put it back in its hiding place. I don't want him to know that I know the necklace is there.

I need something stronger to keep me from feeling this way. I should call my doctor and ask her to fill me a pain prescription. Maybe that will help. I wish I had never looked in that closet.

OCTOBER 13TH

Becky arrived today! I went to the airport to meet her. She's softer, older, heavier, but still full of energy. It was sheer joy to see her again. We didn't talk much because her family was there, and I didn't want to make a pest of myself. It's not that I dislike her family. In fact, it's quite the opposite. I love her family. They were my second family when I was growing up. She said she would call me in a few days to schedule a good time to get together.

OCTOBER 15TH

Today my department was empty. Three of my employees phoned in sick, Mary was out somewhere, and Raj had to get some account information from the sales department, so he was out of our area. It wasn't so bad, because as a team we are caught up and things are running routinely. And the secret project is on schedule, so Brent has given me some breathing room. Thank goodness! However, there will be a rush next week because it will be the end of the quarter and Back-2-Back will be expecting more information. I took advantage of the solitude today and allowed my mind to drift off in a daydream.

My morning was quite nice because Devin and I had a nice chat and that passed the time more quickly. For some days now, I've noticed that he's been down, lifeless, in some kind of funk. I can almost feel his sadness. I like Devin. I think I've written that here once or twice. So today, I put my professional attitude aside and asked him what was troubling him. He came to my desk and smiled (I love to see him smile), but he said nothing about his problems.

"You seem like you're in mourning," I said. "Did someone close to you pass away?" I spoke as a friend, not as a boss talking to an employee. "I can almost feel the hurt you're carrying around with you," I added.

He didn't take this as an act of courtesy, but only looked at me and said, "You're a very kind-hearted person."

Good God! He looked at me like my kids look at me when I say I'm worried about them. Made me feel damn old. Damn old!

I got brave. "The girlfriend?"

Devin looked away from me, shook his head, and stood up. "Excuse me for a moment." And off he went to the men's room while I just sat there staring at my computer screen.

I think I was worrying that I had upset him. I didn't mean to, that's for sure. I felt an agitation I haven't felt in a long time. Agitation? Is that a proper word? I thought about it. The sensation going through me at the time was something and belonged to me. I was witnessing the agitation of my own emotions. Suddenly a light dawned. I'm not some dried-up old woman!

When Devin came back, composed and maybe a little embarrassed, I was still selfishly enjoying my new breakthrough. I'm not all dried up! I looked at him with gratitude. He had made me think. He had brought out this revelation. And then our moment was ruined when Raj and Mary came into the department. Devin and I turned away from each other and went back to work.

OCTOBER 16ᵀᴴ

W hat is happening to me?

All day at work, I was giddy. Devin's on the outs with his girlfriend...yay! How awful of me to hope that someone's happiness is compromised. I'm ashamed of myself. But I'm *not* a dried-up old woman. I can feel that special stirring of wanting. That's what made me feel giddy.

Other good news—the doctor's office called, and, yes, my white count is up, but they don't think its too concerning. My breast exam was perfect, and everything else seemed to be in order. I need to come in for a follow-up appointment and discuss the results, but I am relieved that nothing is "of great concern."

Should I make another appointment with my lawyer now? Is it now the right time to set the divorce in motion?

I need to think about that. I want to avoid thinking about it, but after finding the hidden necklace (that's evidence, isn't it?), I need to make a decision about the proper way to go about it. I don't want either of us to fail financially because of this possible divorce.

OCTOBER 17ᵀᴴ

W ork sucked today. It was so boring! To make things worse, I felt awful. I should have phoned in sick. Besides, it was raining, as if Mother Nature was saying, "Winter is on the way." I love you, Mother Nature, but I don't love the cold of winter.

After work, though, my day got good again. And what made it good? Well, it's a little funny, but when I was pulling out of the parking lot, I looked across the street, and there, walking down the sidewalk and getting drenched, was none other than Mr. Goldsole. Of course I stopped and offered him a ride, which he gladly accepted.

"It's cold out there, looks like winter will be coming soon," I said, making small talk.

"Yes, winter." His face brightened. "I love winter! That's when Santa comes!"

I laughed. Mr. Goldsole looked like a young child who actually believed in Santa. We had a wonderful chat, then he had me drop him off at the corner of Poplar and Birch, where he said his daughter lived. He said he was going to have dinner with her. He also said her name was…what was it?…oh, yeah. Fae. Mr. Goldsole had told me that Fae was old English for Faith. There is that word again. Faith. Anyway, he and Fae were going to have dinner and then she would drive him home. Gosh, she's a lucky woman to still have her father and that he's such a good man. I just love that man. I hope I run into him again.

Something tells me I will.

Anyway, I made it home safe and sound and found Colt there. He was making dinner. He suggested that I take my time and get out of my work clothes and into something comfortable. He'd have dinner on the table. With hot tea, too.

"Take your time and relax," he kept saying.

He is such a good cook, I'm not sure who is better, him or me. We're both pretty good. I hate it that I've made up my mind to dislike him and then he's so nice to me. Damn him for always being the good man he is. I can still feel my resentment toward him.

D evin. I want to have a talk with him, someplace private, away from the office, someplace where we can have a nonprofessional conversation. But I don't want to scare him. I don't even know quite what I'd say to him. Before we have that talk, however, I would like to know exactly what is going on with me, inside me. It can't be what I think it is. Not at my age. But somehow this young man, who is young enough to be my son and who isn't even that handsome, has become the object of my attention. I feel as nervous as an adolescent, yet when I look in the mirror I see skin that has some wrinkles, I see flabby arms, and when I see those crows feet around my eyes and the varicose veins on my leg, I don't feel like an adolescent. I feel ridiculous.

My feelings more or less turned off eight years ago. That's when I resigned to the fear created by the cancer. My grief and anger and fear knocked me off balance, and the indifference I've felt ever since developed into a sense of unattractiveness. So I went looking for confirmation that I'm still a real woman. I'm ashamed to admit it, but I cheated on Colt. Well, he's cheated on me. And doesn't he continue to do so? The man on the bus the other day was a one-time thing. I can honestly say there was no love involved. I enjoyed the sex, but I didn't feel anything for him afterward...or did I?

I want to be wanted. I want to be the focal point of someone's attention. It's completely selfish of me to want that. I didn't struggle with compromising myself, with committing my future to a normal relationship on a permanent basis. I thought that a one-time encounter would fill me where I'm empty. Well, it did boost my confidence, but now when I look at Devin, I lose that fragile confidence. I want to talk with him and find out if there is even a chance he would be interested in me. I'm breaking all of my rules when it comes to this. I should never get involved with an employee, so why am I thinking about doing exactly that?

I'm an idiot.

I need to get a divorce and gain my independence, and that's that. This is the first time I've thought of what follows divorce. It's my first serious step toward being free and being able to make myself available to commit to someone besides Colt. But why would I want to commit to someone else? I just want an independent lifestyle. With that freedom, I could play the field like men do, and go to bed with one man tomorrow and with another the day after that. I want the freedom to have the man I'm attracted to the same way I want to eat what I know will satisfy me.

Why am I so selfish?

I want what I had when I was younger. Surely I'm still capable of that kind of love.

Before the mastectomy, radiation, and chemo, being with Colt was different. We had a special connection, and when we made love, it seemed like every bone in my body was in harmony with every bone his body, that every impulse of mine found itself synchronized to his. It was like having the perfect dancing partner. In the beginning, every movement induced an equivalent response, and every response corresponded immediately to every thought. There was only one person who thought, yet it was two bodies wrapped up in the dance.

That's what I want again.

OCTOBER 19TH

Becky called today. We're going to get together soon. I sure hope so! She is so full of positive energy, I know it will radiate out and fill me up, too. I have a photo of her when she was an eco-warrior. There she is, wearing rappelling gear, hanging on the side of the corporate tower of some oil company. She and another warrior are securing a banner that says in huge black letters SAVE THE PLANET, KILL YOURSELF! Then under that it says, HOW DID OUR OIL GET UNDER IRAQ'S SAND? WE SHOULD BOMB TEXAS, TOO. THEY HAVE OIL. Becky was always in her groove when she had something to protest or save. One time, she lived in a tree house in some forest, either in Washington or Oregon, I can't remember which, but she lived there for a year, sabotaging the logging community. After her third time in jail, her husband filed for divorce. I guess he wasn't up for the whole protest thing. I look forward to seeing her.

I had to meet with Brent and Jerome this morning. That Jerome gets on my nerves! He told me I was stalling, not getting him the information quick enough. I am stalling, but damn him for figuring it out.

Practically the minute I walked into the office, he said, "Have you heard the phrase 'sink or swim'?"

"Yeah," I said. "I've heard that a time or two."

"Well, you are in the deep end of the pool."

This whole macho posturing thing is annoying. I just wanted to tell him and Brent that I wouldn't do any more shady work. If they want to bring down Bio-Sport, they'll have to do it themselves. So I asked Jerome, "What do you want me to give you in addition to the information about Bio-Sport? We have a lot going on here at our own company. We can't just drop everything and work for you. My team's participation in this 'project' is consuming all the time they should be giving to their employer. That's Brent."

"Are you really such a moron?" he said. "You will give me more than data. You'll be a spy like no other. I've been informed that you've met with and become friends with Quintana Adams. That makes you my new best friend."

I looked at Brent for help. I couldn't believe what I had just heard. This piece of crap had his goons following me. Brent didn't say a word.

"Mr. Attwood," I said, "I'm not sure who you think you are, but I don't take kindly to being followed or my personal life infiltrated. As far as I'm concerned, from this moment forward, you communicate with me through Brent. I'll have nothing more to do with you."

Well, Jerome has the best poker face I've ever seen. If my words bothered him, he never let on, he didn't even blink an eye. He turned to Brent and said, "Will you leave me alone with Hope for a moment please?"

Brent left the room. He ignored my expression, my body language, telling him to stay.

I turned back to Jerome. "Should I scream for help now? Or wait until your goons get here?"

"Hope, I think you have me all wrong." he said, his voice so sweet and musical he sounded like some kind of angel. "I just want to do what's best for my company and my stockholders. Back-2-Back is no different from any other company. We want growth and security in our industry. But I'm not like every other CEO. I get what I want, and I can make you do what I want you to do." He gave me this huge smile. It looked like a crocodile. Just before it eats you. "But I prefer that you volunteer your services. Now look here." He took a top-of-the-line Montblanc fountain pen out of his pocket and scribbled something on a notepad on the table in front of him. "This will be the amount I send you. Or I can make it cash if you like. The IRS doesn't have to know about it."

My eyes practically bulged out of their sockets. The figure was more than I make before taxes in ten years. I immediately started mentally spending it. I could pay off every one of my kids' student loans. I could buy a fancy new bicycle I've been admiring. There would be enough left over to...to... to do whatever I wanted to do. But while my imagination was having a great time, my soul was vomiting. My soul dislikes Jerome Attwood. No, that's not a strong enough word. My soul hates him. It's responsible for my gut feelings, and at that moment, my gut was twisted and in pain, begging me to run away.

Jerome leaned back in his chair and gave me a long, calm look. "Perhaps you need some of this money up front to motivate you," he said in his smooth voice. "I can write you a check right now...if you like?"

"Mr. Attwood," I said as soon as I could speak, "I can work with almost anyone, but the name-calling and talking to me as if I'm some kind of idiot commando must come to an end. I don't appreciate it and I won't tolerate it."

"Understood. Now how much of an advance would you like?"

I just looked at him.

"Brent has no idea that we've offered you a bonus," he said with a smile. "He will never know unless you tell him. So how about fifty grand? More?"

"Mr. Attwood," I said as steadily as I could, "I'll take one hundred thousand now, not to be subtracted from the number you just wrote, and that number needs an additional two hundred thousand to be divided among my team at the completion of the 'project.'"

"Agreed." And just like that, he wrote a check and handed it to me. "Now that you've accepted the money, you're committed to me. I will let you know what I need and when I need it." He pointed at the door. "You can go now."

The rest of the day, all I could feel was a mixture of excitement over the money and fear of this creepy guy acting like he owned me.

OCTOBER 20TH

It's Saturday. Earlier, the weather was nice. Chilly, but nice, so I rode my bike over to meet Becky for lunch at the Vegan Haven way over on Cedar Street. Neither Becky nor I are vegans but they do have some great food there.

I'm sure most people think I'm a dyke because I wear a lot of men's clothes. I wore my Merrell hiking shoes, khaki cargo pants, and a sweatshirt and North Face all-weather jacket. At my age, I would rather be comfortable, and if men's clothes are more comfortable than women's, then I'm in them and enjoying life.

Becky hasn't changed. I always felt like she was going to be eternally young. For her size and age she is physically spry. Her spunky attitude and language is entertaining. Her choice of words, her turn of phrase is...I'm not sure if that's the correct way to describe it. She's an old hippie and a veteran eco-warrior so she talks in her own funky language.

I admire her. She's done some amazing things to protect our natural resources. She's still bigger than life, and her approach is helpful, positive, and infectious. She believes in magic. She sees the souls of plants, talks to angels, and smokes dope because it's a natural source for freeing the mind.

"Start using magic," she told me after I'd told her I was in trouble at work. "Magic is the art of knowing the power that lies within us. It's an art that requires ability and awareness to empower us to generate energy. We are living organisms. The human organism is created with several ingredients: soul, energy, and matter, to name three of the important ones. Our energy, soul, and matter help shape our reality. But be cautious. Reality has energy, too, and if we let it, it can shape us."

Is my reality shaping me?

Becky is so advanced in the ways of truly living that sometimes I have a hard time understanding what she's saying.

"Check my words," she said. "Your tangible world, the one you see every day, that is only one reality. There are other dimensions that are equally important, just as real, but less physical. Are you picking up what I'm putting down? Dig it, what you do in your presumed reality has consequences in other realms. When your gut instinct, as you put it, tells you not to do something, more than likely it's a message from another realm."

While she was talking, I thought of Mr. Goldsole and the things he said about my soul. So I told her about him. She found him fascinating. I told her how he reminds me of Granddad. Becky still remembers my granddad, so it excited her to think that someone around today resembles him. I explained to her how Mr. Goldsole thought I should introduce myself to my soul.

"Now he sounds like he has his boots laced up tight!"

"What does that mean?"

"Your old dude is in the know sis." She said. "Now check the audio, seeing yourself as a spiritual being is a way to transform your reality. Drop the past, forget what you've been taught in church, and embrace the freedom to know your soul."

I was eating, listening to her, all the while wondering how coincidental it was that my GP, Mr. Goldsole and now Becky all seemed to be in touch with something I never thought about. The soul.

"You don't need a head skinner to catch this grove."

"What is a head skinner?" I asked trying to understand her funky language.

"A shrink. Duh." She looked at me with a funny face. "Dig it, most people identify themselves by their name, appearance, and occupation. You, my friend, ditch the personal labels and get a grip on who you are. Who you are is only complete when you know your soul man!" She gave me another funny face.

Then we started laughing, and I can't say how much I've needed a good laugh, especially the way my life has been going. We laughed so hard my lungs hurt and my eyes watered. But while I was laughing with Becky, I felt free of pain, nausea, worry, and stress. It was a fantastic high.

So, Who am I?

With the help of others I'm beginning to not only recognize, but also appreciate the invisible, intangible me. Facing inward, as Mr. Goldsole put it, I discover sensations and perceptions, thoughts and feelings, I couldn't have imagined. It's had to describe in words but I could feel my soul and it was connecting with Becky's.

I let our conversation be positive and didn't lay anything heavy on her. That is, I didn't say anything about the doctor's appointments and how worried I have been. I didn't mention that I'm going to divorce Colt. Most of all, I didn't want to say anything about Jolene.

October 23ʳᵈ

I've been thinking about a way to approach Devin. I've come up with two approaches. One is to be frank. Just walk up to him and say, "I'd like to get to know you outside the workplace." Then see where it goes from there. Or I could be more direct and say something bolder. Like, "Devin, I'm an experienced woman. Even though I'm old enough to be your mother, I'm still girl enough to make life exciting."

Gee, it doesn't look as good on paper as it sounds in my imagination.

What would he think of me?

I'm sure he'd see me as an old woman and the thought of the look on his face destroys my courage. I would be so embarrassed if he laughed at me. Or worse. If he didn't say anything.

Up to now, I think he's seen me as a good-humored boss and nothing more. But he's not a kid. His thinking seems to be mature. Maybe he's the kind that likes an adult woman? And maybe his girlfriend is a youngster that likes to play mind games? Maybe he's fed up with the mind games and now wants a grownup, and that grownup could be me. After all, I'm a woman with a semi-good figure. I'm an experienced woman. I have no major vices. I make good money. At fifty, I can be full of life when I need to be. I can be funny and exciting. I can be a lot of things. As for my three children, well, I don't count them in this at all. In any case, he knows I have a family.

Well…now that I've talked my courage up, what are my intentions? The truth is, I haven't thought that far. But I won't fool myself enough to think I'd divorce Colt and marry Devin. Hell, no! I just want to have fun.

Until I talk to him, of course, I won't know anything. I'm only fantasizing. At this stage, I'm not satisfied with finding a man on a bus who rubs arms with me and I end up in his bed. I just feel confused when it's over. I feel perplexed.

I've also thought about having several men. In my fantasy, I get all the way up to the moment of going to bed with another man. The important thing is going to bed with him. After we do the naughty deed, the next thing is to get the hell out of there. We both return to our own places in the world. We lose contact forever. But in that scenario, I don't envision a single comforting conversation, not even a single meaningful phrase.

But what if some man and I are in a bedroom on Cherry Street, and he looks at me and says, "You fuck like a woman on her first of day at work. You're exciting and full of energy, but in the end, well, it's only work." Is he calling me a working girl? A prostitute?? I've been told I'm task-oriented. If anyone said that, I'd be mortified!

Well, in my diary, I can write out any scenario I want to. These are just wild thoughts. What else is a diary for?

I think back to before Colt and the other men I've had, and I remember them, not in detail but just enough to know I've been with other men. I don't recall hearing any complaints.

Devin?

How should I approach you?

OCTOBER 25TH

I've just met Ward, Cleo's boyfriend. First impression: I like him. He has a strong-minded look about him and he speaks with pride and certainty. He seems to have a very solid foundation to his character. He treats me with respect without flattering me and he looks at my daughter with true, unmistakable love in his eyes. In his whole attitude, there's something that pleases me, and I believe it pleased my vanity as well.

Cleo must have said a thing or two to him about me that was admirable. I am truly happy knowing that my daughter has a good opinion of me. It's odd, though, because I don't seem to care much what opinion Junior has of me. Conrad and Cleo's opinions matter to me.

Is that wrong?

Perhaps the reason is this—despite the fact that all three of my children mean a lot to me, despite the fact that all three reflect my own desires and inhibitions, in Junior I note a hidden hostility that he doesn't dare confess, not even to himself.

I don't know which came first, his drawing back or my own retreat. It's clear that I don't love him the way I love the other two. I feel distant from the son who lives in my house but who doesn't ever say anything to me, or when pressed, speaks only obligatory words to me. Junior is like a stranger. I swear he was born angry and hates me. I work hard to offer him love and support. But Junior always finds a way to complain. He will shout loudly how he hates this or that. Then he goes the extra mile to make sure, I not only know, but that I also feel his hatred toward my efforts and me. At this point I'm done with putting out any effort to try and get him to like me. Or am I? I mean, is a mother ever really so fed up with one of her children that she no longer cares? Of course not. I love him and he can't take that away.

Conrad has been acting differently lately. I can't put my finger on it but he seems to be holding back, like he knows something but won't tell me. What is his secret? Why does he have a secret from me or worse, secrets?

Getting back to Ward, I'm happy the boy has character. I see him as a good fit for Cleo. He's three years older than her, but looks four to five years older than that. The essential thing is that she should feel protected. Cleo is loyal. She won't cheat on him. They seem to have a friendship, first and foremost. I like that. Friendship has no substitute. Friends can't be quickly replaced by other people.

I promise I will not interfere with their relationship. I want to be a supportive mother, but not the type that sticks her nose in her daughter's relationships. I do feel protective of Cleo, but not to the point of smothering her.

And I'm still drifting away from the specific subject of Ward. He told us he's been working a good job, something to do with architectural design. I'm not sure exactly what his position is, but he appears more driven than I was at that age.

I think Colt intimidated Ward. He made sure he sat furthest away from Colt and closest to the door. Poor kid. If he only knew I'm the more dangerous one when it comes to our children. Ha-ha.

OCTOBER 26TH

I overheard Devin talking to someone about things he likes to do with his time off. Times and places. It gave me an idea. Perhaps I can *accidentally* show up at one of his usual places. (Oh, crap, am I becoming a stalker now?). I'm hoping the opportunity will present itself so we can talk. Then I could look into his eyes and say—wait, what color are his eyes? I think they're green. Well, anyway, it's a thought.

I've lost some more weight. Now I fit into my skinny jeans again. How great is that? It's strange, I'm not dieting, but I don't feel hungry like I used to.

Becky phoned. We're going to see each other tomorrow. I could use a chat with my best friend. I love the way she talks. She said, "How's your grouch bag holding up? Let's you and me go out shopping. Puttin' on the Ritz." Let me translate. How much money is in my purse? Let's go shopping like we're two rich women.

OCTOBER 27TH

Becky and I did go shopping. Then we came back to my house to make candy for Halloween. I love this time of year, but I think it's going to be a cold Halloween. It's so cold outside right now that if I spit it'll freeze before it hits the ground. She and I were bundled up like it was the end of December. But that turned out to be a good thing because we walked right by a guy that I'm certain was my man on the bus. Did I say this is a small town? Maybe too small. I felt my stomach flip as we walked past him. The embarrassment of knowing what I did made me feel mystified.

Becky noticed, of course. "What's giving you the snakes, sis?" She uses the word "snakes" instead of nervous because snakes freak her out.

"Oh," I said, "nothing."

"It looked like it was gonna rain there for a minute." When she says it's gonna rain, that means someone is going to get arrested.

"Becky, chill out," I said. "I'm not one of your activist, hippie friends. I don't know what you're saying half the time. Speak English, girl."

"Oh, and 'chill out' is sophisticated and very metropolitan?" She gave me one of those looks, but I didn't say anything about the man. Even though she's my best friend, I don't want to divulge my imperfections to her. I think she forgot about it, anyway, because the shopping distracted her. We had a good time, even though we ended up not buying much of anything.

When we got back, I went into the kitchen. I was making popcorn balls and she was carving a jack-o-lantern, and we had the best time talking. Having her in my kitchen was great because I could forget about Jerome and Brent for a while. I also forgot to think about divorcing Colt.

Then we made peanut brittle and fudge. We were pouring out the fudge to let it cool, just having fun and being goofy, and she said, "I haven't blasted this mad since I started going steady with Mary Jane. Laughing this hard is going to put me to bed with a shovel." (Translation: I haven't had this much fun since I started smoking pot. The laughter might kill me.) Then she got cute and flung some fudge at me, and that was it. We had a little food fight. Hah! The kitchen was a mess when Colt came home. He walked in and saw the mess, fudge dripping down the wall, and then he looked at me and then at Becky, and said, "Hey, Becky, it's good to see you again." He grinned and walked back out, shaking his head. We were having so much fun. We sat on the floor and licked the spatulas. Then we cleaned out the bowl with our fingers. It was a wonderful day. I love her.

We also had to clean up the kitchen, of course. I still love her.

October 29th

After work tonight, I went to a cafe near Elm and Willow and sat there from 6:30 to 8:00. I was trying my experiment. It's a Monday night, so I thought I'd look a little less suspicious if I did that. I wanted to run into Devin. I no longer feel like I want to talk to him. I feel like I need to talk to him. So I waited, sipping hot chocolate, watching the men who walked up Elm Street. I thought I saw him in every man that came close to the café. My eyes were playing games on me, of course. Or maybe my mind was playing some idiotic game. I'm not sure, but it was entertaining. Like I said, I thought I saw Devin in every guy that came into the café. It wasn't until each guy came close to me that I could regain control of my mind and stop staring and see what was real.

Then a miracle happened! Devin walked into the café. At first I thought it was my imagination, but it was really him. My heart jumped, just like a schoolgirl's. He was standing two feet away from me, waiting in line to order his beverage, so I waved to him.

"Hello," I said, trying to act casual. "What are you doing here?"

He looked surprised to see me. I believe that he was pleasantly surprised; I hoped he was. "Mrs. O'Dwyer, you startled me," he said.

"I'm sorry, Devin. I didn't mean to." I really wish he'd stop saying Ma'am and Mrs. Blah-blah-blah. "Would you care to join me?" I asked.

He shook his head. "No, I'm sorry, I have a friend waiting for me. I was getting coffees to go."

"Oh, that's too bad," I said. "I would have enjoyed your company." I hope I wasn't biting my lower lip. I do that when I'm nervous. That's a silly thing to write down, isn't it? I doubt I did it, but I did have a brief moment of anxiety that left me out of breath and feeling empty. But at least I was able to say, "Oh, that's too bad."

When he got his coffees, he made for the door, but then turned back to me. "Are you always here at this time?"

I lied. "Oftentimes, yes, I am."

"Then how about we meet another day? Could we do that?"

"That would be fine with me. Will you remember?"

Stupid question! But I was nervous and didn't know what else to say. All I know is that I wanted our conversation to last as long as possible. He left. I finished my hot chocolate.

The girl cleaning the sitting area noticed me watching Devin walking away. She looked at me and said, "Now those jeans wrap up a nice package, don't you think?" We both laughed. She was a homely girl, but so cute in the way she held herself, and I think she noticed every nice package wrapped in jeans.

OCTOBER 31ST

We had our annual Halloween party tonight. Like I said before, I love this time of year. It's just the beginning of all the holiday festivities. Our dinner party was more of a harvest dinner than a Halloween party. We had harvest vegetable soup, baked squash, roasted chicken, mashed potatoes, gravy (of course), and pumpkin bread. Colt helped with the cooking, between the three of us—Becky and Colt and me—everything tasted great. I enjoyed spending time with my two best friends.

Yes, Colt is my best friend. Is that confusing? I suppose so, but I look at it like this. Our marriage is dead or dying, and I can live with that, but I couldn't stand the thought of losing him as my friend. So, yeah, I guess it's a little confusing.

We had a houseful, including some of Colt's friends from the ranching community. It took some time for my city friends to feel comfortable around my rural friends, but once the food was served everyone seemed to be just fine. Food always seems to create a common ground for people. For the most part, no one seems to offend anyone in particular. Well, except for Mack.

Wild Mack and his wife came. That man is certifiable. He's full of goodness, yet his untamed manner is something that you need to dig through to find the domesticated human. Colt and Mack have been friends since the Marines. It's a funny story. They grew up in the same area, yet they didn't know each other until they met in Twenty-Nine Palms, where they were assigned to the same unit. Mack is from the Blackfeet nation. His skin is light like Colt's, but his face is noticeably native. He gained his nickname early on in life, I'm told, but he sure lives up to it.

From the kitchen, I could hear him in a loud voice telling someone how women are too ignorant to work around livestock.

Then his wife Jennifer, who is just as loud, said, "Hey, not only can I outwork you around the ranch, but I can do one thing better than you. I'm like Colt. I can talk to the horses and cattle, and they cooperate with me. Chickens, not so much, but the horses and cattle do."

"Woman," he practically shouted, "I will not stand here and listen to your lies! I'm better at *anything* outdoors than you are. You can outwork me in the house, you know, doing the laundry and shit like that, but that's about it." He laughed, but everyone who didn't know him tensed up, figuring that he and Jennifer were about to have a full-on argument.

Jennifer noticed this tensing up around them. "Knock your shit off, Mack! These good people don't know you're just joking around."

At that, he laughed again. "Sorry, folks. If you knew Jennifer and I at all, you would know that she is better than me working on the ranch. I just don't like it, so I have to make her think I'm better with words." He laughed again, but nobody else was laughing. They were all watching him.

Mack always puts people on edge. When Colt told me he'd invited him and Jennifer, I worried a little, but then I thought the way he talks adds a bit of entertainment to a party. I remember the first time I met Mack. It was a good twenty-four years ago. I was pregnant with Junior at the time, and Mack was following us from his ranch to Colt's family's ranch. He was pulling a horse trailer with his horse on board. The horse's name was Buick. Buick was a beautiful quarter horse, but he had a temperament that matched Mack's. It was always fun to see who was more stubborn. Anyway, we were driving down the road when Colt noticed that Mack had pulled over. By the time we got turned around, we found Mack on the side of the road beating the shit out this guy. When we finally got Mack off the guy, we learned that the guy had been riding Mack's bumper, so Mack had slowed down to a crawl. Of course, this pissed the other guy off, so he pulled out to go around Mack, only he wanted to annoy Mack a little more by getting close as he passed, and so in his attempt to be threatening with his car, he'd accidentally hit the horse trailer. He knew better than to leave the scene of accident, so he pulled over to exchange insurance information. Then, the guy told us that that son-of-a-bitch Mack pulled him out of his car and started beating the shit out of him before any words were exchanged. I thought Mack was going to kill the guy. His face was all bloody.

Two things a person should never do around Mack. One, never, ever sleep with his wife. Two, don't even think of hurting his favorite horse, which at that time was Buick. (Buick has since passed on.)

But the point is, I learned that day that either of these will get a person hurt or possibly killed. The other driver admitted that he was driving aggressively and was being a threat to Buick. When Mack got done with him, the guy was in desperate need of a dentist to fix his missing teeth and a doctor to fix his nose. Yes, Mack is a wild man.

Another funny thing about Mack is that he considers Colt his brother and watches over him. He goes to where Colt's playing on the weekends, not to drink or dance, but to make sure no one gets too close to Colt. I know the bars where Colt plays, and they have bouncers, but Mack insists on going anyway. He brings Jennifer and they get a table close to the band. I suppose I'm grateful to Mack for looking after Colt all these years.

Before I met Colt, he was playing one night at a bar named the Brush Fire (it's closed now and has been for years), and a fight broke out. The way Colt tells the story, the bar was up in arms and the band had put their instruments down and joined in exchanging fists. When the fight was finally broken up and the police were sorting everyone out, one man left with the undertaker and Mack left with the police. I was told that Mack was up for murder, but in the chaos of the fight, no one actually saw who Mack was fighting with so he was released. I've heard from some people who were there that night saw the man who left in a body bag. They claimed he had pulled a gun and was aiming at Mack.

So I know Mack and what he's like, and, yes, he fights and is good at it, but if he ever killed anyone, it was because they had the upper hand and he did what he had to do. Mack is all about living life to it's fullest and is superstitious about the afterlife. He's not a big man, but he has the largest hands I've ever seen. I would hate to be on the receiving end of those clubs, that's for sure.

Anyway, I digress. Everyone at the Halloween dinner party had a good time. I think the kids enjoyed it, too. I caught them laughing and smiling, and it did my heart good to see them happy. I'm glad they'd decided to join us. Now that they're young adults, I know they could go with their friends and not spend time with their family.

Cleo had Ward with her, and I observed how respectful he is of her. He waits on her like he's her personal servant. I think Cleo should have told him to relax and enjoy the party, but she didn't. I think she was a bit nervous. She and Conrad were exchanging funny looks all the time. I would say they're getting along, but something is causing tension between them. I wonder what it is.

And Junior? Junior was being himself; he was enjoying himself, but only on his own terms, one beer after another. But one time I saw Becky talking to him, and he was laughing. She can warm the coldest hearts. She was a champ at getting through to him. At least I got to see Junior with a face that was better than a frown for a while.

Unfortunately, I had to go upstairs before everyone left. I wasn't feeling real good. I hate it when my body dictates what I can and can't do. Hopefully the doctor can figure this out so I can have a normal life soon.

NOVEMBER 1ST

I can't believe it's November already. Where does the time go?

Colt and I had an argument this morning. I told him that I wouldn't file for divorce until after the holidays, that I don't see any reason to disturb the peace of the holidays with one of us moving out and both of us dealing with hurt feelings. He still acts like he doesn't believe me that I'm serious about the divorce. I told him that he's been acting like he's single, so I'm going to do that, too. Then he gave me the same old bullshit about how he's never cheated on me, and that there is no girlfriend. Well, *I can tell he's lying.* All men cheat, and he's got Jolene on the side. For the past few months now, he's spent a lot time away from home in addition to the overnight escapades. Where in the hell is he sleeping if he's not home with me? And that crap about his sister won't fly with me.

I only wanted to talk to him, but before I knew it I was yelling, and then I lost control and said things I shouldn't have. I know, I know, I can't take them back. It's over, anyway, so who cares about what was said? All the bad words are just a means to an end.

Enough of that!

I want to focus on *good things.* Something good happened tonight! I went back to the café and was sitting near the window. This time I wasn't expecting anything to happen. I wasn't watching every man walking in. I think I was trying to balance the pros against the cons of hormone replacement therapy. Menopause. Really? My doctor seems to think I'm menopausal. Since I'm in pain a lot, if this is a menopausal state, it stinks. I hate what it makes me feel like. I don't remember talking to anyone who said it hurt like this. Sure, I know about the missed cycles, the sweats, and even cramps, but this pain is so different. I guess I'll be going to see my gynecologist and the stirrups (oh, fun). And the mood swings! Yikes, they're dangerous. I hate to admit it, but I think I was moody this morning with Colt.

Gee, how did I get off on that tangent?

Anyway, I was sitting in the café and something caught my attention. So I raised my eyes, and there he was, like a dream, like a ghost, or simply like Devin.

"I saw you through the window," he said. "I thought it was a good time to have that cup of coffee."

I stood up so fast, my chair banged into the table and my spoon fell on the tiled floor with such a racket that it made everyone look at us. I felt like such an idiot. Then he sat down, I bent over and picked up the spoon, and before I could get back up, I stepped on my long coattail with my heel and stumbled again. *Idiot!*

He laughed. "It looks like I've startled you," he said.

"Well, yes, a little," I confessed. "I was deep in thought."

"Oh, I'm sorry. I didn't mean to disturb you."

I watched him take a sip from his steaming cup and shook my head. "No need to apologize."

After that, everything went back to normal. We talked about work, shared some gossip, okay, a lot of gossip. I'm guilty. So sue me. I told him the story about Juan at the meeting asking if Brent had a daughter for him to sleep with so he could get a promotion. Devin laughed hard at that. He was wearing a dress shirt and jeans, and his hair was a little messy, as if the wind had blown only on one side. I asked him about it, and he looked at his reflection in the shiny surface of his smart phone and just laughed.

After a bit, I decided to move on to some flirtatious innuendo. "Do you have any idea that you are responsible for one of the most recent crises in my life?" I asked him.

He laughed again. "Social or professional?"

"Neither. Sentimental."

He looked at me and saw that I was serious. "Um, well, uh…." He didn't know what to say.

So I saved him. "Look, Devin, it's possible that what I'm about to say will seem odd to you, maybe even a little crazy, and if you see it that way, just say so. But I don't want another opportunity to pass before I get a chance to tell you that I think I'm attracted to you."

Not a word came from his lips. He sat there, staring at his empty paper cup. I think I saw him blush a little. Was it pleasure or embarrassment?

I broke the silence. "Consider my age. And yours. The most logical thing for me to do would be to keep this to myself; but I believe that out of respect for you I should at least tell you my feelings and give you the opportunity to consider it. I'm not demanding anything. If, today or tomorrow or whenever, you tell me you're uncomfortable, we won't say another word. We will remain friends. And, please, don't be afraid about work, about being disturbed in your job. I'll behave, I promise." I felt myself running down. I stopped and just sat there and looked at him, waiting for him to say something.

But he was sitting there, looking at the table, not saying anything. Whatever he was going to say, whatever attitude he was going to assume, that was going to be the answer I've been waiting for. I sat there, too, still without saying anything. Finally I looked at him a little harder.

"Devin?" I gave him a slightly forced smile. I didn't want him to see that I was afraid of being rejected. "I've just said a lot," I told him. "Could you tell me what you're thinking?"

He looked up. I could tell that the worst had passed. "I suspected it," he said. "That's why I came back."

When I left the café to walk home, it was cold and the air smelled like snow. I was thinking about how good an island vacation would feel. I could see a beach with a warm sun above it. I could hear the rush of the waves on the shore. I was thinking of a beach where failed marriages, mastectomies, and routines at work get washed out to sea and never return.

Yes. Sunshine and me, warm and free.

NOVEMBER 2ND

I didn't want to get out of bed this morning. When I'm asleep, I experience a reality I enjoy so much that it's disappointing to wake up. I was dreaming I was young and still living with my grandparents. There was so much love in our house. I was wanted and loved, feelings that don't seem to exist in the real world these days. Nowadays, I feel like the world is empty, void of love or excitement. Not to mention that odd, sick feeling I have, the pain, the low-grade fever, and the general lack of energy.

I want more in my life than waking up, rushing off to work, going to the grocery store, coming home, doing housework, and doing it all over again the next day. It's like I'm a guinea pig on a wheel running as fast as I can and getting nowhere. I must have snooze-cruised for an hour this morning before I finally dragged my ass out of bed. But I did get up. I'm proud of that because I was so close to calling in sick.

I avoided Brent all day. He kept trying to corner me to discuss the project, but I laid low. In fact, I didn't do hardly any work for the company today. I worked on me. I haven't cashed the check that Jerome wrote me yet. A hundred thousand dollars is a lot of money, yet somehow I've kept it out of my mind. Instead, I've been thinking about Quint. She's really sweet. She really wants to create a positive change for children and in the videogame industry. How could I be a part of destroying her company? It feels wrong to work on Back-2-Back's project.

I also phoned my financial advisor. In the beginning, I trusted him with my money. In the beginning, he reported that my investments were making me a strong portfolio for retirement. But for the past few years, it seems that every time I speak with him, he's telling me how much money I'm losing. And the loss is substantial at this point. So today I asked him what companies he has me invested in. I didn't like what I heard. Sure, I want to make money off my investments, but I also have certain beliefs and don't want to invest in companies that I don't feel are ethically responsible.

So I was happy that Becky came by for lunch. We got takeout and went to the cathedral. I was hoping Mr. Goldsole would be there. I wanted her to meet him, but he wasn't around. Becky and I had a great conversation, anyway. She is so insightful and helpful with things I just stumble over. I was telling her that I'd discovered that some the investments in my portfolio are in BP, Shell, and other predatory petroleum companies. I would never invest in Big Oil (for obvious reasons), but I remember approving those investments when my financial advisor told me the oil companies are hard at work in the green movement.

"They're working on our environmental future, and the future they are working on is green," he told me. "You know— wind generators, solar, hydrogen cars. Hope, the oil companies really have considered your interest as well as everyone on the planet. It's not just about profit to them these days. They know that they need to change. Especially since the fiasco in the Gulf of Mexico."

This is what my financial advisor said to me.

But now I'm thinking about reinvesting my money elsewhere, so I asked Becky, "What would you do?"

"Do you really think investing in greedy gorillas [those powerful oil companies] is dancing in the direction [making a step] toward green energy?" she asked. "Those gorillas got their bankrolls [power] off of the sludge [oil]. Money's their god! And those cats sure as hell aren't going to turn their back on their god. They couldn't give two shits about Mother Earth. They only see dead presidents [profits]. They may talk wind power, but they are committed to petroleum. Here is what I would do, Hope. Invest in yourself."

"What do you mean?" I said.

"Look," she said, "you've invested your money long enough. It's reached its peak by now. All you're going to do now is lose it in the market. The economy sucks! Take your money out and invest it in what you want to. Start by getting rubbed down, fried, and dyed." She reached over and wrapped an arm around me. "I remember when the cancer had you. Your family and Colt and I—we all freaked out. Girl, I thought I was going to lose you to a dirt nap. I looked at you back then, and I remembered all the dreams you had and all the dreams you weren't going to fulfill because you were going to fly it through Endsville before you had a chance to live them out." She gave me a squeeze. "Girl, you've had a second chance at life! But you haven't done anything with it. Roll your bones, Sis. Celebrate the fact that you aren't in marble city. Tap that money jug of yours and spread that gravy on the dance floor."

It's true. I've become too serious about life. Flirting with Devin is a little first step in living better. But Becky, Cleo, and (all right, I admit it) Colt are correct. I need to live life like I did before the cancer. Perhaps live even better. I thought about this for a minute and said, "Hey, you've become too serous about life, too, you know. You're not nearly as much fun as you used to be. What happened?" I was trying to keep a straight face.

"Oh, you're funny," she said. "I dig your dance, but go pick yourself an orchid."

"I know you're right," I insisted. "I've been way too serious. You know what? Now that you're back in my life, you can help me liberate myself."

She nodded like she'd been thinking the same thing. "I was thinking we should get you off the same old and get you into some commando gear for a nice date with Mother Earth," she said. I took this to mean I should get some appropriate clothes to make a fanatical stand against any company that threatens nature. She tapped me on the forehead. "Now check the audio, Li'l Sis. Listen up! One of my posse tells me about a logging camp over the hill. We can go monkey wrench the place and then have a party."

I just shook my head. "Becky, first of all, I don't even know what the hell you're saying. Speak a language I can understand. Posse? Really? And, second, I'm not like you. I don't feel comfortable sabotaging heavy equipment. Someone could get hurt. And going to jail doesn't seem like 'living' to me."

"Ah, you don't know how to live girl. Going to jail is where the party rises. It's all good, I know you're in a different groove than I am but you're still my Li'l Sis. Nevertheless, it's important to me that you are happy in life."

There was a moment of silence. I looked around. The park around the cathedral was beautiful. It was filled with the colors of fall, and I could smell the threat of winter in the wind. "Becky?"

"Yeah, Sis?"

"I want you to know something." I didn't look at her, but continued to stare at the trees in the park. "I love you. I'm not just saying the words. I feel my love for you to my core."

"That's deep, girl. I hear you and thank you."

"Love isn't one of those things in life that's constant, you know. Love moves in waves, but when I think of you, that's when it's been the most constant. You've been in my life longer than anyone else, and I want you to know how much I love it that you're my friend, my sister, and if Colt hadn't come along, probably my lover."

Hearing this Becky laughed so loud the entire park must have heard her. "That's a hoot!" she said when she could finally speak. "You and me being each other's parking pets. Wow, I never thought of you and me hot in the zipper."

We were still laughing. "You know I was joking," I said.

"I love you, too, Sis. And I'm here for you. Always. You do know that?"

"Yep, I know that."

She walked me back to work, and I felt sad to see her drive away. I didn't want to be at work. I wanted to spend the rest of the day laughing with my best friend.

Now it's Friday night, Colt is playing a gig, the kids are wherever they go, Becky is doing something with her family, and I'm all alone. I really need to find something to do with myself. I don't like this lonely feeling. Gee, I'm tired of being me and being such a whining baby. Is that normal, being tired of oneself?

NOVEMBER 3RD

When I was writing about Devin, I didn't elaborate because I wanted the night to finish that way. With an optimistic beat of hope. He didn't say that he thought of me romantically. No, he said, "That's why I came here." He asked me to give him some time to think about it. "I suspected you had feelings for me," he said, "but it's still a surprise to me and I need some time to sort out my thoughts about it."

With that, we agreed to meet Sunday (tomorrow) for lunch. Tomorrow the weather is supposed to be nice. Cold, but no snow in the forecast.

So tonight I'm a little nervous. My mind is racing. At the café I didn't have an opportunity to explain what was on my mind. I had rehearsed in my mind for several days (maybe weeks!) what I would say to him, but when I was actually facing him, it didn't go the way I'd imagined.

Thursday night, when I was sitting there in the café, I wasn't certain how to proceed. After all, he surprised me. I was thinking about menopause and the pain I'm always in, and suddenly there he was in front of me. It was one of those awkward moments. And then I got a notion to tell him the truth of my situation. This was the opportunity I'd been waiting for and it was passing quickly. It was a situation born in my mind and had no basis in reality. I had to say what I was really thinking. I forgot my prepared speech.

Well, I'm not sorry that I followed my impulse. What I said came short of what I intended to say, but it was sincere. Further, I believe that sincerity and honesty are best in my vulnerable moments. And yet I wonder.... If he suspected my feelings, how is it that he could hesitate to reveal his own? Surely he already suspected that I had feelings for him. Perhaps he wanted to tell me I was ridiculous, but thought it would be cruel to shoot me point-blank. But he said he had suspected it. He said that was the reason he came.

Why?

What does that mean?

And what of his girlfriend or ex-girlfriend?

As far as the facts are concerned (do I sound like a detective? what a fool I am), it seems logical that he came because that other relationship is over. Could I provide the desire his girlfriend lacked? Could I be that little push he needs to leave her for good?

At my age, what can I offer that she can't?

What kind of a relationship would I want with him?

All these questions are making me dizzy. I'm wondering, wishing, hoping for...I don't even know what. If this diary were a radio show or destined for a reader other than me, I would end today's entry with a cliffhanger. "If you want to know the answers to these questions, come back for next week's episode."

NOVEMBER 4TH

I waited for Devin at the quaint little restaurant on Spruce Street that he had suggested. I was early. He was ten minutes late. He was dressed in jeans, a sport coat, and a dress shirt and looked as if he had just come from church. All of which improved his appearance a lot, but it's more likely that I was in the mood to find him looking better than his usual work attire.

But he seemed nervous. I think he dressed up to make a favorable impression on me. To show me that he accepted my feelings. But his nervousness showed just the opposite. When the hostess seated us, he chose a booth near the back of the restaurant, and I thought, *He doesn't want to be seen with me.* A bad omen. The service was really slow, so we had a good half-hour to talk after we ordered. We talked about general topics. But then, after our food was finally served and we were eating, he suddenly said, "Please don't give me those expectant looks."

I put my fork down and wiped my mouth. "I'm not looking at you with expectations," I protested. "I'm just looking at you." I felt like an idiot.

"You want my answer?" he asked. "I don't have one. I only have another question for you."

"Ask it then," I said. "We don't need the dramatics."

"What does it mean when you say that you have an attraction for me?"

I just sat there, blinking my eyes. It never occurred to me that he would ask this. Now I had to define my feelings over lunch and in public, not in the bedroom with candlelight and gentle kisses.

"Look, Devin," I finally said, "please don't make me seem more ridiculous than I already feel. Do you want specifics? Like, do I have a crush on you? Or do you want something more…like, have I fallen in love with you? Do you want to know what my love consists of?"

"No, you don't."

"Don't what?"

"Seem ridiculous."

That was a relief! "Well, then…?"

I was feeling vulnerable and it was pissing me off. I knew he meant well and wasn't trying to embarrass me, but feeling that vulnerable always frightens me. And the only way I have to fight back is to get angry.

"So," he began in his defense, "you don't want to appear ridiculous, and I can understand that, but you have no problem if I seem that way. To have an attraction for someone, for me, well…it can mean… well, I only want clarification."

Oops! I hadn't for one moment thought he might feel ridiculous or vulnerable. Here I go again. We haven't even begun a relationship, and I'm taking him for granted. Idiot! "You're right," I said. "I didn't consider your feelings. I'm sorry." He smiled, and I felt more at ease. "Okay, tell me what being attracted to a person means, and I'll admit that's what I meant."

It was nice to see that we'd both lost our verbal equilibrium. He sat there, thinking, trying hard to think of something that would satisfy both of us. It was cute.

But then I said, "Look, there's appearances, and there's reality."

"Ah," he said, shifting in his seat and leaning over the table.

"I'm attracted to you in reality," I said, "but the problem is when I think of the appearances."

"And what are the problems?"

"Don't make me say it. I'm old enough to be your mother. I would have been really young when I gave birth, but still I'm old enough. Don't make me say that. That's the part of reality that bothers the hell out of me. It makes me feel bad, honest to God."

He didn't say anything. That was good. His silence carried the least danger of hurting me.

"My purpose in telling you my feelings, apart from the very natural attraction, is to try and help you feel comfortable with my desire to make you happy." I could feel my face turning red. "That's the difficult part. I'm attracted to you, but I'm not sure I have anything to offer you that you may want or need. I can be selfish and want what works for me, but after giving this some serious thought, I want more than my selfish desires. I want the future." His eyes got big at the sound of *future*. "I'm not talking about marriage," I added, "so don't worry. It would be nice if we both thought of 'us' as a valuable experience. I'm married already and am going through a divorce, so this kind of thing can be considered an 'affair,' but I don't like that term. It cheapens what I imagine for us. I just want us to have the freedom to be together."

We finished our meal and the waiter brought us the check. I took it and Devin wiped his mouth with his napkin. He looked at me with a big nice smile on his face.

When he finally spoke, he said, "I like you, Hope. You're a very intriguing person, probably the most interesting person I've met in a long, long time."

NOVEMBER 6ᵀᴴ

L ast night Colt was on the sofa playing guitar for Sahchi, our big Akita. She loves it when Colt plays and sings for her. He takes songs and changes the words or names and inserts Sahchi. It's quite comical to watch. Here is this big,

120-pound dog pressed as close as she can get to Colt, and every time she hears her name, she looks up at him with the sweetest eyes and her tail wags. That dog loves Colt like no other, and who can blame her, he's so good with animals. That's one of his finest qualities. He's good to mankind and great to animalkind. The only thing Sahchi has a problem with is when Colt is giving more attention to someone else.

I remember back when Colt and I first started dating. It was because of an animal that we fell in love with each other. I was just out of college and thought of myself as an environmentalist, a naturalist, and a woman who would someday change the world. I had grandiose ideas. It was summertime, and I was working with a group of gals growing an organic garden and contracting our produce with two local grocery stores. The garden was hard work, no lie, but the income was a big help. I needed the money because I had the grand notion of some day having a small farm of my own where I could grow organic food. I dreamed of owning free-range cows and chickens for meat and eggs.

Well, if I'm anything, I'm impulsive. I found a mature mare and was certain that I should own a horse. I was going to be a farmer, and every farmer needs a horse, right? Yeah, well, I've been wrong about several things in my life, so this wasn't the first time and it wasn't going to be the last.

The horse turned out to be only half-domesticated. She was hard to work with. Pretty soon I had a real problem on my hands. I was told on several occasions to either shoot her or turn her out to pasture. I had bought her, boarded her, and paid ahead for feed, but I couldn't ride her because she would either bite me or attempt to throw me or both. Usually both. She was damned ornery.

That was about the time I was going to country bars, chasing Colt. The night he danced with me was the first time I got to talk with him. He took my number. We hadn't been on an official date yet, but we did chitchat on the phone a couple of times. During one phone conversation, I mentioned my trouble with the mare.

"I'm good with horses," he said. "Would you mind if I came out and gave you a hand with her?"

Of course I jumped at the idea, and he drove to the stable where the mare was boarded. That's when I got a look at him in the daylight. He looked even better under the sun than he did under the lights in any dance hall.

"Having a horse is kinda like having a relationship," Colt told me. "You don't tell a horse what to do. You ask her. If you ask, then she'll give you what you need. But she won't do anything that feels unnatural to her. Pretty simple, if you think about it."

Colt approached the mare with respect, and to my dismay, she responded to him in the most non-threatening and natural way. She let him saddle her and ride her with no fuss at all. Of course that hurt my pride. I wasn't happy about how my horse liked this stranger better than me. Then he introduced me to her like it was our first encounter. And she was nice to me. Nice to me! No biting, no attitude.

"How much time do you have each week to spend with her?" Colt asked me.

"Less than ten hours." I knew when I said it that that wasn't enough.

Colt looked at me sideways. "Well, you can't expect this horse or any other horse to do what you want it to do if you aren't around." He looked back over at the parking lot. "You drove that Mazda RX7 over here. Do you have a pickup and a horse trailer?"

I kicked the dirt around with my boot, embarrassed. "No, no, I don't. I only have the RX7."

"Do you have money for a vet if something happens to her? A horse needs a vet like humans need a doctor, you know."

"Well, um, no, I don't, but I'm sure I could get some money together if I needed to." My granddad had left me some money, but I had already invested it and would be unable to get to it for two years. But I was sure I could work something out if the mare needed a vet.

Colt laughed at me. "Has anyone given you any advice on what to do with this horse?"

"Yep."

"What was it?"

"Shoot her or put her out to pasture."

He laughed again. "Wow, shoot her!" He turned to the mare. "Did you hear that, you poor girl? No, I don't think anyone will be shooting you unless they shoot me first. People are stupid, aren't they?" He was looking into the mare's eyes and patting her. I could see she was falling in love with him, I could see it, right there before my eyes, my own horse snubbing me for this stranger. He turned back to me. "This is what I suggest. I know some people that might buy this mare from you. Now, before you say no, listen to what I think about your situation." I nodded. "I think you have an image of what it's like to own a horse, but in reality you have no idea what you've gotten yourself into." I nodded again. "You don't have the money or the equipment required to own a horse." I nodded a third time. "You might also think about donating this mare to a good home if I can't find a buyer. And I suggest you act sooner rather than later before something happens that you can't afford and this mare suffers because of your ignorance."

By this time, I had to say something to defend myself. "But her temperament? I mean, sure she's good with you, but she's got a bad attitude. I swear it. And I doubt anyone else would be as dumb as I was to buy her."

"The only reason she has an attitude," he said very slowly, "is because she's in a place where she doesn't feel comfortable. She doesn't trust you or anyone here. Once she finds a home that welcomes her, she'll be fine." He assured me that the problem I'd gotten myself into could be rectified quickly.

And he kept to his word. He found the mare a good home, and they paid me what I had paid for her. I learned later that she was very happy with her new home and the people took excellent care of her.

"I knew when I met you that something good would come from it," I told him a couple days later.

"Life can be funny that way," he said. "We need something, and through life's coincidences, we find a solution."

That was a long time ago -26 years ago. But I remember it like yesterday. Yet today watching Colt sing to Sahchi, I realized how much he gave up when he married me. He had wanted to stay on his family's ranch, but I refused to raise a family there. His family has a large acreage ranch, over 120 acres. Colt and I would have had our own place on the ranch. But I wanted my children to grow up in a city where they would have a quality education, sports opportunities, close to doctors and dentist. And I wanted to work in the city, where I would have a steady job that gave us all insurance and at least one steady income. Ranch wages are unpredictable, in my opinion.

Colt should have been born in the 19th century. He doesn't have a cell phone (he has to be the only vet in the world who still uses a pager), a computer, or anything modern except his truck, his instruments and the amplifiers. Yet he is very knowledgeable in the ways of the modern world. He's no fool and he's educated; he just doesn't go for all the modern conveniences.

Garrett, his father, named him after Samuel Colt, the famous firearms manufacturer, but I think on a soul level his name reveals his true self. He was created to work with animals. He holds clinics for horse and rider teams twice a month. He is co-owner of the Lone Pine Veterinary Hospital. Given that he's no city dude, Colt has done exceptionally well. He has a knack for business and has grown a successful veterinary practice. The best part of his owning his own business is when it's not busy he can come and go as he wishes. How I envy his freedom!

He's also been a great father to our children. If one of our kids is in trouble, they would go to Colt first, and, almost always he finds the solution to the problem, and if not, he finds the least painful alternative for them. They know he's reliable and dependable.

Besides his veterinary practice, he plays with the band at least four nights a week and goes back to the ranch regularly, or whenever they need him. Fortunately for Nina, his sister, we live in town. She was born with severe autism and has been institutionalized since she was young. He's always been a big help to her. Poor Nina. She's sensitive to light, sound, smells, and so on. She cannot speak and can become violent within a fraction of a second. Her situation has been very hard on Colt's family.

Anyway, like I said, last night Colt was playing the guitar and singing for Sahchi. This morning, when I came downstairs to get ready for work, I found him and Sahchi crashed out together on the sofa. I couldn't tell who was snoring, but one of them was really sawing logs. Sahchi was lying on top of Colt and across him with her snout nuzzled under his arm. I just had to snap a picture. They were so cute. I think it will become this year's Christmas card.

When you look at Colt, you see a tall man, broad at the shoulders, and narrow at the hip, the sort of man one reads about in romance novels. His Celtic ancestry shows in his features. He has a lot of confidence in himself, but he also shows an effortless respect for all. He smiles often, and his smile is so damn contagious that no one within eyeshot of him can resist it. Men that don't know him often don't like him because they're either intimidated or envious. On the flip side, women—and I don't care if they're old, young, middle aged—they all love him. I once watched a five-year-old girl fall head over heels in love with him. And I've heard the old gals, church-going gals, make flirtatious remarks. I don't think I've ever been anywhere with him when a female hasn't made a pass at him.

The man is gifted in many ways. Who am I to blame them for being as captivated by him as I was? But I got lucky. He was captivated by me, too. And that worked, our marriage worked for 25 years. But now...Jolene.

NOVEMBER 7TH

I had the most vivid dream last night. The world was dark, and I was about twelve years old, and I was walking through the streets of the city. It wasn't nighttime, though. The world was dim, like the sun had a shadow across it, and the populace appeared to be ill. Everyone was ill. As I walked, I saw people digging graves in their yards and burying their loved ones who had passed away. I'm not sure if I was a ghost, or what, but no one ever saw me. I felt alone and afraid. I could smell the dead, rotting bodies. As I walked along, I looked up at the sun. I could see a blood-red murkiness on the face of the sun. This dark, spider web-looking mask of ugliness was slowly choking out our sunlight. I knew that soon we would be in complete darkness.

"Don't worry, Chief. I'm here."

I turned and saw Granddad! He was a young man in that dream, much younger than I ever saw him when he was alive.

"What's happening here?" I asked him.

"The light has become contaminated."

"What does that mean, the light is 'contaminated'? Is the sun dying?"

"I'm afraid it is, Chief."

"Oh, that is so sad. Everyone will die, and the earth will be in darkness forever." I began to weep, and he put his arm around me and pulled me into him.

"It'll be alright, Chief. You'll get to heaven. Don't worry about all this ugliness. There's something better in store for you."

"Heaven? Granddad, I don't think I believe in heaven. Does heaven really exist?"

"Heaven does exist," he said. "But everyone has their own perception of what heaven is.... What I'm saying is heaven is different for everyone."

"Oh. I wasn't sure if it even existed."

"I can understand that you have your doubts."

"Is that where you and grandmother live now? In heaven?"

"Well, Chief, there's a place, a dimension where the everlasting sun sheds everlasting enlightenment, where the soul drinks from the running streams of love. It's a dimension where the good angels of mankind are free. Come on now, Chief. Open your eyes."

When I looked where he was pointing, I could see glorious sunshine, wonderful thick forests of green trees, masses of animals wandering about without fences and without fear. I could see my grandparents' home nestled neatly under that bright sunshine. Granddad led me there.

When we walked in, Grandmother was baking me a birthday cake. I ran to her and wrapped my arms around her. Oh, how having my grandparents nearby made me feel complete. "Is it my birthday?" I asked.

"No, child," said Grandmother. "It's your completion day."

"My completion day?"

"Yes. Now you're all done with that chore called living. Now come over here and take a seat."

My mind was racing as my granddad pulled out my chair at the head of the table for me. When I was little, I got to sit at the head of the table on special days, so I knew this must be a very special day.

"Close your eyes," Grandmother said, "and make a wish."

I closed them real hard. I was so excited I could hardly sit still. My eyes were shut, and my nose was wrinkled because I had them shut so tight.

"Now open your eyes!" Granddad said.

When I did I heard "Surprise!" Four people were cheering me. I looked around, and there stood my parents. I only knew them from faded memories and some photos, but here they were. In that dream, I could touch them, hear them, smell them.

"It's my girl!" I heard my father say in his deep baritone voice. Granddad had told me that my dad had an unusually deep voice, and it sounded so good when I actually heard it.

"Daddy!" I screamed, and he picked me up in his arms.

"Oh, my pretty girl, how I've missed you." This was my mom.

Grandmother had made my favorite oatmeal cake with cream-cheese frosting. Everyone took a seat at the table and we all ate the cake. I wish the English language had more accurate words to describe how I felt. It was a warm love that touched every cell in my body. Not the ordinary love we talk about, but a more intense kind of love.

After I ate my slice of cake, Granddad stood up from the table and asked me to take a walk with him. I was hesitant, but I went. We walked out of the house and down a long road. We walked for a long time, and when I looked back at the house, it was over the horizon. And when I looked down at my hands and feet, I saw that I was now an adult. I looked at Granddad. He was suddenly very old and walking slowly.

"Chief," he said, "when the time comes, I'll be there for you. I don't want you to worry in the dark times. I'll lead you here to your family that loves you so much. So don't worry, Chief. Can you do that for me?"

"Yes, Granddad. I won't worry about the dark days."

"A choice will be given to you," he said. "Think carefully about what you want before you decide. There is no right or wrong. There are two paths to take."

"Okay, Granddad, I'll think carefully before I decide."

I woke up crying, and when I looked up at my ceiling and saw the painted sunshine, I cried that much harder. I felt so deeply sad, I didn't know what to do with the energy. I was actually pissed off because it was only a dream. I wanted it to be real. Somehow, I was able to drag my sorry ass out of bed, get dressed, and go to work. I swear—going to work these days is killing me. It's painful to get up and go. And motivation? Like is there any?

...

I met with Quint at lunch today at the Purple Lotus on Mountain Mahogany street. As agreed during our last lunch, this was a social lunch, not a working lunch. We talked about cycling. I told her I was a "fixie" (fixed wheel rider) and she told me she had a Seven (Seven is a custom cycle company based out of Massachusetts and they make very fine cycles. I've always wanted one).

"So you like to ride," she said. "Have you ever ridden your bicycle over the Golden Gate Bridge?"

"No, I haven't. I've never even thought about that."

"I turned sixty-two this year," she said, "and one of the things on my bucket list was to ride my Seven across the Golden Gate Bridge."

"Tell me more." I leaned toward her.

"Well, it's not just about riding across the bridge. It's about seeing true beauty. My husband and I stayed at a boutique hotel near Union Square in the city. It was September, and the weather was incredible. We wore shorts and T-shirts, you know that's not all that common for San Francisco, and we started out about ten in the morning. We waited for the fog to burn off. Riding across the bridge is easy, you know. It's getting to it that's a workout."

"I've spent very little time in San Francisco," I told her, "so I can only imagine. San Francisco has a lot of hills. I'm sure they're difficult on a bike."

"You bet they are! I never had to dismount, but there was a time or two when I thought I might fall over from going so slow." She gave a giggle and her face was all smiles. "We rode from Union Square to the Presidio. That in and of itself is a good, picturesque ride. From there, it's a steep ride up to the bridge, but once you're there, the view is spectacular."

"Heights make me a bit nervous," I said. "Did it bother you, being that high off the water?"

"I thought the same thing," she answered, "but once we started across, the view of both the bridge and the city, along with the fact that I was doing something I'd fanaticized about for years, well, all that distracted me from any fear I might have had." She reached over and put her hand over mine. I felt a gentle warmth as she described the joy of her ride.

"I don't know why," she said, "but something in my gut is telling me to encourage you to do this. You have to do this ride! The view from the Golden Gate is spectacular! Like I said, it's not a difficult ride. And then, as a reward on the Sausalito side of the bridge, it's all downhill. I tell you, I get off on speed, and there I was, moving so fast the only thing offering any resistance to my momentum was the huge smile I had plastered on my face. Then, as if the god of cyclers had blessed us, there's a quaint little restaurant near the bottom of the hill. My husband and I had a wonderful lunch on the deck."

"That sounds fantastic," I said. "I think you've sold me. I've got to do that ride."

"Yes, you have to. My husband set everything up for us, but if you'd like, I can get the information from him on where we stayed, the route we took, and so on."

"Would you email me that info? Your husband sounds like a good man."

"He is a good man. I haven't always thought so highly of him, of course, but, you know, every relationship has its ups and downs. The last few years, I realize no one else could ever make me feel as good, as loved, as he does. And not only do I love him, but I'm deeply in love with him. There's a difference, you know. It took me a long time to figure that out, but I finally did.

"What I love most about him," she went on after she took a drink of her water, "is that he's always coming up with these fun things for us to do. I tell you, I wasn't looking forward to turning sixty-two, but up there on the Golden Gate Bridge, I realized how lucky I am. First to be sixty-two and have the energy and interest to do something like that is important. Second, I was grateful that both my husband and I have our health and love for each other. Third, I was so grateful that years ago I had let go of my vanity to embrace my age. And this year I embraced my sixty- second!"

I looked more closely at her. She looked every bit of sixty-two, but she was beautiful in her age. She has short, chopped, gray hair that looked like chaos with an attitude. Her body is larger than mine, really fit, and her smile broadcasts to the world that she both invites and passes along positive energy. The confidence she carries herself with brings beauty to any imperfection she might have. And her words might not have been meant as encouragement, but they were to me. If she could let go of her vanity and embrace sixty-two, why couldn't I do the same at fifty? Why do I put so much emphasis on my age?

We put our menus down then the waiter came over and took our order. Quint asked for vanilla prawns and I requested Hunan eggplant. They didn't offer Mountain Dew so I ordered a Dr. Pepper, she stayed with water.

"That's a really cool way to look at life," I said picking up the conversation after the waiter left. "Let go of vanity and embrace our age. I like that. Thank you for sharing your philosophy with me. What you've said hits home for me."

"Age is such a bothersome thing," she said. "We put so much pressure on ourselves. Unnecessary pressure."

"I turned fifty this year," I told her. "And it's bothered me more than any other birthday. I remember when I was young, and my grandmother turned sixty-three, I thought she was the oldest person on earth! Now I see you, and my mind tells me you're middle-aged. Isn't it funny how our perceptions change?"

"Yes. I remember when I was young thinking the same thing about adults. Now I don't see myself as old-aged or middle-aged. After my kids grew up and had their own families, I started feeling like I've started something new. A new phase with plenty of energy for all kinds of things. My husband and I have a good, healthy, sex life." She laughed. "Is that too much information?"

"No." But I blushed.

"I'm sorry, but I'm proud of it. Sex is something I have always believed would stop after forty. Sure, when I'm out shopping, especially for clothes, I realize my age. I know there are certain ways I shouldn't dress. It's one thing to feel young, but completely another if one tries to dress young. Wearing clothes made for an adolescent at my age? It looks ridiculous!"

"I know what you're saying," I said. "I'm about being comfortable now. My days of towering heels, short skirts, and low-cut blouses are over. I figure what you see is what you get. When I'm not at work, I wear men's clothes because they're comfortable. Whoever designs women's clothes surely doesn't want us to be comfortable or be able to move."

"My husband says that women are beautiful in every stage of life. I agree with him. He's opened my eyes. He's helped me to see my aging process as a positive thing filled with the richness of a living education."

"A 'living education.'" I smiled. "Again, I'm compelled to thank you for your philosophy. I think I'm falling in love with your husband." We both laughed. "It seems like work is all I have at fifty, but my soul is screaming for freedom. I'm not sure how to balance work and my family."

She took a deep breath and let it out with a sigh. "I know where you're at. I was a career-minded woman in my fifties, well, more in my late forties. I was consumed with work. It put me in a place I didn't want to be. It got so bad that I was headed toward a divorce from my husband. I mean it. I had been to a lawyer, I had separated my money from his, opened my own bank account, we had done everything except tell our children. We were waiting for the right time to break it to them. And then one day I locked myself in my bedroom and had an all-out argument with myself."

"You did?"

"You bet I did! I was angry with myself because I was choosing work, my career, money, over happiness, over the man I loved. I'd placed my husband below my career achievements. I didn't value the man I fell in love with and married. So you bet I argued with myself. Like you just said about your soul, I believe it was my soul making a stand. I think my soul put her foot down and made me see how unhappy my future would be without him, no matter how much money I was earning. The thing is, I wasn't losing my husband to anther woman, or because he beat me, or to drugs or alcohol. No, I was losing him because I wasn't making an effort to see the value of him in my life. Now he's most valuable."

"You're smart to have saved your marriage," I said. "We need love in our lives."

She shook her head. "I don't think I was smart. I think something supernatural was at work. I mean that argument with myself behind closed doors changed me completely. Don't think it was all that easy. It took work, hard work, but we saved our marriage. But my marriage wasn't the only thing I wanted to fix. I wanted to change my attitude toward life. Toward money. And I realized that love was the answer. Reach out to my husband with love, approach life with love, only work at a job that I love and believe in. Once I opened myself to love, a cascade of changes came. That's when I decided I wanted to implement learning techniques into videogames. I love the world so much that now that I want to make a difference in it."

"I've thought about your work," I said. "And the teaching within a vehicle that kids embrace. I see your work as important. So different from what I do. My job sometimes has me making companies, and eventually people, uncomfortable. Numbers and money equal heartache." I didn't want to go into detail about Back-2-Back right then, but I thought I might cast out some information to see how she reacted.

"My work is meaningful," she said, "and as I get older, I see that meaningful work is important. Knowing my work is meaningful helps me do my job with dignity and pleasure. If your work is troublesome, I would strongly suggest that you find something else to do. Life is too short to live it in misery."

Our food arrived and the aroma elevated my appetite. Her Vanilla prawns smelled incredible. I hurried a bite of my plate in and the flavor of garlic and sweet basil brought a smile to my face. The taste of sautéed minced chicken and shrimp came a fraction of a second afterward and it was so damn good. I almost forgot what we had been talking about but did manage to ask, "So you're free from work stress these days?"

"I wouldn't say that. The videogame industry is worth over thirty billion dollars domestically, that's not global, just domestic. It's a very competitive industry. I mean very. My life has been threatened. My husband's life, and our kids', too."

"What? When, how...really?"

"In August, I was approached by an arrogant, unscrupulous CEO of a competitor here in town. He told me he wanted me to walk away from my job. If I didn't, he was going to make me wish I had. Then he handed me a picture of my husband. 'I can get to him anytime I want to,' he told me, and then he winked at me and followed it up with, 'or I could cut to the chase and you might have an accident.'"

My eyes about popped out of my head. She was talking about Jerome! Jerome was going after Quint on all fronts, both private and professional. Those threats made me angry. Quint is a great person who is trying to do good with her life, and what does she get for it? Threats. "I'm scared for you, Quint."

"Don't be," she said, and her voice was very level and calm. "Something will happen, sure enough. He'll either get his way, or I'll figure out a way to turn the tables."

"Shouldn't you go to the police?"

"I did, but it's a he-said-she-said situation. He's a respectable businessman worth millions bringing in millions of dollars to our community, so the police weren't too motivated to investigate. Besides, there are no witnesses. Unless I have a witness or something in writing, or any kind of proof, they can't act. So I'm left to figure out what to do."

"Maybe this person was just blowing smoke," I said fiddling with my chopsticks. "After all, he threatened you almost three months ago." I was hoping this was true. I thought perhaps Jerome had decided to use data to get what he wanted instead of hurting Quint.

"Oh, he hasn't forgotten about me! I get frequent reminders. Subtle things. Like the other day, I was getting a coffee and this perfect stranger pushed his way into the line so he could stand next to me. I noticed him, everyone noticed him, he was so rude. Then when he was standing next to me, he whispered, 'Have you thought about quitting your job yet? Be sure to ask your husband how the brakes are in his car.' And like that, he stepped out of line and walked away."

"That is chilling. This sounds like something out of a spy novel, not an industry where kids buy games."

"I'm telling you, people don't realize that the market for videogames is a powerful force in our country. Think about it. Ninety-seven percent of kids from twelve to seventeen own some kind of videogame system. The market is huge. My competitor is the worst in the business. His company designs the harshest, most venomous videogames. Kidnapping, torturing, and rape are common."

I gasped. What did simulated rape look like?

"That's right," she said like she'd just read my mind. "In one game, Rape Play, the player enhances their virtual soul as they rape, torture, steal, and murder innocent people. We obtained a copy of it. I was horrified. The player chooses a victim from a crowd on a busy street and stalks her, it's usually a her, and on one level, it's a mother and her two daughters! Then the player takes his time and learns the habits of the victim and plans the abduction. After the victim is taken…well, I won't even go into to the details because it's straight out of a nightmare. I'm serious. The kids who play this so-called game should have PTSD after playing. If and when all levels are achieved, the conclusion is a ceremonial offering of his or her virtual soul up to the lord of the game. The point of the game is to encourage the most disturbing behavior."

I almost collapsed in my seat. "I had no idea."

"Most people don't."

"What can you do about it?"

"I don't think we can keep kids from playing games like those. If we outlawed them, it would be as effective as Prohibition was back in the twenties. The people who work for me at Bio-Sport share my vision. No, that sounds arrogant. We share the same vision, which is to produce games that are equal in excitement and maintain a level of threat, because that's what the players are looking for, the adrenalin dump, but in our games, the player has consequences or rewards for their choices, just like in life. We keep morality at the forefront creating a game that reduces violent fantasy."

"Is it complicated, designing a game that's close to reality, but has human values?"

"No. I think it's easier because it comes naturally. We perform study after study, and when the results are analyzed, we use the data to help with the design. Our platforms are working, too. At first, we thought we might gain a certain segment of players, but not a large portion. We were pleasantly surprised by the response we got."

"Obviously, you're doing well. But you've gotten death threats! What are you going to do?"

"I'm not sure yet," she admitted. "I know I want to continue doing what I'm doing by being a positive element in the industry. But I'm not sure how to survive in such a violent and threatening environment. That's new for me."

"If you're that important, are you worried about a hostile takeover of Bio-Sport?"

"I can control takeovers. I'm the major stockholder. I pretty much have the say in what happens regarding buyouts."

I was surprised at how quickly Quint and I had become friends. She had really opened up to me. I felt her frustration, fear, and stress. I didn't tell her about my dealings with Jerome, though. I made a decision right then and there to continue to work for him in order to find his weakness. I wanted to help Quint, and I knew that I had an angle when it came to Jerome. From this moment on, I would be his spy, but I would falsify the information going to him, and at the same time I would keep tabs on Back-2-Back, find out what I could about what they might be planning to do to Quint. Besides, if I didn't I work for Jerome, he'd only hire someone else, someone ruthless, and willing to harm Quint.

Together, Quint and I will get her the protection she needs and keep her safe. I also made a decision to take my team off the project. No one else needed to be involved. Or get hurt.

When I got back to the office, I went to Brent and told him to pull my team from the top-secret project and I would handle it myself. I made up a story that my team had come across some questionable information and made a connection between Bio-Sport and Back-2-Back. Brent feared my employee's discovery would cause problems between he and Jerome. He agreed to pull my team and let me handle it all on my own. He said that he would call Jerome and explain it all to him. Thankfully, I hate talking to Jerome. Later Brent came to my cubical and told me that Jerome was also in agreement. Jerome didn't want anything to become public.

I must say, my lunch date gave me an awful lot to think about.

I went to my gynecologist today and told her about the pain and frequency of urination, my suspicion of hormone imbalance, how I'm feeling bloated and my loss of appetite, along with the frequent fevers. Again, more tests were scheduled and more blood was taken. She told me I've been menopausal for over a year and that these symptoms were most likely attributed to that and not to worry. But she also had urgency written all over her face about the tests she was ordering. The urgency made me concerned.

But I don't want to worry, so I will now change the subject.

Devin and I spoke again. We have decided to go slow, to date and get to know each other. There'll be no binding commitments, just the freedom to see each other when we want to.

However, I'm finding it challenging at work, this game of manager and employee. I've made a rule for myself that I won't get out of rhythm and I will maintain my normal habits. I want work to stay routine. In the morning, I delegate the work of the day to Raj, Mary, Blythe, James, Kelly, and Devin. Devin is just another employee on the list. I've told him that when I see him at work, I place a sweet kiss on him. (Mentally, of course. I don't know why I said that, though. We haven't even kissed in reality yet.) He told me my affection isn't noticeable because of my professionalism. At times he attempts to charm me, but I resist the urge to laugh and hold firm to my rule. I'm so good at it that Blythe asked me if anything was wrong. He said I've been "grumpy" for several days. "It's because of Brent," I told him.

And then Blythe said a funny thing, "Don't worry, Boss. Your team is behind you. We will have anything you need as soon as you need it, and this will get Brent out of your hair." What a nice man to support me like that.

If he only knew that if I'm grumpy at all it's because the source of my problem is really Jerome. I've got to meet with him again soon with more data and also a report on Quint and our friendship. That should be interesting.

NOVEMBER 9TH

Devin is with me nearly every day during our scheduled breaks. On the surface we look like friends; at least that's what we want people to think. It's a friendship with something more, though. We speak in code and refer to our affair as the "situation." That is, the situation that bonds us. He will say something like, "The situation has gone unnoticed by the staff," and I might say something like, "Oh, that happened long before the situation came up."

It's a silly game, really. I feel silly. All the flirting and none of the follow-through gets old. It may be my insecurities, but I'm certain my age has stopped us from the actual act of touching. He's hesitant with me, but if I were twenty-five years younger, I wonder if he'd move faster.

Time keeps moving. I think I ought to take Becky's advice and invest in me. Perhaps if I live life to the fullest, I can retrieve some of the youth that passed me by. Like the other day, while a colleague at work was talking to me, she was staring at me like she was examining my wrinkles, even as she said something like, "But you're still young." *Still?* I'm at the age where people say you're still young, blah-blah-blah. How many years of "still" do I have left before I graduate to "are," as in "you are old." I think about being old, and I'm afraid. I feel like my life is getting away from me, like somehow my arteries are slowly opening and my blood is flowing out of me, not around inside me.

Life.

What is life, anyway? It's work, money earned, money spent, health, complications of all kinds. It's exciting moments, friendship, love and children (sometimes that's a good thing, sometimes it's not so good.), island vacations. I remember when someone said (before my mastectomy) that I was "clinging to life," making it sound like life is more attractive in dangerous times than in routine times. But was my life the same, if not more routine, after the cancer went into remission? I didn't see it as more valuable.

Why?

But now, with age, I feel like life is slipping away from me. I think about pleasure (any form of pleasure) and see that's where life is. I feel the tragic weight of my fifty years treading on my heels. Because I'm "still" young, I can forecast a few more years of exciting moments, friendship, love, and time with my children. Perhaps, and I'm hopeful, some island vacations as well. The bike ride over the Golden Gate, as planned by my friend Quint, has become the new adventure

I look forward to. I'm excited to pedal over that bridge and enjoy a day in San Francisco.

Hopefully my remaining years will be filled with adequate health, the usual sentiments, and an impressive amount of pleasures. I want my fifties to be a positive time. I want to forget about cancer and the scars it left me with. I want to move forward with purpose. My life should be *lived*. But then again, fifty is "still" young.

I think about when I was twenty and how young I was then. At thirty, I was still young, and forty brought few concerns for age. But at fifty I'm "still young." Does being "still young" mean it's the *end* of being young? Or better yet, has the deception of youth left me camouflaged by the word "still"? It's funny how one little word can set me off.

Devin and my agreement to take it slow amplifies the reality of time passing me by. *Taking our time* means my time is passing me by. No matter if we do anything or not, time is passing by, and it makes him more attractive every day. And every day that he is maturing, becoming more interesting, becoming more of a man, those same days are threatening me with more wrinkles, more gray hair, less courage, and less energy. Each plus for him becomes a minus for me. Sure, maybe for him I'm attractive because I've lived life, I've exchanged my innocence for experience, my head is full of wisdom. But I understand that experience and vigor exist together for a very short time. I'm living in that brief little time.

November 10th

S aturday. I woke up this morning under my painted sunny sky and felt nostalgic again about my granddad. I lingered in bed for a long time, just thinking about him. Times were less complicated when I lived with my grandparents and I wish so much I could go back, even for just a moment and be with them. I want to ask my granddad for advice on the things that bother me today, I don't care if he had all the right answers or not. I just want to feel his arm around me and to hear him say, "You know, Chief, everything is going to be all right." Oh, what I'd give to have a moment like that! I was such a lucky girl to have had those grandparents.

I was desperate to do something with all that sentimental energy, so, when I could finally drag my lazy ass out of bed, I went to the cathedral. It was bitter cold, with snow coming steadily down, but I wasn't bothered by that. I parked my car in the lot at work and walked to the cathedral. It was warm and dim inside. I found a pew, knelt on the kneeler, and bowed my head in prayer. I wasn't praying to God. I have no image in my head of God, other than a grumpy old man who wants to punish mankind for whatever reason he can come up with. No, I bowed my head and prayed to the man whose image means something to me. My granddad.

"I want to tell you how much I appreciate the times you stood beside me through the years when I was growing up," I whispered to him in my prayer. "I'm here on my knees to let you know, just in case I never said it when I was growing up, how much I love you! Even though you've been gone twenty-eight years, I have not lost the strong feeling of love I have for you. Grandmother, too. Of course, her, too. She was a terrific influence on me, but you, Granddad, had a special connection to me. I don't want to seem disrespectful to her in any way, but you know the connection I'm talking about."

I prayed my heart out. I don't know what I thought would happen. I guess I thought if I prayed hard enough he would somehow reappear in my life. I was truthful, saying things to him that ought not to be spoken in church, I suppose.

"Well, Granddad," I prayed some more, "my life is messed up right now. Colt's been cheating on me with Jolene and I'm getting a divorce. I'm working on a new relationship with a young man. Yep, that's right: a young man. Did you ever think you'd hear your little girl talking about dating a man half her age? I wouldn't mention it, but I'm hurting inside. He won't put his hands on me. Am I ugly? Is that why he keeps his hands to himself?"

I suppose this prayer would have been all good and well if I had kept it to myself, but I suddenly realized I was praying out loud! I heard a woman clear her throat to get my attention. When I looked up, I saw a woman on one side of me and a man on the other, both of them kneeling in prayer, too. They stood up, stared at me, and left. But that's okay. I needed to be alone. So I just continued with my prayer.

"Granddad, you've been gone so many years, you may not know what your little Chief is up to. I can't tell you how much it would mean to me if you were here with me. The cancer was scary. I survived it, but now this age thing has me really freaked out. I don't know anyone who has outrun death by means of old age."

I rambled and blubbered for over an hour, but nothing happened. There were no apparitions, no Granddad, certainly no God.

I've got a problem with God. He gave me cancer, took away one of my breasts, and now he has me facing divorce. What the hell did I ever do to him to deserve this sorry poker hand? I stood up and felt more alone than I did before I walked in. I wrapped up in my coat and scarf and walked out. I was wrapped up so tight and in such a hurry I almost didn't see my friend standing by the tree. Mr. Goldsole was standing in the cold, head down looking as if he, too, were praying.

"What's up?" I asked him, hoping I wasn't invading his space. "God won't let you in where it's warm?"

He raised his head. "Oh, hello, Hope. No, I don't go in. I'd just drag in snow and dirty the place up. I'm better off out here."

"I'm sorry. Were you praying? I didn't mean to interrupt."

"I was, but you didn't disturb me in the least. It's always a happier, brighter day when I see you."

"Gee, I wish I heard words like that more often. You're sweet. Why don't you go on in and pray? It's warm in there. And the bonus is that the place is empty. I made sure of that."

"No, thanks," he said. "God told me that if I ever needed him, I would be more apt to find him under a rock than on the inside of a church. God is of nature and is best found in the woods, near a stream, in the falling snow. That's why I stand by this tree in whatever weather the Lord provides."

"Okay, well, if church isn't where God is, why do you come to the church to pray in their yard?" I asked him.

"Because of the people who might come out. Like you, for instance. I usually find a friend here. What are you doing here, Chief?" He smiled at me. I liked for him to call me Chief like my granddad used to do.

"I came here looking for answers to questions that I doubt I will ever find the answers to," I said. "But praying was all I could think to do."

"God doesn't work that way."

"Hell, I wasn't praying to God! I was praying to my granddad."

Mr. Goldsole laughed and laughed at that, and his laughter was so contagious that I started laughing with him out there in the snow.

"What would you say, Chief, if I bought you some hot chocolate?" he asked, just like my granddad did when I was a little girl. A tear rose in my eye, but I refused to release it. Inside, I felt an odd sensation of familiarity.

"That would be wonderful," I replied. "But I've got money. How about I buy?"

"You know it hurts my feelings that you won't take the simple gift of my money for a cup of cocoa," he said. "I insist on buying."

I took his hand in mine and agreed. I never would want to hurt my granddad's feelings, and I looked at Mr. Goldsole as my surrogate granddad. We strolled through the wind and the sharp cold for several blocks to a café on Mulberry Street.

When we got all settled in, I realized I was the only one with a cup of hot chocolate. "Where's your cup?" I asked.

"I've got a condition and shouldn't have any," he answered. "It brings me joy to see you drinking it. Don't worry about me." No one seemed to notice him. I thought people would disapprove of his outdated heavy coat, his funny little shoes, and his fedora.

He took off the heavy coat and hat and laid them on the spare chair. "So, Hope, what's been bothering you?" he asked.

"I don't know if I feel comfortable telling you," I said. "Maybe it would be better for me if we kept our conversation to a superficial level."

"Oh, come on now. I was at the church, too. Why can't friends talk about their prayers?"

"Okay. If you don't mind?" He nodded as if to say go ahead, and so I continued. "Why does God mess with people? I mean, why is he allowing the things in my life to happen?"

"You think God is allowing bad things to happen to you?"

"I guess so. I'm all mixed up. My husband's cheating on me, so I'm getting a divorce. Now I'm involved with someone, but not exactly. That is, I want to be involved, but he's hesitant. I want him to be as excited as I am about our relationship."

"Is this relationship you are about to embark on a healthy relationship?"

"It's as healthy as any I have! The relationship I have with my children comes in waves. One day it's good, the next, not so much. The relationship with my husband, soon to be ex-husband, is obviously bad, or the 'ex' part wouldn't be in the equation. The worst of my relationships is with God. So, yeah, it's a good relationship."

Mr. Goldsole laughed again. "Well, you know what's best for you. On a deep level, your soul lets you know if what you're doing is right or wrong."

"Yeah, that's right, it does. I have a conscience, and I do listen to it frequently. It tells me not to let this opportunity pass me by."

"By opportunity, you mean the chance to be touched by this hesitant man?"

"You bet! I want his hands on me! Mr. Goldsole, I'm sorry, I hate to be frank, but I also want to declare what I want. Yes, I need to be touched by him. He makes me feel young, in tune with my sexuality, and, honestly, I need a boost. I've been depressed a lot lately."

He nodded. "Yes. Aging in today's world is hard. It seems that everyone, or most people, anyway, are so focused on youth and being young. It wasn't always this way, you know. Not so long ago, in terms of time in the universe, all religions had female deities that balanced their male counterparts. Women were proud to be young, but just as proud to grow older. The female deities offered not only balance but allowed all ages, shapes, and sizes of women to believe in themselves and their purpose on earth."

I was listening, but I was also thinking that Mr. Goldsole was either a nut or a fanatic trying to bring me into his cult. I focused on my cup of hot chocolate, as Devin had done to me. "Sure," I said, "but did any goddess have to go through menopause? Ask her for me sometime." I laughed, but he didn't.

"Hope, the goddesses understand the changes your body goes through. Every step of the way in a woman's life was celebrated."

"Aging and menopause being *celebrated?* That's hard to believe."

"Yes, because you have today's perspective. At this point in time, aging is a bad thing, a thing to be feared, especially for women. The younger and skinnier, the better. Right?"

"Yep," I said. "That's the way it is. Colt has Jolene, and I'm sure she's young, tight, and full of all kinds of energy."

"But, Hope, you are overlooking your own qualities. You've gained wisdom during the time you've been alive. You are very valuable to this world, whether you believe it or not. You have a reason to be here, even though you're getting older and other physical things are happening to you."

"Are you saying I'm getting fat?"

He looked at me and chuckled. "I said much more, but all you heard was me accusing you of being fat? No, you're not fat. But even if you were, you would still be just as valuable to this world. Stop looking at the world *around you* and start looking at you *in this world*. You belong here. You're not obsolete because of age, menopause, weight, height, hair, breasts, fingernails, or anything else."

When I heard him say it that way, I felt so shallow. How vain I've been lately!

"You have a very poor image of yourself," he added, "and it's not healthy. When you say these negative things, you begin to believe them and then you manifest the negative qualities.

That's not good! Before you make love to this man you like so much, I ask you to do yourself a favor."

I shot him a suspicious look "What might that be?"

"Get undressed and look in the mirror. Look at yourself, *really look*. And if you don't think you're attractive, then wait to make love with him. If you don't see yourself as attractive, the love you are trying to create will be out of balance."

"So…if I look in the mirror and I see a fat old woman, I need to wait until somehow I can reverse that? How can I turn back time to make myself young? Well, I could." I laughed. "But that would be a pretty hefty plastic surgery bill."

He shook his head. "No, no, no! What I'm saying is, you have a poor image of yourself. So go and look at yourself until you figure out why you think so little of yourself. Change your mind about what you see. Learn to love yourself. You are as beautiful as anyone on this planet. You deserve as much as anyone else. Stop excluding yourself from living a wonderful life because you think you're too old or fat or whatever."

His words were beginning to make sense. He sure was being direct with me, but if he had presented his ideas in any other way, I wouldn't have listened. I know that. His direct approach was as close to a kick in the ass as I could ever get. Becky's been telling me the same thing. She says I need to invest in myself. I guess I should be open to all this free advice. It's definitely better than paying someone for psychotherapy. Or psychoanalysis.

"You're right," I finally said after taking a long, slow drink of my chocolate so I could think. "I need to change my opinion about myself. I need to love me before I can expect someone else to love me." I smiled at him. "You know what? I'm going home and get naked in front of a mirror. Do you want to come with me? Maybe give me some more advice?" I about died laughing when Mr. Goldsole turned every shade of red a pale-faced man can turn.

"Uh, no, not this time," he stammered. "But ask me again another time?"

"Oh, you're a bad boy, Mr. Goldsole."

We laughed together, and the snow continued to fall outside. "Well," I finally said, "I really should get home before the roads get too bad." I didn't want our time together to end. "Seriously, would you like to come to my place for dinner? I will take you home afterward, I promise. And we are exceptionally good cooks."

"No, thank you," he said slowly, "I've got some place I've got to be, but thank you ever so much."

"When will I see you again?"

"In time. I'm sure our paths will cross again."

"Do you have a phone number so I can call you?"

"Not at this time. I'm in between places. But soon." He wrapped himself up in his outdated clothing and I put on my more fashionable coat, and we worked our way to the door. "Get to know yourself soon, Hope," he said. "Life is short, and regret is a long, long road. Some lives are shorter than others."

"Oh, you can bet I'm working on that as soon as I get home. I plan to draw me a nice hot bath and get started liking me!"

As we walked out to the sidewalk, we said farewell, and he went one way and I went the other way. As I was walking back to my car, I thought I should offer him a ride. I turned to call to him, but he was already gone, nowhere in sight. What a funny little guy he is. But I sense a feeling for him that resembles love. I think I'll invite him to Thanksgiving dinner.

I did what I promised. When I got home, I left a note on the kitchen table asking Colt to make dinner without me, and I went up and drew a hot bath. While the tub was filling, I stood in front of my wardrobe mirror. Sure, gravity has struck, and things have sagged a little here and there, but I did like what I saw. I had one breast, two arms, two legs, ten wiggly fingers and ten stubby toes, a nose, ears, a mouth. Yep, it was all there. I'm not as old or ugly as I thought. Sure, there are some wrinkles, but I could see Hope, and she was looking back at me. I like her, and she likes me, too. I laughed, and she laughed, too. It was like discovering an old friend. I looked right at her and said, "The bath is ready. Would you like to join me?" She nodded and we got in.

I suppose I've gone crazy, but crazy can be fun.

NOVEMBER 13TH

There was some excitement at work today. The woman that was sleeping with Brent's son could be heard throughout the building yelling at him. I don't know what Brent's son had done or why she was mad, but it must have been something pretty big. The whole office was in a dither. For her, the breakup would probably cost her not only her promotion but her job as well, so I'm sure she thought about that before she started yelling. But suddenly the yelling stopped. Then I heard a couple of wallops, and then the door to his office opened, and she ran out. Brent's son chased her, but he wasn't moving very fast and everyone could see one of his eyes turning red and purple. He'd have a black eye by suppertime. We all knew that. Brent turned up to follow her and chase down his son, too. I guess Juan might get his promotion after all. Well, that's the unauthorized version of events, anyway.

Devin and I have been out a couple of times. He has been very cordial. On Sunday, we went to see a movie and he put his hand on my thigh, but that's as far as he has been willing to go. Not even a kiss, though he did hold my hand when he walked me to my car after the movie. After examining myself in the mirror like Mr. Goldsole told me to, I like me now, and I wasn't going to be patient any longer. At my car, instead of getting in, I turned back to Devin and leaned toward him.

"You're very good," I told him. "You have behaved yourself for a good long while now."

"I don't think of myself as a saint," he replied. "I try to have good manners."

"I can see that."

"I was taught that if I was good, I deserved a reward. Do I deserve a reward?" he asked.

"Oh, yes," I said. "You deserve a reward."

His arms came to rest on my shoulders. He must have taken notes from some romantic movie because his moves were kind of choreographed, but the kiss that followed was from no movie, that's certain. I liked his lips, the taste of them and the way they sank against mine. I left mine half open, inviting him to go further. This wasn't his first kiss, but it was the first time he kissed me. It was such a relief to have that first kiss, and I was going to make sure he remembered that he'd been kissed. I don't know what happened, and I don't know who maneuvered whom, but somehow when we finished that kiss, he was the one who had his back against my car.

Progress!

That's all to report. A simple kiss, but a lot to think about. I'm tired now, but I can't go to sleep. At least I can write this happy bit of news.

Oh, I almost forgot. *Jerome.* That bastard came to the office today, and I had to take a meeting with him. That man is walking evil. He was pressing me for information about Quint. He wanted to know her personal schedule, like I know the details of that. I'm not sure what he's up to, but it was very suspicious. After he left, I told Brent that this whole thing with Back-2-Back is making me uneasy, and Jerome's behavior is making me uncomfortable. And what did Brent say? "At least you have a job. Deal with it."

I want out from under this job. But in a comfortable way.

NOVEMBER 15TH

I got a call from my doctor's office today. The result of the CA 125 test came back positive. Or is it negative? Positive for cancer, but negative for making me feel good. That, combined with the pain I've been feeling down there, has elevated the stress in their office and in me, too. My doctor is going to confer with Dr. Bach, the oncologist I had when I went through the breast cancer.

I'm a little freaked out here.

I'm not going to trouble anyone, however, until I know for certain there is in fact a problem. It would only complicate the situation with Colt and me and make the kids worry. I can do enough worrying for everyone. I don't see anything positive happening.

So...given the signs and symptoms, my doctors, collectively, have ordered a complete battery of tests, exams, and plenty of do-over tests, I'm sure. There will probably be another pelvic exam, a transvaginal or pelvic ultrasound, and a confirmation of the CA 125 blood test. Then I'll be having a CT scan or PET scan soon, and then—lucky me—maybe a little surgery and a new biopsy. Oh, the fun of it all! No, this sucks. Big time! I was having such a good time with Devin, and I thought I was getting my shit together, and now this. God hates me! He absolutely hates me. I've already gone down this road once. Why again? And in another part of my body?

I'm going to stop writing now. I'll go take a hot bath and have a good long cry.

NOVEMBER 18ᵀᴴ

I'm wondering if I have an obsession with predictions. In every health crisis cast upon me, I'm never satisfied with intense invasive (alleged curing) therapeutic resolutions. That could be the source of my exasperation. One thing is apparent.

If an intensive approach provokes a positive attitude within me, is that evidence of healing? On the other hand, nonaligned attitudes (regarding illness) are in general inconvenient and at times disagreeable. They hardly seem heroic. But I need a lot of courage to hold myself in equilibrium. I can't avoid the consequences of another diagnosis, but with that diagnosis comes the very fear I seem to live with all the time. It's the source of my cowardice. Besides, the doctors will tell me that a nonaligned (not willing to follow the advice of my physician) attitude is dangerous. They will expect me to be aggressive toward the invader of my body. To be less than aggressive is, in these technical days, an unforgivable fault.

What does all this come to? Ah, yes. The prediction that a doctor uses to subjectively measure the distance between my cancer and death or my cure. I don't want to go through all of the treatments that will surely drag my health down again and cost me all joy in life. It will be the cure that will surely kill me. Yet I don't want the cancer to spread and kill me, either. But I don't want to be condemned to being an old, weak woman loathed by a younger man in the prime of his life. Nor do I want, from fear of such a future, to lose out on the experience of being with Devin. The present is appealing and irreplaceable. I finally feel attractive and wanted.

What should I do?

I think I will take the check that Jerome wrote me for a hundred thousand dollars and buy a little condo. I don't want to completely abandon my home here, of course, but I would like to have a private condo. I fancy a simple place where I can do as I wish without fear of my kids, who come and go as they please, walking in on me enjoying my boyfriend.

This threat of cancer really has me freaked out. The waiting game is harsh. I don't know if I have the patience for it. I've phoned Dr. Bach's office several times today. Am I being a pest?

What I would give for an answer! Either way, just an answer. Just tell me *Yes, you definitely have cancer and these are your options*, or *No, it's all a mistake*. Don't torture me with this *We don't know anything for sure until the results of the tests have come back*.

No matter what the answer, the condo is on! I've got plenty of money, and the place I have in mind shouldn't cost too much.

It's Sunday, and I wanted to run to the cathedral and pray, but it's absolutely treacherous out. We're having a huge storm and the roads are one, big, slick sheet of ice. Colt built us a good, hot fire, and I spent most of the day trying to distract myself by reading a self-help book about women turning fifty. If anything, that book made me feel like shit. It was a collective work and the women in it seemed bitter. They seemed like a bunch of women I wouldn't hang out with, anyway. The book came across sounding like they want to populate the planet with women only and forget about the men. Hey, I'm a gal, but I won't deny that I like men. I see value in them. I'm not of the mind that men are all bad and the world would be a better place without them. I think this world would be a horrible place if there were only women populating it.

Being fifty is a bitter pill to swallow. I can identify that it's our Western culture (though as far as I know, it might be a global problem) that is the cause of my grief and anger over aging, but I refuse to blame it all on men. There are plenty of women out there, young women, who like to rub it in that they are young and tight and can take away your good man. Look at Jolene.

...

Colt and Sahchi were cute to watch today. Colt was lying on the couch, reading some adventure magazine, and Sahchi was sprawled out over the top of him. That big dog kept wiggling, trying to get closer to him, but she was already as close as anyone could get. But that didn't satisfy her. Colt was stroking her with one hand, and as he got lazy and stopped, Sahchi nudged him with her paw until he started petting her again. Quite comical.

I wonder if Jolene has met Sahchi.

Colt and Sahchi are a package deal. You don't get Colt without Sahchi and when the dog is around, Colt must give her all the attention she wants. I don't know, but Sahchi might be a deal breaker for Jolene.

NOVEMBER 19ᵀᴴ

Today was cold and windy again. I dislike the wind, especially when it's a cold wind! To think that when I was young, I liked winter. I remember asking Granddad to take me out so I could go sledding, no matter how cold or windy it was. Well, I'm not like that anymore.

Earlier today, I began sneezing like a fool. I was the perfect candidate for a sniffling, sneezing commercial. My nose ran like a broken faucet, drip, drip, drip.

I went to the cathedral today for lunch. There I humiliated myself again by sneezing repeatedly. As I sneezed, an older lady who was trying to pray turned her head and gave me a look as if to say, "Cover your mouth and be quiet about it." I wonder if the pope has ever sneezed so frequently that he started cussing like I did. I think even he would resort to curses after ten, twenty, or even thirty tiny explosions. Damn cold!

Anyway, I didn't feel any closer to God or salvation in the cathedral, so I got up and took my sneezing nose out the door. Does God ever visit cathedrals? I don't think so. I never see him or feel him, or even feel that he has any indication that I exist. Anyway, I digress again. I made my exit, and there near the same tree stood Mr. Goldsole. I felt better immediately.

He smiled at me with his wide, warm smile. "How are you this fine day, Chief?" He was staring at my bright red nose.

"I've got a cold." I said, covering my mouth.

"Oh, you poor dear."

"Yes. Health seems to be a constant issue with me these days."

"Health," he said, "is in fact one of the few elements of living you can reasonably hope to control. Treat your body good, and your body typically will remain healthy. Everything else, well, life is never perfect, is it?"

"No, it's not. And the not knowing is the scary part."

"Ah, yes. Uncertainty. It is normal to fear uncertainty. The truth is, you are a work of art created by a grand artist, and it's only a matter of perspective for a piece of art to be seen as profound by one person and a disaster by another."

I frowned. "Are you talking about God, Mr. Goldsole? I don't think God knows me."

"Something greater than you and I exists," he replied. "I will not say one god, nor will I say that god is a man, but I will say that you were created, and your capacity to express what you were intended to be by the creator is immense."

"And you are certain of this because…?"

"You are looking for certainty," he said. "And with certainty, you imagine you can control life. If you give certainty a major role in your life, you are less likely to live a satisfying life. It's the risks, the seditious attitudes, the ifs and what-ifs, the spontaneous leaps of faith that are where life's satisfactions exist. You don't need a name for God to know God exists. What is needed is nothing more than the broad sense that you are looking for the supernatural. You need no strategy, no recipe, no preachments of a clergyman. If the creator created you, then he or she—or even a combination thereof—is near you and of you. All you need to do is recognize the signs. Open you heart. Open your eyes. Most importantly, open your soul." He smiled at me.

I was ready to run away, thinking again that he was a religious fanatic. But, as always, the warmth that radiated from him held me. I didn't want to leave. He was so familiar to me, as if he were cast from the same mold as my granddad. I fear to say it, I fear to even write it, but from the first time I met Mr. Goldsole, I felt love for him. Is that weakness?

"My soul," I replied, "Do you think a god recognizes my soul? I doubt it. In fact, I have never felt the presence of God or anything supernatural. I think I must have sinned or done something to offend the creator."

"Of course, the greatness of the artist recognizes your soul!" he said. "Forget about sinning or offending the creator. Embrace your mistakes. Do not think of them as sins. You are human. You can't avoid mistakes, faults, or downfalls. Life is filled with mistakes and surprises. Embrace them, for they are essential, inevitable, and all-encompassing."

I laughed. "Wow, again you are full of philosophy today."

He laughed, too, then put his arm around my shoulders and walked me back to my office building. "Yes, I guess I am full of philosophy," he said. "But let me leave you with this thought. The tolerance for uncertainty is the prerequisite to reaching the creator."

His use of simple language allowed me to expand my mind a bit and reconsider my relationship with God. Being with Mr. Goldsole, I see the possibility of God. And within that possibility, I see that I could develop a relationship of some kind with the "great artist," as he calls it. Also I invited him to join us for Thanksgiving dinner but he turned me down. I'll be honest here. I was very disappointed. It would have been so good to introduce him to Becky and my family. Besides he makes me feel good.

NOVEMBER 20TH

I was warm with a feeling of being spontaneous when I phoned the real estate office and started my search for a condo. I thought about what Mr. Goldsole had said to me and allowed the uncertainty to motivate me. While the doctors try to find out if the cancer has come back, and to what extent, I'm going to live my life.

I'm so sick of being afraid! I wake up every morning afraid of my health, my choice to divorce Colt, and, of course, working for Brent and Jerome. I carry that fear with me all day long, every day, and then at night I lie awake in bed, still carrying that fear. I want to live at least one day without those feelings of anxiety. I even worry about what I'm going to spend my retirement money on. I have a horrible propensity to worry. That sucks.

Earlier today, I liquidated my retirement money. I paid the fees, taxes, penalties, and so on, so the money that's left is mine. It seemed like the thing to do. After all, I was losing more than the fees, taxes, and penalties, combined, in the market. These are some bad financial times. One surprise was that I had gold in my portfolio, and that was the bonus. I bought it when gold was at an all-time low, and I cashed in when gold is at its all-time high. Good for me!

I've been fantasizing about riding my bike over the Golden Gate Bridge in the spring. Quint really planted that idea in me. I've seen pictures and read stories about the ride on the Net. Like Quint said, it's not a difficult ride, but it's a ride worth doing. I don't see it as a challenge, but more as a sight-seeing trip. When I think about it, I get excited. So now I have two things that give me something to look forward to: buying a condo and pedaling over the Golden Gate.

The results from the series of CA 125 tests came back and confirmed my greatest fear. I won't go into everything Dr.

Bach reported. But, in short, it's likely ovarian cancer. Life is going so good, and now this!

I want to scream.

NOVEMBER 22ND

Thanksgiving. An awkward day, but I put the CA 125 test out of my mind the best I could and the day worked out, I suppose.

Colt's parents arrived early, as did my Aunt Agnes. I wish people would stick to the time I planned. Agnes is my mom's sister, and after my parents were killed in the car accident she thought she should fill my mother's shoes. She used to come to my grandparents' house (after all, they were her parents) and boss me around, asking me if I got my homework done, did I do my chores, should I try out for the softball team… blah, blah, blah. She was always on my back. She's a miserable woman. She's done more damage than good in the world. Granddad should have drowned her when she was a little girl. Oops—did I really just write that? I'm terrible.

Anyway, it started when Aunt Agnes asked Cleo if she was pregnant. Out of thin air! She asked and added to it by telling Cleo that she had put on weight and was looking pregnant. Who says shit like that? To come in my home and accuse my daughter of being pregnant, or at the very least accuse her of gaining weight.

Colt was out in the garage with Garrett, his dad. We could all hear the noise of the circular saw and the pounding of hammers.

"Dad's building Sahchi a deluxe doghouse." Conrad said.

"Why?" I asked. "That dog never sleeps outside. She lives in this house more than I do."

But I knew what Colt was really doing. He was hiding from Agnes. She's never liked men with tattoos, and she's always made comments about Colt's various tattoos. Eight years ago, when we told her I had cancer, she thought I had somehow contracted it from Colt because he has tattoos.

"It's all of those dirty needles, you know." That's what she said to him. "They carry all kinds of germs...cancerous germs. Not to mention the ink those kinds of people use. That ink is radioactive to keep the color vibrant. I'll bet all of that transferred from you into Hope and gave her cancer!" That's how ridiculously her mind works.

While Cleo, Becky, and I were working in the kitchen, Agnes sat on a stool munching from the *hors d'oeuvres* plate. We couldn't keep up with her. We'd fill it and she'd munch it all down again.

Then she started talking about cars. "Do you think we could have Conrad situate the cars in a more proper order?" she said. "I had to park my car on the street. I don't like it on the street in this neighborhood."

"Your car will be fine where it's at," I said. "There are no bad neighborhoods in this town." I wanted to add, *you crazy lady*. I wanted to say that so bad, but I kept my mouth shut, and pretty soon Conrad gathered up everyone's keys and began moving the cars. He was a good sport about it. Years ago, he would have jumped at the chance to move the cars, but he's an adult now, and those kinds of chores are just that, chores. He made sure Agnes's car was straight out our front door.

Then she started again, this time at me. "Why aren't you wearing the sweater I bought you for your birthday?" I rolled my eyes. "Sweetheart," she said, "that blouse you have on makes your tummy look as though it's hanging over your waistband. The sweater would cover that up nicely." She grabbed a handful of olives and two deviled eggs. "I will get you some of those slimming elastic undershirts for Christmas. They'll take care of that tummy problem of yours."

That's when Becky spoke up, bless her. "I was going to say Hope, it looks like you've lost some weight. Have you been dieting?" She was speaking clear English for once.

"I have lost some weight," I said. "But it's no diet. I just don't have the appetite I used to."

I went out to the garage to get some folding chairs. Colt and Garrett were rummaging around for something, and their conversation struck me as entertaining. I find it funny how different men talk than women. While Agnes was accusing my daughter of being pregnant and me of getting fat, those boys' conversation went something like this.

They were going through toolboxes, storage boxes and whatever else lives in the garage.

Garrett said, "I didn't know you had one of these." He held something up.

Colt: "Yep, I think I have two. Take it if you need it." Then he said, "I wonder what in the hell this is." He held another tool up for his dad to see.

Garrett: "Oh, that's a crooked dog-legged wrench. You know, it's for tightening or loosening a rear axle on a Model A."

Colt: "What good is it? I don't have a Model A."

Garrett: "Damn, son, don't throw that away. For God's sake, man, that's an antique!"

Colt: "Well, then, you take it home with you. I don't want it. I have too much junk around here anyway."

Garrett held up something else and said, "How about this? Will this work?"

Colt: "I don't know. Let me see it…yeah, that'll work. Are there any more? We need four."

Garrett: "Nope." He found something else in the box. "But you have three of these doohickeys. Will they work?"

Colt: "No."

And I went back to the house laughing. I have no idea what they were looking for or why, but men don't seem to communicate much unless they have a project they're working on.

Back in the kitchen, Agnes was complaining about the chemicals in the food nowadays and Becky was explaining that at one time I had wanted to be an organic farmer.

That made Cleo turn to me. "Really, Mom? You wanted to be a farmer?"

"Yes, I did," I told her. "That was a dream of mine at one time."

"What changed? Why didn't you follow through with it?"

Tammy Jo, Colt's mom, answered before I could say anything. "I'll tell you why. She met your father, fell in love, and had babies. That's what happened."

Cleo frowned. "Our family kept you from following your dreams?"

"No, not at all," I assured her. "Don't you think that for a minute. My dreams changed, that's all. I was in love, and with each birth I became more in love with my family. To have a family, a healthy family, we needed insurance and income. That meant your dad and I both had to work in town in traditional jobs. My dream of farming was far removed from the reality of raising a family."

Cleo thought about that for a minute. "Do you regret it?"

Becky looked at me and winked. She thought I had regrets, but she also knew how much I loved my family.

"Nope," I said. "Not at all. When I see you smile, I see that I made the right choice." I said it and I meant it. I wouldn't have changed my life. At least not until now. But I didn't dare start talking about the divorce and why I want to change my life now. I'm keeping that to myself. I'll save that for another day.

Just then, Colt, Garrett, and Sahchi walked through the kitchen and headed into the living room. Colt was saying, "Dad, I think it's in the second quarter of the game. We should be able to watch the rest of it."

Cleo was making the salad. She bought the ingredients with her own money. I could see that it was expensive for her, but I was proud of her for striving to be independent. One day soon, she'll move out on her own. Everything she bought was organic—spinach, lettuce, carrots, celery, artichoke hearts. Plus she had imported Greek olives and imported bleu cheese.

At the same time, Agnes was whispering to Colt's mom about having that dirty dog in the house. She threatened to be upset if the dog stayed through dinner, so I thought I would forestall that problem.

"Colt," I called to him, "can you please put Sahchi outside for a while? She doesn't need to be in here now."

He came into the kitchen and looked at me like I'd hurt his feelings. "It's Thanksgiving, and she is just as important to me as anyone here, I can't do that to her." he said. "She'll be good."

Agnes gave a disgusted sigh that was so loud they could probably hear it across the street.

Colt ignored her. "Do you need help with anything, Babe?" he asked me.

"You could check the turkey," I said. "It should be about done."

He opened the oven door and bent over and I watched him like a schoolgirl. He was wearing faded Wranglers, and there is something about a man in well-worn Wrangler jeans that always makes me stop and take notice.

"Yep, it's done," he said. "Should I carve it now, or do you want me to hold off?"

I blinked my eyes and turned red from being caught staring at his ass. "Umm, yeah," I stammered. "Go ahead and carve it. Everything else is about done."

In that moment, staring at Colt bending over, for that instant, I missed him. I missed our old traditional Thanksgivings. I was thinking way back to when Colt and I were first married, before the children. Our day-after-

Thanksgiving tradition was the best. We used to gather up leftover turkey, rolls, mashed potatoes, sweet potatoes, and pecan pie on a big tray and carry the tray into the bedroom, where we stayed in bed most of the day. We made love, ate, fell asleep, made love again, ate, and flipped the channels on the TV. It was truly wonderful.

When the turkey was carved and everything else was on the dining room table, we all sat down and Garrett said the prayer over our meal.

"Everything looks great, Babe," Colt said.

"Yes," Becky said, "it all smells and looks terrific." She had decided to have an early dinner with us and then later have another dinner with her folks. I'm glad she came, even though we didn't get to chat much. Her friendship gives me strength.

Then Agnes started again. "Cleo," she said from across the table, "do you have a proper facial scrub?"

I watched my daughter blush. I wanted to kick Agnes under the table.

"Yes, I do," Cleo said.

Agnes peered at her. "I don't know, but it looks like you have some pimples sprouting around your cheek. Remind me later, dear. I have some apricot scrub I can bring over and give you. That scrub should turn your complexion around."

That's when Colt gave Agnes a scowl and spoke up. "You don't need any scrub," he said. "Honey, I think your complexion is exceptional. You're as pretty as any angel."

So Agnes retaliated. "Can you do something about this dog? It's unclean to have a dog around while we're eating."

"Sure, I almost forgot." Colt got up and got an old plastic plate we use for camping. He filled it with turkey, gravy, mashed potatoes, the works. Then he set the plate on the floor next to his chair. "Sahchi," he called, "come on, girl. It's Thanksgiving. You need to eat, too." Then he rolled his sleeves up so Agnes could see his tattoos. After that, he smiled across the table at her. "If I had to name only one thing to be thankful for this year," he told her, "it would be Sahchi. But, thankfully, I've been blessed with much in my life. I feel gratitude for many things. I'm thankful for my wife, my children, my parents. Even for you, Agnes."

I was still trying not to laugh. Poor Agnes. This was the first time I'd ever seen her at a loss for words. But I heard laughing from the other end of table.

It was Tammy Jo. She couldn't hold it back. "That Colt can be such a brat," she said to Agnes, and then she changed the topic. "Garrett told me this morning that he was going to take me to Hawaii this year for our anniversary."

We all congratulated her, and Colt patted Garrett on the back, "That's great, Dad. Real nice."

"It's my favorite place on earth." Tammy Jo said. "I doubt I could live there, but I sure love being there. The Hawaiian islands have a soulful feeling about them."

"I know what you mean," Becky commented. "I was there once on my way over to Japan to protest whaling. I just fell in love with the people that live there and the feel of the islands."

Cleo spoke up. "I don't think I have a favorite place on earth." She looked around the table. "Does everyone have a favorite place on earth?"

"Oh, honey," I replied, "you're young. When you get out and travel around, I'm sure you'll fall in love with some place."

"Where's your favorite place?" Conrad asked me.

I thought for a minute. "I don't know," I said, "but I want to go to San Francisco next spring and ride my bicycle across the Golden Gate Bridge. That might become my new favorite place."

"San Francisco!" Becky perked up. "Wow! Now you're giving yourself some oxygen to the brain."

Everyone at the table looked at her with a blank face. I laughed. Becky just can't stay focused on a language that people understand.

Conrad turned to his father. "How about you, Dad? Where's the best place on earth for you?"

Colt answered without hesitation. "That's easy." He pointed to the couch. "Sitting right over there with my head in your mother's lap. Put any four walls around me, and as long as I can rest my head in Hope's lap, I feel like I'm fine, the world's a good place to live in, and most all—"

He was interrupted as Junior came in.

"Where have you been?" Colt asked him. "I thought you knew what time we were having dinner."

"Gimme a break," Junior said. "I don't believe in holidays. And you know how I hate turkey."

"It's a family meal, boy! I don't care if you like holidays or not. You should honor and respect your family."

"Yeah. Right. Whatever." He did a U-turn and went into the living room. "We're missing the game."

Garrett looked at his watch. "Well, just look at the time," he said. "Half time is over." He looked at Tammy Jo, then at me.

"Go on," I said.

And with that, Colt, Garrett, and Conrad picked up their plates and followed Junior into the living room.

And I just sat there at the table, my mind stuck on what Colt had said about his favorite place on earth. I was touched. I was puzzled, too. Did he actually believe what he'd said? That the best place on earth was lying on the couch his head in my lap? Or was that just to cover up our divorce?

"Where'd your mind go?" Becky asked. "You're staring off into space."

I gave a little laugh. "Oh, Colt. He says the darnedest things."

"I don't know what I would do without him," Tammy Jo said. "Nina has been in a bad way lately, and Colt goes to see her every chance he can. He's the only one who can calm her down."

My eyes started watering. But I didn't have the heart to tell her that Colt wasn't going to see Nina, that he was out with Jolene. I will tell her another day.

Agnes was still smarting from Colt's remarks. I can always tell when she's upset. She doesn't talk, she gets quiet. "Well," she said now, "I should be on my way. Conrad could help an old woman to her car."

Conrad came back in and helped her with her coat, then walked her out the door and helped her get into her car. She didn't even say good-bye, but that's just the way she is. She'll call in the next few days as if nothing happened.

I suppose it was a good Thanksgiving dinner, all in all, even though I wasn't feeling my best. I swear this flu-ish feeling really brings me down. But I made it through, and now, with all the company gone and everyone here in bed (I think), I'm alone in my bed under my sunny painted sky, I'm wondering about many things. I wonder about Mr. Goldsole. Where did he go for Thanksgiving dinner? Was he alone? Did Devin have a nice time at his parents' house?

And then, slowly, my fear began to fill the room as I started wondering about the doctors and the tests. The holiday will just prolong the time before I can talk to the doctors and find out what the plan of action will be. I hope somehow, some way, it's all a huge mistake and this worrying is for nothing.

NOVEMBER 24TH

I've seen very little of Cleo's boyfriend, Ward, but I see his presence in my daughter's face. I'm certain that I haven't misjudged him. He's a good man and he's good for her. I see the brightness in her smile, the lofty attitude, and the general air of love around her. I'm a little envious. My boys seem bitter, but I'm not sure if they are bitter toward life in general, or toward each other, or what. They come home complaining, they eat at odd hours, and they leave the house cussing. If they're in a room at the same time they inevitably fight. I don't mean yelling, either. I mean fisticuffs. I have had to separate them more than once. What could be so bad that they have to fight? They don't even act like brothers anymore. I've asked them individually as to what is going on between them, but they both insist it's nothing for me to worry about. Whatever it is, I hope they work it out before they kill each other.

I'm not fond of Junior's manner or his friends. Call it mother's intuition, but I sense something's not so good with them. Whenever he's with them, he's drinking. And when he drinks, he's not a pleasant person to be around.

Colt and his band, the Wild Bunch, have a gig to play tonight out at the Sour Mash Saloon. Devin has been flaky lately and wouldn't take me out to dinner or on a date of any sort, so I asked Becky to take me out and put a smile on my face. She picked me up and delivered me to the Sour Mash, where Colt had no idea we would show up. He smiled big when he saw Becky and me.

Becky is a hippie through and through, but I can see the way she looks at the cowboys. I hear what she says, too. She spied one tall cowboy and said, "Look at hip pockets over there. He makes me come to life. I hope he doesn't give me the go-bye 'cuz I'm red hot and ready to moan."

"You wouldn't know what to do with a cowboy even if you caught one," I told her. I was busy scanning the crowd for Jolene.

"You just watch," she retorted. "I'm going to knock the polish off his boots, then I'll get him to hop into my car, take off for the fluffy pillow, and then I'll boil his ham bone for him." Her description of sex with the cowboy came with gestures.

"Becky," I said, "let's keep this a nice, cool night. No one needs to leave with anyone and go have sex somewhere. Have a

good time, dance, but get to know the guy first. No overnighters."
I wanted Becky to take me home, I sure didn't want to have to
wait until the band broke everything down and ride back with
Colt. By the time they get packed up the sun could be rising.

"Now that you've laid me out, when are you sending me to
the retirement home?" she asked.

Becky got ol' hip pockets to dance with her, and when I
found Wild Mack and Jennifer, Mack asked me to dance.
One thing about Mack, I've seen him fight and he's good,
I've seen him ride a horse, and he's very good, and I've danced
with him and he is fantastic. That boy can swing. Colt was
playing a cover of Elvis's "Burning Love." I swear, dancing
with Mack was as much fun as being on a roller coaster. After
the first song, the band covered Dwight Yoakam's "Gone,"
and the roller coaster was in full motion. I hadn't danced in
a couple of years at least, and it sure felt good. I could see
Becky was having a good time, too. I hoped the tall cowboy
she was with had enough wits about him not to go any further
with her. He was smart, though, and Becky played it cool.

By the time the band got to a slow set I was out of breath.
They were playing George Strait's "Amarillo by Morning," when
Jennifer, Mack's wife and my friend, asked if she could cut in. I
said yes and sat down. Pretty soon, a man I'd never seen before
stepped up to me. He didn't look like he was from this area.

"You are an incredible dancer," he said.

"Thank you."

"I don't mean to sound prejudiced," he said, "but where I
come from, I've never seen a black girl dance to western music,

let alone master it. I really enjoyed watching you and your husband dance. I wish I could find me a partner like you."

"Well, thank you," I said not sure how to digest his racist comment. "But Mack isn't my husband."

The man's expression changed, and it looked like he thought he had an "opportunity." For a minute, I thought so, too. He was a good-looking man. But I knew it would be wrong to let this guy have one tonight while Colt was watching. Mack and Jennifer and Becky were all there.

"You see that man singing up there?" I asked the handsome stranger.

"I sure do."

"He's my husband."

"Oh. Well, he's a lucky man."

"Thank you. And you know what? I will remind him of just how lucky he is when he takes a break."

He slumped in disappointment (I'm not exaggerating) and walked away. I felt bad for him, but he boosted my confidence. I'm not so old and dried up, after all.

When the band took a break, Colt came over to where Mack, Jennifer, Becky, and I were sitting. "It's nice to see you again, Becky," he said.

"It's always nice to see you, too," she said. "I hope you don't ever get tired of me showcasing your wife. She's my hot little mouse." When Colt looked at her with a confused expression, she explained. "Hey, there isn't nothing wrong with taking your skin off and dancing around your bones once in while."

Now he really was confused. "Huh?"

"You know? It's alright for me to come out and have a good time with your good-looking wife. Everyone needs to drop the reality of the day and dance once in a while. Right?"

Now he understood. He smiled, "Yeah, sure, Becky." Then he sat down next to me. "Hey, Babe. I'm pleasantly surprised to see you here."

I turned to him. "I didn't know if your little girlfriend would be here or not," I said. "But I wanted to dance. I'm tired of being home alone on weekend nights."

"Ahh, now," he said, "let's not start that up again. Babe, there is no girlfriend. How can I convince you of that?"

"Where do you spend your nights when you're not home?"

"With Nina."

"That's bullshit, and you know it!"

He stood up. "I'm not going to argue with you here. I'm going to get a drink and start the next set. We'll talk when I get home. If you want to talk. I love you, and there is no girlfriend." He turned away and got a bottle of water from the bartender, then got back on stage, and in a minute I heard him tell the guys in the band, "We've got a request...." I couldn't hear the rest of his sentence.

He picked up his '58 Gibson Archtop and started picking the cover of the Marshall Tucker Band's "Can't You See." When they got to the second verse, I felt the words resonating in every level of my body, mind, and soul. As Colt sang, I could hear (and feel) the pain in his voice. I know Colt well enough to know when he's hurting. The song lasts about four minutes, and it was like we were the only two people in the room. No one else mattered. It was only him singing to the Lord about me. I don't know exactly who Colt prays to, but I felt like this song was his plea for our marriage to survive. However, I don't know if he expects me to forgive his infidelity, or to forget it, whichever the case may be. I haven't and I won't. When the song ended, I applauded with everyone else, but I had talked myself out of the sentimental feeling.

Mack ordered some buffalo wings, and I started on them and couldn't stop. For some reason, they really hit the spot, so I ordered us another basket. Dipping the wings in bleu cheese sauce, oh, yum!

Note to self: find a buffalo wing recipe and make them at home.

NOVEMBER 26TH

I found a condo! It's perfect, exactly what I'd pictured in my mind, and it was unbelievably priced. It's a two-bedroom, bath and a half, living room with a fireplace (I love a cozy fireplace), and a remodeled kitchen. The appliances are top of the line. The condo has its advantages, but the complex is also great. There's a swimming pool, a sauna, and an exercise area. Not bad, considering that before the recession, it was worth over $190K and I picked it up for $55K. And it's only three blocks from work on Hawthorn Street.

It all happened so fast. I went to a realtor at the beginning of last week, and we looked at several condos. When I saw this place on Wednesday and fell in love with it, I told my realtor my offer. It was accepted. I had cash, so things went smoothly and quickly. We met at the title company this morning, and before my mind had time to register what was happening, they handed me the keys. My first big step toward freedom!

I have a date with Devin tonight, I'd like to take him back to my new condo, but I still have to buy a bed. Plus furniture, dishes, things like that.

Mary (at work) and I had a funny conversation today. I told her that I was thinking of getting divorced, and she asked me if I was going to get my naval pierced. "Where did that come from?" I asked her.

"Hey, that's normal for women who are getting divorced these days," she said. "Last summer, I was out to dinner with my husband and his friend from work and, wouldn't you know it, while we were walking through the parking lot, we ran straight into the friend's ex-wife. They'd been divorced for three years, and this was his first time seeing her since the divorce was final. And there she was, fifty-five years old, and she was wearing a half shirt and shorts. She did have a firm body. Evidently she had been working out, and there was a shiny ornament pierced right through her navel."

"Oh my gosh!"

Mary laughed. "My husband's friend asked her what she'd been up to lately. She answered that she was dating a younger man and had just returned from a surfing trip. She had plans for several snowboarding trips with him this winter. I don't think she was acting or being hurtful, either, because she was so honest about it. She asked my husband's friend how he had been and sounded genuinely interested in what he had to say. After our little, uncomfortable chat, she went on her way. My husband's friend told us that in the thirty-two years they had been married, he'd seen her in a swimsuit only a handful of times and never in shorts."

"Well," I said, "maybe that's why they got divorced. He never took her to the beach!" I laughed, but Mary didn't. "You know, on second thought," I said, "I think a nice two-carat diamond in my belly button would look nice. It might be the right sort of thing for me to kick off the last third of my life!"

I said this sarcastically, but Mary didn't seem to hear the sarcasm. "You may start with piercing," she said, "which is disgusting, but you won't stop there. Then you'll have to get a tattoo."

"Don't worry, Mary," I said. "My mind may be messed up, but I'm not going crazy!"

She actually looked relieved, as if she'd thought I might actually get my belly button pierced. Now that's a laugh. I had to go to the bathroom, and while I was in there, I lifted my blouse and looked at my belly. Funny thing, the belly. No one's belly is their own is it? It's like landscape. People look at bellies. They notice bellies, they talk about strangers' bellies, like, wow, that girl sure is fat, look at her belly sticking out, or, wow, look at that girl, she's hot and her belly is nice and flat. It isn't only men that do this, either. Women do it, too. They check out guys and say, hey, did you see his six-pack? Or, damn, look at that dude, he hasn't seen his shoes in years. All of this over a belly.

It's landscape. Maybe I should put a monument on my belly so people could stop and give me some attention. Yeah, they could admire that thing that was pierced into me. It would be sharp and it would have to be painfully pushed in. I could tell people I was tough. Getting my belly button pierced didn't hurt. That I liked it.

What then?

Would they be impressed?

My belly is thankfully flat. And the issue of piercing it would be my ego wanting to show it off. *Hey everyone look at me, I'm fifty, but I'm still young enough to do stupid shit! Wisdom has somehow failed me, but don't I look chic with this gaudy jewelry hanging out of my belly button hole?* Nah. That's not me. I know why my belly is flat, and, believe me, it's nothing to be proud of. I'm ill and my illness takes away my appetite.

I could market this as a new diet plan. I could name it the Get Cancer And Lose A Bunch Of Weight Quickly Diet!

NOVEMBER 27TH

My date with Devin was interesting. Devin, Devin, Devin. No one would believe that I'm fifty by the way I'm acting. I'm acting like a teenager. But that's what's so wonderful about it, I feel young and wanted. After we took in a movie, we went for a walk. He spoke freely and the subject of our conversation was the future. Our future. He hinted we should take a blind leap of faith and see what happens. Then, after some time passes, we would reevaluate our situation, and if neither of us was unhappy with it, then we should continue.

"After your divorce is final," he said, "then we can see how we feel about each other. Until then, let's just enjoy each other."

I'm certain that I stumbled. I blamed it on my heels.

It's not even been a month since he met me at the café and showed some interest in me. Now he's discussing the future!

"I have a surprise for you," I said.

"What is it?"

"I bought a condo. It's a place for you to be with me comfortably. It could be our place. If you want to live there." I wasn't sure if he was completely broken up with his girlfriend, but I figured if they were sleeping in separate beds, he could handle an option. For me, living with Colt can be difficult and awkward at times, not to mention confusing.

Who knows what men think? I for sure have no idea. There have been times when I thought Colt was criticizing me, but then I'd hear his frustration and realize that he was merely asking me a question. And Devin? Like tonight, when

I couldn't tell if he was upset with my suggestion or what. He didn't say a word.

"Jesus Christ, Devin," I finally said. "I asked you if you wanted to live in my condo. I didn't ask you to marry me!"

"I'm sorry," he said. "I didn't mean to offend you. This is so sudden! I thought we would discuss things before acting on them, so I was taken aback. But I'm thinking about it. I haven't seen the place and I don't know how much stuff you have and how much stuff I have. I doubt you'd want me to move in and take up all of your space."

"I'm a spontaneous gal," I told him. "You need to get used to it. I see what I want and I take it. The condo was ripe for the picking." I was telling him more about what I wanted to be than what I actually am, but at least he didn't say no. Yet he didn't say yes, either. He just walked me back to my car. Under the street lamp, I could see his clenched jaw. He looked at me through squinty eyes, and it was as if he were wearing a mask.

"I didn't mean to upset you." I said again.

"It's all right," he said. "I was just thinking it's too bad that things weren't different."

My mind was spinning. What the hell was *too bad?* Too bad that I'm fifty and he's twenty-eight? Too bad I have children? Too bad his girlfriend took him back or he took her back? My passion was fading quickly into humiliation. When he wiped my eyes with his finger, I realized I didn't even know I was crying.

"Is it over then? Before we even had a chance to start, are we over? Is that it?"

"I'm not sure what it is you're looking for," he said. "Hope, I thought we would take this slow and see where we'd go from here, but you're thinking of us moving in together. That's a huge step for me! I like you, and I want to see you again…if you want to see me, that is."

"Of course I want to see you again!" The hurt in my stomach wasn't easing up. He didn't even want to see the condo. I was embarrassed, so I got into my car and drove home. Sahchi and Colt were crashed out on the couch again, with one of them or perhaps both of them snoring. Thank God for dogs and boys who love us! Nevertheless, I felt the pain of defeat with each step up the stairs to my bedroom.

NOVEMBER 29TH

They fired Brent's son's ex-girlfriend today. I'm not too surprised. But it's a little disheartening to watch it all go down. The only mistake she made was dating that boy. The gossip is that Brent and his son set her up by reprimanding her often enough that HR could legally fire her.

She must have been embarrassed, though, when she came to work this morning. Two security agents surprised her. They escorted her to her work area in the cubicle farm and watched her carefully as she packed her personal belongings into a box. Then they walked her to the door and out to her car. It was quite a spectacle. Everyone was watching. We all realized that any of us could lose our jobs at any moment if we didn't follow both the written and unwritten rules.

But I can't say the girl had many friends. Most of the staff thought of her as a kiss-ass for dating Brent's son. But who are we to judge? She may be a wonderful person. But we will never know because we didn't give her an opportunity to be friendly. I was right there with my coworkers, believing she was trying to get ahead fast by dating Brent's son. I regret thinking that.

I have to admit that when I watched them escort her out the door, she looked scared and defenseless. She looked like she could have used a friend. I should have walked out with her to give her support. Poor thing, she was in tears as she was walking down the aisle with everyone watching her. What a sad day for her. I hope she'll find some happiness wherever she ends up.

It's a shame to think that the state of affairs at work boils down to the satisfactory orgasms of one powerful man. Brent needs to pull his head out of his ass and fire his son. I think he fired the wrong person.

Devin came to my cubicle a bit later after she was escorted out of the building. He said he was stopping in to say hi. He was being very discreet, which I appreciate. We have agreed to keep work on a professional level at all times. But it was so nice to see him smile at me. I like him, not only because of our romantic situation but, honestly, because he's a likeable person. He's just a good guy.

Of course I went to the cathedral today for lunch. It was a cold walk, but there was no wind. Someone was hanging Christmas lights on the gutters of the building, and the familiar manger scene was already set up in the yard, minus one Wise Man. I read in the paper when it was stolen last year that a prankster was suspected of taking it, but the figure was never recovered.

I love Christmas. Not because of its religious meaning, but for the good time of year with the pretty lights, yummy, homemade candies and cookies, and the snow (if I'm not out in it). The little things about Christmas mean more to me than the big religious Mass to Christ.

Does that make me a bad person?

I went into the cathedral, and when my eyes adjusted to the dim light, I lit a candle and then knelt and prayed. I don't know why I pray. God is as far away as anyone or anything can be. I suppose I'm scared of the cancer, and when I'm scared I pray a lot. It's not really a payer, to be honest about it; it's more of a conversation with myself. I talk to myself and invite God to listen if he wants to.

Since I don't know God very well I thought it best to invite him rather than to assume he automatically shows up when a person prays. Besides, my grandmother told me in my dream to ask for God to find me. She's right, I've never asked God to come find me, I just have assumed he was there watching me, judging me, taking my parents, giving me cancer.

I have a picture in my mind of what God and heaven look like. Heaven is an old, rustic, log cabin high on a mountain with a fire burning in the fireplace. It's near a lake, and it's always warm there because the sun is always shining bright. It's warm, and there's a girl in cutoff jean shorts and flip-flops (me) who lives in the heavenly cabin. God comes to visit her (me) regularly, and I love his company. He looks just like Granddad, and he can fix anything that I break, even my heart, and he loves me, no matter how broken I am. There are no streets paved in gold, for gold has no value in my heaven. And my God doesn't wear a white robe or have a long white beard. My God wears well-worn coveralls and has a wife, and she's the perfect balance for him. My God is lovable, conceivable, and full of understanding, but most of all he is the essence of love.

After my prayer, I went in search of someone in charge at the cathedral. I found a man who was volunteering his time to put up the decorations. "I want to donate some money for the missing Wise Man," I said.

The volunteer explained to me the three men in the nativity were wise men but were also and more importantly they were all kings. And when Christ was born, he became the King of Kings so the Three Kings knelt before him. Evidently I wasn't using the proper term for the missing figure. Whatever. I just wanted to buy the figure, I didn't need a Sunday school lesson!

"I'm not aware of any donation being collected," he said. "I think the church is working it out with the insurance company. But I can ask."

"Do you know how to obtain a King?" I asked him.

"Yes, yes, I do. I had the privilege of ordering the whole nativity scene four years ago. I ordered it and set it up. It's a shame someone stole one of the figures. What is the world coming to?"

"Okay," I said, "here is what I want you to do. Here's my name and cell number. Order the replacement Wise Man, King, whatever you want to call him, and I'll pay for it. Shipping and everything. Please keep this between us, though. No one needs to know. I want my charity to be anonymous."

"That's very nice of you," he said. "But those figures are expensive. Are you sure?"

"I'm more than sure."

He agreed and said the replacement figure should be here before Christmas. I feel so good about this! Between Jerome and my retirement money, which had been just wasting away in investments, I have plenty of money. I might as well do something good for the community and myself.

After I made the agreement with the volunteer, I went out and stood by the manger. I was admiring it when I heard a familiar voice.

"Hello, Chief." Mr. Goldsole came and stood next to me.

"I knew you would be here," I said. "It's good to see you again."

"Did you have a good Thanksgiving holiday celebration?" he asked.

"It was good. A little interesting and good. How about you? I wondered about you. Did you spend Thanksgiving with Faith?"

"Your memory is good but not completely accurate. Her name is Faye," he said with a smile. "Yes, Faye and I spent the holiday together. We had a very nice time."

There was a moment then when neither of us said anything, and in that moment, I felt the warmth of his energy. It was like everything was going to be okay. I took a deep breath and held it. I didn't want the moment to end.

"How are you doing?" he asked me. "Is everything all right?"

"Of course," I said. "Everything is good." I was lying, perhaps more to myself than to him, but then I felt a rush of conscience flow through me and I felt the urge to 'fess up. "Well, I guess I'm a little scared."

"What are you scared of?"

"I had cancer in the past. After treatment, it went into remission. But I had some tests done the other day, and it looks like it has come back."

"I see. Well, that would concern anyone. I think fear is the most natural response to such news. Is that why you come here so often?"

"I guess. I mean, I go in and I try to communicate with God, but I usually make a fool out of myself." I told him about the time I was praying out loud and the time I had the sneezing fit and, of course, the time I banged my knee and swore out loud. "Why is life so complicated?" I asked him.

"It's not that complicated, Chief."

"Oh, it's simple, is it?"

"Sure it is." he began as we started walking back toward my office, "It's all rather basic. You are born into a body. You might like it, or you might hate it, but it's your body, either way. Then you live a life, and life is nothing more than an education within a divine school. As with most schools, you are expected to grow while you're there. Your growth is nothing more than learning by trial and error. You may do well and live your lessons without a single mistake. But it's more likely that you'll make mistakes. You're given more than one chance every time. You're also given information to use to correct your mistakes. More importantly, mistakes don't equal failure."

I stopped walking. I wanted to hear what Mr. Goldsole was saying, you know really listen. So I stopped. When I stopped he stopped talking for a moment. We looked out over the snow filled Washington Park. There were people making their way up and down the sidewalk and I wondered if they had things they worried over. I further wondered if they all had someone like Mr. Goldsole to help point the way on life's road.

"What were you saying about failure?" I asked.

"There is no failure here. Every day, your life is filled with lessons. You encounter every one of them. You learn that lesson and move on to a new one. Or maybe you don't learn and you have to repeat the lesson until you get it right. Whenever you feel that you're doing the same thing over and over again, it may be a lesson worth learning and you're not getting it, and so you're repeating it. The divine artist gave you life. What you do with your life is up to you. You have everything you need to live your life. You have all the tools you need to live life. They're all in your soul. It's up to you how you choose to use your tools…it's up to you how you live life. Again, I tell you that you have the gift of free will."

"That's pretty deep for simple," I said after I thought about what he'd said.

"You have your body and your soul to guide you through your life. You once asked me if you had a soul, and the other day you told me you'd found her. Do you still believe in your soul?"

"Yes, I do. I feel more connected to it more now that I've identified it."

"It's important to live life knowing your soul. If you never know it or acknowledge it, that makes for a long and hollow life."

I thought about all this for a few minutes. "Is this the same for all these people in the park, I mean for everyone?"

"You bet it is! Everyone has a soul. It's the divine energy of higher purpose, given to them by the divine artist. Souls shouldn't be ignored because they connect us to our higher purpose. Wouldn't you agree?"

"Sure."

We regained our step and walked toward my office. While walking he suddenly changed the subject. "I'm sorry to hear about the cancer resurfacing, Hope. I'm sure it's a scary time for you, but if you live in faith, you'll find your security there."

"Live in faith?" I repeated. "I don't have any faith. I don't think I ever had any faith. What should I have faith in?"

"You are here for a reason, Hope. Have faith that something created you and placed you here for a reason. Whoever or whatever created you, I call it the divine artist, loves you. And even though you are going through something as terrible as cancer, remember that you are loved and that the divine artist didn't do this to you, but is here to help you. Have faith that whoever or whatever you believe in has your best interest in mind because you are here for a reason."

Faith?

I'm here for a reason?

Had anyone other than Mr. Goldsole told me that, I would have told him or her that they were full of crap. But hearing it from him relaxed my mind. I could honestly feel like something greater than myself did love me and had my best interest, or the best interest for the greater good, in mind. Mr. Goldsole walked me back to my office, and we discussed faith. I liked that. It pacified my mind. Still, when it comes to my fear of cancer, faith doesn't come so easy.

I can see that I need to work with my soul and figure out this faith thing. I'm curious. I need to do a real soul check and see what I do believe in.

Thank you, Mr. Goldsole.

We parted on the sidewalk outside my building. I always feel empty inside when he's away from me. I swear he's so familiar to me, like he's my granddad's brother or something. I feel so safe and comfortable with him.

Where do you go, Mr. Goldsole? Where do you go when you leave me?

NOVEMBER 30TH

I called in sick today. I feel like shit, mentally and physically. Being sick so often bothers me. I want to be better.

I went back to bed and slept till noon, and then I went to the condo. The furniture I ordered was delivered late this afternoon, and now the place looks great, just like I want it to look. It's cozy. The majority of my furniture is bookcases. I have so many books, and now I get to bring them out of boxes and display them. I will sort them by the ones I've read, the ones I'm going to read, and the ones I'm going to reread.

In addition to the bookcases, I have an easy chair that reclines. I look forward to spending a lot of time in that big chair, wrapped in my favorite blanket and reading peacefully. I love the smell, feel, and weight of a good book. I have one of those electronic gadgets that can hold hundreds of books in its memory, and I use it often. But I still continue my love affair with actual books.

...

I had an odd dream last night. It began with me waving goodbye to people boarding a white, yellow, and blue cruise ship. Among the passengers were my granddad and grandmother. They were in the middle of a huge crowd moving up the gangplank.

Across the street was a rail station with people getting on a luxury train like you see in old movies. The people getting on the train were also excited. Once the ship had departed and the train had gone, I was alone, standing there and looking around. Then I walked into the city, where people were walking up and down the sidewalks. Some were going north; some, east; others, west. But no one was going south toward where the ship and train had been loading their passengers. Then the city was suddenly empty. All the people had left, and I was alone on the abandoned streets. Then I heard a voice coming from behind me.

"Hello, Chief."

I turned around and saw Granddad smiling at me. "Is everything all right?" he asked.

"No," I said. "Everyone is going someplace but me. I'm all alone here."

"Well, Chief, some people are thieves and take things, and some are kind and generous. What kind of person did I raise you to be?"

"I'm just me," I said. "I'm not the best or the worst, I'm not more than some people, nor am I less than anyone else."

"That's right! You are who you are. Be who you are. Don't hurt anyone, and don't let anyone hurt you. Some people want to leave the city, some want to stay, and some are just following others. What do you think you should do?"

"I don't know! I'm afraid. I want to leave, but where is it safe to go? Life is difficult, Granddad. I've got cancer, and that scares me. Where should I go?"

He smiled down at me. That's when I noticed I was a little girl in my dream. "Life is difficult compared to what?" he asked. "It's only as difficult as you make it."

"That's not true! I didn't create the cancer that threatens to kill me."

"Don't worry, Chief. I'm right here to take care of you. If that cancer wants to live in you, then you might need to live somewhere else."

In my dream, we walked through the empty town back to where I had come from.

"Why are you here?" I asked him. "I saw you leave on that cruise ship with Grandmother."

"We did leave, but the captain turned around when he learned you hadn't come with us. He dropped me off here to fetch you and then he steered the ship back on its course. I'm here to get you. Together, you and I will wait for the ship to return."

We sat on a bench by the water. I was little, about seven or eight, and I was wearing a yellow sundress with cute little black shoes on my feet. The sun felt warm, and I felt safe because Granddad was with me.

Strange dream.

DECEMBER 1ST

I went shopping with Becky the other day and told her the cancer has come back. I spoke in the same casual way that I would use to tell her when I needed to stop and get a box of tampons. We were eating soup and salad at the Chilled Tomato over on Ash Street. She was taking a drink of her Dr. Pepper when I said it, and all of a sudden I was showered with fizzy pop.

"*What?*" she yelled. "What do you mean, the cancer is back? What? Where? How serious?" The worry in her voice and her use of standard English were signs that she was disturbed by my words.

"I've yet to come to terms with it myself," I said. I wasn't using the word "cancer" yet. It was "it." "Don't worry about it."

I said patting my lower stomach. "They suspect it's ovarian this time. I'll probably have a hysterectomy. And that will be that."

"No, no, no," she said. "Tell me you're kidding. Please tell me you're kidding."

I nodded and grinned, but then I couldn't restrain my tears.

"How long have you known?" she asked.

"I've suspected it for a couple of months," I said, "but the doctor didn't confirm it until just before Thanksgiving."

"Cancer again! Oh, Hope, this isn't fair! I was certain you had it beat."

All I could do was shrug my shoulders. "I guess my body hates me for some reason. I know it does."

Now she got mad. "It's just like you to sit on this and worry for months without telling anyone. For some reason, you think you deserve this. You punish yourself. You don't ask for help. You try to go at it alone. Dammit, Hope! I've been here since September, and you never once thought to talk to me about this. Never once!"

"I'm talking now, aren't I?" I wanted to be honest with her. With myself, too. I guess I needed to vent. It's been building up in me, the worry, the fear, and the stress. I was feeling overwhelmed. I didn't mean to blurt it out like that, but that's how it came out. Once I said it, the dam burst and the tears flowed. I was wiping tears and sticky Dr. Pepper spray off of my face while Becky was talking.

"Does Colt know? The kids?" I shook my head. "Of course not. *What*, Hope? You think it will be easier to tell them when your hair is falling out and you're puking in the toilet again? Come on! Think about your family."

"There won't be any puking or hair falling out this time," I said. "I refuse to go through the radiation or chemo this time. Like I said, it will probably be a hysterectomy. And that will be that."

"That simple, eh?" I could tell she didn't believe me. "So when are you gonna tell Colt and the kids?"

"I'm not," I said. "There's no need to worry them over this. The kids need to stay focused on starting their own lives. The last thing they need is for me to be sick and needy like last time."

"Then I'll tell them."

"Becky, please. I need you in my life, but if you do that, I will never speak to you again. I need you, so please be kind. Just cry with me."

"Good God, Hope. You need to at least tell Colt."

"I can't. We're getting divorced and I don't—"

"What!? You're getting divorced? Do I even know you, woman? Since when did the two of you decide this... this...oh, let me guess. Last year, and you're just now getting around to telling ol' Becky."

"Gee, you make me feel awful about myself."

"Well, goddammit, I'm your friend! Or at least I thought I was. But you're all shut up. You don't let me in, you don't let anyone in."

She was right about that. And hearing her words opened a hole in my stomach that hurt with deep, agonizing pain.

"Becky," I said when I could talk again, "I'm sorry. I thought I could handle it, all of it, by myself. But it's too much. It's just way too much."

She reached across the table and grabbed my hand and held it tight. We were both sobbing by then. I didn't think about where I should tell Becky, so here we were in the Chilled Tomato crying at lunchtime with people all around us watching and pointing.

"I'm here for you," she whispered through her tears. "I'm here, and we'll beat this again. I don't want you to feel like you're alone. It's a tough row to hoe but hoe it you will, and you will do it with me right beside you. I'm here with you, do you hear me? I'm here for you."

"I hear you. I love you, Becky."

Becky has a loud voice, and, well, I get loud, too, so I suppose we were causing a bit of a scene in the restaurant. People were staring at us. I heard a man saying, "What are those two bitching about?" What a pig! I got up and went to his table and threatened to deck him. "I just found out I have cancer," I shouted at him, "and you wonder what I'm *bitching* about! *Really?* You're an asshole."

And that was that. Becky and I got asked to leave the Chilled Tomato.

I never had the chance to tell her about the lump under my arm and how afraid I was that the cancer has already spread. I'll ask her to drive me to my biopsy follow-up appointment next Friday. I'll tell her then. But I don't dare mention Devin. Not yet.

DECEMBER 2ND

Sunday. My day to do whatever suits my fancy. I love Sundays! I've been feeling a bit of fatigue, so I slept in. When I woke up, I just lay in bed reading, trying to keep my mind off things that bother me. Eventually my mind refused to be distracted, so I got up, showered, and went downstairs. I had a chance to talk for a minute with my kids before they headed out of the house, each one going their own way. They seem to come and go about the same time, but they never come and go together. Well, I don't stick my nose into their business. They have their own lives to live. I only hope that I have some time in the near future to be with them without distraction.

I went to the condo again today. I love it there! It's so comfortable. I feel free there. It's as if the cancer can't reach me at my condo. This was also my first date with Devin at the condo. He agreed to meet me here and see it. After spending the day making the condo and myself look our best, I waited for him.

He was a tad late. I was both excited and apprehensive when I opened the door. He walked in slowly, as if was he was paying the utmost attention to everything. He was careful as he walked deeper into the condo, absorbing what he saw as he went along. He passed his hand across the titles of some of my books, then over the upholstery on the couch and the recliner. I noticed that he avoided looking toward the bedroom. After a look around the kitchen, he found his way back to the living room and sat in my recliner. Then he looked out the window at the view of the park. I sat across from him. He turned his attention from the window to my exposed legs.

"Hemingway, Fitzgerald, Whitman," he said finally. "I didn't picture you as a reader of modern American literature."

"And I doubted you even knew who they are."

"Why? You think I'm not capable of knowing about modern American literature?"

"I'm guilty," I said. "I thought your generation would be too young to know those writers. I expected you might reach back as far as Kerouac, but not farther than that."

He laughed softly.

The sun, as it does in the winter, turned a reddish orange color as it began to set. Devin looked around my living room again and said, "I like it." He was stiff and uncomfortable, and I regretted inviting him over. He didn't even take his coat off. He was sitting there as if he were ready to run out the door at a moment's notice.

"Do I frighten you?" I asked him.

"No, no, I'm not frightened." He stretched nervously.

"Then what is it?"

"Do I look uncomfortable or frightened?"

"I've seen fear," I said, "and I would say that you're scared."

"Where have you seen fear?"

"In my own face. Many times."

He looked confused, but I didn't want to press him, so I made myself relax and allowed the silence to return. Finally, he took his coat off. I don't know if it was because he was getting too hot or because he was relaxing.

Dinner was ready, and the table was set. I served pork roast with mashed potatoes and gravy, corn, and salad for the side dish. I served dinner with my dignity in place, not knowing how this dinner date would go. He liked everything. I knew he had an appetite, but he really put the food down. I took that as a good sign. But the tension in the room kept either of us from really enjoying the food.

He told me he'd had a conversation with his mother on his cell phone on his way over. She knows about our dates and me. That can't be good, can it?

"You told your mother about us?" I wasn't expecting this. His girlfriend, maybe, but his mother? No, that was something I didn't calculate. I'm sure she and I are closer in age than I care to learn. I felt exposed, like one of those dreams when you show up to work naked.

"My mother and I are quite close," he said. "I tell her most everything."

"And your father? Did you tell dear old dad, too?"

His eyes narrowed and he looked a little pissed. "My father is a workaholic. He only notices what goes on in his world, and I'm not in his world."

"So what does your mother say about me?"

"You? She doesn't say anything about you. It's me she worries about. She lectures me about my lifestyle. She thinks I'm a cougar hunter."

I slammed my hand down on the table. "I'm no cougar!"

"I respect you, Hope. I'm not accusing you of being a cougar. Please don't get angry about that. My mother has her ideas of how life is. She's afraid that I will miss out on true happiness in life because of my desires."

That stopped me in my tracks, so to speak. "What?"

"She thinks I will have regrets later in life because I spent my time on frivolous relationships. She claims I act on urges rather than good judgment. She wants me to find someone to marry and start a family with."

"I'm sure some context is needed here," I said. "Your mother sounds a little off. You are a grown man, you don't need your mom to tell you whom you can date. I'm sure she's a great person, that's why I think I missed the context of her remarks, especially the part about me being a cougar."

"She didn't call you a cougar," he protested. "She said *I* was being a cougar hunter. She was accusing *me* of not being moral."

I wasn't sure what to say. "So," I finally asked, "are you here as a moral, stand-up guy, or are you here on the low down as an amoral trophy hunter?"

That made him blush. He wasn't prepared to answer that question. After a while, he got up and cleared his dishes, taking them to the sink, rinsing them, and putting them into the dishwasher.

"Before I answer that last question," he called from the kitchen, "can I ask you a favor?"

"Yes," I called back. "You can ask anything of me."

"Could we let tonight end now? Like this?"

"Yes." I felt my disappointment expanding in me.

He came back to the dining room. "We can make another date," he said, "and I'll come back and answer your question."

"Of course we can do this again another time."

What could I do? Nothing. I watched him put on his coat and leave.

I feel ugly.

DECEMBER 3RD

I left work at three-thirty, got home and changed, then gathered up a few things. Colt was putting up Christmas lights on the house and our lone pine tree in the front yard as I left. I wanted to get to the condo and sit awhile and relax before starting dinner. Devin was coming over at six-thirty, and I didn't want to feel rushed.

He came by my cubicle earlier today and, speaking in code, apologized for yesterday. He actually asked if he could come over again tonight.

So when I got to the condo I turned the furnace up. It was cold and snowing outside, and I was perfectly content to wrap up in my blanket, drink a cup of hot chocolate, and read a book. I was so content, in fact, that I no longer wanted Devin to come. I kept hoping he would call and tell me he was stuck in the snow and couldn't get out. I read for far too long and didn't get dinner started on time, but I didn't care. I knew if he came at all, he would soon be in a hurry to leave again. So why worry about fixing dinner for him?

My attitude toward him was poor to the point that I just nestled back into my blanket and read some more. At a quarter to seven, I heard him rapping on my door. When I opened it, he seemed genuinely happy to see me. He came in, took off his coat, and hung it up in the closet without any inhibition. And then—big surprise—he gave me a kiss!

"I'm embarrassed," I said.

"Why?"

"I invited you over for dinner, but I haven't prepared anything. I must have dozed off."

"Oh, well," he said, "that's not so bad, we can order in. I know a Chinese restaurant that has good food and delivers. Do you like Chinese food?"

"I do. Moo goo gai pan is one of my favorites. Oh, let's order some hot and sour soup, too."

I was getting hungry just talking about it, so while he was calling the restaurant, I set the table and my mood began to change. Here I was with this young man and a candlelit dinner in my own little, cozy corner of the world where it's forbidden to mention cancer. Our dinner was delivered within the hour and we ate it, not saying much, mainly gazing at each other. After dinner, we let the candles light the room as we sat together, looking out the window and watching the snowfall. It was very quiet. Neither of us said much, but only stole glances at each other. At some point, he reached for my hand and I gave it to him. The warmth of his hand reassured me and my mixed emotions dissipated. I could feel a connection stirring between us. It can't be described in words, but existed in the absence of our words. It had a life of its own, an energy that expanded and contracted with a sort of throbbing I could feel.

At some point, I made the commitment to myself that he wouldn't leave this time without making love to me. Something uncontrollable and dangerous had returned to my life, true, but I was going to amplify my life by living, not dying. I wanted the experience of Devin. I wanted passionate kisses, and not just on my mouth. I wanted to be touched in tender areas. I wanted to be held in strong arms. Why shouldn't I have these things in the face of a devastating disease?

The bathroom is off the bedroom, so I made the excuse that I had to go. Once there, I undressed, found my new lacy underthings, and donned the entire set, including garters and stockings. It was my fantasy to have my first time with Devin dressed like this. When I picked up the bra, I paused. Should I use the prosthetic? Should I fill the bra, or should I not wear it and let him see me for who I really am? I left the bra on the dresser. I was going to show him the real me, no surprises, me with one breast. I stood in front of the mirror looking at the imbalance in my reflection, at the scar I had instead of a breast, and then I remembered how Mr. Goldsole had told me to look in the mirror and learn to love myself. I looked, and I liked what I saw. I liked me. Sure, there are imperfections, but everyone has imperfections of some kind, and I accept mine.

"I'd make love to me if I were him." I said out loud to my reflection.

I walked back into the living room, feeling a bit naughty and very vulnerable. He glanced up at me and then did a double take. "Oh, my God!"

"Devin, how about you follow me back to the bedroom?"

He didn't say a word. He got up and took my hand, and I led him into the bedroom.

And there I took control. I unbuttoned his shirt and pulled it off, then took off the layers of winter clothing we all wear underneath, until he was standing there in his black briefs. Sexy. Then I took his left hand and placed it on my scar. "I want you to feel this," I said. "I want you to be on familiar terms with who I really am. I've had breast cancer. This shouldn't seem ugly to you. It's part of who I am. I also want you to know that I'm not fragile. Touching me here doesn't hurt, so don't be afraid."

I watched him look me over carefully, and I could see by the rise in his briefs that he wasn't turned off. I kissed him passionately, as I had imagined doing, and he put his hands around my neck and kissed me back. I wanted this. I wanted to have this younger man make love to me. I felt that somehow it would validate me, that it would give me a strong life force.

Then I pushed him onto the bed and straddled him. I kissed his chest and teased him, making him believe I was going all the way down, but at his waistband I made a track back up to his lips with my tongue. I had never taken control like this before, and it was him that was trembling, not me. I took off one of my stockings and bound his hands to the headboard. Then I pulled his briefs off and let him out. I dressed his little fellow with a rubber that I'd bought especially for this occasion. I had cancer, true, but I sure as hell didn't need to catch anything else that could make my life ugly.

There is so much power in the human touch. I didn't surrender anything to him. I gave him admission to the best ride he's ever had up to that point in his life. I didn't want him to love me anymore. I just wanted his attention, and maybe he needed someone to hold on to. Ever since the cancer resurfaced, my feelings toward him have lessened. I understood my loneliness and my yearning to make love to him, but I wasn't in love with him. And the more we touched, the more we explored each other, the more I came to understand how temporary he was to me. But in that same short-term love lay an adventurous sensual fire fueled by our desire. That very desire was akin to need, and I believed that it was essential for me to give my best.

One thing was certain. He was never going to pull that shit on me again like he did last night, when he asked if we could end the evening and then he left. He would be back. I would be the one who decided if the evening was at an end or not from now on.

DECEMBER 4TH

B ecky took me to the office of Dr. Bach (my oncologist) today to discuss my prognosis. He gave me a short examination, then excused himself for a moment. I was trembling, my fear growing into panic. I could control it, but only barely. I wanted to run, but run to what, to where? Becky held my hand, and when Dr. Bach retuned, he introduced me to my future. My new reality.

"Hope, listen carefully," he said. "After going over the test results, biopsies, scans, and so on, the collective information is hard to report. As you know from your previous bout with breast cancer, cancer cells grow and divide chaotically. As a result, they can form tumors. As a tumor grows, it can invade other tissues and organs."

"I don't remember it exactly that way," I told him, "but what you say makes sense. To be honest, I've put almost anything I've learned about cancer out of my head. But go on."

Becky just sat there quietly. She was so good, she just held my hand with one hand and with the other she rubbed my back. It helped keep me more or less calm.

"Yes," the doctor said, "well, portions of a tumor, or tumors in this case, can also break free and enter the blood stream or lymphatic system. Once it has access to either of these, the cancer can be transported from the primary site to the lymph nodes or other organs, where they can form new tumors."

"Are you telling me that the cancer has spread?" I asked him.

"Unfortunately, yes, I am. Luckily, the symptoms are minimal."

"So, I don't have just ovarian cancer then?"

"No. It's not that simple."

Of course I cried. My worst fear had just materialized. Becky whispered sweet, tender words in my ear.

Dr. Bach began again. "Let me explain the treatments available to you—"

I interrupted him right there. "No, Dr. Bach. There won't be any treatment this time. Last time, the treatment was worse than the illness. I think I'll refuse treatment this time."

"Hope, don't you want to fight for your life?" Becky asked. "Don't you want to live?"

"Yes," I told her, and the doctor, too. "Yes, I want to live, and I want to live my last days in the best health I can so that I'm able to enjoy the little things in life. If I take the treatments…

well, you know what that was like for me, you were there, you saw what the chemo, radiation, and cancer drugs did to me, to my quality of life. If I go for treatment again, my days will be filled with appointments and illness, not to mention the costs that reach further than my bank account. I won't bankrupt my family. No matter what, the outcome will be my death. I know the treatment will make me sick and I'll spend most of my time in bed, dying, anyway. I want to live to the fullest life I can in the short time I have left."

Becky turned to Dr. Bach. "Doctor, tell her! Persuade her that the treatment will save her. Tell her there's a chance to overcome this new cancer." She was practically crying.

"It's my professional obligation to explain the options to her," he replied in a mild, professional voice. "And I'm obligated to attempt to do all I can to save her life. That is what I am supposed to do as a physician. But as a human who cares just as much about people as the M.D. in me...well, I must agree with Hope. Her cancer has spread and the chance of us getting it under control is very, very slim. We could prolong the inevitable, but while we're prolonging her life, she will be very ill from the treatment. Knowing how hard the treatment was on her last time, I strongly doubt that she will respond differently this time. Like Hope said, the outcome will most likely be the end of her life."

As Becky began crying, he turned to me, "I respect your decision, Hope, and I will support you all I can. I want to make you comfortable, whether it be psychological, physical, or spiritual, or all the above. I have resources for services in all those areas. When the time comes, I have information for hospice care."

"Hospice?" Becky looked at him. "Blast yourself, Doctor. She's not dying! Look at her. She looks as healthy as I've ever seen her. This is a nightmare! Somebody wake me up. This isn't happening. This is the worst croak sheet I've ever heard of. I'm not going to sit here and listen to the two of you reserve a home for Hope in marble city. You two are giving me the snakes! It's gonna take a lotta giggle water to lift me out of this conversation. Jeepers!"

"Becky," I said, "it's okay, I had a suspicion I'd be facing this."

Somehow, in some deep place in my mind, I knew this day was coming. My dreams, my sixth sense—haven't they been pointing to this day? I've been afraid of it for a long time, so it was good to finally hear the news, to no longer just suspect it, but to confirm it. I wasn't happy to hear it, of course. In fact, I was in shock. My mind drifted out of the exam room and I somehow found myself back in time, back when I was a young girl.

Becky and I met when we were in grade school. I was always excited to get back to school in the fall. School was fun for me. Becky lived not far from me, and so we walked to school together all the time. I showed her my Scooby-Doo lunchbox, and she let me read her Captain America comics. That's how we met. She was such a tomboy. I suppose that's what happens when you've got three doting big brothers. She and I walked to school all by ourselves, safely. This was at a time in our country before everyone was so afraid all the time of predators.

I didn't know back then that Becky and I would be best friends for…well, for the rest of my life.

Becky's parents were what my granddad called hippies. They loved the Beatles and said "groovy" a lot. Her dad drove a '69 Charger and her mother a '67 VW Bug that they had painted with spray paint in tie-dye patterns. I loved that car! It was, like, the grooviest car in town. Her mom was cool, too. She always smelled like spices, primarily sandalwood, cloves, and cinnamon. She was the one who inspired me to be an organic farmer.

My grandparents were just plain old country folk. They listened to George Jones, Tammy Wynette, Loretta Lynn, Merle Haggard, and all the rest. Yes, Becky and I came from vastly different worlds, but our realities melded very well. When Elvis died, Becky and I were together and comforted each other. Three years later, when John Lennon was shot, I spent two days at Becky's home. Becky and her family took his death very hard. As high-schoolers, I think she and I were too immature to quite understand it all, but we knew that the world would be very different without Elvis and John in it.

When Becky turned sixteen, her dad and her brothers built up a 1971 Plymouth Duster for her to drive. It had a 383 six-pack (whatever that means) with a four speed, and she knew how to drive it. All the boys at school wanted to get know her, partly because of the car, partly because of Becky's chest, hers being bigger than mine. High school for me was a whole lot more fun with Becky and the Duster, which was jet black with thin, blood-red pinstripes in the Von Dutch style that ran down the edges of the fenders and then blossomed on the hood and trunk. It had a black interior and a cassette stereo that she often used for jamming to the Doors. I don't think Becky could ever get enough of Jim Morrison. His posters were plastered all over the walls of her room. He'd died when she was only nine, but somehow in her mind, she still thought she would meet him some day.

We went to our senior prom in her Duster. Ian Henderson asked me to go, and I said yes on one condition: that we go with Becky and her date in the Duster. Dale, her future husband, had asked her, but she told him on the same condition, that they go in the Duster. Becky drove, she never let anyone drive her car, and I was in the back seat with Ian, and she was in the driver's seat with Dale in the passenger seat. He didn't mind that.

We went to the dance and had a wonderful time, but afterward we had some more unconventional fun. While most of the students went out drinking or getting laid, we drove out to County Road 50, where the drag racers hung out on the weekends. There we were, in our prom dresses and the boys in their tuxes cheering Becky on as she raced for twenty, thirty, sometimes even fifty bucks a race. I bet she raced at least a dozen times that night. She won almost all the races. The girls were jealous of her, and all of the boys wanted her for their girlfriend. Yeah. Those were good times.

Those memories buffered what the doctor was telling me. And, you know, I let myself focus on those memories instead of the cancer. I think Becky was upset with me because I didn't take it as hard as she thought I should have.

"Are you going to tell Colt and the kids?" she asked me.

"Yes, I am. But not until the time is right."

"I respect that." she said. (What is this, I wonder, with everyone saying they respect what I've decided to do?) "Let's blow this joint," Becky said, "and find a gargle factory or a smoke house. My knowledge box has sprung a bearing. Where do you want my riding rubber to drop you? This boy's vomit on the table stinks. Do you still want me to take you back to the chop house?"

"Work?" I said. "Heavens, no! I want to go to your mom's house. I want to listen to the Doors. I want to sit with you and just be with you. You're my best friend and I want to just be with my best friend right now. Can we do that?"

"Sounds like a plan," she said. "That fits the beat of this groove…let's bounce."

Becky, I thought, *I need my true friend right now, complete with all hipster banter.* I gave her a grin with watery eyes and we left.

When we got to Becky's parents' house, I had to laugh. There in her mother's driveway was a new turbo VW Bug painted in the old tie-dye design. It was very hip, but in a modern way. As soon as we got in the door, Becky's mom gave me a hug. I let her hold me for a long moment and breathed in the smell of cinnamon that seemed to sweat through her pores. I swear that scent is the essence of love.

She had come to the door in her bare feet, tie-dye dress, and long, flowing, gray hair. "What a gas it is; you've come to visit." she said as she opened her house to me. Becky's mother is in her late seventies now, but she is still so cool. She wears round sunglasses, like Janice Joplin did, and peace sign jewelry and smokes a joint every now and then. "I haven't seen you since..., well, gee how long has it been?"

"Whatever it's been," I said, "it's been too long."

"Come in! Come in and make your self comfortable. Jimmy's gone out and I'm here all alone. Still smiling, she turned to Becky then slid her sunglasses down to the end of her nose. "Becky, I can tell by the look in your eyes that something's wrong.... What is it?"

"Let me tell you." I said. When I began to tell her about our discussion with Dr. Bach, she put her hands over her ears as if to say, *No I'm not hearing this.* But she listened, anyway, without saying a word till I finished.

"You poor girl," she said, and I could see her tearing up. "I know this news hurts my Becky to the core. She loves you, you know."

"I know," I said putting my arm around Becky and kissing her cheek.

"I'm honored," her mom said, "that you came to see me after news like this. How can I help you?"

I told her about wanting to hear Jim Morrison and how I felt such a strong need to spend time with her and Becky.

Her eyes lit up. "I know just what we need!" She was only too eager to run the needle through some old Doors vinyl. While the records were playing, she rolled a hefty, tight joint, lit it, and passed it around. I don't drink, nor do I partake of any kind of drugs, but at that moment, I felt like a toke was exactly what I needed. It relaxed my confused mind and put Becky at ease, too.

I've been losing sight of who I am. I keep feeling like there's a noose around my neck, especially at work, that's choking my dreams out of me and leaving me struggling to breathe. What I needed today was a breath of life. The THC was helping to erase that anxiety.

I certainly didn't feel as sick as my prognosis might suggest. The smoke played around the room, and my mind seemed to float up to the ceiling as I watched Becky's mom laughing and dancing her groovy dance to the Doors. I knew she was doing it not because she was happy, but because I was sad, and she wanted to cheer me up.

Well, it worked.

"Jim is so dreamy," Becky's mom said.

"The most sexy man to ever live," her daughter said.

"Oh, no," her mom argued. "The most sexy man was and still is Robert Plant. I can't even drive my car if Led Zeppelin is playing. Plant's voice is more dangerous than drinking and driving."

"Now, girls," I drew in another big toke, "let's not argue over our men."

"Who's your dream daddy?" Becky asked.

"I thought you'd know. My best friend should know who my fantasy man is."

She shook her head. "Shake up your business and pour it out for us to see."

"Well," I began, "Jim Morrison is too much like a god, he's unreachable. Robert Plant? He's pretty hot, I admit. But I've always seen myself wrapped in the arms of Sam Elliot or

Chris LeDoux." I lifted my hands into the air in a gesture of surrender. "I know those cowboys aren't from the era you two are talking about, or even in the same realm of existence, but a man in faded jeans who can ride a horse and work a rope makes me go all flush. I'm a romantic. What can I say?"

"A romantic? Really? That's your fantasy guy? *A cowboy?*" I could hear the surprise in Becky's voice. For once, she was speaking in plain English.

"Why not?" I replied.

"A cowboy! Hell, Hope, you have one of those already! And he even sings in a band. For god's sakes woman, you have the Marlboro Man at home! Besides, you don't want to listen to me comparing Colt to the sexiest man that ever lived, who is Jim Morrison. I could see Jim and me in a room taking some kind of mind-altering drug and then me letting him do things to me that I can't even imagine. Out-of-this-world-type stuff."

"I saw him once," her mom said. "I saw him in the nude, and I will tell you two girls, Becky has chosen well. If my memory serves correctly, he was hung just right." She inhaled again. "Just right. Let's just say that he had *the tool for the job.*"

"What!" Becky screamed. "I've known you all of my life and you never saw Jim Morrison of the Doors naked. Why the fib? What are you talking about, old woman!"

"I did so see Jim naked. Your father and I left you and your brothers with your grandparents so we could drive to San Francisco to see the Doors in concert at the Winterland Arena in December of '67. Now that's a trip, driving a VW Bug in the winter from here to San Francisco. We froze our asses off, but, damn, we had a blast. I don't think the promoters knew how heavy the Doors were at the time. So many people showed up for that gig. Man, there were people everywhere. It was freaky."

"Mom," said Becky, "just get to the part about Jim being naked. And why haven't you ever told me about this before?"

"I knew how crazy you were about him. I didn't want you to get jealous."

Becky rolled her eyes. "Oh, brother."

"Anyway," her mom said, "after the show, the people who couldn't get in were still outside, so we walked into this huge mass of people doing the free love thing, even in the cold. Your dad and I wandered around, sharing puffs off the doobies and so on. We got lost. We were nowhere near the Bug. Then some dude saw us and asked us if we had any acid on us. We told him to be cool, we didn't know if he was a dick, or what." She grinned at me. "Meaning an undercover detective, not a penis." She laughed and laughed, then went on. "So when we felt that the dude was cool, we went with him. Turns out he was with the Doors. A promoter or something, and he took us to where the crew was staying. Jim was there on one of the beds with no clothes on and enjoying some girl."

"That's it?" Becky cried.

"Well, isn't that enough? Okay, I saw that he was erect, if that's what you want to know. Had it been Robert Plant, I would have run over and jumped on him! Is that what you wanted to hear?"

And that's why I love Becky's family. They make me laugh, and laugh often. I knew her mother wouldn't disappoint me. She said all the right words, did all the right things, and smelled the right way. Oh, how I needed that. She isn't my granddad, but she'll do in a pinch.

Then the record came to a new song, "The End," and our mood changed. We felt the seriousness. That song has some gravity to it. Becky's mom looked uncomfortable. Then she proceeded to tell me how she didn't enjoy this song much because it reminded her of the war and her son.

She was born in 1934, married her husband, Jimmy, in 1950, and a week later he was shipped off to Korea. She was scared that she'd never see him again, but he made it home. However, when Becky's dad returned from Korea he was disabled. Not physically, but mentally. I had never realized that until Becky's mom told me today. Jimmy is functional but suffers from a nervous disorder; I guess today we'd call it PTSD. Because he is functional I never suspected it, and was sad to learn about it. It was difficult for the family to deal with. It was because of her hatred of war, all wars, really, and what that war had done to Jimmy that Becky's mom became an activist. Even though she was in her thirties at a time when most activists were much younger, she was right there standing tall for her beliefs.

She explained how the sixties was a fearful time and that she and Jimmy felt they had to do something about the U.S. involvement in Vietnam. Becoming activists came almost naturally to them. And then, in 1968 her eldest son turned eighteen; was drafted; and in 1969, killed in a night ambush. All that's left of him are some pictures and a folded flag that still rests on her mantel.

"It seems like life is always dangerous," she said in a sober voice. "There's always a threat. A threat just sitting and waiting to spring at you. Like you, Hope, I've never felt safe. Our life is beautiful at times, but then it can turn into the worst thing ever. We have to recognize and relish the best moments and also work to survive through the worst moments."

Even though we were high, I heard what she was saying. I agreed with her. We must recognize all the moments in our lives and be present in them. Celebrate the good ones and defend ourselves and the ones we love against the bad ones.

DECEMBER 5TH

A fresh blanket of snow greeted us this morning. It was delightful to see my little town covered by a huge white quilt of snow. Of course I had trouble getting to work. I had to shovel my car out (well, actually, Colt did it for me) and buck my way down the side roads with my front bumper until I got to the main streets that were plowed and glazed with a combination of salt and gravel.

I like adverse weather. It gives people something in common to bitch about so we don't complain about each other. And snow hides the ugliness of the manmade litter under a beautiful white blanket. This time of year it reminds me of candy canes, giggling children, beautifully wrapped presents, and, of course, decorated trees.

When I walked into the office, I noticed immediately how lackluster the place always looks. Same old, same old. Four years ago, someone in a corner office made the decision that we could no longer decorate for Christmas. *It sends the wrong message to our investors,* the suits said, *some of whom are foreign and don't celebrate Christmas.* Like our foreign investors ever visit this crumby place. But, as a consequence, now we all look like robots without emotions or celebrations.

Where I work reflected how I felt after my trip with Becky to Dr. Bach's office. I felt stripped of being in control of anything, especially my emotions. But on a deeper level I wanted, no, I needed to see color—bright lights, colorful bulbs on trees, shiny reds and greens, tinsel, men in Santa suits, department stores with display windows full of festive themes and people telling each other, *Merry Christmas.* I didn't want to hear about being politically correct or incorrect or worry about how any investor felt. *Invest in the human soul!* That's what I wanted to yell from our rooftop.

I didn't, though. I just walked in and made my way to my cubicle. Devin was there. He smiled at me and I smiled back. I entered more data into the project for Jerome, but I was gritting my teeth because I loathe the man. When lunchtime finally came around, I couldn't get out of there fast enough. I put on my knee-high boots and walked through the snow to the cathedral. I didn't go in this time. I stood out by the tree and prayed. I was hoping to see Mr. Goldsole, but he was nowhere in sight, and I felt the disappointment grow within me. My bottom lip started trembling, and I didn't know why.

Big clumps of snow fell out of the tree and piled up on the ground. The nativity scene by the door, half hidden in the virgin snow, looked like it was frosted. It was noticeably quiet there, and I felt my soul, the deeper part of me, listening to the sounds of nature around me. Pretty soon, I understood that Mr. Goldsole was near.

And, sure enough, he walked around the corner. "Hello, Chief," he said.

I turned and saw him through the tears in my eyes. He was in his same, old, long coat, his suit, his brown shoes, and his hat. Not really an outfit for walking in the snow.

"Why the tears?" he asked.

"Tears?" I said. "I have no tears. I guess the wind's blown something into my eye."

He looked around. "There's no wind today, Hope."

"Oh. I guess there isn't."

"What are you doing out here by the tree?" he asked. "Don't you usually go inside?"

"Not today," I said. "I was looking for you."

He smiled and wrapped his arms around me. "Do you want to tell me about it?"

"Not really." I looked into his brown eyes that seemed to sparkle like the stars. "I want to talk about the snow," I said. "And the time of year. And love and life."

"Oh, yes, the snow," he said. "It is quite beautiful. This is the time of year when the cheer should be felt by everyone. Yet this time of year has a way of making some people feel absolutely cheerless."

Something occurred to me. "Mr. Goldsole, do you think my grandparents became angels?"

"No, Chief. I don't think they did. Angels are angels, and your grandparents were human beings, not angels. I'm not saying your grandparents aren't good people, but people don't become angels."

I thought about that for a minute. It made sense to me.

"Why did you ask me that?" he asked.

"You know, I see them in my dreams. I thought maybe they were my angels, that they keep coming to me to give me messages."

He considered that for a minute. "I think perhaps your grandparents are your sprit guides," he said. "When people die, their souls become free from the human body. We say 'dead,' but the soul lives on. We live on after all of what we call life is over. And you're right—we do have angels that watch over us. But we also have spirit guides. Most adults don't see angels, though children see them quite often. They have a better heavenly connection, I suppose."

"When I have a dream abut my grandparents and they tell me things," I said, "should I put more effort into remembering what they say? Are they giving me messages?"

He answered my question with another question. "What are we here on this earth for?"

I don't know. I shrugged my shoulders.

"To gather information," he said. "We are elaborate recording devices. We record everything we see, hear, touch, smell, taste, and experience. We interact and process that information as it is being recorded with our emotions. We share the information with a collective intelligence. Our dreams hold valuable information. I would suggest that you take some time to ponder your dream and process the information in it."

I had to frown a little bit. "We are processing data and we download that data into a mainframe. Like work? Is that what you're saying?"

"Not exactly, Chief. You are part of a collective intelligence. You, Hope, have a purpose greater than merely living in this life. When your time comes, like your grandparents, you will find that your life was very basic compared to what comes next. And what I'm saying is that your grandparents will communicate with you in whatever way you will accept it. It appears that you accept their communication in the form of dreams."

I stood there in the snow and cold and thought about what he was saying. I didn't want to debate with him. I wanted to see life from his perspective. "So...if I were comfortable with communicating with my grandparents as ghosts, they would appear to me as apparitions?"

"Sure. If you identified with Mother Mary, she would come to you, or if you identified with Christ, he would come to you. You see, the spiritual universe communicates on a level that is comfortable for you. So if you don't have the preconceived notion that ghosts are scary, you might see a ghost instead of seeing your grandparents in your dreams. But in this culture, ghosts are considered something to fear, so most of them don't communicate on that level. It didn't used to be that way. In ancient times, a spirit could manifest itself and communicate openly with the living. In those days, people considered a visitation a good omen."

"It's funny how things change.

"It sure is. Something considered a blessing from God in one era will be considered a curse by the Devil in another."

I nodded. "Remember when you told me about a goddess?"

He nodded. "I do."

"Do you believe she exists?"

He nodded again. "I do. I pray to her as much as I pray to my god."

"She understands menopause and growing old, right?"

He chuckled. "Yes, I suppose she does."

I had to tell him. "Mr. Goldsole, the cancer is back. It's spread. The prognosis isn't good. I was wondering if she would take a moment and listen to me. Do you think she might help me?"

He gave me a squeeze and held me close and I cried into his shoulder. Yes, I did. As I'm writing this, I feel a little embarrassed about it, but I did cry on his shoulder. And it felt good. It felt good to have him there holding me.

He was patient with me and held me while I let it all out. "You know, Chief," he said after a while, "she is who I pray to.

She is who I consider one of my focal points in the spiritual realm. She may not be who you're comfortable with. Hope, you pray to whomever you feel comfortable praying to, and whoever you pray to probably won't be able to change the prognosis. But your soul and the universe can definitely help you deal with it."

"You know," I said, "it's not me who prompted all this. It's my soul. She's the one who brought me out here to find you."

He smiled. "She almost sounds demanding."

"Oh, she can be, but she gets that from me, I suppose."

His arms around me felt wonderful; and standing in the snow was unreal because when I peeked over his shoulder, I didn't see anyone. The park, the whole town, seemed to be motionless. Frozen, like a frame in a movie. There was no one in sight, nothing moving except for smoke rising from the chimneys of people's homes. I guess the cold and snow were keeping everyone inside close to their fireplaces and hot beverages. That's okay, though, because I wouldn't have wanted it any other way. His warm hug. My face buried in his shoulder. And he smelled like cookies baking in the oven, fresh chocolate chip cookies.

Cancer is like a wave or particle that comes from miles away. It picked me out from everyone else. It hit my body like a bolt of lightning. It's devastating and it has the capability of taking my passion for living out of me. It's scary, and sometimes it feels like I'm walking alone through the darkest tunnel. And there are times when the fear causes my mind to lose control. Cancer is not transmittable. It's not viral or bacterial like a contagion, so I can't say I caught it like I'd catch a cold. I can't say I should have taken my vitamins or should have used antibacterial soap. Cancer is devious. It seems to choose a person, and when it does, it becomes an enemy that takes over your cells and turns them against your body. So now I have cells that are out of control recruiting other cells at an unforeseen rate, building up an army with, well, nuclear weapons of mass destruction. There is no escape.

"This feels like a vicious joke," I said aloud.

"Yes," he said. "I can see where the news of something so dreadful could appear that way."

"I'm afraid! I don't want to die."

He continued to hold me, and soon he spoke again in a gentle voice. "You have established a relationship with your soul at a very important time in your life. You've embraced the opportunity to connect your body with your soul."

"I do find it comforting," I admitted. "Just knowing that it exists helps me feel complete."

"With your soul, dying needn't be so scary," he said. "The image you have of dying isn't the same as the real experience of dying. There is a vast difference between what we observe when someone close to us dies, and the actual feeling that comes to us when we ourselves die."

"Why is that?" I asked. "Shouldn't I be able to rely on my past experiences to inform me of what to expect in the future?"

"It's culture," he said. "You live in a time where the common culture fears death. It denies death. The popular focus is on youth. The dying experience is characterized as victimization, as if we are the victims of death, as if death is taking something away from us. The only thing people are victims of regarding death is the superficial, distorted, outlook toward dying. Now that is tragic."

"So it's possible to change my attitude toward the inevitable? At some point I can relax and not feel so scared?"

"One can look at dying as a process," he said. "Biologically speaking, the body comes to an end. Every body comes to its natural end. It's natural, it's expected. That's a small way to look at death. In life we find things, lose things, break things, establish new life within our lives. Dying is basically the same thing. We are ending the old way of existing and being born to a new way of existing. You see, our bodies know how to die. They've been programmed to do so, and it's nothing evil or sinister. It's routine. Two very important events happen to everyone. Without exception, we are born and we die. I say both events are more than physical. To me, they are divine events."

"How can I think something as common as being born as routine, like you said, as death? How can either one be routine?"

"Because neither event can happen without something greater than mankind being involved," he said. "Don't take either birth or death for granted, Hope. No child comes to this earth without a fingerprint of the Great Artist on him or her. And no one dies without another fingerprint."

"Fingerprint?"

"Yes." He saw I wasn't getting it yet, so he added, "Think of DNA and RNA. We say they are unique to the individual like a fingerprint. Yet, it's more like the finger of the Great Artist places the DNA and RNA within the individual."

As I thought about his words, I could feel my soul acknowledging them and endorsing them as true.

"Death and dying are very different things," he continued. "Dying happens here on earth. You observed it when your parents' lives and again when your grandparents' lives came to their ends. However, the real death is unknown to us. All we see of death is a motionless person lying there in a casket. I can tell you that death should be known as a new beginning, not an end."

"You make it sound like a vacation," I said. "Something to look forward to."

"Not exactly," he said. "I'm hoping to extinguish your fear of death. Death is good. It's the natural progression for all of us, but you shouldn't let it stop you from living. Whether you are afraid of dying or look forward to it, it shouldn't distract you from living your life."

I had to shake my head. "Words. This all comes down to words. Death. Dying. Living. I should accept that I will die and that death is a celestial experience, but before I worry about any of that, I should concern myself with living. Is that right?" I asked.

"Yes. While you're here, live your life to the best of your ability. Take on the attitude that every day is your last day and ask yourself, *Have I lived today to the best of my ability?*"

"How do I reach this mindset? How do I convince myself that my death will be a good thing?"

"Think about what you've been taught in this culture," he said. "You've hardly been taught how to deal with the death of your body. Also, little has been taught about how to live, I mean really live. You, like many others, have been taught that the body is some kind of tool, a slave, a suit of clothes, something to rise above. Your body is forced to live the life that your mind has decided it wants it to live. I'm not surprised that you're afraid to die. Your mind is afraid, not only because it fears the unknown, but because it's losing its vehicle. The body that has housed and transported your mind will come to an end, so logically you want it to survive."

"Yes," I said. "Logically, a mind needs a body to complete itself. I understand what you're saying. I see the mind and body as one, and you're saying the mind and soul work together, and the body is just a constituent for a certain period of time."

He smiled at me. "Chief, you do understand!"

"I'm not so dumb after all."

"But don't forget about living before you die," he reminded me. "We are conditioned to avoid death to the point that we live partial lives. We stress about premature ageing, feel guilty about what we eat, feel angry because we put on a few pounds, deny how old we really are, and fear what will happen when our time is over. All of this is unnecessary because it robs us of living. Liberate yourself! Eat what you like, do what makes you feel good, and (most important) do what makes you feel that you have shared love."

"Love?"

"The greatest gift anyone person can give to another person, animal, plant, any living thing. *Love.* Its power is timeless and powerful. It takes the whole of you to give it or accept it."

"What do you mean the *whole of me* to give it or accept it?"

"Love is given only through a combination of our free will (conscious mind) and our soul's desire to express it. It takes the same kind of effort to hate as it does to love."

Our conversation felt like it lasted for hours, yet in actual time, it was relatively brief. In that short time, I came to understand what he was telling me and, within my soul, I was further confirming my trust in him and his words. Even though he is a small man physically, his energy is larger than that of any other person I've ever met. Mr. Goldsole helps ground me to this earth, to this reality. He helps me to see things more positively. At the same time, he elevates my mind to lofty places where I get a peek at the holy universe. Somehow, in a mysterious way, he gives me strength.

Thank you, Mr. Goldsole.

DECEMBER 6TH

Quint and I had lunch together again today. She picked me up in her perfectly restored 1958 Cadillac. That car is an honest work of art—pearl ivory, beautifully streamlined, all the chrome and the big grill like a shark's mouth. It's a heavy car that pushes through snow and ice like an army tank with white-walled tires. The interior is lipstick-red leather with modern heated seats that are warm and comfortable.

"Wow, what a ride!" I said. "I'm surprised you'd take something like this out on a winter day."

"Three hundred-sixty-five cubic inches of beast," Quint said. I could hear the pride in her voice. "Nothing can stop her. She's built to be driven, not to be stored away in a garage or to be driven only on the summer days. I'm a practical gal. I don't buy something only to look at it."

"Well," I said, patting the leather, "She's a beauty."

"You should have seen this car when my husband and I bought her. She was a pile of parts. You couldn't even tell what it was. My husband and I took each piece and cleaned, replaced, and/or restored it. This Caddie is what saved my marriage. I tell you, Hope, this car was pure therapy."

"How so?"

"Remember when I told you I almost got a divorce from my husband?"

"I do."

"Well, at the time we bought this car, my husband and I weren't even sleeping in the same bed. He was in our bedroom and I had moved into one of our kids' rooms. She was grown up and had moved out. My husband and I decided we wanted to do something together to see if we could make our marriage work. We discussed going on a trip somewhere, then we thought about maybe hiking the Appalachian Trail."

"Travel or hiking both sound like good options," I said. "Why didn't you try one of those first?"

She turned onto Evergreen Street and she had my attention. The similarities of her marital problems freaked me out. Could it be possible what was happening between Colt and I was so common?

"We didn't think we would be able to hold long discussions about our marriage and other issues while we were hiking. We'd run out of breath. We were also afraid if we went on a trip, we would treat it like a vacation rather than a means of rescuing our marriage. So we bought a pile of junk and invested our time, money, and love in rebuilding this car. It was fun! It was soulful work, putting this car back together. My husband and I came together every night after work and on the weekends, getting our hands dirty, cleaning parts, fabricating the parts we couldn't buy, and all the while communicating from our hearts. The result is this piece of Americana."

"I like your idea of building a car for therapy," I told her. "That isn't thinking out of the box -that's thinking outside of the warehouse that stores all of the boxes!"

"It worked like a charm," she said as we both laughed. "We fell in love all over again in our garage. I rediscovered my soul mate, not in some clean office with a marriage counselor but in the garage, in the piles of bits and pieces and the dirt and grime of this old car. I wouldn't have had it any other way. We built a classic and practical car for our needs.

"My husband is an engineer," she continued, "and I don't know a thing about mechanics. Or didn't. But he took his time and taught me. That's why I can tell you the engine size, the horsepower, the torque. We built it and dyno-tested it. After the engine block came back from the machine shop, I slid the pistons in one by one. I helped put on the dual-carb manifold as well as the new shiny carburetors. I'm not joking or exaggerating. We put everything in this car together and we did it properly."

"I love it," I said.

She could have bought this car and paid for it to be built. I had already crunched the numbers for her company, so I knew what kind of money she made (an astounding number), not including her husband's income. Quint is a wealthy woman, but like she said, she's also a practical gal and her personality is the kind that would rather build a classic car than buy one. Good for her.

No, Quint isn't some rich chick with deep pockets who likes to show off what she could buy. She isn't anything like Jerome with his $5,000 suits. She's an old-fashioned girl, genuine, and true to her word, one who got in with the grease and workings of things to understand better how they worked.

As we drove along, I looked at her and realized she is just as beautiful as the car she was driving. Her beauty is natural. She doesn't wear makeup, and her short, chopped, gray hair is thick and full of attitude. Her eyes are sky blue and she was blessed with high cheekbones. She doesn't make any attempt to hide her age. To her, age seems to be something to be proud of. Her age gives her strength. She doesn't see it as weakness. She isn't thin, but she carries herself with such confidence that she could be severely obese and her beauty would still shine right through. The wrinkles in her face (not that there are many) accent her features. What an on-looker sees is a wonderful human being.

I'll be honest, though. Looking at her, I began to feel angry with myself for giving Jerome any information that would harm her. Guilty! How could I hurt such an honest, hard working, positive woman? I wanted to come clean, but I didn't think lunch today was the place or the time.

As we drove along, her expression changed from amused to serious. "We replaced so many things on this car," she said, "that the question has to be raised: Can we really call this a 1958 Cadillac? I mean this is hardly the same car GM put out in 1958." She had a sense of gravity as she spoke. She pulled the big car into a parking space. "I'll bet you know people that are like my Caddie."

We walked into the restaurant and took a booth with a window that looked out over the river. "I'm not sure what you mean," I said.

"You know. People that live an average life style and then they find they aren't comfortable with being average anymore. They need more. So they set their sights on more money, and they start to change who they are to achieve their goals. They change so much that they aren't themselves anymore. It's like this Cadillac. We changed so many parts that we began to wonder if the car is really what it was to begin with."

My stomach did a flip-flop as she said that. We weren't just talking about her car anymore. We were talking about me? I wasn't sure. Does she know about my deal with Jerome? Does she know about the $100,000 check and my condo?

"You know," she was saying, "the kind who go from wearing jeans, T-shirts, and tennis shoes to expensive suits. They become refined. They add etiquette to their persona. They get all prim and proper. They also change the people they associate with, always looking to better their situation, no matter who they betray. They used to buy drive-thru burgers, but now they brag about being on some fashionable diet like the South Beach and eating expensive and trendy things like exclusive sushi." She was speaking with passion now. "And at some point, Hope, at some point, a person has to ask herself, *has the money changed the core of who I am?* The costume has changed, the bank account has grown, and all the new things being bought have a higher quality indeed. But what about integrity? Does the person have natural integrity? That stuff deep down, the stuff that makes our soul come alive? What about our integrity to our soul?"

I looked down, staring at my menu but not really seeing it. Shit, was she talking about me? I felt my face go flush, as if she had caught me out. What specifically was she talking about? I nodded and hid behind the menu. "Exclusive sushi?" I forced myself to ask.

"Here." She reached over and flipped my menu around. "This might help." I had the damn thing upside down! What a moron I am! "It's very expensive," she said. "Supposed to be delicacy fish. I say it tastes like crap, but that's just me. Anyway," she continued, "my point is that a person has to respect herself enough not to sell out to things she doesn't believe in. Right? How about you? What is your purchase point, Hope?"

"I'm not sure I understand. What are you saying?"

"We all have a purchase point. The point where we're willing to sell our integrity, the point that would make us turn our backs on what we believe to be morally correct."

I gave my head a tiny shake. "I have no idea. I don't believe I've had a proposition to compromise my morals." Liar! Liar! Pants on fire! My mouth was lying, and my soul knew it.

Our waitress came by just then to take our orders. I was hoping the interruption would calm Quint down. We were in the old Jefferson Street Station, an old rail station converted to a restaurant back in the seventies, when the railroad discontinued this route. Off to the side of the restaurant was an old fashioned rail car that had been converted to a large banquet room. I love this old place. It's cool.

I ordered salted-sea bass and a Mountain Dew. Quint opted for cedar-planked salmon and hot herbal tea. Our booth was oak with Naugahyde upholstery, and the table was Formica with scalloped stainless steel trim. There was a bank of phone booths made of solid oak against the back wall, well-preserved, and straight out of the old days when passengers wandered around the depot waiting for their trains. There was even an antique, but still functioning, cigarette machine, the kind a person had to pull the handle out to disperse a pack that dropped onto a stainless steel ramp and slid down for the customer to retrieve. I remember those from when I was little girl, before Granddad stopped smoking. I used to get excited when he let me pull the handle and make the pack drop down.

Quint started again. "I don't think people know their threshold until a proposition has been made. It's those times when the money tempts you and your mind starts spending it before you even have it. You start to imagine a new custom home, another car, travel to Paris, and so on. All the while turning your back on what you believe to be right."

"Quint, you've been going on and on," I broke in. "To be honest, I feel like you're having a conversation with yourself. I don't even know what you're talking about. What's bothering you?" I figured I could cut to the chase and find out what she knows.

"I'm sorry," she said. "My mind is all over the place these days. Do you remember when I told you I was having trouble with a competitor?"

"Yes. You said they threatened you and your family."

"That's right. Well, that same company, I've found out, has been paying some of my employees to give away our company secrets. People I've known for years and believed were my friends. Not just employees. Friends. It hurts to get news like that."

"I suppose it does. I'm sorry to hear that."

"This competitive CEO will not stop until he gets what he wants. He's going after the company. And after me personally. He's paid me another visit and threatened my husband and me again. If I were a man, I'd handle him physically, you know, the proverbial *ass kicking*, that sort of thing. But I'm not a man, and I'm not that kind of person. I don't know how to get him to stop."

"Quint, are you in danger from this guy? Is he really going to harm you or your husband?"

"I don't know. Lately there has been a black SUV parked outside our home at night. Two men sit inside and watch our house. Watch us. They're so obvious about it. They don't try to conceal what they're doing. We've called the police, but every time, they drive off before the police arrive. And the other day, when they drove off they waved at me. I was watching them through the window."

"How do you know this CEO guy is behind the SUV?"

"Because the CEO called my office and told me those men worked for him. He said the nightmare could end if I presented to my shareholders that a buyout would be the best thing for Bio-Sport."

That's when my blood began to boil. Jerome is an awful man, and for him to use intimidation on Quint just twisted me the wrong way. I wanted to come clean with her, to get it off my chest what Brent and Jerome had me doing, but I didn't have the courage. I'm such a coward!

"I'm sorry," she said, "I didn't want to talk about work. How are you doing, health-wise? How's your family?"

"I've been on a roller coaster lately," I admitted, "but I think I have a handle on it now. My doctor tells me it's menopause." Even though I wanted to share my personal life with her, I didn't want to throw out the cancer card, at least not yet. That's my situation, and I want to keep it mine. Private. Besides, menopause is happening to me. It's just being overshadowed at the moment.

"Oh, yeah." She hit the table with an open hand and gave a sigh of relief. "The fear of menopause. I remember that. Is it the end of my youth? The end of my sexuality? The end of my energy? Was I now an *old woman?* I remember the conflict within when—I think I was forty-eight when I went through it, and I kept it a secret, hoping I would slip through it as quietly as possible. My kids didn't act like they even knew me. I felt so alone. Those damn hormones can make a person feel lousy."

"Tell me about it. My kids, too. They walk past me and keep walking like I'm some sort of stranger."

"Actually," she said, "menopause went pretty smooth for me after I went to my doctor, and she told me about estrogen therapy, and I listened to her recommendations. Rather than focusing on the harm hormone replacement therapy might do to me, we focused on the good it could do. My doctor was older than me and had gone through it herself, so she was my pioneer, my champion. I started taking estrogen; I still do, along with the progesterone supplements she prescribed. And now, thirteen, no, fourteen years later, I feel balanced. I've known so many women who struggle with their fears and suffer because they refuse to admit it's happening to them. Why? After all, we have the technology these days to make it easier."

"My doctor and I have been discussing it," I said. "She's doing some tests to see what is compatible with me. Heck, I don't even know what all the tests are she's doing. It's all Greek to me." I tried to laugh it off.

She changed the subject. "Say, how about that ride over the Golden Gate? Have you thought anymore about it?"

"Oh, yes, I have. I look so forward to the summer and riding my bike again. I haven't made any real plans yet, but I think about it a lot. It's an escape to daydream on."

Quint nodded. "It's the sort of thing you can't read about or see pictures of and get the effect," she said. "You have to actually experience it. You have to be there, be in that moment when you hear your soul shout 'Holy shit, this is great!' You know what I mean?"

"I sure do."

"Every day we move with people," she said. "We move through and pass over things people have made. Yet rarely do we move *with people* and through or over things people have created that impress the mind in the way the Golden Gate Bridge does. It's not a spiritual structure, but if I had to attend a church, I would claim the Golden Gate Bridge as my church and I would attend as frequently as possible."

"That's a little extreme." I laughed. "I'm sure your trip was fun and exciting, but a spiritual experience?" Then I felt bad. Quint flushed with embarrassment. Evidently the ride over the bridge *had* been spiritual for her, and she no doubt felt vulnerable sharing her experience with me.

"Well, I guess it was spiritual for me," she said softly.

"I'm sorry, Quint. I was out of line. I didn't mean to laugh or joke about it."

"No worries. I've learned recently that for an experience like riding to the other side of the Golden Gate Bridge to have any value, we must see the value in ourselves. When I did the ride, I felt that I had value. I could visualize that I had value here on this big, beautiful planet. The ride was almost ceremonial for me because as I pedaled, I was aware of each muscle that was engaged to forward my progress and that my forward progress was symbolic of my moving through the sixty-two years of my life. And like the bridge and its scenic views, my lifetime has some breathtaking views in it. I see them as memories. Sixty-two years, I've been a part of this earth, and for sixty-two years I've made an impression on the world around me. Up there, up on that massive bridge, I realized that I've done a lot of good in my lifetime." She leaned forward and looked into my eyes. "But, Hope, don't fool yourself into thinking I'd come to think of this little philosophical exercise on my own. Something had a hand in it. My mind was never the kind to believe in spiritual stuff before. While I was pedaling, my soul connected to God, Goddess, whatever, something greater than I am, so, yeah, it was a spiritual experience for me."

She was glowing. She had overcome her vulnerability with faith. I could see that my friend had faith that her experience was indeed spiritual. I had challenged her faith for a moment, and for that moment she may have doubted it, but after she took a minute to revisit her memory, her faith reclaimed the experience.

Mr. Goldsole had suggested to me that I can live either in faith or in fear. I could see how Quint maintained her faith. I wished I could be as strong as she is. I envied her just then. She is a proud, strong, and confident woman. Again, just like with Mr. Goldsole, I had a sense of familiarity with her. She seemed like the big sister I never had.

"I can understand your experience," I said. "When I'm riding my bike, I feel my soul come to the surface. I feel connected to the world around me. And you know what? I like the feeling of being small in God's eyes, or like you said God, Goddess—my friend Mr. Goldsole calls it the Great Artist, whatever it is that is greater than us. I like knowing that what is beyond my comprehension has taken the time to see me and the little things I do. I, too, see value in them."

"Exactly! Oh, Hope, you have to go and see what's on the other side of the Golden Gate."

I promised her that I would, and she promised that she would get the information from her husband regarding the hotel and the best route to take up and over the bridge.

So lunch was great, the food was exceptional, and then Quint took me back to work. Back at work, I became very depressed as I stared around my dull cubicle. I wanted to get out and go somewhere and think. Why should I stay at work? Why should I even continue to work?

The truth is…I have an exit plan. I will do Jerome's bidding and collect as much money from him as I can so I can leave my family with something other than a funeral. But I will also figure out how to do his bidding without hurting Quint. Is that possible? Am I being a fool? I will keep working for Brent for the medical insurance. But at some point, I will leave this all behind and go out to enjoy life before my death arrives. Yes, my exit plan includes a trip to San Francisco.

DECEMBER 7TH

I was a little afraid about dinner tonight. Cleo had mailed actual invitations to Colt and me to meet her and Ward for an early dinner at the Hunter's Steak Pursuit restaurant off of Sycamore Street. When Colt asked me what the dinner was all about, I confessed that I had no idea. But I was afraid. (My default emotion is fear.) My head was in a terrible place. I was thinking, What if Cleo had something bad to tell us and this dinner was her way of breaking the bad news to us? Yet, Colt, ever the optimist, figured it was just that Ward was going to propose marriage.

We arrived at the restaurant and were escorted to the table where Cleo and Ward were sitting. They both were dressed rather nicely, but this restaurant is a little upscale, so Colt was wearing a dress shirt, new Wranglers, and his good hat.

The waiter handed us our menus, then left us alone.

"So, Cleo, what's going on?" I asked because I couldn't bear to wait any longer.

"Oh, nothing," she said airily, "it's just so hard to coordinate everyone getting together, so I thought it would be nice if we had dinner together."

Oh, no, she didn't! Did my daughter just lie to me? She did. I know her well enough to know when she's lying. But I played along. "Well, honey, we could have had a nice dinner at home. All you had to do was ask. This place is a bit pricy."

Colt interrupted me. "Babe, this is good," he said. "We never go out anymore. I'm glad Cleo invited us here."

Ward had a look of pure apprehension. Colt was sitting closest to him, but I think the boy—the young man had expected me to sit next to him. He didn't say a word; not one word. He only nodded when someone asked him something. It was only after we had eaten our salads and we were working on our entrees that I found out what this meeting was really for.

"Mom, Dad," Cleo began nervously, "Ward and I are going to have a baby!" She smiled while I choked on my chicken.

No one spoke for a moment. The silence was painful.

"I've wanted to tell you since Thanksgiving," she said, "when Aunt Agnes made the comments about me gaining weight and my skin."

I blinked, realizing the truth had been right in front of me the whole time, but I've been so wrapped up in my own problems that I never took the time to notice anyone else.

"Congratulations!" Colt bellowed, and he threw his big arm around Ward, who was more nervous than Cleo. "Some of my happiest moments were when my children were born. Ward, my boy, you're in for a good time! And I'll be right here if you need any help." Colt squeezed the poor boy's arm. I could see that Ward wasn't sure if Colt was being sarcastic or genuine.

"Thanks, Dad." Cleo stood up and went around the table and wrapped her arms around her father and kissed him on the back of the neck. "I knew you'd understand."

Even though she didn't mean it to, that comment hurt me. I won't lie. Colt, the perfect man, the man who is always healthy, the man my children hold in higher regard than God, the man who can do no wrong—I hate him and love him at the same time.

With tears in my eyes, I leaned over and hugged Ward. Then I walked around the table, too, and kissed Cleo. "Honey, I'm so happy for you." I said.

Colt was really happy. He smiled all through dinner, and every now and again he would reach over and whap Ward on the back with his heavy hand and congratulate him again. Ward kept flinching in both pain and fear. Poor guy.

Cleo explained that she'd wanted to tell us formally like this because, to my surprise, her brothers already knew. I learned from her that Conrad was the first person she confided in, even before Ward. She looks at Conrad as the wise man of the family. She knew he wouldn't pass judgment on her and would guide her to make the right decision. It was Conrad who encouraged her and told her that our family would be happy about the coming of a new member. I agree. Conrad is the wisest of us all. He looks after his sister. He helped calm her and held her hand when she told Ward. But she wanted to tell us, her parents, alone to show Conrad that she was a mature woman.

I learned a lot tonight. When I got cancer the first time, Cleo told me she was convinced I was going to die. She was afraid to tell me or her father how scared she was, so she confided in Conrad. Even at that young age, he took care of her. She was thirteen and he was seventeen. Even though he was only a teenager, he always seemed older and more mature. I learned tonight how my cancer affected my three children eight years ago. I thought I knew everything, but evidently I didn't. As parents, as adults, there have been times when Colt and I were not there for our children because we were caught up in treatments, doctors' appointments, and so on. So the kids supported each other. Well, Cleo said that she and Conrad did. Junior did what he's always done. He stayed on the periphery and observed, but did not participate.

As for current events, I also learned that Conrad is now dating a girl that Junior dated for a long time. This bit of news was a bombshell. To have my two boys in a situation over the same girl is very bad news. Evidently, one night Junior was out with a bunch of friends, and he was drinking—he likes to drink. He drank too much, and then he started running his mouth like he does when he's drunk. He said one too many negative things to the girl. Called her names and embarrassed her in front of everyone. So she left with Conrad. To hear Cleo tell it, Conrad really likes this girl. (I wish I had a name to put here, but they never told me her name.) Cleo even thinks her brother might pop the question to this girl. Wow, I had no idea my son was in love. How did I overlook that?

To sum it up, as Cleo put it, Junior is angry with Conrad and feels that Cleo has taken sides with Conrad, so he's mad at her, too. Not to mention that Junior thinks Colt and I stand behind Conrad and support him more than we do Junior. So he's got a grudge against us all.

Why would he think something like that?

He's my son, and I love him, no matter what. Yeah, I wish he didn't drink because he's a mean drunk. He has no idea how he acts or what he says when he's drunk. To him, he's the life of the party when he is drinking, but in reality, he says terrible things to everyone when he's drunk. But I don't love him less because of it. I will always support him.

This is awful. Bad karma? Why would Conrad fall in love with Junior's girlfriend? No wonder they've been fighting all the time. I doubt I'll ever get my two sons to make up over a girl. They've fought about all kinds of things, but this is the first time one of them has taken the other's girlfriend. Yikes!

Over dessert, I turned to my daughter. "I want to ask you something," I said, "something that has been bothering me for a while."

"Sure, Mom. What is it?"

"I saw you and Ward in Washington Park when I was riding my bike, and you ignored me. You turned away from me like I was stranger. Why did you do that?"

"Oh, that. Um, well, I wanted to introduce you to Ward properly. Not in an accidental meeting. I had just missed my period and wasn't certain...but I had an idea that I was pregnant. I hadn't even told Ward yet, so that was...well, it was the timing, Mom, the timing was bad, and I didn't have enough emotional reserve to include you. I'm sorry."

Cleo has always been an organized person. When she is faced with doing something spontaneous or without planning it, she freaks out. That's why I understood what she was telling me.

"Honey," I said, "I don't ever want you to feel like you have to avoid me. That hurts me to my core. It hurts me to see my little girl turn away from me." I put my hand up to my cheek, ready to catch a falling tear.

Her eyes welled up, too. "Mom, I never meant to hurt you. You mean all this time you thought I had avoided you because I was embarrassed by you?"

"Yeah. A little." Now my eyes were doing the full-on waterworks thing.

"I'm so sorry, Mom. I hope you can see it was a misunderstanding."

We hugged and kissed, and my heart felt so much better. It was good to hear she had a good reason to turn away from me.

If turning fifty didn't bother me, then becoming a grandmother absolutely freaked me out. I identify the word *grandmother* with my grandmother, who always seemed advanced in age, overweight, white-haired, and sweet. But me? A grandmother?? Well, I'm just not ready to be a grandmother. How selfish is that? I'm not ready! Cleo is ready to be a mother. She and Ward are committed to the baby, and it's not like I will have to provide for my grandchild. I can relax and be the doting grandmother.

I'm a grandmother!

How did I get here? Where did the time go? I don't feel fifty, and I certainly don't feel like a grandmother. I'm afraid. I know I will never be the good kind of grandparent that my grandmother was to me. Have I failed in life? Have I failed to mature properly?

I look at Colt. He is confident about life. Nothing seems to jar him. He never freaks out like I do. He heard what Cleo and Ward had to say and was instantly happy for them. No hesitation, no pause for thought. He's an optimist. He's confident. Oh, how I envy him. I wish I had those qualities.

In truth, well, I am excited to see a little one come into our family, and beyond that, I'm excited that my child wants this baby. *This is a wanted baby.* Not everyone can say that. Just looking at Ward, I can see that he has good qualities, and I know in my heart that he will be a good father. The good outweighs anything that frightens me. I need to face it. I'm so self-absorbed that I didn't congratulate my daughter straightaway because I was worried about me feeling old. *Self-absorbed*. That's me.

At the very least, though I just got some answers to some questions. No wonder our house has been so full of drama. We've got Colt living in the guest room, Cleo hiding her pregnancy, and the boys fighting over a girl. The only person acting normal is Sahchi. The *dog*.

December 8th

I had a bothersome dream last night. At first, I was sick in the dream, ill beyond any ailment I have ever really had. I was in my family home in my bed under the sky I had painted on my bedroom ceiling. Colt was holding my hand, Cleo was rocking a baby boy, and Ward was standing behind her. Conrad was sitting on the bed holding my other hand. Junior stood at the foot of my bed, distant and withdrawn. I was weeping.

I felt my body go weak and fall away. There was absolute darkness for a bit, but then I could see something…it was like opening your eye after you rub it real hard. I could see, but everything was out of focus. In a minute, I had focus again, and, to my amazement, I was viewing my body from above. Below me were my family and my lifeless body. I hovered there for a while, but then something caused me to turn around and when I did, I was immersed into a sort of florescent bright tunnel. It was like a tube, but it was a tube of motion that blasted me out of the bedroom to somewhere else.

When I landed, I was in a familiar place. I had been here once before. That was in a dream, too. Just last week. I was young again, a little girl, and I was standing between a railway station and a pier where a blue, yellow, and white ship was docked. Again, I saw my grandparents standing in line to board the ship. I was waving. Tears were flowing down my cheeks because I thought I would never see them again.

Like before, passengers were getting on a beautiful train across the street. People were sending them off with waves of farewell. Where I stood, it was crowded with all kinds of people bidding farewell to their family members. Then the ship moved away from the dock and the train left the station. Like before, I was all alone. The feeling of absolute solitude was unbearable in this dream. I was filled with dread. I felt like I didn't belong anywhere, not to anyone. It was an unearthly feeling, an unnatural sensation.

But just as in the earlier dream, my granddad came to find me. To retrieve me. As he and I sat waiting for the ship to return, I felt like a little girl sitting in the sun and feeling warm and happy with my granddad and wearing my favorite yellow dress and black shoes. The ship returned, and we waited for the gangplank to come down.

"You know, Chief," Granddad said to me, "the decision is yours. You don't have to come with me if you don't want to."

"I want to go with you and Grandmother, I really do!" I said. He smiled and the gangplank came down and we walked up it and boarded the ship. Grandmother was there. She swept me up in her arms and kissed me.

It felt so real! My cheek rested against her ample bosom and the top of my head was snuggled under her chin. I could hear her heart beating. Her wonderful, generous heart was beating for me, and she smelled of fragrant powder, perspiration, and cookie dough. The safest place in the whole of my existence had always been there, wrapped in her arms and listening to her heart beating. It was in this place that I had fallen asleep many times as a child. This was where I cried many other times. Her voice coming from her chest sounded rich and seasoned by the reverberations and filled with comforting tones.

In this dream, she began singing "Where the Soul Never Dies," and the weight of her arms embraced me and sheltered me from my insecurities. As she sang, I could hear instruments, angelic harps or string instruments of some kind. The sound was soulful. It was a calling that rang deep in me. I couldn't resist it. I needed to hear it, to be part of it. Grandmother rocked me back and forth as she sang and the music played. If bliss is achievable, then I reached it in this dream. The ship sailed on, and I was sailing on it with my grandparents.

Then I woke up in my bed.

When I woke up, I had my arms wrapped across my chest. The feeling of being alone washed over me. Then I felt the flat space where my breast used to be. That's when I realized that when Cleo's baby arrives, she or he won't know the feeling I had known as child; the safe place in the bosom of a grandmother. Knowing that bothered me. It made me angry. I wasn't just angry because of that, though; I was also angry that I woke up alone after feeling the most wonderful feeling I've ever felt. I must have lain in bed for an hour, just yelling into my pillow. I screamed, I cussed, I screamed about injustice, I ordered God (or whoever is in charge) to materialize so I could present my case.

Some of my noise must have slipped under the door because Colt came barging in the room. "Are you okay?" he asked.

"I'm fine." I tried to act causal about it. "Why?"

"It sounded like someone was suffocating you with a pillow."

I looked around, all innocent, "Hmm. I don't know what could have made a noise like that." Colt went into the bathroom and lifted the lid on the clothes hamper. "What are you looking for?" I asked.

"I thought maybe a cat got stuck in the hamper and was covered with clothes. I definitely heard muffled screaming. Or crying."

"Hmm," I said again. "We don't have a cat."

"I know. But *something* made that muffled wail."

"I have no idea what it was. What you might have heard. What you thought you heard."

He looked at me funny and reluctantly left the room. I got up and showered and made my way downstairs. Since it was Saturday everything around the house was in relax mode.

Colt sat reading while I dug through my old vinyl albums until I found one of my grandparents' gospel albums. When

I set the needle down on "Where the Soul Never Dies" by Hank Williams, chills ran over my skin. When I looked it up online, I learned that what I thought I heard in my dream as angelic harps were actually an autoharp and a dulcimer. The old record popped and crackled, but I loved to hear those instruments making that heavenly music. I couldn't resist, I played that song over and over again. Every imperfection in the record held an energy left over from the people who raised me and that energy connected me to them. They gave me a wonderful childhood, absolutely wonderful.

Poor Colt just about went crazy. He was good for the first ten or fifteen plays, but after that, he gave me another funny look, called Sahchi, and headed for the garage. I couldn't help it. The more I heard the song, the closer I felt to heaven, or at least to my grandparents. But I couldn't bring myself to confess this to Colt.

Oh, well. I guess I gave him a reason to go out to the garage with Sahchi. He probably worked on something out there and enjoyed the peace and quiet and the time to himself.

DECEMBER 9TH

It's Sunday. Devin has put me off the whole weekend, something about his pal's, football games, and something else. To be honest, I quit listening to him after he said he couldn't meet me this weekend. When the excuses began to fly out of his mouth, my ears shut down. I know I don't love him, and I know on a deep level that our attraction has calmed down since we slept together that time. I'm selfish, I suppose. I wanted him to want to be around me, to want my affection. For him to make excuses not to see me hurts a little. I don't like feeling this alone.

Colt asked me if I would spend the weekend before Christmas with him at his family's ranch. I wanted to tell him no, but deep inside (in my soul?) I wanted to have the opportunity to talk with him. We had discussed having Christmas at Tammy Jo and Garrett's house, but not the weekend, too. I agreed, thinking it would be a good opportunity to tell him about Dr. Bach and the diagnosis. Anyway, the additional time up at the ranch should be fun for all of us.

"I'm going to visit Nina on Thursday the twentieth," he said. "I'll probably spend the night with her. Then I want to leave before noon on Friday. You can come whenever it's convenient for you," he said. "Come up Friday, Saturday, or even Sunday, if that works best for you."

I got hot when I heard him say he was spending the night with his sister. I know what that means. He's going to spend the night with Jolene. But I didn't want to let that upset me. I still love him on some level, and this was going to be a time when I could let him know what Dr. Bach told me. Colt will be the best one to help when the time is right to tell the kids. He is such a good father. He has a knack for conquering difficult situations.

"Sure, I'd like that," I said with a smile on my face. "Are you going for the whole weekend and will you stay up there through Christmas?"

"Yeah. My brothers and I are going to meet up there. We'll decorate the house for Mom and Dad, set up the tree and the whole bit. I purposely didn't book a gig for those two weeks. It'll be a special weekend, you know, getting ready for the big holiday. It'll be fun. On Sunday, we were thinking of hitching up Calypso and Orion [their draft horses] and going for a hayride, complete with hot chocolate. I know how much you love hot chocolate." He smiled at me.

"And the kids?"

"Well, I invited them. They'll for sure be there for Christmas, but I didn't see any excitement about the whole weekend from them, so who knows? I hope they come out, but it's up to them. I love them so much, you know, but sometimes I wonder if they love me anymore."

I looked at him and suddenly saw a man who questioned the world he lived in. Suddenly he was uncertain about everything, even his children.

"Oh," I said, "the kids adore you! They just don't show it much, I admit, but you're their favorite. I don't doubt their love for you. Look at Cleo the other night! She was thrilled to tell you about the baby."

He seemed to find some reassurance in my words. I think they had a positive effect because they were words from my soul to his. He looked at me with a funny little smile. "I'm going to be a grandfather!"

"Yes, you are," I said, "and you'll be a good one."

"You think so?"

"No. I know so."

"So...will you be there Friday?"

"Yep. In fact, I think I'll take half a day off so I can drive up there with you. No need for us to take two cars."

He gave me a wide smile and packed a few things into his pickup.

"Where are you going now?" I asked him.

"I'm headed out on a call. One of the Jamisons' horses is down. I'm going to see what I can do. After that, I'm headed over to see Nina. Unless you need me here? I can change my plans. Just say the word."

"No. You go on. I'm fine." I didn't want to seem needy, but I was kicking myself because I did want him to stay with me. I was too proud to tell him how much I wanted—no, I needed the friend in him to spend some time with me. I owe too much to my pride as it is. Sometimes I really hate myself for not speaking up and asking for what I want.

He wrapped his arms around me and gave me a big kiss. "I'm so glad you're going with me to my parents for that weekend. I love you, Hope."

Sahchi jumped up into the cab of his pickup, and then he climbed in and gave me a wave, and I watched them drive away. I thought about calling the facility where his sister resides. I thought about how I wanted to catch him in a lie. But then again, I don't really want to know the truth.

Jolene, will you become my children's stepmother after I'm gone? If so, I hope you are good to them. I know they're adults now, but they can still be fragile and in need of guidance. Colt is quite a prize, but my kids are, too. Collectively, they're the grand prize!

I fixed myself a salad, but I had no appetite to eat it. I was alone in an empty house with a salad sitting in front of me and staring me down. It won. I've lost interest in eating. I looked around my kitchen and a huge wave of sadness came over me. On the refrigerator were photos of my family. One was of Cleo and Conrad acting goofy, another was of Junior being serious about texting on his new smart phone at the time. Making sure it wasn't smarter than he was. The kitchen connects to our dining room; it's actually one big room, and on the bookshelves in the dining room are the books I've read and the books members of my family have read or intend to read. The kitchen has always been where our family comes together. So many good times have happened here, so many decisions agreed upon, and so many birthdays celebrated. And now it's in the kitchen where I feel the saddest and most alone.

Becky called, thank goodness, and asked if I was all right. I lied and told her I was. She wanted to come over and visit for a while, and I told her that I would love the company. Only then did I realize that I had kept Devin a secret from her. I wanted to tell her about my night with Devin and how he's currently making excuses not to see me. But how can I? She doesn't even know he exists. I can't bring it up now. She would consider it a false reality. Besides, it pales, compared to what has really been worrying me. At any rate, I've become comfortable keeping Devin secret. After all, it's for his protection. Or is it for mine? I don't want news of our affair to spread around at work. Even if he didn't work with me, I think I would keep him hush-hush. Maybe I'm selfish that way, too.

Becky came over a little later with Christmas cookies and brownies her mother had made special for us. I made hot chocolate, docked my iPod, and played my hippie playlist. The cookies were good, but the brownies were fantastic. The more I ate, the better they tasted.

"I can see you like Mom's magic brownies." Becky said with a laugh.

"What are magic brownies?"

"You know…made with special ingredients that make you feel good."

"Becky! I get high with you and your mom once, and now you're trying to make me an addict!"

"Yeah, right. You get high twice, and look out! Now you'll be breaking into houses and stealing from the neighbors to support your brownie habit." She started laughing so hard I couldn't help but laugh with her. We were laughing ourselves to tears and spilling our hot chocolate when Junior came in.

"What's going on?" he asked.

"Nothing," I gasped. "We were just talking about old times. What are you up to?"

"I'm just going to hang out tonight. I don't feel like going out." And just like that, he disappeared up to his room, showing no interest in Becky or me. He was rude. Where did he learn to be rude? I know it wasn't Colt who taught him to be rude. Colt has never been nor will he ever act in a disrespectful way like that.

Becky looked at me, shrugged her shoulders, and laughed. "Maybe he needs a brownie?" She laughed some more.

"Becky, he's my son. We don't get my son high!" I said trying to be serious, but then I said, "Hand me another brownie."

They were magical, all right. They went right to my mouth and I began gabbing. I spoke slowly when I said Devin's name. It was the first time I had spoken to anyone about him besides Mr. Goldsole. I pronounced his name slowly, as if it were mine and mine alone, not to be shared with anyone. I was amazed how territorial I felt about his name. In my confession, I seemed to be seeing myself as if I were outside my body, as if I were a witness rather than a participant.

Becky listened to me with serious attention. "Oh, Hope, you fry my wig, girl, you are so full of secrets. I get the snakes thinking about the next time I interview your brains, but I've got a lot of room left in my ears."

"No more secrets," I said. "Honest. That's the last one."

"But why? You're cruising with your lights on dim with Colt and this Devin. You're married to the Ace of Daddies, and I can see that you're flipped over him. With that kind of perfect man, you shouldn't have room in your heart for anyone else."

I couldn't understand her. Why couldn't she see what was so clear to me? "I know my age and his age matters," I said, "and that I should be considerate of his future."

"Whoa—before you bump your gums one more time, stab that thing in reverse and riddle me again. You didn't say anything about the cat being a Ricky. How young is this poor devil?"

I turned red. "Am I being ridiculous?"

"No. In my book you're way upstairs. I get it. I know what it's like to be in a bluesy groove and then have a Ricky give you the glad-eye. No, you're not being ridiculous."

"We did it...I slept with him."

Becky about choked on her fourth brownie. "Why do you always do that?"

"Do what?"

"Tell me a gasser with the weight of reality hanging on the end of it when I have a mouthful of something. Girl, you're gonna make me aspirate something one day and take a dirt nap." She cleaned the spatter of brownie off the front of her blouse. "So you flashed your welcome sign for this Ricky, eh? Go into your dance and don't leave out a single detail, you naughty girl, you."

"Oh, no. I don't kiss and tell."

"Don't treat me ugly! You started this. You better finish it or I'll take my brownies and go home."

"Becky, please, please, please, don't take the brownies! Not the brownies! Please, not the brownies!" Hysterical pleading over, I said, "Wait a minute. Let me eat another one. Then I'll tell you." We were laughing like damn fools. I felt light as a cloud. The seriousness of life had been banished. I believe that Becky moved back to town because something greater than me sent her home to be with me in my time of need.

"I don't get you girl." Becky said in a serious voice. "Why? I mean Colt is the MAN! He's that Daddy any woman would like to play house with. What Gives?"

"It's complicated."

"Oh no, that won't fly. I've done a lot of skull work on this and I've come up nil. What did Colt do to you that would make you want to leave him?"

I looked away from her. I didn't want to tell her, I didn't want to hear my own mouth say the words. "He's got a younger woman."

"Well, Crazy, you have just fried my wig...I've heard the wind blow before."

"What... You don't believe me?"

"Look, I know Colt, and he's so sharp he leaves me bleeding. There is no way that man is cheating on you! He's an honest john from alpha to omega." She gave me a stern look. "If I were you I would get my fact checker calibrated."

"But Becky...."

"Don't!" She said. "I've sang my song, now I'm done regarding Colt. Let's chat about something upbeat. I'm done being your sob sister."

And like that we left the subject of Colt and Devin. I love that Becky will listen to me complain, but she will stand up and point out my fault in the situation. She called me on it with Colt, pointed out that she didn't believe me. I appreciate her for being honest with me and not candy-coat her opinion.

After she left and while I was cleaning up, I thought about things. It took a while, but I came to understand why Junior was shocked when he came home. He hasn't heard his mother laughing or having a good time in years. No wonder he asked what was going on. He couldn't understand what was going on. I've got to change the impression my children have of me. Perhaps I've worried over them too much and made sure they had a good life while I absorbed the things they should have worried about. It's possible that I've spoiled them and stolen the life lessons they needed to learn for themselves. I've been wound so tight for so long that it feels nice to unwind a bit.

Further, I made the supposition that Junior was home and in his room because he was depressed about Conrad taking his girlfriend. I gently knocked at his door. When he opened it, I went in and sat on the edge of his bed.

"How you doing, Junior?"

"I'm fine. Why?"

"Why? Because every time I see you, you don't smile, laugh, or seem to have any pleasure in life."

He walked around the room awkwardly, shifting his eyes, his face red, his brows furrowed, his arms tense. "I'm happy."

I couldn't help it. I giggled. "Oh, I can see how happy you are." Blame it on the brownies. "I wish I knew what you needed in life. Don't take life for granted, Junior. Time moves one way and before you know it, it's over."

"I'm not an idiot, Mother. I know time moves in one direction!"

"You see, that's exactly what I'm talking about. You're angry because I'm asking you questions. Maybe you're mad because I care what happens to you. Am I a bad mother because I want my children to be happy?"

He stopped walking. "Who said you were bad mother?"

"Colt Jr., goddammit! Just stop with the pouty attitude for a minute. Come on. Talk to me. I'm your mother, not your enemy. Is there something bothering you? Anything I might be able to help with?"

"You're my mother, that's it, nothing more, nothing less. Just because you're my mother doesn't mean I have to like you. I just want to be left alone."

I felt my face turning red. My stomach sank and my eyes welled up. The tears, however, were not sad ones. I was angry. All I could see was my son's angry face. I stood up and put my face right in his. Our noses were almost touching.

"That's right! I'm your mother. You don't have to like me. But look at yourself now! Just look at yourself. You sure can hate me with great effect. In fact, I feel your hatred like I feel my own skin. I don't know what I've done, if I've actually done anything to you, but one thing is for certain. You feel like you have the freedom to hate me, but let me warn you of something, Mister. It may not be today, but one day you will regret that hatred. I'm going to leave you alone as you wish, and when I walk out of this room, I will no longer bother you. You won't catch me asking how are you doing. I'll keep my care, my love, and my interest in you to myself. But you're my son and I can't help but love you."

Colt Jr. was born angry. I don't know where it comes from. Colt has never mistreated him and I don't think I have either, but maybe I haven't been a good enough mother to him. I just don't know. I'll give him space and respect him, but I'm not going to avoid him or walk around in fear of his anger. He'll have to learn to button up his attitude around me. Respect is earned and a two-way street.

Wiping my tears, I stormed out of his room and went to my room. When I had calmed down a little, I drew a nice hot bath and lit some candles. It took a lot of effort to calm myself down, but I sat in the hot water in the candlelight and finally felt myself relaxing. The flicker of the candles hypnotized me and took me away from that moment of rage. Of course, the effects of the herbal brownies added to the relaxing effect of the hot bath. I let my mind drift and thought about how different Becky's family is from mine. Her mom and dad are old hippies. My husband is a country boy who grew up on a real ranch and plays in country band. I love both worlds. I love the smell of the livestock on the ranch, the feel of the rustic way of life. The scents of the ranch are as comforting to me as the smell of cinnamon, sandalwood and clover coming from Becky's mom.

These are the little things in life that I value. I know I've felt this way and said it before but, again tonight the more I thought about it, the more I realized that Devin doesn't fit anywhere in my life, other than as a momentary visitor. He makes me feel young, in control, and above my condition, but there's nothing of greater value in him. Does that make any sense at all?

Note to self.
Work on clarity.
This confusion is
uncomfortable!

DECEMBER 11TH

Devin came by the condo tonight. He was out of sorts. Is that the right way to say it? I'm not sure. He had been acting funny at work today. His eyes were on me constantly and he stayed close to me, which is unusual. And then he came to my cubicle and asked if he could come by the condo this evening. I mulled it over for a millisecond but said yes. I'm such a fool! After the weekend, when he didn't even have time to call me, I still said yes. Why?

I went home, picked up the things I thought I would need, and headed over to the condo. I arrived with plenty of time to sit in the recliner and read. I'm reading a collection of poems by Elizabeth Barrett Browning, originally written in the middle of the 19th century, though the edition I'm reading was printed in 1921. They're old poems, sure, but her thoughts seem to apply to my life today. Her stanzas are far-reaching and soulful. I had a hard time putting the book down to start dinner, so I carried the book into the kitchen and read while I was cooking. I made pomegranate pork chops with lime cilantro rice and steamed zucchini. I must say that the dinner was excellent. I think Elizabeth helped in some odd way. Or at least I'd like to think so.

Devin was late. As usual. Why is that? He's punctual at work, but when it comes to being on time with me, he's very lackadaisical. I didn't mind very much tonight, though, because his lateness gave me more time with Elizabeth's poetry. I think my favorite poem is "Irreparableness"—"I have been in the meadows all the day/And gathered there the nosegay that you see…." In the poem, Elizabeth sits in the evening realizing that after all of the work she had done throughout the day was a waste of time as the flowers she picked during the day have already begun to decay. She says she's too tired to start collecting them all over again. That seems to me to be a metaphor for life, the comparison being that our life, like the flowers, wilts in the "evening" (as we get older) and our imperfections make us tired and then we don't have courage to try again.

Did Elizabeth know imperfection like mine? She certainly was sick almost all her life.

I feel a connection to her. This poem is the one that brings me to her the most.

Is that crazy?

In addition to Devin and poetry, I was having a hair day. Not necessarily a bad hair day, but just a day where I'm finicky about my hair. I don't know why but I wanted it to be perfect and presentable for Devin. I have this pride about my body. I've already written about my vanity. I like the curve of my butt and the shape of my legs. I've written so much about my remaining breast, of course, that it's like beating a dead horse. But my hair! Because I have this mixed race heritage, I have a complex relationship with my hair. I inherited coarse, nappy hair from my dad, but with today's hair products, I can make it look how I like it. Plus, I know the limitations of my hair. But when I was a child? Oh, boy! Growing up in a small town in the seventies, it was hard to find product, let alone find someone to teach me how to use it. I remember when I was ten, I wanted to look like Tanya Tucker. That's because my grandparents listened to country music, and Tanya was young, not much older than I was. I looked at her picture on her album and saw her long, bouncing, blonde hair and thought it was the most beautiful hair in the world. Would that be a good look for me? I didn't care about the dark color. I liked my hair color. But I wanted that bounce. So I devised a plan. Becky and I pedaled our banana-seat bikes down to the beauty shop where the popular girls went to get their hair done. I walked in all proud-like. I was doing my own shopping, I felt grown-up. I looked at all the boxes of products until I saw what I thought resembled Tanya's hair. I grabbed that one and showed it to Becky "This is it," I said. "This is the one."

"Do you know how this stuff works?" she asked.

"How hard can it be?" I said, still acting grown up. I pushed by her and walked right up to the counter.

The lady behind the counter may have thought twice about my purchase, but she didn't say a word. I bought chemicals that no fifth-grader should ever have in her possession without parental guidance, and we rode our bikes home.

I also convinced my grandparents that Becky and I knew what we were doing. "We know all about the fashion world," I said. "You just wait. My hair will be just like Tanya's."

We mixed up the frothing chemicals, and Becky slapped the mixture on my hair. "My hands are burning," she said. She looked at her hands. They were red. "I don't think this stuff should burn my hands."

But I didn't care about her hands. "That's what will straighten my hair," I said. "It's all in the heat." I was convinced we were going to make me look like the lady on the box. "Go on," I said. "Make sure you cover all of my hair, I don't want any squiggly parts."

To this day, I'm still not sure what we were doing. There was Becky, standing in front of me with her foaming hands, rubbing the mixture all over my head and saying, "I don't think this is working." Then my hair began breaking off in bunches and sticking to her hands!

"Your grandmother is gonna kill me!" she said. "What should I do? Oh, God! This is bad."

I will never forget her standing there with that thick frothy muck running down her arms and dripping on the floor. That muck was my hair! But the chemicals had liquefied it.

"Your grandmother is going to kill me!"

And the next day? The next day, I walked to school with hair so short and butchered I looked worse than Buckwheat from The Little Rascals movies we saw on Saturday mornings on TV. All the other kids, of course, had fun teasing me and calling me names. But you know what? That never bothered me. I held my head up and told everyone that short hair was *the* style because I'd seen an article in a New York magazine that said so. When we were kids, if anything happened in New York it had to be the thing. That's how I covered up my calamity. And Becky, my dear, best friend Becky, she made a fist and threatened to punch out any boy or girl who didn't heed her warning to not tease me.

You have just got to love Becky. She's always been the one to stand up for justice. When we played superhero, I always wanted to be Catwoman. Becky always wanted to be Captain America. Captain America carried a red, white, and blue shield that he could also use as a weapon as he fought the bad guys, so Becky's dad, being the cool dude he was, had painted a trash can lid to resemble that shield. She carried that damn thing all over the place until the principal made her stop bringing it to school. That's because she split Bobby Parker's nose wide open with it when he was teasing me about my hair. That's her. My best friend.

Oh, my...how did I get off on that tangent?

When Devin finally arrived, he was immediately affectionate, hugging me the minute I opened the door and pressing a passionate kiss on my lips. I was taken aback. He's just not that way. He might kiss me, and he did kiss me the last time he came to my condo. But not like this. He was needy tonight. I wouldn't sit for a minute before he got up and came over and put his arms around me and kissed me somewhere, my neck, my cheek, my lips. It didn't seem to matter to him.

After dinner, but before we cleared the table, he took me by the hand and led me back to the bedroom. He was slow, taking his time touching, kissing, and looking at me. One night of love doesn't make up for all the nights I've spent alone, but having his hands on me sure felt good. We didn't say anything. We just let our bodies move.

I was confused. Part of me didn't want to make love to Devin. But the other part of me couldn't ignore how good he felt.

We made love, starting slow and quiet. My health, my illness—none of that mattered. I don't know how long I have left, so even though I'm kind of leaning toward not going through with this love affair, I've persuaded myself to do it. I've coaxed my mental self into believing that my life was limited and that I should never let an experience pass me by. Well, guess what. Tonight I was wrong. It wasn't my mind that I was trying to convince me. It was my soul. It was pulling back, or was it? Why am I so attracted to Devin? It must be more than I can understand at this time.

So tonight it was too late when I realized that I didn't really want to do this again with Devin. He and I were already in bed, and he was in me, between my thighs, increasing his rhythm. His face had a strange look, and he was saying that he loved me over and over again. But he wasn't saying it like he meant it. He was pumping away and saying it like he was trying to convince himself of it.

"What is going on with you tonight?" I finally asked him.

"I wanted to see you," he said. "I knew you would welcome me. You have a way of pushing away my loneliness."

"Your loneliness?"

"I didn't want to be alone tonight."

He didn't want to be alone tonight? Did that mean he hasn't been alone the other nights?

He was still pumping away. "You've been so good to me," he sort of grunted. "And I know at times...I've overlooked the love you've...offered me...so, so tonight I wanted—"

I stopped moving. "Wanted what? You thought tonight you might as well come over because you were *alone? What?* Your girlfriend kept you busy this past weekend, but tonight she's out so you thought I might as well go ride Hope?"

He stopped too. Then he tried to defend himself. "No! It's not like that at all."

"I needed you this weekend," I said. "But you were busy. You said you had to be with your friends. You were going to watch football. Well, that was a load of crap, wasn't it? You were with your girlfriend, weren't you? You two aren't having problems." I could see him looking guiltier and guiltier. "You've worked things out, right?"

He withdrew and turned away from me, and I knew I was right.

"What was with all this 'I love you' tonight?" I asked him. I was getting madder and madder. "You don't love me."

"Hope." He was still on his knees above me, but he had backed away. "I want to love you."

"Wanting to and being in love are two very different things."

"I know." His voice was very quiet now.

"You love her, and you're trying to convince yourself that you don't."

Now he moved away from me. He stood up, then sat back down on the edge of the bed. He wasn't looking at me. Finally he said, "Am I that transparent?"

"Yeah." Suddenly my mood changed. At first I had been angry, but then that soulful thing kicked in. It was as if I could feel his heart and all the confusion in him. He was hurting, and his pain was pushing him toward depression.

He stood up again, but he still wasn't looking at me. "I'm sorry, Hope. I don't mean to hurt you."

"Don't be silly," I said. "You haven't hurt me. I don't believe you could hurt me. But I believe that you are hurting. Do you want to talk about it?"

Finally he turned around. He looked down at me for a long time, then he sat on the bed again and opened up and told me everything. He explained how he had proposed to his girlfriend, but she had asked him to wait. Her request for time had made him think that their relationship was over, that maybe she wanted to be with someone else. I told him that sometimes a girl needs time to process, time to prepare her family, time to organize. I was thinking of Cleo and how she didn't do anything unless it was all planned out.

By this time, I was sort of feeling like his mother. "Give her some time, Devin," I said. "She didn't say no. She just asked for some time. Don't stop giving your love to her. Go back to her," I told him. "But don't tell her about me, this condo, or anything we've done together. Don't ever tell her. Let's keep this moment as a memory just the two of us can share."

He looked surprised. "You think so? That she still loves me?"

"I do. She loves you, Devin, and she will say yes very soon."

He lay down on his side next to me and took my hand in his. "Thank you for understanding. I guess I expected you to be angry with me."

"Oh, Devin, I was angry at first but out of respect for love itself, I can't be angry with you. You can't force love. I can't force you to love me. You have to go where your heart leads you, where your soul takes you."

"I don't deserve to have your arms around me," he said, "but I thank you for being the shoulder I can cry on."

As I watched him get dressed I knew I'd done the right thing. When the door closed, and I was alone again, and even though I knew Devin's departure was the right thing, I cried.

DECEMBER 14TH

I've been sick all week. I spent Wednesday and Thursday in bed with a fever, aches like none I've ever felt before, and I won't even mention the other things going on in me or coming out of me. Let's just say I've been damn sick. Becky has taken it upon herself to be my nursemaid. Bless her heart. She means well, but, damn! That woman can drive me crazy. She's been badgering me about telling Colt and the kids that I have—no. I'm not ready yet. I'll tell them when I'm ready.

When Becky isn't tending to me, she's been helping Colt. He's been very busy. He put up our Christmas tree and decorated the house. I've been downstairs to see the decorations a couple of times. They're so beautiful, I doubt Santa will pass our house by this year. Cleo and Ward came over and helped Colt, too. I heard them all laughing. Since Colt found out that he's going to be a granddad, he's sparkling with energy. He keeps coming up to my room to see if I need anything. He is such a good man. Our grandchild is going to have the best grandfather...well, next best after the one I had.

Cleo came up to visit me yesterday. She's suspicious about my illness. She asked too many questions about it. She even asked if I thought my cancer had returned. I wonder if Becky has been talking to her.

DECEMBER 15TH

I woke up this morning feeling great. It's strange, but my fever broke and the aches were gone—just like that. Last night, I had a dream-filled sleep. I dreamed about my granddad and woke up with the strongest feelings. I just couldn't shake the feeling of missing my grandparents. I guess I was homesick. I got out of bed (finally) and after a good, hot shower and a substantial lunch with Colt, I got in my car and did something really weird. I drove out to my grandparents' old home. It's still there. I walked up to the door and knocked.

A woman a little older than me answered. "Can I help you?"

"Hello," I said. "I hope so. My name is Hope O'Dwyer, and when I was a little girl I lived in this house. This is where I grew up."

The woman had kind eyes. She smiled when I told her who my grandparents had been. "So how can I help you, Hope O'Dwyer?"

"For this Christmas, I want nothing more than to revisit the house where I grew up and hopefully touch a little bit of my past. Would you mind?"

"Well," she said, "I don't normally let strangers into my house, not even the cable man, unless my son is here." She looked at me up and down. "But if what you say is true...well, in the holiday spirit, come in."

I wiped my feet on her doormat and stepped in. The house looked very different from how I remembered it.

"Feelings are strange," the woman said. "I have those moments when I want to go home, too. I can relate to what you are going through. If only I could go back and see my parents again. If only I could see the place where I grew up. Yes, I can relate."

I smiled at her. "Down that hall and to the left," I said, "is the little bedroom where I spent much of my time." She walked with me back to the bedroom and opened the door. I saw boxes stacked against the walls, an ironing board with clothes draped over it. All kinds of odds and ends cluttered the room.

"It's more of a storage room for me," she said.

"I remember it being bigger," I said.

She laughed, "We all see things as bigger when we're children. We're smaller."

I looked up. The ceiling was partially painted over, but I was happy to see a piece of baby-blue sky and what was left of a puffy white cloud that my granddad had painted all those years ago. My eyes welled up.

"Are you all right, dear?"

I wiped my eyes. "Yes, of course. It's just so good to see that some of the old paint is still up there. My granddad painted the ceiling like a sunny day for me." I backed out of the room, closed the door, and wiped my eyes again. My bedroom was near the back door, so I looked out into the backyard where the old oak tree used to be. "My granddad hung a swing for me in the oak that used to stand back there."

"That old tree was dead when I bought the house," the woman said. "It cost me three hundred bucks to have it cut it down."

I can still remember being small, and my grandmother making lunch for us to eat on a blanket out there in that backyard, and Granddad pushing me in the swing that he'd hung from that old tree.

The tree is gone now. I closed the door and turned up the hallway. I remembered that hallway as being so big and long. And now? It was only a few steps for me. We walked back to the kitchen where my grandmother baked cookies and bread, and made countless meals. The kitchen had been remodeled, complete with new appliances. It was so different, but there was still an air of familiarity about it.

"Would you like a cup of tea?" the woman asked me.

"I would love a cup of tea."

"I got this new flavor," she said. "And I'm excited to taste it. It's called 'holiday treat.' I'm not sure, but I think it will probably taste like a candy cane."

"That sure sounds good," I said. I was still surveying the kitchen. We went into the dining room and sat at the table and talked. She told me about her life and living in the house that my grandparents used to own. Finally, she put her empty cup down. "What were you expecting to find here, Hope?"

At first I shrugged. Then, "I just wanted to touch some part of my past." I told her about the cancer and how uncertain my future was. "Life moves us in a current and tows us in and out of directions we don't always expect to go in," I said. "The flow of life has taken me further away from who I was than I care to admit."

She smiled and patted my hand. "I hope that this old house was able to give you back some of what you seem to have lost." she said. "I wish I had some way to offer you comfort for your uncertain future. I wish I could say something, anything, that would help your situation."

"Thank you," I said. "You've been very kind. You've said plenty that helped me. You allowed me to peek into the past for a bit, and that's the greatest gift of comfort you could have given me. You could have just as easily turned me away when

I knocked on your door. I'm grateful to you for letting me in. Thank you again."

"Well, I'm glad I did! It's nice to have some company. Someone to share my tea with." The tea did taste wonderful, just like a liquid candy cane. "Oh," she added, "I almost forgot, I baked some cookies for my son and his family, but I doubt that they'll notice if you and I have some." She went into the kitchen and came back with the teapot and some decorated sugar cookies. We dipped them in our tea.

The familiar feelings, flavors and smells of the old house... they offered me a sense of being home. I've heard the phrase *you can never go home again*, but I had to go there. I had to try and touch the past. I thought if I could touch our old place, if I could only touch the past for a moment, then maybe, just maybe, this ailing, cancerous, body might start healing itself.

DECEMBER 17TH

Another Monday. I hate Mondays! Work sucked today. Have I said that before? I'm sure I have. It's true, work sucks! Today it *really* sucked. What is this world coming to? Here we are, close to the biggest and most expensive holiday of the year, and work has to become problematic. When Brent called a meeting just before lunch, I was thinking he was going to tell all of us managers about giving our employees a turkey or gift cards, something like that. Boy, was I wrong! Brent told us that the consultant that worked with us on October 4th has turned in his report and observations. What Brent announced is that "working in conjunction with consulting recommendations, we were going to go through a reorg." That "reorg" is corporate-speak for a company-wide reorganization. Actually, it's verbal camouflage for layoffs. To make the meeting real exciting, all of the managers were handed a list of employees to be cut on Friday.

Juan raised his hand. "How can we fire our employees on the Friday before Christmas?" he asked Brent.

"Easy," Brent said. "You send them an email that you want to see them and within ten minutes you should have those five people on your list on their way out the door. We'll cut their last check and HR will handle the rest. If you're a coward, Juan, you can let HR do all of the dirty work."

"I'm no coward! I'm thinking of the timing. What kind of a company puts people out of work over the holidays?"

"A strong company, that's who! After all, it's what the shareholders want. Who's going to argue with shareholders?"

Juan did not back down. "Well," he said, his voice getting louder, "I hope those fucking shareholders have a very merry Christmas!" He looked around the room to see if anyone was with him. Some of us were. Then he turned back to Brent. "First, I get passed over for a promotion because your son's dick was stuck in the cunt you promoted instead of me. Now this. Brent, you tell the shareholders to go fuck themselves. I quit! And to show you I'm not a coward...."

As we watched, Juan stood up, walked around the conference table, and stood right in front of Brent. Then he punched Brent in the nose. Brent hit the floor.

Juan turned to us. "I wish you all luck in the future. I cannot—*will not* in good conscience work here anymore." And he stalked through the door and out of the building.

Brent looked like a kid curled up on the floor. None of us went to his aid. We picked up our lay-off lists and quietly filed out of the room, leaving him alone. I went to my cubicle and sat down to read my list. Blythe was at the top. Poor guy. He's my most loyal worker. Sure, he's overweight and, sure, he takes his restroom breaks, but that doesn't make him either a bad employee or a bad person. He was going to take this layoff hard, I knew that.

I thought hard about what to do next and made a phone call. Then I went to lunch. When I returned I sent Mary to get Blythe.

A few minutes later he came to my cubicle. "What's up, Boss?"

I gestured for him to have a seat. "How are you doing, Blythe? How's the holiday season treating you?"

"Oh, you know.... We're getting ready for it. The kids are excited. We got the shopping done for all five kids. Now I only have the little lady to buy for."

"What were you thinking of getting her?"

"Gee, you really want to know? It's not a traditional present."

I smiled at him. "You don't have to tell me."

"No, it's all right. We've been together for twelve years. Can you believe that? I've been married to a woman so far out of my caliber for twelve years. Look at our family picture," he said, pulling his wallet out of his pocket and opening it to a family photo. "See? She's way out of my league!" There was Blythe posing proudly, his wife (beautiful like he said) next to him and their children in front of them. "To show her how much I love her, I'm going to do something special. Remember when I put in my vacation request for this coming year?"

"You were going to take quite a bit of time off. You bet I remember."

He gave me this huge smile. "True. I'm building a trip for her and the kids. She's a Hans Christian Andersen fan, maybe his biggest fan. She's read his books over and over again and then again to every one of our children. She reads and rereads his work more than any other author. So I'm going to fly all of us to Denmark! Yep, I've got the whole thing planned. We're going to see where Hans Christian Andersen grew up, where he wrote his books, the streets he walked on...the whole thing. For my wife, it'll be like going home. I'm just waiting for Friday, payday, and I can pay for the trip."

My eyelids fluttered as I reflected on my walk through my grandparents' house and how important it was for me to feel like I was going home. "That sounds wonderful, Blythe. She's a lucky woman."

"Well, she isn't near as lucky as I am. I mean, look at me. I'm no Speedo model, but she loves me for who I am." He looked around my cubicle. "So, Boss, what did you want to see me about?"

The phone rang. As I picked it up, Blythe sat there, clueless, he had no idea what was about to happen to him. It was Brent on the phone. He was wondering what had happened since he woke up on the floor in the conference room and there was no one there. I told him we had concluded the meeting and he was fine when we left. He started to say something about Juan, but I interrupted him. "Brent, I'm sorry. I have to go. I'm working the list right now."

"The list?"

"Yes, you remember the list. Blythe is here. I have to go."

I hung up the phone and looked at Blythe. "We've worked together for a long time," I told him, "and you have always exceeded my expectations. You know I'm a straight-shooter. I don't mince words. I tell it like it is."

He nodded. "That's true. I've always respected you for your management style. So what's going on? I've got a bad feeling all of a sudden."

"Well, the company is going through a 'reorg,'" I said, "and we have to let some people go."

"At Christmas time?"

"Yeah. I'm sorry, Blythe, but to be honest with you, this place is falling apart. You don't want to be a part of it anymore. You need a better job. A change of atmosphere. You need a place to work where you're appreciated for all of the effort you put out. A place that still has some respect and that does good for the world."

"I suppose you're right." He started to get up. "I'll go dust off the old resume."

"Wait," I said. "There will be no need to do that. I got you a job at BioSport. My friend Quint is the CEO there. She's thrilled to have you."

He sat back down in the chair eyes wide. "Are you serious?"

"You bet I am! You've been my best employee, hands down. So I couldn't ruin your holidays. I had to do something."

He stood up and grabbed my hand and shook it, then just kept holding it. "You know, Boss, I've always enjoyed being around you. Every morning when I saw you here, no matter what, you always asked me how I was doing. And if I wasn't doing very well on a particular day, you always took some time to talk to me. You're a real people person." His hand was warm and his face was full of gratitude.

I picked up something on my desk. "Here. This is a map of how to get to BioSport. Quint would like you to start on January seventh. I told her wonderful things about you, so don't let me down."

"No way, Boss! I'm your man! I won't let you down. In fact, I'll make you proud of me." He turned to leave.

"Blythe," I said, "one more thing."

"Yes, Boss?"

"I told Quint about your request for time off, though I didn't know about your plan to go to Denmark. Well, she's going to honor it. You make sure you get your wife that gift."

He looked like a little kid meeting Santa for the first time. "I will! You can rest assured of that."

"OK. Now, why don't you go down to HR and go through the process of getting out of this place. They'll want you to finish out your scheduled work time, but don't listen to them. As your boss, I recommend that you take the time off right away and enjoy your family. I'll handle HR. They have to pay you, anyway."

"You bet I will!" Blythe may be a large man, but I swear he was walking on air when he left my cubicle.

It felt awesome to help him out. What I hadn't told him was that Quint was giving him a higher position with more pay, better vacation time, a company car—the works. I had also told her about how Blythe needed his restroom break about ten-thirty every morning, and she'd told me it wasn't a problem. As he left I watched him float across the office knowing he had dodged a negative life-changing event, the layoff. Good luck to you, Blythe.

After that, I went down to HR and negotiated the reassignment of my two other victims to other departments. The transfers might not be ideal, but at least they've still got jobs. It's the season to give, dammit. Not take! We shouldn't have to be worrying ourselves with this mess.

When I'd called Quint, I'd also told her I needed to talk to her right away. We agreed to meet for lunch at the Jefferson Street Station.

"What is so important?" she asked as soon as we both sat down at the table.

I told her about our restructuring and the layoffs on the way in. "What I want you to know as a friend," I said, "is that my company has lost its moral bearings. Since we're getting rid of some very good people, I have a suggestion for you."

"I'm listening."

"Drop my company and let Blythe do your accounting. I'll help you get a good team together so you can bring your accounting under your own roof, where it will be in a more trustworthy and reliable place."

She raised an eyebrow. "You sound convincing. I'm still listening."

"Well, there are several things going on at my company that aren't at all good for our clients. I could get fired for telling you these things." Remembering Juan, I smiled. "In fact, we had one manager quit this morning over the direction we're headed in." I told her how Juan had punched Brent out. "I know I don't have much more time there myself. So while I'm still there, let me help you."

After we ordered, we returned to Blythe and his new position at BioSport and discussed starting up an in-house accounting department for BioSport. She was open to it, with one exception.

"Hope," she said, "all this sounds great, but why would I spend the money on making a good position for Blythe when it's so much cheaper for my company to outsource?"

I shook my head. "On the surface it may appear to be cheaper, but in the long run, outsourcing is costly. I can't tell you the specifics at this point, but I know for a fact that upper management has been bundling valuable information that belongs to our clients and is selling that data to their competitors."

Her expression was all I needed to see. "You're right," she said. "It's less costly to give Blythe a good position and bring the accounting department in-house. It's more secure."

"Blythe has worked on your accounts for years. The transition will be seamless. And I will personally stand by him and his honesty. He's been my most loyal employee. He's a forward-thinking man, and he's honest to a fault."

That settled, we ate lunch and chit-chatted about family, the holidays, and (of course) shopping. She gave me some wonderful ideas for Conrad and Junior, the two I have the most trouble buying for. And then, about midway through lunch, she handed me a Christmas card. "Speaking of Christmas presents," she said, "I got you something."

It was a handsome Christmas card and when I opened it a sheet of paper fell out.

"Here you go," she said handing me the paper. "It's all set up for you. This is all of the information you'll need to pedal over the Golden Gate Bridge. I've taken care of the whole thing, even your hotel reservations. When you check in, they'll have an envelope for you. Inside it, you'll find tickets to the theater for you and your fella for Valentines Day. That should give you enough time to plan a real vacation. There will also be some cash for you to shop with and eat lunch on. I have reserved specific restaurants for dinner each evening."

I didn't know how to react. "Oh, my God, Quint! Such generosity!"

She merely smiled. "I consider you a friend now, and I wanted to do something special for you. What good is money if you can't spend it on the people you care about?"

"But—but…you didn't have to pay for the whole thing," I sputtered. "I have money, I can afford this trip, you didn't have to do this." Then I thought about the date. "Valentines Day?

Isn't it cold in February? I don't think I want to pedal across the Golden Gate Bridge in the cold."

She laughed. "You know, San Francisco is never what I would call a warm place, but, actually, in February it's quite warm...considering. The average temperature is fifty. Not bad. And, besides, you'll be generating a lot of heat pedaling. The other advantage is that there will be fewer people on the bridge that time of year."

"I'll do it if you let me repay you."

"Not a chance. And I won't take no for an answer. You go to San Francisco, Hope. Go and see what's on the other side of the Golden Gate."

DECEMBER 20TH

H ow do I describe what just happened? How do I find the words? I doubt if anyone would ever believe me, but this really happened! I decided to go Christmas shopping. Our little town is in the grip of a deep freeze, but the atmosphere was still festive. Excited shoppers were rushing about, holding presents to be paid for and wrapped. People had full shopping bags. Shop windows were trimmed with decorations, fake snow, and flashing lights. I was excited, too, though I wasn't feeling altogether well. But I had to go shopping. I had in mind several things for Cleo, her baby, and Ward.

I was walking from my car in the parking lot to the shopping center and enjoying the joyful feeling when suddenly my eyes couldn't seem to focus. People's shapes began sort of melting together, making a sort of shadowy mass. Then I felt a deep flooding, an overwhelming feeling of weightlessness. I tried to keep walking normally, but I couldn't even take another step. I was frozen, and not by the cold. I just stood still. Then the air around me began to glow. A shower of what I can only call celestial dust came flowing down on me. In the sparkling dust that sprinkled down on me, came relief from my feelings of being sick. My nausea disappeared, all the aches and pains in my body went away. All my earthly burdens—work, family, illness, everything went away.

Does that make sense? It doesn't even make sense to me yet.

I was just standing there, enveloped in the glowing air. I noticed that no one was moving, everything around me was motionless. Time was standing still. Time had stopped! And then from the heavens above came a beam of bright, intense light. It hit me. I mean, *it physically hit me*. I felt it vibrate right through me. The light was so bright that I was blinded for a moment. When I could see again, I was no longer in the parking lot, no longer in my town, no longer on earth. (Do I sound crazy?) I was somewhere, but where? I'm not sure. Well, I have an idea, but I have no proof.

Where I was, was in this place of peace. How do I describe this place of peace? It's a place where the warmth of peace of mind is automatic, where consciousness is free of any limitations. It's also a place where I was able to think and analyze my thoughts without external opinions or judgments interfering. It was like a magical isolation cell in which I had total privacy. Then I thought of Mr. Goldsole and what he had described when he told me that I was facing the wrong way by always looking outward. So here I was, possibly somewhere inside me, possibly deep inside my mind. Wherever this place of peace was, I was facing inward. I was facing *me*.

What I saw was the cancer. It was big. But I was able to look at it more clearly, without all the fear and mythology that go with the "C-word." Of course, the diagnosis scares me, but just then I had the overwhelming emotion of feeling grateful because I understood that most people die without warning. They don't have any opportunity to say or do things that need to be said and done before they go.

Even though the cancer has come back, I can see how lucky I am. I have a valuable opportunity, a priceless one, really, *to live before I die.*

That place of peace? I can only say that it is either in my mind or in heaven, I didn't have any control over the thoughts that came to me, but at the same time, the thoughts I had were my own. I know that doesn't make much sense, but it's the only way I can say it.

The next thought that came to me was *Colt.* What the world looks like through his eyes. I got a glimpse from his perspective, and I didn't like what I saw. Here is a man that takes care of me, who took care of everything when I had cancer the first time. He never said no to any request I made. He took care of me, tended to our children's needs, cleaned the house, cooked every meal, did all of the laundry, kept track of all the doctors' appointments, paid all the bills. All of this in addition to working his job! And I took him for granted. Yes, I'm guilty for taking him for granted. In the place of peace I could see plainly that I took him for granted and I never relieved him of any of those chores after my cancer went into remission. I just let him keep working hard for me. I even had the gall to complain when he didn't do something the way I liked it.

This revelation wounded me to the core. If I were Colt, I would leave me for another woman, too! I would run to someone, anyone, who would recognize the effort I was making. Not only recognize the work, but a person who didn't take me for granted and thanked me every now and again.

Poor Colt!

He is an amazing man. He deserves a happier life. I decided right then that I will talk to him about Jolene. If she makes him happy, I will step aside.

At the same time, being in the place of peace, I had no choice but to be honest with myself. I have to face the fact that I love Colt. I have to think about how much I miss him. Now, in that place of peace, I could see that my loneliness, the emptiness I've blamed on him for all these years is actually my own fault. I'm the one who's isolated myself from him and the kids. That was a painful realization.

I have to face the fact that my real problem with Colt is my resentment of him. I have to face the fact that I resent him for being healthy when I was diagnosed with cancer the first time. And my resentment grew every year afterward because he not only stayed healthy, but he stayed young, too. I could see my grudge. It was like a real, living thing. It looked like a monster. How awful and ugly and harmful it was.

I say that I was in a place of peace because there I was given the opportunity to view these things and analyze my own actions without interruption. I was able to focus on my weaknesses, my oversights, and my transgressions. It was a place where I could make a truthful review of my life, where I had to hold myself accountable.

I don't know how to explain what a wonderful experience this was. It was freeing. I could see all this and I didn't have an option to ask for forgiveness, as if being forgiven were an escape hatch of some sort. I was seeing my faults and wondering how I can be a better person. How I can repair any damage I may have done.

Looking at my mistakes was no fun. That's for sure. It was painful in ways I can't begin to describe, but the only person judging me was me. And from my judgment, I wanted desperately to rectify my obvious errors. I felt as rotten as a person can for mistreating the man who loves me unconditionally. I realized that I needed to come clean with Colt, tell him the truth I've been hiding from him. In this place of peace, I could sort of see the future. I realized I would have a chance to come clean, and that thought brought me to my knees in gratitude.

In that place of peace, I had the sensation that this is the natural process of judgment. I was taught in Sunday school that in our last days God will judge us. But in the place of peace, I saw that that biblical belief was clearly not right. God wasn't judging me. I was being judged *by myself*, and it made perfect sense to me that I was—that I am my own judge. I was born with consciousness and my mind has recorded all of my life's events, so who better to judge me than myself? Who better to judge anyone than themselves? Right? I was full of gratitude because I realized that now I have a chance to change. I have an opportunity that most people don't have (or don't know they have), and that is to right my wrongs. I will have some time to do this before I die.

After my review of my life and judging my experiences and feeling judgment stretched all the way to enlightenment, I saw areas of my life that I haven't necessarily understood.

Like, what about my children?

Issues and events independent of my problems and my existence complicate their lives. I've felt that they have built lives for themselves that exclude me. Don't they trust me? What have I done to break their trust? I was granted the ability to see and feel from my children's perspective, much like I was granted with Colt. And I looked and saw my children and the love that still lives in their hearts for me. It's strong, like their father's love, but they show it in different ways. I could see that even Junior loves me.

I could see from their perspective how my breast cancer eight years ago had consumed me. I saw how the illness isolated me from my children. They had no choice but to grow closer to Colt and to each other. They believed I was going to die. That's what the word cancer does to people. Because they believed that they had no choice but to prepare a life for themselves without me. They were only teenagers when they were preparing for their mother to die. Their teen years should have been filled with scholastic and social activities, not spent worrying about their mother. Understanding that now hurts me deeply. I never wanted to be one to have caused them such hardship. In this place of peace, I could see, feel, and understand how hard it was for them, even though my illness taught them, for better or for worse, to be independent. They are truly capable of engaging in life with a strength that not many young people have.

In my vision, I saw Conrad and Cleo bonding and supporting each other. Just like Cleo had said at dinner the other night, they've always had each other.

With Junior, my vision was darker. I could see that the fuel of his life, for his strength in difficult situations, is his anger. I couldn't see the source of his anger, but I sure could see the depth of it. It was overwhelming to see how deep-rooted his anger is. Where most people like to smile and laugh, he thrives on being unpleasant and angry.

Then, in the place of peace, I realized that I'm not alone. It was as if a star, a tiny, dense, bright, star was flickering with energy near me. The tiny star hovered around me, growing bigger until it formed the shape of a person. The light was so bright, however, that it was hard for me to look directly at it, so the person standing in it (if it was a person) had no face, no identity that I could make out. It wasn't male or female. It wasn't frightful. Just the opposite. All I can call it is a Being of Light. It was comforting to be in that presence. The warmth and love I felt were so great they overwhelmed me. My body started vibrating with a feeling of contentment. Is that strange to say that I vibrated with contentment? One would think that person would be calm with a feeling of contentment, but that's not what happened. I want to be honest here, I want to report it exactly as it happened, and what happened is that I trembled in the presence of that Being of Light. I was shaking like I've never shook before.

From the Being of Light came a direct ray of energy like an energetic umbilical cord, a lightning bolt of energy that connected me to it. From the what, for lack of a better term, I'll call it a spiritual umbilical cord I heard, no, that's not right, I *felt* a connection, some kind of communication. Yes, the Being of Light communicated with me. It welcomed me to this place of peace.

"Why is my son this way?" I asked. I was sick in my heart for him. I could see all of the joys of life passing him by. I saw his future, and it was dim with alcoholism, self-destructive behavior, and loneliness.

There was no answer yet.

"I don't want this for him," I said. "What can I do? Is there anything I can do to help my son find the joys in life and love?"

It's up to him, Hope, the Being of Light said. *Your son has the gift of free will to do as he chooses. You may influence him, but you can't change him.*

No! "I don't want to see this! I can't take seeing the darkness in my son."

And my vision changed, just like when you change the TV channel.

The next channel showed Devin. My honest mind took hold, and I had to confess the disappointment I felt because our relationship wasn't at all what I'd fantasized it would be.

"Why did I do such a dumb thing as to pursue him?" I asked.

You, too, have free will, said the Being of Light. *You chose to be with him.*

"It's that simple?" I asked.

Actually, no. You haven't considered all elements of your existence.

"I'm sorry? I don't understand." I didn't even understand how I was having a conversation with a Being of Light.

Look, the Being of Light said. *You seemed to recognize him. He was familiar to you for a reason.*

And I looked as a new vision that played out before me. I saw a couple in love, making passionate love. Their throes of passion were almost athletic, and then I saw and felt their exhaustion. As they relaxed into the high that people get after really good sex, I noticed the bedroom. It was old-fashioned. I saw oil lamps and a rope bed rather than box-springs. The clothes that littered the floor were old-fashioned. High-button shoes, her long skirts, his long johns, his detachable collar and studs.

"Who are these people? What era am I looking at?"

Feel the vision. Feel what you are seeing.

And then it hit me. I could feel it. I was seeing a far memory! This vision was coming from my memories of another lifetime. The man on the rope bed was Devin and the woman was me, both of us in a former life! He and I were married in a previous lifetime.

It's common to run into people that you once loved deeply, the Being of Light said. *You also run into family members from earlier lifetimes. Look again.*

This time I saw the anonymous man I met on the bus. He and I were in his bedroom, and then, parallel to this vision, I saw the memory of us in another previous lifetime. He and I had loved one another; we'd lived a life together once. And now, in this life, that distant attraction was still recognizable, it still had energy, it still had gravity. He and I may have not understood in this lifetime the feeling we felt on the bus when our elbows touched, but our souls sure did. We were granted a moment. We were granted a point in this lifetime to share our love once more. The vision touched me emotionally.

I tried to look at the Being of Light. "I am grateful," I said. "I am truly grateful to have had those special moments with the man on the bus and with Devin. Thank you."

In those visions in the parking lot of the shopping center, the Being of Light had allowed me to see how important those memories were. Both of these men in my current life were attracted to me by the memory of previous lifetimes. Both encounters—reunions?—were thrilling, but now the mystery has been solved, so the thrill has subsided. These men and I had on a soul level had been together in past lives. Now I've been blessed to have an opportunity to experience them again. Those experiences satisfied me, sexually and soulfully.

Do I regret my lovemaking with those men? In all honesty, no. It's strange to think so, but I *needed* to experience them. My sense of it is that I needed them on some kind of soulful level. When I saw the visions of my previous lifetimes with those two men, any guilt I felt about those moments with them was lifted off my conscience.

I never believed in reincarnation before. Not until this experience. After being in the place of peace, I can see how our present lifetime is only a continuation of our life energy. I can see that when the time comes for me to die, whether it be from cancer or whatever, my true life will go on, only at a different frequency.

This tiny bit of knowledge is comforting.

I have no idea how much earth time it took, but the instantaneous examination of my life continued. I wasn't afraid. I was feeling almost calm about what I've been afraid of for far too long. The first time I had cancer, I went through all the typical stages—denial, anger, bargaining, and so on. But this time, the Being of Light somehow told me that I wouldn't be alone. I was being shown things. Being told things. In this sacred moment I realized that I won't need denial, anger, bargaining, depression, or acceptance this time. The Being of Light is helping me focus on what is truly important. What is truly important? To love and be loved. There's no time for me to bicker and obsess over the small things in life. The most important thing is to reaffirm my love for the people in this life, my current life. It's important to forgive them and to be forgiven by them.

It's all so clear.

Look again.

I looked and saw myself after I left Becky's mother's house the other day. I was crying.

Do you feel that? the Being of Light asked me.

I saw myself crying, but the emotion I felt wasn't sadness. I was crying that day because I love Becky and her mother for loving me. I love them for supporting me. I can sense that through their love that I was connected to them in my past. I can see where my grandparents' love originated, too. The power of love is far-reaching. Endless. I can see that the love we experience every day is a tiny fraction of the larger, universal love that we are capable of, the great love we are meant to experience. I can see that when I touch people like Becky, she connects me to others, like my grandparents, and the love given to me thirty or forty years ago is still alive in me. I can feel the love flowing to me and through me.

It was the Being of Light that got me to feeling better on Sunday. And it was the Being of Light that instigated me to get out and go to my grandparents' house. The Being of Light connected me to the love I needed now. The link to my family's love was there in that house and in that nice woman's company.

Love!

Just like the spiritual umbilical cord coming from the Being of Light and connecting to me (done so with love), so does our love connect us to others. I could see it plainly. I could sense that this is the way of our souls.

Look here.

A new vision opened up, and I could see Quint's face and a wider view of her troubles with Back-2-Back.

You love her like a sister. Feel the love between her and you. With that, don't you think it's time to be a better friend to her?

The vision expanded, and now I saw Jerome and his goons. I could feel his intent to harm her. Not just ordinary harm, but cruel harm that made my stomach start aching.

You need to be honest with her. The information you are holding back from her is very harmful. She's a good friend to you. She has love for you, you can feel it. Receive her love, but also return it. Jerome might be scary, but it's his time to learn a lesson.

"You want me to try to intimidate Jerome and his goons?" I asked. "Now that's a laugh. Those boys are all about hurting people, whether real or virtual. How can I do anything to them? I have no power."

Have faith and move with love in a positive way.

I have a choice! When I saw Quint in my vision, I knew that the love I feel for my friend is strong. It's stronger than my fear of standing up to Jerome. I've made my choice now. And it feels wonderful to commit to doing the right thing.

"I have faith," I said. "We will help Quint."

Being in the place of peace was extraordinary. I could see my faults in all honesty. I was getting a fear-free review of my life, but I also saw my strengths, all of which help me gain a true perspective of myself. I saw everything about myself, the good and the bad. I learned that I like me. All of me. I see the wrongs I've done, and I want to change them. After all, Mr. Goldsole says that mistakes in life don't equal failure. I haven't failed! I have time to right my wrongs. Isn't that a huge blessing?

Again, *Look here.*

Then I was shown the cathedral. *Thank you for calling out to me*, said the Being of Light. *I've heard you. I'm with you always.*

Looking at the cathedral, I took a deep breath. I was embarrassed for it hadn't crossed my mind who this Being of Light might be. Hesitantly I asked, "God?"

That is one of the names man has chosen to give me. I am beyond mankind's understanding, however, so men have created many words and names for me.

"I'm in the presence of God? Really? Am I in trouble?" I think I said that out loud.

Trouble? The Being had heard what I was thinking. Or saying. *You choose to look at me as an authority figure? There is nothing more gratifying to mankind than power or dominion over others. However, I'm not only authority I am many things. For you, and in your situation, what I am is love. I think the better question for you to ask is, 'Am I here because of love?'*

At that moment, I felt love as a huge waterfall, an overwhelming Niagara of love flowing over me. It was such a powerful force that I could do nothing but weep with gratitude.

Then the Being spoke in my granddad's voice. *I love you, Chief, and I don't ever want you to feel like you are alone again. When you feel depressed, I want you to stop what you're doing and look within. Think with your soul, connect with your soul, and it will help you.*

Like Moses, like the prophets of old, I fell to my knees and hid my face from this Being. God. I was sure that there must have been some mistake. I wasn't worthy of this visitation. I wasn't pure of heart or any of the other religious stuff that goes with a visit from God. I didn't even go to church, not really.

You were created with two legs to stand on, the Being said. *You have been given a body to be proud of and a face that should be seen. Stand with pride. Stand like a woman who deserves the good in life. You deserve this as much as anyone. You are not better or worse than anyone else. Stand with me. Don't hide from me.*

What could I do? I stood up and held my head high. I felt as comfortable as if I were standing next to my granddad. This Being of Light had just called me Chief. In fact, the air around me smelled of my grandparents, and their familiar energy was present, too. I couldn't see them but I knew on a soul level that they were in attendance.

I stood in tune with my soul. I liken my soul to the better part of me, or maybe it's the greater part of me. In that vision, I understood that my soul is the celestial element that makes up my complete self. I know that my soul was not born of earth, but higher. I've heard much talk about the redemption of the soul, but I've also learned that the rediscovery of one's soul is more important.

Hope, said the Being of Light, *I've waited in hopes that you would recognize your gift, your soul. Thank you for questioning your reality enough to be curious about it. Finally, you can work on life as a complete person, as it was meant to be.*

I couldn't believe it! The Being of Light was actually thanking me!

"I'm sure this is a dumb question," I ventured to say, "but does everyone have a soul? I mean, is that what we are supposed to do as humans? Work with our souls?"

It is a certainty that every human will come to seek out their soul at least once in their lifetime, the Being of Light replied. *However, it's up to the person to choose to see the soul or ignore it.*

"I was ignorant of my soul and of you," I said. "I'm sorry for not working toward my soul or you sooner in life."

I thought I felt a divine chuckle. *No worries. As a human being, you are blessed with free will to choose what you want to believe in.*

Then I was aware that I had a choice—a choice to employ this moment in my reality or let it go. I had the choice to refuse the experience, and if I did, I would return to my reality having no recollection of this vision. I chose to embrace it, to honor the experience.

You must go back. Now that you have chosen this experience as your reality I want you to know this: you're never alone.

Divine love overwhelmed my senses. All I could say was, "Thank you. Thank you. I love you, thank you."

The umbilical beam of light intensified, and then it made me giggle, and then in a flash I was returned to my body in the parking lot of the shopping center. I found myself laid out flat on my back and foggy in my thinking. When I managed to open my eyes, I could see that there were people gathered around me. Evidently, my physical body had collapsed. I was gone from this plane while I was visiting the Being of Light. It seemed like a really long time to me, but to the people around me, it was only a few seconds of our time.

I immediately went from being so happy and giddy to being embarrassed. Like I said, I was lying flat on my back in a pile of snow in the parking lot with onlookers worrying over me.

"How long have I been lying here?" I asked.

"You collapsed right in front of me a few seconds ago, " a gentleman said. "How do you feel?"

"I think I'm all right."

"You gave us quite a scare," someone else said. "It looked like you were having a seizure." I sat up, and someone leaned over me. I felt hands on my hands and forehead.

"No, she's sitting up now and talking to us," I heard a woman say into her phone.

"Who are you talking to?"

"I called 911."

"Oh, you shouldn't have, I'm fine. Tell them not to bother. I must have slipped on some ice and banged my head. Other than a headache, I feel fine. Really, I'm fine!"

"She's telling us that she's fine," the woman said into her phone. "She looks all right. Oh, okay, then. Thank you."

She closed her phone, and I got to my feet. I did have a headache, but I actually felt fine. Well, not really. What I felt was a little out of sorts. Going from one reality to another is strange enough, but coming back is disorienting. I reassured all the people around me that I was fine and they finally went on with their shopping. I sat there, blinking my eyes, trying to focus and establish my bearings when I heard another voice.

"Chief, what are you doing sitting there in the snow?"

I looked around. "Mr. Goldsole! You're a funny guy. Always showing up when I need you, but never when I expect you."

He walked closer and looked down at me. "What happened here?" he asked.

"You wouldn't believe me if I told you. It's hard for me to believe it, and I experienced it."

He laughed, took my arm, and pulled me up. "Try me. I've heard some wild things in my time.

"Did you ever hear of a person that was made of only light?"

"This is going to be a real good story, isn't it?"

DECEMBER 21ST

I cracked a Mountain Dew, poured it over a glass of ice, and finished packing. Colt had his big Ford pickup loaded and was waiting for me. Sahchi was in the back, wagging her tail with excitement. She knows the ranch and loves it there. That dog has one of those faces you can read. To her, "ranch" is spelled F R E E D O M. On the ranch, there's no leash law. She can shit wherever she likes, and she likes to do it in private. You don't feel like an idiot until you've walked Sahchi on a leash in Washington Park and she does her business. You'll be going along, and she starts walking faster, as if she can get away from you. She wants some privacy, but she obviously can't get away to do her thing, so, she looks at you looking at her and you can almost read her mind. *Pardon me, but I'm pooping here.* But the situation becomes hilarious when you pick her poop up with your hand draped in a plastic bag and carry it to the dumpster. She watches you with this look on her face that screams, *Hey Dumbass, that's my shit, didn't your mother ever teach you not to play with shit? What a Dumbass!* She always has to get one more *Dumbass* in there.

Well, anyway (how did I wander off to the subject of shit?), it hasn't been pleasant at work since the 17th. That's the day the layoffs were ordered and Juan punched Brent. So today I left at noon. It didn't take me long to pack my things into my all-weather backpack and throw it into the bed of the truck. I set my big travel mug filled with the Dew into its cup holder, and I was ready to get out of town. Colt started the engine, but I happened to look at my hand and I yelled, "Stop! I forgot something." I ran back into the house and went right to the kitchen windowsill. My wedding ring was still sitting there. I picked it up, gave it a quick buff with a dishtowel, and then slid it back on my finger. It was a little loose. More weight lost? I ran back and jumped into Imp.

Colt named his pickup Imp. He says this covers all the attitudes the truck has. Like, *important* (we need it to get us where we want to go), *imperfect* (it's a diesel and it belches smoke from time to time.), *impecunious* (it's old and has no creature comforts like GPS, though I think Colt would rather die than own a device that gives him directions), and *impressive* (it sits high on its big wheel and has four doors. Also, it's loud. It sounds like two trucks, not just one).

Now Imp was loaded, I was settled in (wedding ring and all), Colt was grabbing gears, and we were off. I could tell he was excited. We were at the county line when it began snowing hard, so we pulled over and brought Sahchi into the cab. God forbid, that precious dog should get cold or wet unless it's her own idea. She crawled around on the backseat and shook cold wet snow all over me. With these weather conditions, I figured we had an hour on the highway, then at least another hour on the winding, narrow, secondary gravel roads that led to the ranch.

Now was the time for Colt and me to have a chat.

"So," I began in the most casual voice I could summon up, "tell me about Jolene."

"Who?"

"Your little girlfriend."

"What?" He almost drove off the road.

"You know. The girl you've been spending time with when you're telling me you're with your sister."

"Jesus, Hope! Sometimes you frustrate the hell out of me! I don't have a girlfriend. I have been at the Good Shepherd residential facility with Nina." He turned and looked at me. "Do you *honestly* believe I've been having an affair?"

"Of course I do. You won't admit it, but I know you're having one, and she's young and cute with two perky tits and blonde hair."

I watched him take this in. He was quiet for a couple of miles. Then he pulled over again, turned to face me, and exploded. "You are full of shit! That's what you are. Who in this world do I know that is young with blonde hair and two perky boobs?" He adjusted himself in his seat and took a deep breath. "Look, Hope," his voice was marginally calmer now, "it's impossible for me to be with another woman, and that's that. *There is no girlfriend.*"

But I wasn't done yet. "Why can't you be with another woman? Who's stopping you? I certainly haven't been able to."

I could tell he was holding his temper in. "Are you serious? Is this why you've been threatening divorce? Babe, how can you doubt me? I can't love anyone except you. I swear—there isn't anyone else. Honest to God!" He slammed his hands against the steering wheel and stared out at the falling snow for two minutes.

I turned my head and looked out my window. The snow was so thick it looked like it was falling out of the sky sideways. Is it possible that I've been wrong this whole time? Can he be right? No Jolene? Can what he said be true? I felt a terrible rush of doubt falling over me like a dark, heavy blanket. I felt like the Being of Light was frowning at me over my judgment of Colt.

"Nina has never needed you to stay over all night before," I finally said in a tight voice. "But lately you've been telling me that's where you're spending your nights."

He didn't even look at me. "And you honestly think I've been with another woman?"

I didn't answer him.

After another minute, he said, "Well, maybe I can see where you might doubt me. But every time I've asked you to come along to see Nina, if only for a few hours, you've always refused. The doctors don't tell me much, but something has changed with her. She has these huge behavioral swings. She's attacked and hurt some staff members at Good Shepherd. She's even harmed herself on several occasions." He paused, and I could tell he was thinking about what to say. "You know how good I am with horses. I can break the most stubborn horse without any pain if I can help it."

"Yes," I said.

It's true. He can. I've even seen him walk up to a strange horse that was giving its owner fits. He'll say something quietly in the horse's ear, and next thing you know, the horse is following him around like it's smitten, and it'll do whatever he asks it to. It doesn't matter whether it's a stallion, a gelding, or a mare—they all fall for Colt. And it's not just horses. He's that way with any animal. Just look at Sahchi.

Anyway, I'm digressing again. "Yes," I said, "you can communicate with any animal."

"Well," he said, "I seem to be able to do it with Nina, too. I swear she calms down when I walk into the room. When she looks at me, I believe she knows I'm her brother. Babe, it's hard on me to see her condition getting worse. It's painful to know my sister has never had a normal life. Sometimes I feel guilty because I live a normal life. I get to experience new things all the time. But Nina? She only knows Good Shepherd. Sometimes I bring her dinner that I cooked at home. You know, a real home-cooked meal instead of the institutional, nutritionally measured, unflavored crap they serve. You should see her face change when she tastes it. Even though she can't talk, she sure can go 'yum' loud enough."

Suddenly I was holding back my tears of guilt. I could hardly believe what I was hearing. "You mean there really is no Jolene? No girlfriend? Honest? You really have been going to see Nina?"

Now he took his hands off the steering wheel and turned to face me. "Hope, how can these two hands hold any other woman when they're desperately trying to hold onto you. There isn't anyone I'd rather be with. You're my lover, my best friend, my life-long companion. I don't ever want to lose you. I wouldn't ever do anything—"

Oh, my God! I knew he was telling me the truth. I could feel it in my soul. I punched him in the shoulder. Hard. "Then why did you lead me to believe that you had a girlfriend?"

"Ouch! That hurt." Sahchi poked her head around the seat. She didn't like me hitting Colt. "You've got some sharp little knuckles!" He rubbed his shoulder. "I'd rather be hit by a man with broad fists anytime than your little fists." He rubbed his shoulder again, but I knew he was just putting on now. "What is it, Hope? Why have you been going on about a divorce? What have I really done to push you away from me?"

"You won't like what I have to say."

"If it's going to hurt me," he said, "then tell me some lie. I'd much rather hear a lie than a truth that'll cause irreparable damage to our marriage."

I didn't even want to mention Dr. Bach now. I just wanted to focus on our marriage. "Well," I said, "I feel like you haven't been attracted to me since the mastectomy. I feel like the ugliest woman in the whole world when I'm around you."

"Oh, Babe, no! You are attractive. Very attractive. We discussed this awhile back, remember? And I wanted to discuss it further, but you shut me out. When you were diagnosed, I believed you were fragile. I didn't want to hurt you. I guess I saw you in so much pain and sickness with all that chemo and radiation that I just assumed they made you weak."

"But I'm not weak," I protested. "I'm strong, and you wouldn't hurt me if you just picked me up like you used to do and kissed me hard. I need to know that the passion hasn't died. The chemo and the radiation killed so much of my life, but they didn't need to kill our passion. I live for you to take me swift and hard like you did when we first got together. Grab my remaining breast and hold it. Suck on it if you want to. And touch my scar. Feel it. Don't avoid it. It's a part of me."

He started the truck again and we got back on the road. He was quiet for several miles. I could tell he was thinking about a lot of things. "I had no idea," he finally said. "Hope, I'm so sorry. I can see how right you are. I've been avoiding your scar. And I'm guilty. I was waiting for you to initiate lovemaking. I thought I was being a gentleman. Now I can see how I was hurting you. I never want to hurt you, Babe. You're the most important person in my life."

"If, and when, the mood strikes you, I want you to take me just short of rape."

"*What?* Listen to you. I've been aggressive before, but I don't think I've even come close to raping you. I hope not, anyway."

"I'm serious, Colt. If we're out shopping, and the mood strikes you, take me right there and then. Don't you wait, don't you hesitate. *Take me.* We'll deal later with the consequences of being nude in public places. What's important to me is that you love me and that you express your love passionately."

"Sahchi, cover your ears back there. Momma's talking dirty up here." His face was turning red. He had never heard me talk like this before.

But I had to. My time was now on a clock that was ticking faster than everyone else's. Colt and I are guilty of not communicating. I should have talked to him about all of this a long time ago or even gone to marriage counseling, or something. It's my fault we got into this mess.

Something strange happens when you learn that your life will really end. Morality takes on a new meaning. I decided that I wouldn't tell Colt about Devin, not because I wanted to avoid admitting to an affair of my own, but because I had to repair the damage to my marriage without causing further damage. Being honest is only worth it if the harm it causes is repairable. I knew I would only hurt Colt if I said anything about Devin or the man from the bus. It's better to let sleeping dogs lie.

"Promise me this," I said to him. "Promise me you won't hold back anymore from showing me that you love me, whether it's a kiss, a soft touch, or making full-out love to me. Promise!"

He grinned. "Be careful what you wish for. I can become a nuisance. You might start feeling smothered. But you got it. Babe, from this point forward, I will show you that I love you. I promise." He put his hand on my thigh. I can't describe how good it felt to feel his hand on me. I also felt like another weight had been lifted off my shoulders. An old, heavy, dusty weight that I'd been carrying unnecessarily for far too long.

"Does Becky know you wanted a divorce?" Colt asked.

"Yeah."

"Crap!"

"Do your parents know?" I asked.

"Yeah. And my brothers, too."

"Really? How long ago did you tell them?"

"Before Thanksgiving."

"Oh, shit! You mean I sat with your parents through Thanksgiving dinner pretending that everything was okay, and they knew?"

He gave a laugh. "Yep, we sure did. Remember I was there, too."

Now I had to laugh. I looked at him, I mean, I really looked at him, and I saw that he was a country song come to life. He had his four-by-four pickup, his big dog, and a song in his heart. And he was the man that was my best friend and the love of my life. He has his faults, and God (the Being of Light, eh?) knows I have mine, but sitting in that driver's seat was the same man I fell in love with twenty-seven years ago. And I remembered how when we first met, he always seemed to be so eager to see me that he jumped out of his pickup and ran up the stairs to my apartment. He'd pick me up and hold me in the air and give me a twirl. It may sound like a cliché, but when he picked me up I felt like I was part of the ether, a spirit in touch with the universe around me.

It was still snowing hard outside and it was getting colder, too, but Colt had the heat turned up. He knows I get cold easily. I took off my boots and wiggled my toes in my thick wool socks. Colt started singing a song to me, "Country Roads" by John Denver. The lyrics described a man who had been away from his wife too long and was coming home to her. At that moment I knew he realized how lonely I've been, how empty my heart has been. Even though we've been living together, it was when he was standing right next to me that I felt the loneliest.

"You know what I love most about you?" I asked him.

"No. What?"

"You *get* me. You really listen to me, and you heard me when I told you how I felt."

"Of course! Babe, everything you say is important to me. But you've got to realize that I'm only a man. It seems as if men usually only hear every other word a woman says. You know when I nod a lot in our conversations and say *yep?* That's that masculine cellular makeup kicking in. It can't be helped. I'm a man."

I punched him on the shoulder again.

"Ouch, damn your sharp little knuckles."

"You don't do that to me, do you? Not hear every word I say?"

"It can't be helped. I swear."

"When was the last time you did that to me?"

"Let me think. Oh, I know. When we were shopping for Thanksgiving and you forced me, that's right, you heard me, *you forced me* to go into that shoe store with you. Warehouse of Ladies' Shoes. Now there's every man's dream." He rolled his eyes. "Not a good pair of Tony Lama boots in the whole place. But yeah, that's where I only paid attention to every other word you were saying. But that didn't matter much because every other word was 'shoe' or 'cute.'"

"Asshole!"

"You've probably never said a truer word."

Cold as it was outside, I was starting to melt inside. "But you got a cute ass."

That made him smile. We'd come to the gravel road that leads to the farm, and he turned onto it. It was covered with snow, but I wasn't worried. I feel safe with Colt, and the fresh snow added to our Christmas spirit.

"Sing to me again," I said. A woman never feels like she's living the fairy-tale dream until her man sings to her, and my man's smooth baritone pacified my uptight mind.

When we went through the ranch's gate, there must have been ten inches of snow on the ground. The minute we stopped, I let Sahchi out and she shot off like a rocket. I knew where she was going—to find the privacy she requires when she's taking care of her business. "Have a good time." I shouted after her. You know what? That dog, going in a full run, looked back at me and smiled. I swear she did.

Colt's parents' house is a big place. It's an old homestead, built maybe a century ago and well maintained, meant to last for generations and to accommodate multiple family members. His family was warm and all smiles when we walked in, but I couldn't help but wonder if they'd have rather seen just Colt and Sahchi, and not me. But I couldn't tell. They all treated me very well.

"Colt," Garrett said after the hugs all around were finished, "we need to get the tractor out and plow the road. The blade's already on it." There is always another chore to be done on a ranch.

"Sure, Dad."

"Monty's on his way with Agnes. I'm sure he's already had a time of it. We don't need to make it any more difficult for him."

That got my attention. I looked at my father-in-law. "Agnes? Why is my aunt coming here?"

Colt answered. "Babe, it's the holiday season. We don't want to leave anyone out, no matter how annoying they are. I invited her, so blame me."

I walked over to him in front of his parents and punched him on the shoulder again. "That woman drives me nuts," I told them. "I barely got through Thanksgiving—"

"Good," said Garret. "That means there'll be some entertainment around here." He laughed and patted Colt on the back. "Son, you want me to call you a doctor?"

"Dad, she's got those damn sharp little knuckles, the kind that stab right through the muscle."

We got situated with everything we brought, our backpacks, presents and the groceries we brought to add to the meals, and then I bundled up and went out with Colt to plow the road.

"Where are you going?" he asked.

"Doesn't every girl want to ride on your tractor?" He whistled for Sahchi, who came at a dead run from the wooded area behind the barn. "I think your tractor's sexy," I added, referring to a song I knew Colt detested.

"Oh, you're turning me on now," he said. "Keep it up."

I made a snowball and threw it and it hit the back of his neck and drizzled down his collar. When he slowly turned and looked at me, I squealed and ran away, but he caught me and gave me a snow bath from head to toe. It was wonderful. Devin was fading ever so quickly from my thoughts. His youth and office-smooth hands had nothing on the rugged man I was married to. Guilt was poking at me, but I ignored it. I was being selfish. I wanted to do what Becky's mom suggested— recognize the good moments and relish them. Wrestling in the snow was such a turn-on. Even though I would have frozen my ass off; I wanted him to take me right there and then. When I got really cold, though, I changed my mind.

Sahchi joined in the fun, jumping around us. She's so smart. She plays and acts like she's going to bite, but when she gets her mouth around an arm or hand, she's so gentle. "You want some of me?" I said pulling her down, but she jumped up again and pushed me down with her front paws. She weighs nearly a hundred and twenty pounds, so when I fell down, she stood on me and looked down into my eyes.

"I love you, girl," I told her. "I really do." After my transcendental experience at the shopping center parking lot, I really do feel and want to express my love openly toward everyone and everything. I appreciate everything more now, and I don't want to hold it in; I have the urge now to say it, be a part of it, and offer my affections freely.

There we were, the three of us lying in the deep snow, and I was telling my husband and my dog how much they meant to me. I'm so thankful for that moment.

We eventually got the road plowed, and about a half hour after we finished, here came Monty and Aunt Agnes. Monty was looking a bit troubled, and Agnes was running her mouth as usual saying something about his bald spot and how some product she saw on TV might help. I had to laugh at his frustration. He looked at me but didn't laugh.

We all came inside and got settled around the fire with Garrett and Tammy Jo. We were having a pleasant chat, and— what a surprise—Aunt Agnes added some pleasantries to the conversation. We were all lost in the conversation when, much to everyone's further surprise, all three of my kids came through the door. Right behind them was Ward. I was so full of emotion that I thought I was going to burst.

"You all came in one vehicle?" I asked.

"Yeah, Junior drove his 4Runner, and we all fit in it," Conrad said. "Luggage, too."

"I never imagined that the three of you could occupy the same space at the same time for more than half a minute." I turned to Ward. "Were they nice? Be honest. Did my kids all behave themselves?"

"Yes," he said. "They were good."

"Good job, Junior," said Colt. "How were the roads?"

"They're getting bad. The temperature's dropping, so it's getting slick."

Tammy Jo was glad to see that everyone had arrived safely. She and Aunt Agnes settled down for a game of cribbage and a long, private conversation. Agnes is especially good at cribbage and Tammy Jo seems to keep her toxic attitude at bay better than most of us.

The house is big, but not big enough for everyone to have their own room, so Colt and I gave up our room for Agnes and we slept in our sleeping bags in the living room next to the fireplace. Our kids were right there, too. It was fun. Like a big family slumber party.

Yes, I said to myself, *relish the moments! Relish them.*

DECEMBER 22ND

I woke up this morning to the loud, boisterous voice of Wild Mack.

"Is everyone going to sleep all day?" he was yelling. "I didn't plow my way over here to sit on my ass! Come on, get up. Let's get going!"

My hair was going in every direction but the one direction that made me look human. I kept pushing it down, but it just kept springing back up and out. Looking up from my sleeping bag on the floor I said, "Good morning, Mack."

"Good morning, Sunshine. Where's that no-good husband of yours?"

I looked at the empty sleeping bag next to me. "I have no idea."

"If Jennifer weren't here," Mack said, "I would jump in that sleeping bag with you and we would have us a real good time."

"It would be a good time, all right, Mack. A good time with me beating your ass! I'm not a morning person. Now go away."

He smiled real big, and then went off in search of Colt. I made my way to the bathroom. There is only one bathroom, so with four women in the house, I felt lucky it was free. The day became a constant motion of bringing out decorations, mending strings of lights, dragging ladders around the house both inside and out, then cutting, trimming and setting up the tree.

Tammy Jo and I started working together. We would move our ladder, and she would hold it steady while I scampered up (that's what I do, I scamper) and hung more strings of lights around the porch. Aunt Agnes was actually useful, too. She kept the hot, spiced cider coming out to all of us. I love that spiced cider.

"So it looks like you have forgiven my son," Tammy Jo said to me with a smile. "I saw the two of you wrestling around in the snow yesterday."

"Oh, uhh..." I stammered, "I guess you know about our... our situation." What else could I say?

She nodded and picked up another string of lights. "Colt told me you wanted a divorce. He sure was busted up about it. He came over here one day after spending the night with Nina. I don't think I've ever seen him so upset."

"We had time to talk on the drive up here yesterday," I said. "What was going on was...well, it was all a huge misunderstanding. I was wrong about so many things. But now things look like they are finally getting back on track."

"I hope so! You're like my own daughter. I was a hot mess, thinking I was going to lose you." She threw her arms around my neck and gave me a long hard hug. "Colt is my son, but don't think for a moment that I don't know he can be hard to live with. If he needs straightening out, you just give me a call. Then send him home to me. I'll stitch a knot in his ass so tight he'll run back to you with a whole new attitude."

"That's generous of you," I said, "but it was my mistake. I'm definitely the one to blame. I could have never been more wrong about Colt. I'm sorry I ever doubted him. You raised the best guy in this world just for me. No one makes men like you do."

"Believe me," she said, "I didn't do it all on my own. I had some help from that one over there." She pointed to Garrett. "Because Colt is so different from anyone else in this family, sometimes I wonder where he really came from. You know. On a soulful level. His approach to life is different, and not everyone, including he himself, understands it."

Garrett was walking around with a limp after being kicked by one of his beloved heifers. Colt's dad is always a sight to behold. He had open-heart surgery four years ago, and when he talks about it he calls it the time when he 'got his valve job,' like he has some kind of V8 engine under his ribs. He had back surgery last year, but he didn't do any of his physical therapy. "It's too damn far to drive for some little ol' exercises I could do at home," he's famous for saying. So he was making his limping rounds and supervising all the work being done by everybody else.

I've always been fond of Garrett. One time, oh, maybe six years ago, when I was still in remission, he had some calves that were born late so they didn't get tagged and branded along with the other calves. That was the summer when Colt and I came out to give Garrett a hand. I don't like that part of ranching. To me, branding is too violent. I don't consider myself a violent person unless I'm punching my husband in the shoulder. But that's just in fun.

But Garrett and Tammy Jo needed our help, so we came up to lend a hand. There were a half dozen or so of these good-sized calves to be branded, and they weren't as easy to handle as the small calves are at branding time. Those little guys are so cute, and that damn branding iron burns them so much, they cry out in pain. I just don't like it. Anyway, the men herded the cows and calves into the round hold. Colt was on his horse, the one named Mr. Personality. He was roping the calves around their hind legs and dragging them over to me. My job was to tail them down. Garrett calls it tailing. Basically, what that means is you can control a calf by manipulating its tail. You pull and twist its tail to get it to lie down on the ground. I had never tailed a calf down before, but that was the task I was given, and with a little coaching from Tammy Jo and Garrett, I was getting it going pretty smoothly. Colt and Mr. Personality were catching and dragging them out, Tammy Jo and I were tailing them down, and Garrett was cutting, vaccinating, and branding. It was a system. I just did my job and didn't watch what Garrett was doing. I had no stomach for that.

After a while though, Garrett started bossing Colt around too much. I could see that Colt was getting irritated. I know he could whip his dad in a fight, but at the same time I could see fear in his eyes when his dad got upset. Maybe it was respect, but Colt held his tongue and did what he was told. He rode back to get another calf, the largest one. He caught this one around the neck and one leg. Mr. Personality didn't hesitate. He just dragged the big calf right out. Garret was coaching me, but then he saw Mr. Personality and Colt spinning around, trying to avoid getting tangled up in the line.

That's when Garrett turned and started yelling at Colt. "Son, quit dilly-dallying with that calf! Get it under control!" The calf was spinning around, frantic to get away, but it wasn't bawling for its mother. It was getting good and pissed. Garrett was still yelling as he was marching off toward the round hold. "Goddammit, son, watch what you're doing!"

The calf charged toward Mr. Personality and the rope went slack. Garrett, still yelling, walked between the horse and the calf. In a flash, the calf darted the other way and the rope went around Garrett and then it went tight, and it threw Garret a good twenty feet, heels over ass. Like I mentioned, that calf was good and pissed. And I swear it waited for Garrett to hit the dirt. Then it ran run over and started stomping the shit out of him. Snot from the calf's nostrils was flying around, and Garrett was down under it in the dust getting the worst of all four hooves.

Colt and his horse finally got that big calf pulled back, but the calf still looked pissed off, like it wouldn't be satisfied until Garrett was stomped six feet under. Tammy Jo ran to Garrett and lifted him up. His shirt was torn and he had a rope burn across his chest and he wasn't breathing too good. Colt jumped down off the horse.

"Dad, are you all right?"

"I've had the shit kicked out of me before, son. I know what this is all about. I've got some bruised ribs, but I'll be alright." And he waved off any assistance Colt was offering.

I looked at Garrett, then at Colt, and I put my hands up. "I'm done," I said. "That calf over there is free to do whatever he wants. After the ass kicking he gave your dad, there is absolutely nothing I can do that would help."

As Colt cut the calf loose and got back on Mr. Personality, Tammy Jo helped Garrett back to the house. Then she came back out, and the three of us finished up with the last calf. It was much smaller. We left Mr. Badass alone.

I thought Garrett would come out of the house with his hunting rifle and shoot the calf, but he didn't. He kept it as a pet! He respected it so much after the ass whipping it gave him that he gave it its own pasture to graze on and used it to mount the cows. That calf's name is Whiskey Punch now, a name taken from the Battleship *Wisconsin* that Garrett served on in his younger days. I look at Whisky Punch today and as a bull he's almost loveable. He's even tempered and even enjoys "talking" to Sahchi when she visits.

Isn't that what I should do in my last days? Remember the

people I love so fondly? That was a rough time for Garrett, but the kindness and goodness that came out of a bad situation are a blessing, and now Whiskey Punch is a big, healthy, proud, old bull. I'm glad he didn't get cut or shot.

After the Christmas decorations were finally up, we girls retreated to the kitchen. I was the last to walk in. Tammy Jo, Aunt Agnes, and Jennifer were cooking up a storm. It didn't look like there was any room for me in there. Ward was outside with Cleo. She was introducing him to Whiskey Punch. Junior, Conrad, Wild Mack, Monty, and Clint (Colt's other brother) were out shooting cans behind the barn. I wrapped myself up in my heavy coat and walked around the porch, watching everyone doing their thing, and I felt good, like this was exactly where I should be. The wind had died down, the air smelled fresh, and the sun was as bright as the painted sky on my bedroom ceiling. I thought of my granddad and how much I would have liked it if he'd been able to meet my children. To meet Colt and his family.

Then Mr. Goldsole came into my mind, and I thought of how much he reminded me of Granddad. I hoped he and his daughter would have a nice holiday together. He was kind of a stranger to me, but he was also more important to me with each new meeting. Something told me I would see him again. Just like always, I would run into him, maybe at the grocery store or outside the cathedral or maybe in a shopping center parking lot.

Then I thought about Becky and her mom. That made me laugh. They're special people, both of them. They've been a special part of my life since I was a child. In fact, they're the only people left from my childhood.

Standing out there in the cold, I even thought about my parents. I never knew them, really. I have hardly any memories of them. I've always wondered about them. Did they have special moments like I was having? Did they recognize those moments and see the value in them? I like to think so. My grandparents were so exceptional; they had to have made my mother and father feel special.

I watched the snow falling on the ground, and the new layer of virgin fluff became a symbol to me, a symbol of sacred ground on which no one had walked yet, of the unknown waiting to be discovered. It symbolized my own future, too—virgin territory, the unknown - but a soft, peaceful unknown. In my visit to the place of peace I'd gained the knowledge that death is soft, warm, and comforting. And that thought brought me the feeling that everything will turn out okay.

As I was standing there, Colt came onto the porch and kissed me. Then he leaned against one of the pillars. "It's nice to have everyone here."

"It sure is," I said. "I'm so glad the kids showed up. I had my doubts they would come. I thought if any of them came, it would only be Conrad."

"I was surprised, too," he said. "You know, they don't need us anymore. They're adults. They have their own lives. I guess with all that independence, they don't even want to be around their parents. It's like we embarrass them somehow."

"No," I said. "They need us more than they realize. After all, they're all still living in our house. They didn't seem to be too embarrassed when they each needed a place to stay."

He nodded. "You're right about that."

"Colt."

"Yeah?"

"I've got to tell you something."

He looked at me, and I could see the sudden worry in his eyes, probably just from hearing the tone of my voice. I could have told him any number of things then that would have confirmed his worries, but on a soul level I had to say this. I had to do the right thing and I couldn't hold it in any longer.

"I need to apologize to you," I said, "and ask your forgiveness."

"No, Babe, you don't need to apologize to me. It's all right."

"Listen to me," I insisted. "Yes, I do, and it's important that you understand why. When I got diagnosed with cancer, you stepped up to the plate. You really did. You took on so much—raising the kids, doing the housework and laundry... everything. I want you to know that I'm aware that I took you for granted. I did, and I'm so sorry. I never relieved you of your duties when I went into remission. I just sat back and let you continue as if you were my servant."

"Oh, Babe, I did it out of love. You don't need to apologize. Really."

"That's bullshit! I should have loved you enough not to take you for granted. I need you to get that. I need you to understand and forgive me for not loving you properly. Think about what

I'm saying, let my words settle in that thick skull of yours. I promise I will not take you for granted from here on out."

I could see the confusion in his face. My words must have landed somewhere in his mind. I could almost see him thinking.

Finally he said, "If I had to do it all over again, I would do it the same way. But if it's important to you, I can see where you took me for granted. I'm not bothered by it, but evidently you are. So, Babe, with all the love I have for you, I forgive you. I accept your words of contrition. I thank you for respecting me enough to explain what's on your mind." He started to give me a kiss, but I ducked and backed away.

"No, not yet," I said. "There's more."

"More? Crap! I don't know if I can handle any more."

I put my hands behind my back so I wouldn't reach out and touch his face. "I have to get this out or I feel like it will kill me," I said. "Really, it's suffocating me. I was so wrong to accuse you of being with Jolene."

Now he frowned. "Who is Jolene? Where on earth did you get that name? As far as I can tell, I don't think I have ever known a Jolene."

"Well, um…" how was I going to explain this? "When I thought you were cheating on me, I didn't know who with, so I named her Jolene after the Dolly Parton song."

"Woman, you are certifiably crazy! You know that? You put me through hell with this damn Jolene!"

His voice was so strong that I took another step back. "If you stop and listen," I said, "I'm trying to apologize for that."

He stood still. "I was very wrong about that. And I'm sorry. My goofy mind almost got us a divorce. I've not only hurt you, but I've hurt my soul, too. So, please...please, don't be angry with me."

He just stood there, shaking his head. Finally he looked straight at me. "I was angry, yeah, but I can let go of that. I can't stay mad at you for very long."

"Besides that, you can't blame me too much," I said. "I love you so much. You're the best man on earth, but my head has a hard time believing I'm the only one you love."

"Do you really love me, Hope? Really? I mean, do you love me now as much as you always have?"

"Of course I do. I never stopped loving you. My mind fooled me into being an idiot. But my heart and soul aren't that stupid, and they have never stopped loving you. So...you forgive me?"

"Yes." He touched my cheek. "Yes. And I mean it."

I stepped forward. "Okay. You can kiss me now. If you still want to."

He kissed me and held me for I don't know how long out there on the porch while it was snowing. How different this weekend was turning out! Just days ago, I honestly thought Colt and I were over and done. I was certain I would tell him about Dr. Bach and that would be that. We would figure out how to tell the kids. We would figure out all the end-of-life stuff. But now? Now I was swimming in the waters of desire and excited about my future with Colt.

He looked around. "Everyone else is busy doing something," he said quietly.

"So?"

"Come on. I have an idea." He grabbed my hand and pulled me into the house and up the stairs to Aunt Agnes's room.

"No, Colt. This isn't a good time. We should wait."

"It's as good a time as any," he said, closing the door. "Besides, you told me when I get the urge to act on it and we could deal with the consequences afterward."

"You're right. I did."

He kicked off his boots, pulled his shirt over his head, yanked his jeans down, and came toward me. It was adolescent, it was passionate, it was exciting, with the added risk of our family catching us. He kissed me hard. I'm not sure if he did it to distract me from his hands pulling at and unbuttoning my clothes or if his hands were doing their own thing and his mind was on that kiss, but whatever his intent, before I knew it, I was undressed, with my back on the bed and legs around him. There was an urgency to it. We didn't want anyone to notice we weren't working anywhere, and there was also a ferocity, like it was our first time together. God help me, I arched my back to his rhythm, but I also held back my cries. Colt had a fever, the hunger of an animal... and, well, I must say there is nothing like making love like an animal. The intensity, the pleasure, the pumping, the sweat... it was all so overwhelming. I couldn't think about what we were doing. I could only comprehend it with my soul. If I ever doubted it before, I was certain today that Colt is my soul mate. He mated with my soul and the explosion that followed was amazing.

As he withdrew, he smiled down at me. "Later," he whispered. "Later we'll take our time."

"There's going to be a later?"

"Yep."

"How much later? Like when we get home?"

He tweaked my nipple. "No, silly. Tonight."

Shit! I knew he was going to say that. "But we don't have a bedroom."

He winked at me. "We'll think of something. We're on a ranch with all kinds of buildings, and at the very least we've got Imp."

"Oh, hell, no! You're not making love to me in a pickup truck that smells like wet dog!"

He only laughed and got dressed as fast as he'd gotten undressed. Leaving me on the bed, he went out in search of his brothers and sons, who were still shooting at tin cans out behind the barn.

Before I got dressed, I stood in front of the mirror and took stock of what I looked like. In my reflection I think I saw my soul peek at me and give me a wink. My hair was a ratty mess again. I'd never be able to deal with all of the tangles. But my face! That was where the problem really was. My cheeks and forehead had a reddish glow. It had to be from windburn or sunburn. Or both. I liked the added color, but the grin was a dead giveaway. I was grinning from ear to ear. I looked at this damn fool in the mirror. "Stop it!" I exclaimed. "They're all going to know." No matter. Whatever I did, it couldn't be helped. Sure enough, when I went into the kitchen where Tammy Jo was, she gave me a quick look. Then she grinned. I knew she knew.

Agnes, thank God, was oblivious. "Did the two of you find whatever you were looking for in my room?" she asked.

I blinked at her. "What?"

"You and Colt up there in my room. It sounded like you were tearing the room apart looking for something."

"Uh, no...no, we didn't find everything, but we're gonna look again. Later." I winked at Tammy Jo, and she laughed and laughed. Aunt Agnes just looked puzzled and went back to whatever she was doing.

DECEMBER 23RD

Winter looks different on the ranch, like it belongs in a storybook. The ranch is a place of nature and simplicity where the wind can howl all night and all day and push the mercury down below any human comfort zone. And when the wind blows, it can bring down fragments of storm fronts or full-on storms that most people would like to stay up in the mountains. But then, with a quick shift, the wind will also push the storm clouds back up to the mountains and leave crisp, white, untouched snow. The scene becomes something anyone can get lost in...pure beauty.

The earth, Mr. Goldsole told me once, uses its scenery to communicate. It's our responsibility to read its message.

Earlier today, I became aware of my responsibility to the earth. I read the landscape. Last night, we had a storm of heavy, wet snow blown in by strong winds. I came to the conclusion that the earth is female. She is full of intuition. She's perfect but also has the capacity to be moody and defensive. That's when we get those storms.

The winter solstice was Friday. In the winter, days are shorter, nights are longer, and the lack of sunshine drives the temperatures down below zero around here. My nose and ears turn red and burn from exposure to the wind and the cold. That reminds me of the burn of the radiation and chemo I had eight years ago. If a person were to remain exposed to this cold long enough to get frostbite, the physicians might have to remove frozen body parts, just like they had to do when I had breast cancer. I shudder at the thought of the removal of body parts. However, the wind seemed to make me feel that the earth was trying to communicate with me. Somewhere deep inside me, I'm beginning to feel more connected. The connection stretches from the earth to me and my family and friends, then it keeps going to strangers and then finally to the place of peace.

I was so caught up in that mystical connection that I didn't even hear Colt coming out the door.

"What are you doing out here in the cold?" he asked.

"Just looking around. Admiring the beauty of winter."

"It is beautiful, isn't it?" He wrapped his arms around me and I leaned back against him.

"It truly is," I said.

"But it's cold," he said, "and you don't like to be cold. Do you want to come sit by the fire? I could get you some hot tea."

"No," I said, "not now. But I wouldn't mind just talking with you out here, away from everyone else. Would you mind talking to me?"

He nodded. "I woke up this morning, you know, and I had the feeling that you're back. Like the old Hope, the Hope before the breast cancer. It's not a dream that we're together here, that we want to talk to each other." He turned me around so we were face to face. "It's been a while since we've been able to have a good conversation. I'm greedy for talk."

We walked down the front steps and waded through the snow and sat on the rails of the trap. The trap is the holding area between two of the four pastures. Garrett uses the traps for calving the heifers. Other times, he uses it to put cattle in when he's working in one of the pastures.

Looking around at the snow, which was as smooth as velvet, I took it as a sign that now was a good time to talk to Colt about Dr. Bach. He knows Dr. Bach very well from when I was first diagnosed with breast cancer. Dr. Bach was wonderful about helping Colt. He was so afraid of losing me that he couldn't even pronounce the word "cancer." He kept saying things like "the condition," "the diagnosis," or "the problem." Anything to avoid saying the name of the disease.

"Colt," I began, "I've wasted precious time that we could have been happy in. It's all my fault. I should have opened my eyes sooner."

"Babe, don't sweat it," he said. "We're good now. We can spend the rest of our lives loving each other and making up for any misunderstandings."

I was trying to be grown up about it, but I was really feeling like a child that's afraid of the dark. I looked at him, and tears were already running down my cheeks. "The rest of our lives?" That was all I could say.

"Yep! I will spend the rest of my life making sure you never have a doubt about my love for you again." He tried to put his arm around me, and I pushed it off.

"Don't touch me right now," I said. "I—I can't have you touching me right now."

"Did I do something wrong?"

"No, no, of course not." I shook my head. "I'm trying to hold it together, is all, and when you touch me, all I want to do is for you to wrap both your arms around me and let me just sort of explode."

He looked a bit puzzled, but all he said was, "It's all right, Babe. If you need a good cry, I'll hold you till you're done." He opened his arms wide. "Come on in here. Let me put both arms around you."

Still sitting on top of the top rail of the trap I had to pull back from him. "I can't!" I took a huge breath, and when I exhaled, I sounded like a wounded animal. Colt became visibly nervous. "Colt," I said in a tiny voice, "honey, I've got some bad news."

"What is it? You're scaring me."

"I don't know how to say it. I've been to see Dr. Bach. The cancer is back."

"No! No, it can't be. You beat it, Hope, you're in remission." I saw him look away from me in an attempt to hide his own tears.

"Believe me," I said, "I wish I could tell you something different, but it's back. And this time it's worse."

I could see the pain in his face. It hurt me to see it. Sometimes I feel like I've come to terms with my diagnosis. Death doesn't frighten me so much anymore. But what I simply cannot do is explain this to the ones I love and not hurt them. Colt's a good man, probably the best man there ever was. He didn't deserve to hear that I've got cancer again. He deserves to have a wonderful, loving wife, a wife who'll be here with him in all the years to come.

Eight years ago, he didn't take the news very well, either, and the scar on my chest has always been a reminder to him that there are things in this world that he can't protect me from. When they cut into my body and removed my breast, in some ways they cut into Colt's soul. Unfortunately, the surgery that saved my life back then also cut into places in him that were impossible to heal.

Now he had questions. "When did you talk to Dr. Bach? What if he's wrong? Maybe it's a mistake, maybe they mixed up the results." He was searching for logic in places where there is no logic. Cancer has nothing to do with logic.

I shook my head. "There's no mistake. I've done all the tests. We've checked and rechecked. I didn't want to tell you. I know that's extremely selfish...but, well, I just didn't want to tell anyone."

Now he sounded almost mad. "That's just like you! Keep it all to yourself. I'm not sure if you're brave, or what, but I don't like it." His anger suddenly went away. "Babe, I would have been so pissed off if you hadn't told me."

I tried to smile, but it was hard. "Becky said the same thing. She said I close people out."

"What? You told Becky? Goddammit, Hope!" His eyes were full. "Well, she's right about that. You do keep everything in."

"I'm sorry. I don't mean to."

He turned away for a minute, then turned back to me. "Please don't shut me out, Hope. I want to be there for you. I want to help you fight this thing. We've been there before! You beat it once, you can do it again. You are the strongest person I know." He suddenly grinned. "Remember when we went to Alaska and you showed those guys that you were tougher than they were?"

That's when I got down off the fence rail and went over and rested my head on his knee. "There's no fight this time," I said, not looking up at him. "There will be no treatment. No chemo. No radiation."

He was on the top rail looking down at me with a face full of fear. "Why the hell not? What are you talking about? There will be no fighting this time?"

"It's in my bones," I said. "In my lymph glands. In my ovaries. It's in too many places." I knew that every single day I was alive, I was making memories for him, and this day, this moment, wasn't a memory I want him to have. It wasn't a good memory for anyone to have. It wasn't kind. Selfish me, I only want him to have good memories.

He put one hand on my head and began stroking my hair. "Are you sure? I don't mean to be disrespectful, but you don't seem that ill. You were so sick last time. I don't understand how you can have cancer in more places and seem so healthy."

I looked up at him. "I was sick because of the treatment. The chemo, the radiation. Don't be fooled, Colt. There are days I don't get out of bed, there are times when I feel horrible, but it's nothing now compared to what I felt eight years ago."

"So what now? How much time are we talking?"

"Dr. Bach said he can't predict the future. But he said...he said less than a year."

And as soon as I said "a year," Colt just stopped. He stopped everything. Time stopped. Then, I don't know how much later, maybe a minute, maybe a thousand years, he came down off the fence rail and put his arms around me, buried his face in my hair and started crying. We wept together. We wept so hard that we went weak in the knees at the same time. Kneeling in the deep snow, we held each other up and kept crying. There were moments when he told me he loved me and moments when I told him I loved him. But when he told me he couldn't live the rest of his life without me, I just gave up and collapsed against him. My sorrow overwhelmed me.

The earth has signs she uses to communicate with us. Some of her signs can be interpreted as life or death. I can see that water follows a descending path. That seems to me to lead toward death. Right? Or water can rise. A fountain can be a sign of life, sexual vigor. Yes, water can be a sign of life or death. It can signify the unconscious, intuition, or whatever else we want to make it a symbol of. I've come to think of water as a symbol of the body. And right here, right now, at this moment, all the water is frozen. Immobile. And that's where I feel I am. And I'm thankful for temporary frozenness, for immobility. At this moment, I feel relatively healthy, and even though I'm flowing toward death, right now I'm frozen in time and I have time to express my love to the people I love.

"I need you, Colt! I need the strength in you to help me live the happiest I can before my end. Can you give me your strength?"

"You bet I will. I'll do everything I can to make you happy until.... Well, *until*."

We got up, dusted ourselves off, and walked hand in hand back to the house. Halfway there, Colt broke away from me.

"Where are you going?" I asked him.

"To the woodpile. I really need to chop some wood right now."

Well, I thought, that made sense.

Garrett met me on the steps up to the porch. He had been out tending to the cattle and was in good spirits. "Good morning, little girl! How are you doing?"

"Not bad," I said. "It's hard to have a bad day when the world is so pretty."

Then he heard the sound of wood being chopped. He looked and saw Colt swinging the axe. "Uh oh, that's not good."

"Why not?"

He shook his head. "The only time I've seen Colt chop wood like that is when he has a problem. Say, are you two getting along all right?"

"We are doing just fine."

"Well, then, the good thing about Colt being upset about whatever it is, is that I won't have to worry about my woodpile for a long time. That boy will have me stocked up with split logs and kindling. Whatever it is, I sure hope he gets it out of his system."

"Yeah," I said. "He's good that way. Even when he's at his worst, he does something good for someone."

"You know," my father-in-law said, "I love my three sons. They each have their way about them that is likeable and loveable. But Colt? He's different from his brothers in one way. No matter what he does, he gives his best, and when it's done, you'll be hard pressed to hear him brag. He's a capable man. When he was young, he not only worked with me on this ranch, he helped ol' Pete on his ranch, too. One year, he wove us all hatbands out of horsehair he been saving throughout the year." He took his hat off and showed me. "Look here. I've still got mine." I've seen Garrett's old, worn-out hat countless times, but I never paid any attention to the hatband. Garrett put his hat back on. "He's a good ranch hand. He knows animals. Not just cattle or horses, either. I swear that boy can talk to any animal."

Yep. There was Sahchi, sitting in the snow and watching Colt swing the axe. She watches him, never takes her eyes off him, or, if she does, she doesn't do it for long. We could hear Colt grumbling with every swing of the axe.

"This isn't good." Garrett said again.

"What isn't good?"

"He's cussing God out. Colt doesn't usually cuss God, but when he does, something is bad, real bad."

Even though I couldn't hear them, I knew the words coming out of Colt's mouth were bad, ugly, and explicit. Sahchi knew he was cussing, too, because her ears were flattened out. She only flattens her ears when she's in trouble.

"I better go talk to him." Garrett said.

"Wait," I said. "I know what the problem is, and it's best if you just give him some time. Let him work it out on that woodpile. You'll have a good supply of tooth picks if that's what it takes for him to work this out."

"Damn, I hope he isn't mad at you."

"No, he's not mad at me."

DECEMBER 24TH

Earth and all of her creatures exist in natural, healing sunlight. I understand that now. I have a better understanding now that the cycles of the human body revolve around the movement of the sun. Even my skin color, I've been told, is due to some of my ancestors living in more direct sunlight. I also understand that our personalities are affected by sunlight. We require oxygen to breathe and food to build cells and keep them going, but sunlight is just as essential. Not only is light one of the most basic components of life—it's essential to the survival of everything on the earth—but it may also be the most basic source of spiritual healing available to us.

Like most people, I've taken sunlight for granted all my life. After my experience in the place of peace and with the Being of Light, I understand light differently. Phrases like "living in the light," "you're the light of my life," or—more applicable to me these days—"I saw the light" have a whole new meaning.

I woke up this morning and felt the rays of sunshine pouring in on me through the window. I just lay there in the sunlight and felt it. When I say that I felt it, I mean *I connected with it*, I exchanged energy with it, I shared love with it. It may sound crazy, but when I interacted with the rays of light, I witnessed a color change. They were bright and yellow coming in the window, but when I consciously shared my energy with them, they turned copper in color.

Light!

How precious light is! I don't know if I've been so busy in my life that I never noticed it before or if I just assumed that light is constant and it needs no attention from me. Whatever the reason, now I believe it's a sin to never notice the light. When I was in the company of the Being of Light, I felt the energy between us, and today I noticed energy in everyday sunlight. Within the sunlight came the energy that chased away the depression that was threatening to take over my mind.

It's funny, the things we take for granted. People don't often talk about being born. They just know that they're alive. We all take for granted that we're born. We never think about how amazing birth is. When I look at Cleo, I see my daughter, a girl, and I also understand now that the Being of Light has touched her, helped her develop into a mother that will give birth. Light comes to our earth with great and consecrated energy; and life comes to us also with great and consecrated energy.

If life is energy…then what is death?

I think of dying as an exchange of energy. Like the sunlight this morning. What is difficult is keeping this speculation to myself. Death and any discussion of it—that makes people uncomfortable.

Should I share my dying with the people in my life?

I feel free, as if some heavy burden has been lifted from me. My dying is charging my living with vigor. My awareness is amplified. I feel good, and I want to talk about death, but I understand that my enthusiasm toward something as grim as death should be best kept to my diary.

But living is so different now.

Colt has been keeping to his word. He has made love to me four times since we arrived at the ranch. We have stolen time here and there and slipped into vacant rooms. Just like the rays of sunlight, when Colt and I come together, I feel his energy on a soul level. I feel us exchanging love. People use the word "love" as a catch-all—in an "I love you" kind of thing. And yet, with little effort, I see love as the essence of our being. And when love is aimed at a person with an intended purpose (like love-making), its magnitude grows. I believe that from this ranch I can focus on my love for Mr. Goldsole and he will feel it.

Love!

Monte and Colt hitched two of the draft horses, Calypso and Orin, to the flat hay wagon for us all to go on a hayride. Aunt Agnes made three thermoses of hot chocolate, and Tammy Jo packed some pumpkin bread with a tub of cream cheese frosting for those of us who want to add more calories. I painted my pumpkin bread with a thick layer of frosting. Hell, yes, I did! Now that is finger-lickin' good right there.

As the horses pulled us through the snow, the sun was making the snow sparkle, and winter never looked so good. I felt as giddy as a little kid waiting for Santa Claus. Colt sat next to Aunt Agnes and me on one of the hay bales. We had a blanket wrapped around the three of us. Clint and his wife sat across from us with Wild Mack and Jennifer, and Monte, Conrad, and Junior sat at the back end of the wagon with their legs hanging off. Cleo and Ward found a space on the wagon floor between our feet, and Garret and Tammy Jo were on the spring seat guiding the team. As we rode along, Colt led us in Christmas carols. As I wrote before, I was aware of the sunlight and its energy. As we sang, I swear I witnessed an exchange of energy between us singing and the sunlight. I could see the rays of sun light sparkle and change color as we sang. And perhaps only I perceived it, but I think I saw individual rays of light reaching out to my family and friends. As the ray of light touched them, I saw each person respond to the energy with laughter or smiles. Sure, it might have been my imagination, but I saw *something* on the hayride. It was magical.

I looked at everyone in the wagon. I saw my strong, handsome husband, my beautiful children, my soon-to-be grandchild. I've got my aunt I've not always liked but who I do see value in. I look at my in-laws and consider them a wonderful part of my life. I was so happy today to have the sunlight, the love of my family, familiar Christmas carols to sing, and hot chocolate and pumpkin bread. I may not have all the riches that Jerome has, but I've got these wonderful things in my life.

I leaned into Colt and said, "Before we go home, I want to go out to Good Shepherd's with you to see Nina."

"Babe, that's a great idea."

Deep inside I knew I had to go and see his sister. She's the only family member missing from the festivities and she deserves to have family around her this time of year. I owe her that at least.

DECEMBER 25TH—CHRISTMAS

Some people might say that it's nuts for a person with a terminal illness to keep a diary. What's the point? I might agree with that. If I were a healthy person looking at an ill person, I'd ask them, what might be the purpose of documenting the days going by? What could possibly be the motivating factors for being tasked with the upkeep of such a collection of ramblings?

Well, every new day has newfound value for me. My diary is the therapeutic vehicle that carries away my anxieties, worries, and confusion. I can write down my thoughts, no matter how grim they are, how depressed I'm feeling, and I can see the state my mind is in. And if any given state isn't to my liking, I can make up my mind to change the course of my thoughts.

This is not ego. I doubt that anyone would find my day-to-day life interesting. Perhaps it's my soul pushing me to keep writing. I feel that my diary has a greater importance than just being the ramblings of a cancer victim.

It's late, or early, depending on how one looks at the predawn hours. Everyone else is asleep, but I'm awake. Inside me, I feel energetic. Sleep is nowhere in sight. I love this moment. Christmas has just arrived, the feast has been eaten, the presents opened, our love shared.

The Christmas lights are still on, blinking in all their colors on the tree. The contrast between the darkness and the pretty lights tickles the child in me. I can't stop smiling. I've received the greatest gift of all this year. I've been blessed with the ability to go back, to return to my family, where only days ago my family was fragmented and splintered. The Being of Light and my connection to my soul are responsible for my Christmas being so special. I know that. I'm truly grateful.

I can see the angel on the top of the tree. She's a symbol of the grace we are granted. Angels. They exist! I know that. They walk around in places where we don't often notice them. But they're around us, and we don't know how lucky we are to be blessed by the grace they represent. The Being of Light does love us, as I was told in the place of peace. The Being of Light showed me the ever-expanding energy that love is. In return, I feel my love extending out past this room, beyond the ranch, up into the stars until it reaches to the limits of the universe. To know that I am capable of reaching out that far with my love is awesome! Yes, I'm fifty years old. I am fifty! My age should be celebrated. Quint and Mr. Goldsole were right. I can see that now. And, yes, I have cancer, but I also have a forecast, a prediction of my end. There are tears, I've written about that. There is pain, I've written about that. And, yes, there is illness, I've written about that. But there are blessings in this situation, too.

Most people just drift through life. I know. I've been one of those people. But to live knowing death is close has colossal value. I honestly hadn't lived until I had my experience in the place of peace. I mean *really lived*. By really living, I mean living as a whole person who feels everything on three levels of consciousness—intellectual, emotional, and spiritual. This Christmas, I've touched the people here, my family and friends, and I have touched them with all of me. I've been engaged in ways I never have been before. I may have felt love for each person here before now, but now my love is on a new plane. When I talk with each person, my soul sees and hears their soul.

The Being of Light touched me and left a mark on my awareness. I confess it here and now. I have experiences. Supernatural experiences. Today Cleo and I were sitting in this room. Everyone was in this room, actually, having their own conversations, and Cleo and I were talking about her baby and some of the names she and Ward had chosen. And then she suddenly leaned over and embraced me and told me that she loved me. She also said she thought I would make a fantastic grandmother.

Anyway…while I was talking to Cleo, everything stopped. I swear time didn't move. I was able to see the future. I had a vision of Cleo giving birth to a boy. I was in the delivery room, but as a spirit, not as a person, and I saw the face of my grandbaby. And more—Granddad's spirit was there with me.

He's got your eyes, Chief.

"He sure does."

I felt the exchange of love between my grandson and me. It was a level of communication that I can't really describe. He was—will be—a healthy baby, and I was assured by the Being of Light that he would never know cancer in his life.

Granddad spoke again in my sudden vision. *He looks just like you when you were young. He looks at Cleo with eyes that shine with happiness.*

I could feel my hereditary strings stretching from my grandmother to my mother then on to me and now to Cleo down to my grandson. In my vision, I saw Cleo as a perfect mother in her own way. I saw her rocking her baby when he was crying, I heard her sing to him. Her voice was beautiful, her voice is the sweeter part of Colt's voice.

That all happened to me while Cleo was still talking as if nothing had happened. But I changed. Now I see her in a different light. She is a woman, a mother, and I am happy for her. Knowing she has a bright future gives me joy beyond anything the material world can ever give me.

Later I found myself unexpectedly alone with Junior. He was awkward, as he has always been with any intimacy. I can say although he hasn't been angry this Christmas, he hasn't been happy, either. The stress he conveys touches everyone, especially Conrad.

"Junior," I said to him, "do you know that I love you?"

"Sure." He didn't even look up at me.

"No," I said, "don't give me *sure* as an answer. I need to know for certain that you not only know I love you, but that you *comprehend* my love."

Now he looked up, but he still wasn't quite looking at me. "What are you talking about?" he asked the air somewhere near me. "I know what love is and, yes, I believe you love me. So?"

"You see right there? I know you don't understand love. If you and I had love for one another, you wouldn't respond to me in that curt way. Junior, you've got to get to know love. You need to know that you're vulnerable when you love people, but that's okay. Sometimes it's good to be vulnerable."

His gaze came a little closer to me. "Oh, God, Mom, cut the crap. What do you want from me?"

"I want you to find happiness."

"Jeez. I *am* happy. You just don't ever see me happy. Come out with me and my friends sometime, and you'll see the happy me."

I wanted to grab his face and force him to look at me. But I didn't. "I don't mean intoxicated," I said. "I'm talking about happiness. True happiness. I don't think you know how to be happy."

"A person doesn't learn to be happy," he said. "It comes naturally. Everyone is happy, one time or another. It comes naturally! I'm happy a lot, just not around you. Besides, you act like I drink all the time. *Intoxicated!* That's such a nice thing to say."

"You do drink a lot," I said. "And you're not a nice person when you're drinking."

Finally he looked at me. "The last thing I want is to do argue with you," he said. "Knock this shit off. Don't talk to me like you know happiness. You've been unhappy for years and years. So shut up!"

"You're right. I've been unhappy for years. And part of me is unhappy because you're so miserable. As your mother, I want you to find love in the world. Find happiness. But it starts with you! No one knows that more than me. Happiness starts with the individual. I had to make a choice to be happy. I want you to know that I'm very happy that you spent Christmas with me. With us."

He looked me in the eye for a second and quickly looked away. "Whatever." And he walked off.

But in that moment, the Being of Light touched me, and I had another vision. In it, Junior was several years older, and he was alone. Over time he had made everyone feel so uncomfortable around him that no one wanted to spend any time with him. As time moved on, he slowly isolated himself until he was completely alone. He had made antipathy into an art. How can anyone hate so much? As far as I know, Junior hasn't been victimized by anyone that would make him so angry. I could see that his soul was in agony because he would never recognize the hostility that he projected. I understood in my vision that what lives in Junior was an element of evil.

He finds joy in making people uncomfortable and fearful of him. He actually relishes the pain of others.

Granddad was there again. I turned to him. "How can this be? How can my son have evil in him?"

We are blessed with free will, he said. *Junior has had plenty of opportunity to choose the light, but he prefers the dark. He enjoys it. He chooses to see the world as bad and all the people in it as an antagonist, or at least unpleasant. The joy he gets from hate is much greater than the joy of love.*

"But, Granddad, what can I do? I can't let him live out his life this way."

It's his choice, Chief. I know you want to help him, but he doesn't want any help. In fact, he's convinced himself that everyone except him needs help because they don't see the world the way he does.

"Have I failed as a mother? Could I have done something different?"

Hope, you're a good mother. You did the best you could in raising your children. But this isn't about you. *You can't blame yourself for your son's actions, his disdain. This vision is a gift for you so you can come to terms with Junior before your time ends in this lifetime.*

At that moment I was returned to consensual reality, where everyone else seems to be. As I thought about Junior, I felt a shift in my maternal desires. Junior was his own man now. I had raised him the best I could. I could love him, but he had the choice of accepting my love or not. Him disliking me, or whatever he thinks of me—that won't change the fact that he is my son.

After Junior walked away, I sat still, quietly observing everyone else in the room. I saw Conrad and Ward talking together. My awareness has changed, and now I could see energy being exchanged between them. Where Junior has consciously blocked his brotherly energy from Conrad, I could see that Ward was filling in those empty spaces. Ward's not connected only to my daughter. He has love for my son, too, in a brotherly sense. These two young men were talking and laughing. On a soul level, I could see that the baby linked them in ways they might not understand. Ward's the proud and excited father, and Conrad's excited for his sister. He'll be the doting uncle. Conrad has felt responsible for his little sister for years, and now I see that his love has been rewarded with the knowledge that his sister is happy and has a good soon-to-be husband. He is so proud of her.

The energy I saw today reassured me that my family will heal after I'm gone. Next Christmas, though I won't be here, they'll have a happy holiday because Cleo's baby will heal their pain, Colt's most of all. He will see his grandson as someone very special. Tonight I'm thankful that this beautiful grandson will be arriving soon. My grandson will know love like my grandparents gave to me, and I know how far-reaching that energy is.

Around my neck lies the necklace I found in the guest room back in October. Colt had bought it for me. Poor Jolene didn't get it! No, that's not funny. I felt like a real idiot when I unwrapped it and opened the box and realized that all along it was for me. A little while ago, I confessed in secret to Colt that I had found this necklace in the closet.

He said, "Babe, let's do something right now. Let's call all the good times we had in the past *living* and let's call all of the mistakes we have made *learning*. So you had one of those famous *learning experiences* when you found the necklace in the closet."

I had to smile. "I like that. You're good."

"Nah, that's not me. It's from a country song. I just like the idea of not blaming each other for things we've done."

"Well, I'm excited to keep *living* with you."

Colt and I decided we wouldn't tell anyone about my new diagnosis until after the holidays. We, more me than him, didn't want to overshadow the celebrations with my bad news. Somehow, I now have the faith that I will know when the time is right to tell everyone. It's not the time yet. I can feel it.

Oh, the memories we made here on the ranch this holiday season! It was truly a sterling moment. I'm so grateful to the Being of Light for these moments. Somehow I also know that these memories will be valuable to me even after I'm gone. I don't think when a person dies they get amnesia. In fact, I think it's the opposite. I believe that our memories are living energy that go with us after we die. I have a suspicion that when we die, we not only carry our memories from our most recent lifetime but we gain our memories from all the lifetimes we've lived. And our collective memories are precious energy on a soulful plane.

I conclude tonight's entry and smile at the angel up there on the top of the tree. She is a symbol of grace.

December 27th

When we arrived at Good Shepherd's, I felt a shiver go up my spine. It was chilly out, sure, but my shiver had nothing to do with the weather. The institution is soul-chilling! Walking toward the building I finally understood why I've been so reluctant to visit Nina—the institution she's in bothers me to my core. It's almost as if I can feel the pain of everyone locked up inside. From deep within me, I felt their fear. I am not exaggerating. I was so reluctant even to step through the front door that it took tremendous self-control just to get myself in.

Colt was proud that I wanted to see his sister. The staff all know him, of course, and are on a first name basis with him, but for some reason most of them doubted that he was married. I heard some of them whisper about that as he introduced me to them. We went directly to Nina's room. On the shelf near her bed was a framed photo of me and Colt. The glass was broken, evidently from one of her outbursts.

Nina was sitting on the bed, staring at her fingers when we came in. She didn't hear us at first. She looked so childlike, moving one finger at a time and examining it.

"Hey! How's my little sis?"

She jumped when she heard Colt's voice and ran toward the door. She doesn't like human contact, however, so she stopped just short of him and stood there, fiddling with her pant leg. It reminded me of how Sahchi trembles at the sight of Colt. I don't mean to be disrespectful and compare Nina to a dog. What I'm trying to do is show that she is unable to show her affection so she trembles with excitement. She also made a grunting noise that Colt interpreted as a greeting.

"I brought you a Christmas present," Colt told her. He handed her a small, wrapped gift.

Her eyes grew big and she grabbed it and threw it on the floor. Then she got down on all fours and attacked the gift. She ripped the paper and the box to shreds. What we'd brought her was a braid of hair from the two horses, Orin and Calypso. Orin is blonde, and Calypso is so black his hair is almost blue. It was a braided bracelet, about nine inches long with a simple knot that slipped through a hole on the other end to latch the bracelet in place. She took it up and examined it closely, grunting and smiling all the while. She handled it as gently as if it were a small pet. Colt was pleased. He had told me that he was afraid she would try to eat it. The staff at Good Shepherd's doesn't like him bringing gifts to her because they're afraid she might find a way to hurt herself or someone else with it. But Colt turned on his charm and they relented.

As Nina played with the braided horsehair, Colt sat in a recliner that a staff member later told me was his home away from home. I learned that because of institutional rules they couldn't put a second bed in the room, so he made do with the recliner. I looked at him sitting there and it broke my heart. I've been so wrong about him.

Nina was nervous with me in the room and I was nervous about being there, but Colt reassured me it would be all right. "Don't worry, Babe," he said. "She does this for a little bit, but then she'll calm down." He spoke to Nina in a quiet voice that

I rarely heard him use. Eventually she did calm down and sat in her chair, still fidgeting with the braid.

Then…well, I don't know what came over me. Normally, I would never speak to Nina for fear of setting off an episode, but today I believe the Being of Light had hold of my tongue. "Nina," I said, "I've got something to talk over with you."

Colt looked at me funny, but he sat still and let me go on.

"Well," I said, "I guess I can only tell you that I've not done good by you. Colt has told me that you've had a hard time lately, but I didn't believe him. He even invited me to come along to visit you, but I always refused." I paused. She was just staring at me. Finally I said what had to be said. "I'm here now, and I want you to know that I'm sorry. I never meant to hurt you, but I understand now that by refusing to come and visit you, I wasn't supporting you. In my book, that is intentional harm."

She was still just staring at me, and for a moment I saw her in a way I'd never seen her before. She looked like she should have the mental capacity of a forty-five-year-old woman, which is what she is. She didn't, of course, but her moans and grunts told me she was listening to me.

I went on. "I guess I was hoping that you might forgive me for my trespasses. If you and Colt could both forgive me. I promise I will become the sister-in-law that you once knew. I will come to visit you. I won't become so fixated on my own life that I forget you. Nina, I'm so sorry." I slowly reached over and touched her hand with the tip of my index finger. "I love you, Nina, and in my love, I take responsibility for hurting you and Colt."

She looked down at my finger and blinked her eyes. I believe she was noticing the difference in the colors of our skin for she looked at my face, then back down at my finger. My heart ached for her. Her hair was stringy and frazzled from her pulling on it all the time.

The moment passed. Then she looked at Colt and rubbed her stomach. This was an indication that she was hoping Colt had brought her dinner from home, a special treat for anyone confined to an institution. We had made a big plate, and it was warming in the facility's kitchen. This was against the rules, of course, but Colt had again charmed his way through the red tape. I can't say he breaks rules. No, he charms people into breaking them for him.

When the nurse's aide tapped on the door and handed the plate of food to Colt and Colt showed it to her, Nina smiled and grunted and clapped her hands together. Colt got her to sit down at her little table. Never letting go of the bracelet, I watched her eat. Handfuls of food went into her mouth. She smacked her lips loudly. Her eyes were focused on the plate of food. I could see that she enjoyed the flavors, and as fast as she was shoveling the food into her mouth, for her, she was taking her time, savoring the meal. It was amazing to watch.

I suddenly empathized with Colt. He'd once told me that he felt guilty because he was able to live a normal life but that Nina has only ever known institutions. Now I felt sad for her, too. I wished that somehow, some way, she could be free. On the walls in her room hung photos of her family taken on the family ranch. That was home, not this institution. How sad it is that a human being like Nina will never know what it feels like to have a real home.

Nina doesn't seem to recognize the people in those pictures. It was hard for me to wrap my mind around the idea that someone is incapable of what we call "normal" human functioning and emotions.

I was busy comparing her reality to mine. I wished for happiness for her. I wished that she could have the ability to feel the love of her parents, Tammy Jo and Garrett. I wanted her to feel the love that Colt offered her, the love I now felt for her.

In comparing myself to Nina, I was granted a vision. I saw Nina bathed in light and love from the Being of Light. She wasn't as tortured as I had perceived, but her reality is nothing I can relate to. What I saw, however, was that she does, on a soul level, know the love that Colt, Tammy Jo, Garrett, and the rest of the family give her. And however distorted her emotional functioning might be, Nina loves them in return. It's unfortunate that what is happening to her only in her soul cannot be expressed in her physical condition — It's her disorder that restricts her from expressing her emotions in what we would call normal ways. Nonetheless, Nina loves, lives, and functions as a human being. She is not less than human. Nor is she to be looked upon as less deserving because she is different.

Then I heard the voice of my granddad. *Chief,* he said, *you're thinking about Nina with a human mind. When it comes to the workings of the universe, you are as incapable of comprehending the 'why' of Nina's situation as you think she is.*

"But why is she this way?" I asked him. "Nina has never had a chance to be normal. She doesn't deserve this punishment."

Whose will should be done? he replied. *Yours or that of the Being of Light?*

That stopped me for a minute. "Not mine," I finally answered. "The world would be all kinds of messed up if it were up to me."

I could feel his smile. *Yes, you understand. Not everything is for you to understand. Don't worry yourself trying to reason the 'why' of this situation. Let's not judge or question the workings of things we don't understand. When you look at Nina, pray for her, but pray that the Being of Light's will be done, not yours.*

"I understand, Granddad. There's something greater than me at work here. Thank you for telling me, for addressing this with me."

And then my vision suddenly changed again, and I could see the real, true Nina. I saw her soul, and it was wonderful. She is bright and filled with energy. And I could see beyond her, out into what I understood were her past lives. She was a special being that in small ways had a huge impact on human development. Her love for mankind was so large that she was willing to be incarnated into this life, a life of great challenges, so that she could help others find their way.

I was astonished. She chose this life on purpose! She chose her family before she came into this life. She chose her disability. She knew that this lifetime would be frustrating and painful, yet she chose to do this in order to help others.

Then my vision changed again, and I saw an alternate reality in which Nina wasn't born. And what I saw I couldn't believe. Tammy Jo and Garrett divorced each other early in their marriage because their commitment to each other wasn't as strong as their commitment to family. In our present reality, Nina, in her way, has given them strength, and they have committed their lives to her and through their commitment to her, have grown into having a strong commitment to their other children and to each other.

In this vision where Nina did not exist, Colt and I never met because Colt didn't return to the ranch after his discharge from the Marines. In our present reality, though, he, too, is committed to Nina. She is a large influence in his return to the family ranch. In my vision, Nina didn't exist, I never met Colt, and therefore I never had his support when I had breast cancer the first time. Without his love and support, I died. But what disturbed me the most was *I died lonely.* I didn't have Colt there to love me, so I met my death alone, without ever having known his love or the love of my children.

Granddad watched this vision with me. Now he spoke again. *You see, Chief, Nina has been a blessing for many people. Without her love, many of you would have never known love.*

The vision began to fade, but I didn't want it to go away. I wasn't ready yet. Everything was fading too quickly, and yet the image of Nina remained until she filled my vision.

I consider you my sister, she said in my vision. *I say this because in a previous life we were sisters.*

"We were?" I asked her. Somehow that felt true. "I like knowing that. Perhaps if I think about it long enough, I'll be able to remember our sisterhood."

Hope, said the Nina in my vision, *I heard you today, and I forgive you. And please know that I feel your love and that I have much love for you.*

And in that moment the vision dissolved altogether.

Are these moments only my imagination?

After visiting the place of peace, I know my visions are real and true. But our society conditions us to doubt such things. I have faith that my visions are real and true. I get angry with myself for allowing doubts to creep in.

Nina, my sister, I am grateful for your courage to come to us in a difficult life and bless us with your love.

DECEMBER 29TH

I woke this morning under my painted sky with Colt sleeping next to me. Did I awaken in love? Did I awaken feeling content? Or did I awaken feeling depressed or lonely again? Well, it's wonderful to report that I woke up knowing that the man I love was next to me and that even though life isn't perfect, I felt damn good. I couldn't feel any hint of doubt or depression.

Was that because Colt was lying next to me? Was that why I felt so good?

I'd like to say yes, but it's not totally because of Colt. I had a dream last night. I dreamt that I was walking to work in the dark. The whole town was dark. I was returning to work after the holidays and filled with dread. With every step I took toward work, I had the feeling that something horrible was going to happen. When I got to my cubicle, I sat in my chair and Brent came rushing in and told to me hurry up and follow him to his office. We ran. We flat-out ran! I'd never do that in that office in real life.

When we got to Brent's office, Jerome was waiting for us. Jerome's goons had Cleo and Conrad tied to chairs. Jerome was demanding that I kill Quint, and if I didn't, he would kill Conrad and Cleo. I begged for my children's lives, but Brent slapped me across the face and told me to calm down and do as I was told. Then Jerome put a pistol in my hand. "Now," he said, "call Quint and ask her to meet you for lunch. After the two of you have eaten, follow her to the parking lot and take care of her." He looked at my children tied to those chairs. "If you do as you are told," he said, "and when Quint is dead, then I will release your children."

This was an awful dream but I couldn't stop it. Feeling scared and alone, I left Brent's office in a panic. There's no way I could kill Quint. But how could I let my children be killed? I tucked the pistol into my purse and walked back out into a colorless world. But instead of calling Quint and asking her to meet me, I went to the cathedral. I didn't go in, though. I went to the tree where Mr. Goldsole always prays.

In my dream, with tears streaming down my face, I began to pray by that tree. I prayed out of the love I felt for my family, the love of the friendship I had with Quint, and the love I felt for the Being of Light. In my prayer, I called out for guidance. And then the tree lit up with energy and morphed into the Being of Light! The light radiated from the tree and gave color to the world. I was standing before the Being, basking in the rays of its sacred light.

Then I heard a voice. *Hope, you are never alone. I'm connected to your soul. I'm so glad that you reached out to me.*

"Oh, thank you," I said in my dream. "Thank you for answering my call. I'm in a terrible position. I'm being forced to do someone's evil bidding."

You came here to engage with evil and the tool you chose to use is love. I'm proud of you, Hope, for you understand the universe in which you live.

The Being of Light was shining not only with pure white light but also with shades of deep purple and gold. And when the purple rays touched me I felt comforted and warmed. When the golden rays touched me, I felt that there might be a way out of this ugly situation.

Love is the word you have chosen to use at this time, said the Being of Light. *You are correct. Love is the answer. Life is more than this problem. Life is more than any problem. Every problem has a solution. With faith and love the solutions will come.*

Now I saw some shadows among the rays of light as the

Being of Light said, *The lengths that people will go to in order to manipulate you to do their hideous duties may seem unavoidable, yet you have a means to end this evil.* The shadows grew and the light dimmed when the word *evil* was spoken.

"What is the answer?" I asked in my dream. "Jerome has my children. He'll kill them if I don't shoot Quint. Not only is love my avenue of prayer, but it's also what makes my situation impossible. Because of love, I can't kill Quint, nor can I stand by and let harm come to my children."

I will help you, said the Being of Light. *Go now. Take the pistol Jerome gave you and find Quint.*

"You want me to find Quint and shoot her?" As I asked this question, I could hear my grandmother singing "Where the Soul Never Dies." At first it seemed to be coming from far away, but then it seemed to be coming from all around, or maybe from inside me.

No, said the Being of Light. *Find Quint and show her the pistol. Show her the tool Jerome wants you to use to bring her down. Be honest with her. Tell her about the love you speak of here with me. Together, you will find a solution to this problem.*

As my grandmother's singing grew louder, and the song brought forth ideas that turned into answers, I knew what needed to be done. Then I looked again at the Being of Light and saw that in order to fight Jerome's evil, I already had the answer! Moreover, the Being of Light would be there to guide me.

Remember the ones you are protecting, said the Being of Light. *Remember that what you are doing, you are doing with love. Love has great strength.*

And then I woke up.

When I woke up, I could hear a strange sound. It replaced my grandmother's song. As with her song in my dream, this sound was a sound that came from within, from inside my body on some microcosmic level, and it was stimulating specific thoughts. I saw memories that contained information I needed. I heard the voices of people that cared about me, and their words began to weave together into a plan. My dream had created the solution of my problem with Jerome. I was instantly excited. Love! Yes, love is the answer.

I looked at Colt sleeping beside me and at Sahchi snoring away at the foot of the bed. I understood that love is so much more than what he and I shared. Love is a celestial power given to us. We receive it and broadcast it. Yet in its most basic form, it's the love that Colt and I share. This basic love is just as important as the larger love. With that concept of love in my mind, I opened my heart this morning and willingly allowed Colt's love to wash over me. It filled me with excitement, the bubbly kind of excitement you get when you're young and in love for the first time. Fresh love. I couldn't resist. I woke Colt and told him, "Wake up! It's time to make love."

DECEMBER 31ST

I was so sick today! It's awful to be sick on New Year's Eve day, although by early evening I was beginning to feel better.

While I was lying there and feeling like shit, Conrad came to my room and sat on my bed. He looked worried. "Mom, I hope you know that you have me if you need anything," he said.

"Thank you," I said. "Sometimes I need to know that you care. I know it's silly. You always care but it's still nice to hear it."

"Mom, is everything...I mean, are you doing okay? I've got the strangest feeling that this isn't just a fever or something simple, like a cold. I've been fighting it for a long time. I keep telling myself it's just my imagination, that you're fine, but my gut tells me to pay attention to you. So. Are you doing okay?"

What's a mother to do? The truth is the way of life, isn't it? Aren't we supposed to be truthful in our way? Conrad is connected to me like no one else is. I couldn't lie to him. Crap—here it is, New Year's Eve, and I was about to drop a bomb on my son. I thought about how to say it, then, "Conrad, I don't want you to fuss over me. Nor do I want what is going on with me to alter your life in any way, shape, or form. You have a good, healthy life to live. You don't need me bringing you down."

Now he looked more worried. "What are you talking about?"

"Do you remember when you were young and I used to walk all three of you to school every morning?"

"Sure. How could I forget?" He moved closer to me.

"Well, do you remember the time when you told me it was time for you to walk to school by yourself? When you told me that you were older and older kids walk themselves to school? Remember that?"

He nodded. "Yeah. Vaguely."

"That was a day I will never forget. That was the day I had to let go and allow you to grow. You've grown more and more independent. It was heartbreaking to do the right thing by letting you go, but I had to do it. It hurt. But it was the right thing to do."

"Mom, what does this have to do with my question?"

I had to say it. "I, too, need the freedom to grow. There will come a time when I will also need you to let go of me so I can move forward and grow."

"What are you saying?" he asked. "Are you dying? Is that what you're saying?"

"My cancer is back, Conrad. It's spread to other places in my body, and there isn't much that can be done."

I can't even express what it's like to tell my son something that I knew would shake his mind and rattle his bones. I've never wanted to hurt any of my children, but I can't lie to them, either. They all deserve to know the truth. I laid my hand on his hand. "I don't want you to pity me," I said. "Please don't do that." He nodded, but I could see he was choking up. "I've decided to live the rest of my days doing things that make me happy. It's important to me that you do your best to wrap your mind around this and be with me. Spend some time with me. I don't want either of us to have regrets when the time comes...."

He put his arms around me and held me for a while. "I just told you that you have me if you need anything. If you need me to wrap my mind around this, I will. I can't say it will be easy." He tried to laugh. "And...and...well, you can forget about me acting normal. There is no normal behavior when your mom tells you she's dying!" He paused again and gave me a squeeze. "But I will tell you this. I'll do everything I can for you."

"Thanks," I said. "That means the world to me. Cleo's pregnant, you know, and your dad and I are so happy for her. So you can understand why I haven't made an announcement yet."

"Sure."

"Conrad, let her be happy for a while. Let's let her have the precious moments of being pregnant before we tell her about this. I know there won't be any good time to tell her, but it kills me to take even one second of her happiness away from her. And Ward. I couldn't ask for a better man to be by her side."

"Cleo is happy!" he said. "And I'm happy for her. Just like you. You're also right about Ward. He's a fantastic guy." He smiled. "He's like the brother I never had."

Silence came between us. We both felt awkward as we faced the obvious next step in the conversation. Conrad, bless him, took the lead.

"Have you told Junior yet?"

I shook my head.

"When are you going to tell him?"

"I don't know. I've tried talking to him, but he's so filled with anger. At me. At the world. For what, I don't know. But he's angry, so we don't talk much. I've thought about writing him a letter."

"That's a perfect idea. Yeah, write him a letter. Tell him everything you've ever wanted him to know. Tell him he's been too damn stubborn and he's shut you out so much that he's unable listen to you when you try to talk to him. Write about how you feel. Tell him about the diagnosis. That way, he can do what he wants with the information."

"You really think so?" I asked.

All he could do was shrug his shoulders. "I don't know," he said after a minute. "I don't know if there's a right way or a wrong way to reach out to Junior. He really is pissed off all the time about everything. I think a letter is your best option."

Then Conrad's face twisted with the pain he tried to keep under control. He turned away from me in an attempt to hide his emotions. I stuffed my emotions down so I wouldn't cry, "So, I hear you have a girlfriend? Cleo seems to think she is the one for you. Is that true?"

"Oh, she told you." His voice cracked. "She's great, mom. She's my best friend."

"Then she is the one. That's how I knew your father was the one for me. He became my best friend and I loved him so much I couldn't function when he wasn't near me."

"That's how it is with Sam," He said.

The change of topic worked. Conrad regained his composure and was smiling. "I feel like I can't breathe when she's not with me," he said. "We were friends at first, but my heart fell for her right away."

"Sam? Is that her name?" I asked.

"Yeah. Samantha, but everyone calls her Sam."

"You should bring her around so I can meet her. She has to get my approval before this gets too serious." I laughed as I said this.

"Sure, Mom. I'll bring her around. You'll love her, too. She'll fit right in with this family...." He paused. "Well, except for Junior. I haven't brought her around because she was kind of his girlfriend first."

"Don't bother explaining, I know about it and I understand. Cleo's real good at explaining our family dramas."

We continued talking about Sam and Conrad's dreams of the future with her. He had already decided when and where to ask her to marry him, and he had the ring picked out, too. How wonderful, to see my son in love. He spent the better part of the day with me. After a while, Colt came in to check on me. He sat on the bed, too, and joined in the conversation. He was relieved that I'd told Conrad and surprised to hear about the upcoming nuptials.

I think Colt needs someone to talk to about my diagnosis. He understands that I need time alone with our children before I get worse. After a little while, he left Conrad and me alone again. I appreciated that. Conrad is intelligent, and he was able to reason away his sadness. Oh, he was sad, all right, but his foremost emotion is his concern for me. That's so kind.

...

We had planned a small party for New Year's Eve, but Colt wanted to cancel it because of my illness. I insisted that we have it. By six-thirty, I was able to get myself up and about. I wasn't exactly overflowing with energy, but I was able to be the hostess I wanted to be.

Pretty soon, I heard Agnes's voice. "I just hate parking my car in this neighborhood," she was saying. "Conrad," she said as she came in the door, "would you be a dear and move your mother's car and park mine in the driveway?"

I shot a look at Colt and he smiled his best professional smile. "Agnes! I'm so glad you could join us." He wrapped a loving arm around her as Conrad ran out and rearranged the cars.

Tammy Jo, Garrett, and Clint arrived a little later, Becky and her parents arrived, and last came Wild Mack and Jennifer. There isn't a party until Wild Mack is in attendance.

"I know you like to drink the hard stuff," he said, handing me a paper bag with a six-pack of something inside it. "The rest of us can't handle those kind of stiff drinks."

I opened the bag. He had brought me a six-pack of Mountain Dew. "Thanks, Mack! You sure know what my vice is."

Colt had taken care of everything for the party, including a spread of food and coolers filled with bottles and ice. It was a casual party. Prior to this year, we usually went wherever his band was playing. I've always liked the Wild Bunch, and now I'm sad but also a little happy to know that Colt has quit the band for now. He told me yesterday that he wants to spend all his free time with me from now on. That means there will be no more lonely Friday nights for me. I feel a little guilty to admit that I'm pleased. In return, I've committed to go and see Nina with him and added that we'll go often and regularly.

The first topic of conversation at the party was Christmas. I told everyone how much I appreciated them for getting together at Garrett and Tammy Jo's. Almost all of them had something to say about how special this Christmas had been. But then Aunt Agnes piped up and said, "I do believe the Christmas season was invented by the Devil."

Everybody went quiet. What on earth was she saying?

"Why would you say that?" Tammy Jo finally asked.

"To annoy me! It's a horrible holiday for those of us who are widowed and lonely. For those of you who have families, it's a source of delight, but it's torture for me to endure it alone."

"Aunt Agnes," I said, "you weren't alone. Are you forgetting that we invited you to the ranch?"

"Well, yes," she admitted, "but even if I share a holiday, I still feel bitter because I have to go home to an empty house. I'm all alone."

I hadn't thought about Agnes being the keeper of a lonely heart, but in that moment I understood her crotchety ways. She was lonely. She still missed her husband, who had died nineteen years ago. But time has not softened her. Poor old woman! She's as healthy as an ox and has many long years ahead of her, but she has no one except the people at our party and some friends from her church. When my time comes, I'm going to ask the Being of Light to be kind to her and find her some companionship. Happy New Year, Aunt Agnes!

JANUARY 7TH

It was back to work today. Actually, I think things are working out for the best. I was finished collecting the data Jerome had requested, so I took the external hard drive with all that secret data up to Brent's office. Here's my secret. What they think is good data is really a mixture of numbers, some real, some crap, and Jerome and his people won't be able to separate factual data from fictional. The numbers are logical and will function in his equations. I bet they won't even notice.

Then Brent told me I had to deliver the data to Jerome in person. I begged not to go but he said Jerome was firm about it. When I arrived at Jerome's office, he was on a VersaClimber (that's a resistance machine that works out the whole body), sweating through his tank top and shorts. He has a great body, no doubt about it, and I can't lie about enjoying watching him work that machine. Hey, it was a free show! He had a Bluetooth stuck in his ear and was doing his usual tough talk while he was working out.

I imagined or fanaticized, wrongly, of course, that once the data was collected, compiled, and given to Back-2-Back, I would get paid. Then I would be taken off his leash.

But Jerome had other ideas.

"The development of Rape Play 2 is behind schedule," he was saying into the Bluetooth, "and I've told you time and again that if you didn't get that project on the fast track, you'd be taken off the assignment." Sweat continued to pour off his body but he wasn't even out of breath. He hadn't noticed me yet. He was up there on that machine like he was climbing a ladder, and his ass was flexed tight.

"Tom, stop!" he barked. "Tom. Tom! Don't worry about it. You don't have a job here anymore." He paused, listening to whoever Tom was and what he was saying. Then, "You're damn right I just fired you! I'm sending security to your office this minute. Don't move until they get there. Remember the surveillance cameras, my boy. Don't let me catch you taking so much as a paper clip or I'll have you prosecuted for stealing." He disconnected that call and dialed up another number. "Alex, this is Jerome. Get a security detail up to Tom Roundtree's office right now. I just let him go. Also mark the time on the surveillance camera in his office. I want you to analyze it. He's been working on some sensitive material, and nothing leaves with him. Got it? Good." He disconnected.

He dropped off the climber and was wiping his face with a towel when he finally noticed me. He didn't so much as say a polite hello.

"You have something for me?"

"I sure do!" I filled my voice with confidence. I wasn't about to act like I was unsure.

"Just put it on my desk. I'll be out in a minute."

Out? What is he talking about? But then he opened a door next to some floor-to-ceiling shelves (piled with video games and stacks of paper, but almost no books), and I could see a bathroom that would have been right at home in a five-star hotel. It was all marble, with a deluxe shower, the kind with multiple showerheads coming out the walls and ceiling. A freshly pressed suit was hanging on a mahogany valet stand. Jerome closed the door and I heard the water come on. I sat on his fancy leather couch, feeling very uncomfortable. I shouldn't be in a man's office alone while he's disrobing and showering. He knew I was coming. He should have taken care of his crap before I got here. He was acting like my time wasn't valuable. That irked me.

I waited and waited and waited. Forty-five minutes later, here Jerome came out of his five-star bathroom, talking into his Bluetooth again and looking like he just finished a photo shoot with GQ. I stood up and said, "Have a nice day," and headed for the door, but he snapped his fingers at me and pointed to the couch. *Snapped his fingers at me!*

Oh, no! I thought. *No one snaps their fingers at me. Who the hell does this guy think he is?*

He sat behind his big mahogany desk and muted his BlackBerry and laid it on the desk. Then he looked at me. "Sit. We have a meeting."

Now I was getting good and pissed. When I'm angry, the tough chick that lives somewhere inside me fights back. I'm not sure where the strength comes from, but it's great to have it there.

I barked back at him. "Then get off the phone or I'm walking out of here!"

"Let me call you later about this," he said into his Bluetooth and disconnected the call and looked back at me. "Hope, why the attitude?"

I was not sitting down. I walked across the office and stopped at his desk and looked down at him. "Look," I said, "you're an important guy, people need you, I get that. But me, I don't need you for anything. You need me. So I'll just make more room in your world for you and go back to mine. You got what you wanted." I pointed to the external hard drive. "It's sitting right there. You don't need anything else from me."

"That's where you're wrong," he said. He didn't even look at the drive. "Remember I told you that you were my new best friend now that you and Quint have become friendly? I need you to use your friendship to help me."

"What makes you think I'm capable of helping you?" I asked. "And, further, what makes you so sure that I want to continue helping you?"

He gave me a big smile. "Oh, you will help me. Everyone does what I ask. I can be very persuasive if I have to be." He hit the intercom: "Kelly, could you bring me the O'Dwyer file?" He has some balls to have a folder with my last name on it.

The bimbo-secretary came in. I had doubted that she was capable of walking and carrying a folder at the same time, but she did it. She almost tripped, of course, but she recovered prettily. Good for her. She was getting smarter by the minute. She handed him the folder without a word and left us alone. He flashed it like some kind of weapon. I knew from talking to Quint what a folder like this contains, but I was still surprised to see how thick it was.

"Here in this folder," he said, "is your life. I have all the information I need to get you to do anything I ask."

I rolled my eyes. "Jerome, do you think this is a movie? I'm in no mood to play with you or listen to your threats. If I were you, I'd start at the end of the negotiations and offer me a lot of money. Threaten me, and I won't do a damn thing for you. But put down some money, and, yeah, I will most likely do whatever you want."

He smiled again. "Do you know what is in this folder?"

"I do."

"Really? I doubt it."

"You have pictures of my husband, my daughter, and my two sons. You have locations and schedules of where my children work. You know that my husband is a veterinarian and is half owner of a successful animal hospital. You probably have a list of my friends and members of my husband's family. All of my family is dead, so I doubt you have much information on them. However, you are a very creepy guy, so you might also have information on dead people. I'm sure you have the makes and models of the cars we own. You have the location of the house we live in. You have confidential bank information that shows you that in nine years we will have paid off our house. You also have information on our dog, and that her name is Sahchi. Is that about right?"

"Well, well, well. You do know what's in this folder. So you know I could use this information to hurt you or someone close to you."

"Wrong! You might be naive enough to threaten me, but you forget that I know a lot about you, too. True, I gathered data on Bio-Sport for you, but come on, Jerome, I don't play any nicer than you do. To protect myself, I did plenty of research on you. Not Back-2-Back. On *you*." I pointed my index finger at the middle of his chest.

He actually looked uncomfortable. He laid the folder down and tapped it with his fingers. "I'm clean," he said. "You don't have anything on me."

"Jerome," I said, not moving, "we're a firm with many customers. Because of the economy, many companies are outsourcing their accounting these days, and many companies don't like to, um...shall we say, air out all the numbers. You know they'd rather put a little gray ink where the red ink is supposed to go. In return, they offer favors, so I get a little something for my time. One of my clients owns a private detective agency. Let's just say that this agency isn't so on the up and up, if you get my meaning. They work for some colorful characters, in particular, an organized crime family. This private detective agency owes me a BIG favor. Do you want to play who has a bigger dick? Maybe you've noticed that I don't have a penis, but I have many friends that have big dicks. Bigger ones than yours." I was lying through my teeth, but it sounded so good I kept going. Jerome looked like he had a red laser sight painted on his chest.

"Hope, Hope," his voice was so sweet and friendly you could spoon it up for dessert, "you've got me all wrong. Let's play nice now. Sure, you can make a lot of money if you play your cards right."

"Like I said, money is my language. But when I leave here, I'm leaving with that folder, and don't let me catch you with a copy of a single article from it. If I think you've threatened my family again, you'll be in marble city [I stole that graveyard term from Becky] faster than you can say, 'I'm sorry.'" I figured that this guy talks tough, but if the tables were turned he'd fold.

"Yeah, sure, no problem. Here, take it." He handed me the folder.

I didn't even open it. I just held it in one hand. "And the check for the work."

He raised his arms like he was surrendering. "I can write it now or we can add to it to the next one. It's up to you."

"I want the money you promised me from the beginning. I want it now. After you pulled this folder shit today, I'm not sure if I can trust you anymore."

He took out his checkbook and wrote out the biggest number I have ever seen on a check. It was exactly what we had negotiated. Even though that number practically made my legs melt, I kept my cool.

"Well, Jerome," I said as I tucked the check into my purse, "what do you have in mind next?" He started to answer, but I interrupted him. "Before we even begin, I want another hundred thousand up front."

He frowned. "I just wrote you a check for eight hundred and fifty thousand," he said. "And now you're demanding another hundred grand?"

"It's earnest money," I said. "I mean, I find cash makes everyone honest. You might try and fuck me over. You wouldn't try to fuck me over, would you, Jerome? Nah. You wouldn't want me to call my friends with big dicks to come over here and take you in that nice bathroom you have over there and paint the walls with your blood...." He could imagine what those big guys might do to him. "Besides, once Bio-Sport goes down, you stand to make over three hundred million. My fee is small in comparison."

"Hey, I'm good for it."

"I let you slide before with all your tough talk," I said. "Hell, I even tried to let you go free, but it was you who insisted on getting on top." I gave him a showgirl smile. "You are such a fool. Do you actually think you're the first dirty company to proposition us? We work with all kinds of shady companies these days. You gotta love capitalism and data. Data's worth more than gold! Even your data, Jerome."

I let him think about this for a second while I pulled up one of his chairs and sat down. "But, hey," I said, almost leaning across his desk, "let me hear you speak my language. Tell me what you want me to do, and I'll tell you how much I want."

I'm really good at this! My mouth was moving and the words were coming out, and, truth to tell, I was as surprised as Jerome was. I wasn't only standing up for myself, but I was pushing Jerome all over in his own office. If I hadn't gotten mad, this wouldn't have happened.

He told me what he wanted. "I want to take Bio-Sport off the map. I want your friend Quint disgraced. You can use your friendship to get this done. I hear she trusts you. I'll tell you what to say and when to say it. She's the brains behind Bio-Sport, and I want to get into her brain. You help me, I help you."

I nodded. "I can do that, no problem. Quint means nothing to me except that now she's my mark. I'll get you more information than you ever dreamed of. And you're going to pay me for it. Here's how I see it working. You break down what you want in segments. I'll meet with you once a week. You give me a segment, and I'll get what you want. The next week, I'll bring you the information and you'll pay me then. After we settle one segment, you can give me another segment. No multiple or segment stacking. Nice and neat, one at a time. At minimum, a segment will cost you a hundred thousand, so make it worth my time and yours. I'll let you know if a segment will cost more, but I'm telling you now, it's no less than a hundred."

I was proud of myself, but, yes, also ashamed. I was lying. No way was I going to hurt Quint. I love her and the good she's trying to do. However, I figured if I broke off my dealings with Jerome, he would only find someone else. Someone truly ruthless who would do real damage to her.

I stood up and picked up the folder. "Write the check, Jerome. One hundred thousand, and we have a deal."

He wrote another check and handed it to me. Jerome's evil was going to come to a halt. And as for the release of Rape Play 2, well, if my plan worked out, that, too, would come to halt.

I took the second check, tucked it in my purse with the first one, and shook Jerome's hand to seal the deal. Then I walked gracefully out of his office. Stopping at the receptionist's desk, I said, "Jerome asked me to tell you that he needed you to copy a file for him." The bimbo looked confused, but got up and walked down the hall to his office. The other bimbo wasn't at her desk. In the minute I was alone, I inserted a storage drive in the receptionist's computer and copied Jerome's calendar and any files I could access at that moment. It was an impulse, almost done by instinct. I have no idea what exactly I got, but I hope the information will offer me an edge.

I was out the door before the receptionist was back to her desk. As soon as I hit the sidewalk, I phoned some friends and set up a little dinner party.

JANUARY 9TH

Today was an odd day at work. Devin avoided me all day until it was time to go home. Then he came to my cubicle.

"Here." He handed me an envelope. "This is for you."

I opened it and pulled out his letter of resignation and read it. It was one paragraph long. "Devin," I said, "why are you quitting?"

"I don't feel comfortable here anymore. I wish I could say it was something else, but I find it hard to be around you now. There's a part of me that still wants you. A part that still wants us to have that special something."

"If this is about me," I said, "please don't quit. It will work itself out. I swear."

"How can this work out?" he asked. "I want to marry my girlfriend, but when I'm around you, I want you. I want you bad! That will never 'work itself out.'"

I had to think of something fast. "Would you please walk me to my car?" I asked him. When we got to my car, I opened the door and gestured for him to have a seat.

"Devin," I said, "I want you to know something."

"What?"

"I love you. You are kind and good. You have the qualities any woman would want from a guy. Now don't be freaked out by the word love. I don't, like, 'love you' like you love your girlfriend. That's a special kind of love. I love you with respect to who you are as person. Do you understand the difference?"

He considered this for a moment. "Sure. But knowing that you love me on any level makes this all the more difficult. I am so attracted to you! I spent the holidays thinking about you, wondering what you were doing. Who you were doing it with." His hands were shaking as he brushed his hair back off his forehead. "I'm so attracted to you, I want to make love you to you every time I see you. I dream about you."

That actually made me blush. "Really?" I asked.

"You're damn right I do. So I have to quit. I can't go on like this day in and day out."

I leaned toward him and looked him square in the eye. "Listen to me." I said. "I'm leaving soon. No one knows it yet, but I'm quitting, and when I do, I'm recommending you for a promotion. So you won't be bothered with this…er…mess any longer. Just be patient."

That made him frown. "Why? After all the years you've put in here, why would you quit? That makes no sense."

"I'm taking early retirement," I said. "Some investments have suddenly paid off quite well, so now I have the funds to do what I would like to do."

"That's great!" He kissed me on the cheek. "But I don't like thinking I won't see you anymore."

"It's for the best," I said, drawing back from him. "Just give me some time to work everything out. Can you do that?"

"Yes, I can do that. But how do I suppress how I feel about you?"

"We all have our earthly tests. You'll have to find your own solution."

He nodded, but I could tell he didn't like my answer. "Do you feel the same way?" he asked. "Do you ever want to make love to me again?"

"I can't answer that right now. But I do love you, like I said."

Looking confused and sad, he stepped out of my car, closed the door, and began walking alone across the parking lot. I felt bad for him, but I also felt that I wasn't the source of his confusion. I keep getting the feeling that he and his girlfriend are struggling with the whole marriage thing. But at least I talked him out of quitting. Being unemployed in this economy would only add more stress to his already stressful life.

I just sat in my car for a couple minutes, not really thinking or anything, and then I drove to my condo. I had invited Quint, Becky, and Wild Mack over for an evening of dinner and discussion.

I'd asked Becky to arrive earlier than the others. I'd told her I needed her help in preparing dinner. Well, that's not entirely true. I wanted to talk to her alone. She's so dependable she was waiting for me when I got there.

"How goes it, Sis?" she asked as I got out of my car.

"It's been a mighty strange day so far," I said.

"Go ahead! Fry my wig. I've turned out my hearing flap."

I told her about Devin and the confusion he was going through. I also told her real quick that I didn't want any advice from her regarding him.

"Becky," I said when we got inside, "I didn't ask you here to discuss work or relationships. I want to have a real grown-up conversation. A serious conversation about my wishes for after I'm gone."

She blinked her eyes and sat down on the couch, then started looking around. That's when I realized it was her first time there and I hadn't even offered her a tour of the place.

"I'm so sorry!" I said. "That was awfully rude of me. I guess I'm all caught up in what I want to talk to you about. Since this condo is part of what I want to discuss, how about a tour?"

She grinned. "Now you're getting some oxygen to your brain, girl. Bounce up outta that chair and show me this dump." It doesn't take long to walk around the thousand and fifty square feet, but Becky seemed to like what she saw.

"This place is over the top," she said. "I dig a pack, shack, and stack like this."

"I was hoping you'd like it."

"Are you kidding me? This pad here is real uptown. *Real* uptown."

We were back in the living room, where my books are shelved, and she was sitting on the couch, admiring the view out the window. I picked up the legal-sized envelope lying on the coffee table. I had gone to my lawyer's office earlier and had all the paperwork taken care of. I handed her the envelope and said. "I'm glad you like this place," I told her. "Because it's yours now. I'm giving this place to you."

That sure got her attention. "Come again? My ears are playing tricks on me. It sounded like you said—"

"You heard me. I'm giving this condo to you. It's all legal, all taken care of. It's paid for, the annual taxes are about eight hundred and twenty five, and the homeowner's dues are only eighty a month."

"Sis," she looked puzzled, "why would you give me your condo?"

"I don't have to tell you that my time is limited," I said. She hadn't opened the envelope yet. "I have to think about where my material possessions will do the most good. I want you to have the option to stay in this town. Your parents aren't getting any younger. They'll need you more often. This condo will give you your independence, but it's also close to where you can take care of them."

Still not opening the envelope, she went back to staring out the window. Without turning her head, she said, "Sis, I don't like to think of the day you won't be here. It kills my heart. I don't want to have this conversation and I don't want your condo."

"Like I said," I replied, "I want to have a grown-up conversation. Avoiding or ignoring my death isn't the answer. And if you think by not accepting this condo, I will somehow live longer, you're wrong. If you don't take it, well, I guess I'll have to give it to Devin."

She didn't get the joke. "*What?* Don't you talk ugly to me. Tune in to this! Do you think I'll sit here and let you hand this condo to that fall-down-juvenile? I can fall into these digs just fine. Just understand that I'll take it in a bluesy groove."

"Yes, I can understand that it bums you out. I'm just happy that I'm able to do this. I've given things a lot of thought. I know this is the right thing to do."

"Well," she said, "what about Cleo and Ward? They have a biscuit in the oven, you know. They're doing the whole domestic thing. Why not give them the condo?"

"I thought about that," I said, "but this is only a one bedroom and, besides, I have other plans for my children. Believe me, I've considered all the options. Giving this condo to you is the right thing to do."

She was quiet for a long time. "Wow. This is really happening."

"What do you mean?" I asked.

"It didn't really hit me until right this moment. Hope, you're processing out. This whole terminal cancer thing is really happening. But you seem so healthy...I just don't believe it."

I laughed. "I have my days when I have to believe it! And then I have others when I feel healthy. It's not at all what I imagined it would be, at least not so far. I'm so lucky to have you as my best friend. I'm honored that you will live in this condo. It's a special place, and I just know you'll feel at home here. Besides, I'll also know where to find you when I come back to haunt you!"

Becky shook a finger at me. "Not funny, Hope. That's not funny at all. I don't like ghosts, not even if they are my best friend. Ghosts give me the snakes!"

We both laughed, then I got serious again. "I need to ask you not to tell Colt that I bought this condo. He still doesn't know about it. I'd like to keep it that way. For obvious reasons."

"Sure, Sis. Your secret's safe with me. We don't want to hurt the ones we love."

Then Becky and I got dinner going and waited for the others to arrive. I had asked each person to come at an arranged time. Like with Becky, I could speak to each of them with the proper audience. Wild Mack was the next person to arrive. He looked very apprehensive.

"Okay, Hope, what the hell's going on?" he said. "Jennifer told me it was a matter of life and death that I come here at this specific time."

"Mack," I said, "you know my friend Becky."

"Of course I do." He looked at her "It's good to see you again."

"You, too," she said.

"This is Becky's condo," I told him, "and I thought it might be the best place to have this meeting, rather than at my home." Mack was staring at me. "Relax," I said.

"Sooooo, where is that no-good husband of yours?" he asked looking around.

"At home. He needn't be bothered with this."

Mack's eyes went wide. "You mean he doesn't know about…about…" He looked around again. "About this?"

"Correct. And if you let me explain, you'll understand."

"Well," said Becky, "get your gab on. I'm dying to get wise to your game."

"What? You don't know, either?" Mack asked her, and she shook her head.

I gestured for them both to be quiet and listen. "This isn't easy for me," I said, "so just listen up. Soon a woman will arrive in time for dinner. She's my friend, and she needs our help. I met her under some strange circumstances, but recently I've learned that they were dangerous circumstances." And I explained about Jerome and how he wants to push Quint out of business. I explained that Quint's business is worth several hundred million dollars to Jerome, so, resorting to force is nothing for him. I told them about the men who have approached Quint and threatened her family, also about the goons who sit outside her house in a vehicle and watch her and her husband.

"Hope," Mack said, "I can understand that you care about this woman, but this is a matter for the police. What do you expect me to do?"

"Jerome has threatened me," I replied. "Colt and the kids, too, if I don't cooperate with him. That's why I want to keep this on the down-low from Colt. Jerome showed me a file that had all kinds of information on my family...you know, when they're at work, when and where his goons have the best access to them, etcetera. If I went to the police, Jerome would only order his goons to harm my family. I can't have that. So I've got a plan." I looked at Becky. "How far have you gone to save a whale or a forest?" I asked her.

"Sis, you know me. I'll put my life on the line for what I believe in."

"Well," I said, "Quint is a good person. You'll find out when you meet her. She's really trying to make a difference in our world." I explained about the videogames like Rape Play 2 that Jerome's company produces, then I explained how Quint was inserting educational elements into her games and how they were being accepted by young players.

Becky nodded. "You got my vote. I'm in! I have no idea what you want me to do, but I'm with you. Let's bring this asshole down! I hate him for threatening you, but I hate him even more for his bully attitude."

But Mack looked skeptical. "What can we do? I know nothing about the videogame business... I'm a ranch hand. You need someone more qualified than me."

"I need muscle," I said. "I need someone who can take hold of Jerome. I want to snatch him up and take him to your ranch, and there you and I will beat some sense into him. You're a smart fighter. You know how to hog tie a calf or a man. That's knowledge very few people I know have, and that's what I need."

"You want me to kidnap this guy?"

"Yep."

He was reluctant, and looked more closely at me to make sure I was serious. "I'm not sure about this," he finally said.

Becky looked at him and nodded. "Yeah, Sis," she said, "I agree. You're getting a little wild here, kidnapping this guy. You don't wanna be front page news."

"But he's a bully. He's threatened my family. I want to make a statement that he will understand."

"Umm, what do you plan to do to him when we have him tied up and at my ranch?" Mack asked.

"I plan to knock the shit out of him! In the end, I expect to have permanently damaged one of his knees so he'll never walk the same again."

"Are you sure about this?" Mack looked at Becky. "Once we cross this line," he said, "there's no coming back."

"I've got it all planned out," I said. "We will be fine. Besides, I just need you to tie him up. I'll do all the bashing myself. I have a specific hammer in mind."

Becky looked shocked. "Sis, really? I never knew you were so radical."

And Mack said, "I trust you. If you think this is best, then count me in. But I don't want it to go too far. No entanglements with the law."

"Good," I said. "It's settled. Now let's wait until Quint gets here. Then I'll tell you the rest of my plan. I didn't want to tell Quint about it until I knew for sure you two were on board. Now that I have somewhat of a commitment from you, I can let her in on it."

"She doesn't know, either? God damn, Hope, you did this all on your own?" Mack asked.

"I had no choice. Jerome put me in an impossible position."

By the time Quint arrived, the three of us were on another subject. Becky was telling us about the times—plural, *times*—she was thrown in jail for protesting, vandalizing, and sabotage. Becky's stories had Mack and me laughing so hard we were crying.

Quint was as elegant as usual. I introduced her to Becky and Mack and she shook hands with them, and then we sat down at the table and had dinner. As we ate, I told Quint about the task I had been given by Brent. I asked for her forgiveness, which she gave me immediately, and I told her I thought Jerome was going to take his ambitions to a new, more violent level.

"When I left his office," I said, "I left him with the impression that I was going to carry out his dirty deeds. I figured if I couldn't convince him that I'm capable of doing it, then he'd only hire someone more capable."

She nodded. "Okay, now that you have informed me, what is your suggestion for Jerome and Back-2-Back?"

"I've asked my friends here to help me. They both have unique skills to carry out what I propose."

"I'm listening."

All three of them paid close attention as I explained what I intended to do. They threw out some interesting ideas that either added to my plan or changed it for the better. They also said they were committed but very skeptical about the legality of kidnapping Jerome. I did my best to convince them it was the only way. We finally made some concrete plans.

"This is a great gig!" Becky exclaimed. "And I have just the people we need for this...this...this—oh let's give it a name. Let's be the Guy Fawkes Raiders!"

"Whatever," Mack said. He was all business. "When will you need me?"

"Soon," I told him.

JANUARY 11TH

It's so cold today! Winter seems to be coming on hard. I don't mind, of course. I like adverse weather, not cold weather particularly, but the snow is pretty. I almost called in sick today. Instead, I made an appointment to see Dr. Bach next week. I guess it's time for the pain management meds and probably a heap of other stuff to choke down.

I've been praying for strength. I only need a month or so of full strength. Colt and I go to San Francisco on Valentines Day. (Thanks, Quint.) I'll need my legs to pedal the bike so I can see what's on the other side of the Golden Gate. Not to mention I need to execute my plan so Quint and her family are safe. So my family remains safe, too.

Just a little bit longer.

JANUARY 13TH

S unday again. I spent most of the day in bed. Colt was so sweet. He knew the minute I woke up that I wasn't feeling very good. When I woke up, he was sitting in the chair next to the bed, watching me. I asked him what he was doing and he said the nicest thing. He said, "Babe, I'm afraid to sleep because I'm afraid I'll miss a single moment with you. I know our time is limited, so I don't want to waste it. So I sit here and watch you sleep."

All I could say was, "Colt, that's so sweet. It is. But I'm fine. We have plenty of time, so don't put yourself through this. I need you, and I sure don't need you acting strange. Sitting there watching me sleep is, well, kind of creepy. You give me more comfort when you're sleeping right here. Right next to me. I need you here beside me."

I can see that my situation has him on edge. He doesn't want me too far out of his sight. He's already begged me to quit my job, but I can't. Not yet. Not until I've finished taking care of Jerome.

Colt brought up some breakfast and came back to bed with me. It was so nice to lie in bed most of the day with him next to me. I slept off and on, and every time I opened my eyes, he was there with me. Just to have him next to me soothes me and makes the pain almost go away. My pain and illness today have me concerned for what lies ahead.

Late in the afternoon, Colt got dressed and went out to get us some take-out for dinner. I asked him to stop at the gift store and pick out a card for Junior.

"What in the hell am I getting Junior a card for?" he asked. "It's not his birthday, it's not any kind of special day that I can think of."

"Hush," I said. "I'm going to write him a letter explaining my condition. I thought it would be nicer if I put it in a card."

"Are you serious? Shouldn't it be you telling him about the cancer and then *he* sends *you* a card? This is ass-backward."

"You know as well as I do, when it comes to Junior, we always have to do things a little different. Just do it for me. Please!"

Colt brought home the most hideous card. It was a sympathy card. When I asked him why, he said, "Because my son is a sorry ass. Such a sorry ass that his mother has to send him a card when she has bad news."

I spent the rest of the evening writing a very careful letter to my son. I wanted him to know the love I had in my heart for him. I wanted him to see that the future isn't set in stone, that with free will he can change and find happiness. I wanted him to know that I hope he finds life in my death. I swear, it was one of the most difficult letters I have ever written, but I did it and I mailed it. I know it's weird to mail a letter from a house addressed to the same house, but that's how I wanted it. I was afraid that if I handed it to him, he'd just toss it in the trash. I prayed over it and put a stamp on it.

JANUARY 15TH

At five o'clock in the morning, I was standing in the company parking lot and freezing my ass off. I had left a note for Colt taped to our bathroom mirror explaining that I had to go in to work early. Thank goodness I was feeling better after a long weekend of illness. A little after five, I heard the loud chatter of a large truck.

"Hey, Sis, are you ready for this?" Becky opened the door and I climbed into the passenger seat.

"This heat and air-conditioning truck ought to be convincing," I said.

"The truck's nothing," she said. "The equipment is the ace. It's amazing what you can buy when you have no limit on your dead presidents. Where did you get all the loot for this plan of yours?"

I had to laugh. "That's the funniest part. Jerome's financed it!"

She handed me a pair of service overalls with Charlie Simms HVAC embroidered on the back. "Slip these on over your clothes," she said, "and put on your rubber soled shoes. Damn, girl, you can't go in there looking like an office drone."

Becky drove around the building and backed into the loading dock.

"You drive like you've done this before," I said.

"I have, a time or two. Remember, you're in my world now. I know what I'm doing. I got this.... I got this." Becky got out of the truck and walked over to security and talked to them. Before long the loading dock opened and a hydraulic ramp came down. Becky rolled up the back door of the truck, and

I put on a goofy-looking ball cap that had the Charlie Simms logo on it, too. Becky was cool; I was scared out of my wits.

"Who is Charlie Simms?" I whispered to her as we pushed a cart full of tools and two stuffed nylon bags toward the service elevators.

"Oh, he's just some dude that needed some cash. The guy that sells me the good stuff [her pot] told me about another dealer who sells crystal meth, and evidently Charlie likes the meth and has dug himself a hole. We came along and bailed him out. Maybe saved his life even. Maybe he'll go clean after this."

The elevator stopped and a security guard got on, a short, fat guy with Steve Washington printed on his nametag. His radio was buzzed with static, probably because there was no reception in the elevator. He had a clipboard and was jotting something down on it. He turned his volume down. "Is that squealing bothering you?" he asked.

"Not bad," I said.

"I get so used to it I hardly pay any attention." He went back to his clipboard. "What are you guys working on so early this morning?"

"We got a call that there's a bad heating unit," Becky said, "so we have to go topside and check it out. It needs to be fixed before all the office dwellers come in."

"In these temperatures? You're going up on the roof?"

"Hey, at time-and-a-half, we'll work in any conditions. Am I right, or am I right?" She gave me a big whop on the back. Jesus, can she act the part. I was practically shaking in my pants that this security dude was going to bust us. But Becky was talking the talk and walking the walk.

"Well," he said as he got off at the tenth floor, "don't freeze to death up there."

A couple floors later, we got off the main service elevator and pushed our cart over to another elevator that went up to the roof proper. When we got to the roof, I hesitated. We were eighteen stories off the ground and the wind was whipping around us.

"Here, put this on." Becky pulled a heavy coat out of one of the nylon bags and handed it to me. "Now that we're out of view, we can cover up our good ol' Charlie Simms embroidery." She laughed and began stringing up some lines, shoveling snow out of the way where she clamped some anchors to where the widow-cleaning scaffold would be set up on warmer days. "Are you ready for this?" she asked.

"Shit, Becky. I'm terrified!" I looked over the edge. The ground was forever away.

"Well, I could say you only live once. Come on, girl! Now I get to say something I've always wanted to say to you. Put the harness on and let's scale this bitch!" She threw the lines over the edge and we watched them go down the building. Then she tossed the other nylon bags over. They were anchored and hung waiting for us.

I didn't exactly feel like getting killed while falling off the roof of Jerome's building, but I also wanted to be a part of this.

"Remember, this is your brake," Becky said. She showed me again how to stop myself. "Are you ready?"

"I'm not sure."

"Oh, come on. This is a major rush. Let's get our paint on!" She swung one leg over the wall, getting herself in position to drop.

I may have looked like I was motivated, but I was freezing. I decided that the fastest way back to the warm truck was down the cold wall. Rappelling is difficult, and I don't recommend it. The worst part is leaning back away from the building until the slack in the line is taken up. It's an awful, unnatural feeling, leaning off into empty space. But I did it.

We lowered our selves to about seven stories and then went to work. In the other nylon bags were smaller ziplock bags holding sponges impregnated with bright orange florescent paint. Becky had spent a whole day preparing the bags. The paint was resistant to the cold, but it was also thick. We had good gloves that protected us while we were rappelling and also while we were painting. Our work required almost seventy bags and sponges, but we finally got it all spelled out. We noticed some of the employees who were arriving for work were looking up at us as we were putting on the final touches. As soon as we finished, Becky cut the lines holding the nylon bags, and they dropped to the ground. Then we rappelled down and pulled our lines through the carabiners, leaving them behind along with the cart of tools up on the roof.

We scooted behind the building and took off our harnesses, coats, and gloves and stuffed them into the black nylon bags. After which we calmly walked back through the building to the loading dock. We noticed Steve Washington and some other security guards scrambling off to elevators as the oncoming shift of employees started reporting what they had seen, but no one seemed to notice us as we got back into Charlie's truck and drove away.

I can only imagine the expression on Jerome's face when he arrived and read what we'd painted in giant orange letters on his black glass windows:

BACK-2-BACK RAPES THE MINDS OF OUR CHILDREN
DOWN WITH RAPE PLAY 1&2

Becky had put out a call to her friends who had been a big part of Occupation America on Wall Street and told them about Back-2-Back. As we were pulling out, I noticed a group starting to assemble in front of the building's main entrance. They were carrying wonderful signs.

This Corporation is brainwashing our youth.

Society must protect its children. Big business is feeding off of them.

And my favorite—*When videogames teach our kids to rape, murder, go to war, and to fight zombies, who is teaching them to love?*

Becky assured me that there would be over a hundred protesters by the week's end and more the following week.

"Really? Over a hundred protesters?" I asked her.

"For sure. Mom and Dad said they'd be here by noon today. Mom actually hopes she'll get arrested again. She loves getting reservations at the iron bungalow."

It makes me happy to know that Becky's parents, even though they're in their late seventies, are getting involved. I know for a fact that her parents will not actively protest anything unless they believe in the movement completely.

She even had one of her Occupy Wall Street-eco-warrior friends hack Back-2-Back's website. Here's what he posted:

> *Warning, Parents! If you buy, or allow your children to buy, Rape Play 1 or 2, this act will be considered traumatic input. It is punishable by state and federal laws prohibiting child abuse. Stop the negative input. Don't allow Back-2-Back to hide behind the First Amendment. THIS IS NOT FREEDOM OF SPEECH. This is encoding. Boycott Back-2-Back. Free young minds with education!*
> (Signed) *The Guy Fawkes Raiders*

I changed back into my office clothes while Becky drove and was at my desk by my company's starting time.

Phase One complete!

JANUARY 17TH

B rent is getting curious. I had to call in sick again today. I called in yesterday and hoped I would be better today, but it didn't happen. I just couldn't get out of bed. Tammy Jo came over at lunchtime and made some chicken noodle soup for me. She definitely has a mother's touch. The chicken soup was so comforting. It made me feel better, too. I'm sure hanging off a building in the wee hours of the morning in the freezing cold didn't do my situation a whole lot of good, but on a soul level? On that level, I feel great.

I'm sure Jerome's already feeling some pressure from the protesters and the website intrusion. Hah! Becky is good.

Tammy Jo is so sweet to me. She loves me as if I were her own daughter. We had a good talk and, yes, I told her about my illness. It's hard for me to talk about my cancer without getting all gloomy and doomy. I don't like bringing people down, but I also think it's disrespectful to exclude the people I care about from the truth. Tammy Jo is good people. It's no wonder Colt is such a good man. He has a great mother.

She took the news well. She just drew up a chair and sat next to me and we chatted for a while. After, she let me rest while she cooked the homemade chicken noodle soup.

Later in the day, she and I were talking about Becky and her adventures as an eco-warrior. "She's always been about the environmental movement," I said. "She was recycling before it became mainstream."

"I guess back in my youth, everyone was evolved in the environment," Tammy Jo said. "Back in those days, we all returned our glass milk bottles and glass cola bottles to the store, where they were sterilized and reused."

I told her I also remember that our milk was delivered to our door at my grandparents' home when I was little. We didn't throw away the bottles. They were recycled.

"We didn't think twice about washing the babies' diapers," Tammy Jo added. "Everyone used cloth diapers back then. Disposable diapers are as strange to me as an escalator in a grocery store. They just don't make sense." We laughed, and then I asked her if she remembered the grocery store we went to one time when were on vacation. The store had two escalators, one for the grocery carts, one for the customers. Tammy Jo laughed about that for a long time.

"Times sure have changed, even in my lifetime," I told her. "People talk about solar power and wind power as if it were a new idea. My grandmother and I always hung our wash out on the clothesline. We didn't have an electric dryer. Year-round, our clothes hung out to dry in the wind and the good, old-fashioned sunshine. And in the summertime, Granddad used a push mower to mow our lawn, not because he couldn't afford a gas-powered one, but because he couldn't understand why a man would spend his hard-earned money on an expensive tool and pay for gas when he could just push it himself. Besides, he liked the exercise. It wasn't until he was ill that he let me hire a boy to mow for him."

"And my father used a straight-edged razor," Tammy Jo said. "He couldn't understand that whole disposable razor thing. No, recycling isn't a new concept at all. Every child of mine wore recycled clothes. We called them hand-me-downs."

"Recycling seems to be a business rather than an environmental movement now," I said. Mankind has developed technologies that offer us benefits, but in other ways we're returning to what we used to do. It turns out that the folks of the older generations had it right to begin with. Wind power. Solar power. Recycling. They just didn't have fancy names.

Tammy Jo distracted me so skillfully and kept the conversation interesting enough that I almost forgot how awful I felt. She also took me to see Dr. Bach. He examined me and prescribed some more pills. Isn't that the way of things in life? A pill will fix it. Well, let's see what those pills do for me.

I want to see Mr. Goldsole. I miss him. He's as familiar to me as my grandfather. I hope I get to see him again soon.

JANUARY 18TH

I had to force myself to get up and go to work today. I felt like the walking dead. Everything hurts. Even my hair is painful to the touch. How can hair have pain? I mean, I've always been told that hair is made up of dead cells. I don't believe they have any dendrites or any way of conducting nerve impulses, so how can I be feeling the pain from my hair?

Anyway, I made it to work. But I struggled all day. Devin noticed that I had phoned in sick the past few days and saw what a wreck I was today. He was sweet, tried to comfort me the best he could, and asked me to lunch so the two of us could talk privately.

"Are you all right?" he asked when we were settled in a far corner of the lunchroom.

"Yeah, I'm fine," I said. "I'm just a little out of sorts today."

"Is it stress? Is your divorce stressing you out to the point it's making you ill?"

"Uh, no. Stress might be a factor, but it's not what you think."

He leaned forward and lowered his voice. "Hope, I'm here for you if you need anything," he said. "Anything at all. It's hard to see you so ill. I've noticed that you've been losing weight and I'm concerned."

I had to look away from him. Even though my mental state has been good and I'm confident of my fate, there are still moments that reach out and make me hurt. Having Devin sitting at the table with me provoked some sentimental feelings. I realized every time I see him, it might be the last time. I had no intention to stay in contact with him after I resigned and left the company. And I had no plans to tell him about my cancer. I suppose I was worried that he might show up at my funeral.

My funeral?

Wow, that's something I haven't thought about. How should my funeral go down? Should I be planning it now? I don't even know what to think about that.

He cleared his throat and got my attention.

"There won't be any divorce," I told him. "My husband and I have worked things out."

"Oh...I see. Well, that's for the best isn't it. Things are as they should be."

He didn't sound enthusiastic, so I made a stab at it. "Exactly! Things are as they should be. And when you and I were together, it was as it should have been then. I'm happy to know you, Devin. You brought a necessary change to my life, and I don't regret a single moment with you. In my opinion, you and I shared real love. And the love we shared has taken up residence in my heart and it will be there for a long, long time."

He reached for my hand and touched it. "It was love for me, too. I have no doubt that when we came together, it was love. I admit it's not the same kind of love my fiancée and I have, but it's still love, and I still feel it." With his other hand, he reached over and turned my head so I was looking at him. "I'm glad to know you, too, Hope."

I remember when I was with the Being of Light, I had a vision of Devin. We have had a previous lifetime together. Now, sitting with him at lunch, I began to have a greater recall of that lifetime. It was a lifetime spent well lived and full of health and love. If I were to write the details of our previous lifetime, it would fill volumes, so I won't even attempt it here. However, ours was a strong and passionate love, so strong that it bridged two lifetimes. I'm not sure if my meeting him in this lifetime has been a gift or a curse. I'll lean toward it being a gift, and because of that I am thankful.

"I will always hold your memory in high regard," I told him.

"I'm not sure, but I think I will always love you," he said. "I think you're part of me in some way I can't comprehend completely."

I had to smile. "That sounds nice. Real nice, in fact. But don't obligate any part of yourself to me. Give everything you can to the one you love the most here and now. Don't hold back anything from your fiancée. Give her all your loving energy. I'll pray for you. I'll pray that you have a healthy, passionate, loving relationship for the rest of your life."

He looked past me, as if seeing the rest of his life, "How is it going to be after I lose track of you?" he asked. "What if I want to talk to you? I wonder if there might be times when I want to see you, to hear your voice. I don't like to think about the future without you being near me. The times when we laughed, the times when we made love, the times when you kissed me.... I don't want those moments to fade into memories. You are special, Hope. I can't see my future without you in it. You are always so wise. What will I do when I lose track of you and want to hear your sweet voice?"

"Oh, Devin, you always say the right thing - you're a real charmer. Life tends to fill in the blanks, though. You might have a moment in the future when you miss me, but then you'll hear a baby cry from another room in your home, and you'll go to your baby, look in her eyes, and you'll see new love. You'll see your purpose, and then the momentary pain you felt for me will be gone. Erased by the gift granted to you. God gives us what we need."

"God? Do you believe in God?" he asked.

"I believe there is something greater than mankind. I believe that you and I have a purpose in life, and our purpose is derived from God. Or whatever you want to call it."

He thought for a moment and a smile came across his face. "So with faith that I'm doing the right thing in my life, I'll heal the wounds you and I have created?"

"Yes. With faith."

Time seemed to stand still then. It seems to me as I write this entry in my diary that we discussed so many things they couldn't possibly have fit into a mere hour. We were there forever. When we went back to our cubicles, I don't know about Devin, but I sensed we had closure. I was sad, but I felt good letting him go completely.

And then, in the middle of my sweet thoughts about eternal love, Brent called me to come to his office. I wasn't completely feeling myself yet, so it was with great effort that I dragged my sorry ass into his office.

He didn't even greet me. He just looked up from some papers and said, "The timekeeper reports that you have had an increase in sick days. Is there anything I should know?"

"Yes. Yes there is."

"What?"

"This will surely be hard for you to believe, but I've been sick." I sat down without being asked to.

"Funny." He sifted through the papers on his desk and said, without looking at me, "Jerome called this morning. He's not happy."

"So? What else is new?"

"He wants to meet with you ASAP. He told me that he's phoned your desk, but you haven't been answering."

"Brent, I've been sick. What part of *I've been sick* don't you get?"

He looked at me again, and his look was not friendly. "Hope, Jerome seems to think you've been avoiding him. He's not happy about it."

"He'll get over it."

"Just go over and see him. I told him you'd be there within a half hour."

"Are you crazy? I've got a lot of work here to do. You're making me and my team fall behind, all because of Jerome demanding that I do this, that, and the other thing."

"Don't fool yourself, Hope. Jerome is a powerful man. If he says jump, I say how high."

I made a bit of a fuss in Brent's office, but that was all for show. I actually wanted to go see Jerome. I wanted to see the results of Becky's and my work on his building.

When I pulled up at Back-2-Back, I could see men out on scaffolds in the bitter cold, scraping off the paint. That made me laugh out loud. The next thing I saw were the cops trying to muscle the protesters. Yelling that this was private property and the Guy Fawkes Raiders were trespassing. I had to laugh again because I could see Becky's mom standing firm in front of a police officer. She had her arms folded and was glaring at him, daring him to touch her. She wore her tie-dye dress, a heavy sweater, and thick wool socks with Birkenstock sandals. Most of the snow had melted, but it was still cold. She's one tough lady. I slipped past the cops and the protesters without saying a word. I sure didn't want anyone at Back-2-Back to know that I knew some of the protesters. At least, not yet.

When I arrived in Jerome's office, he wasn't there. That was no surprise. I had to wait, of course, so I watched his two bimbo receptionists doing absolutely nothing. I get so sick of seeing these young bimbettes who get by in life by being cute in their revealing clothes. I hope they age poorly. I hope they get fat and wrinkled. Oops! Did I write that? I'm a bad person for wishing ill on another person.

Anyway, Jerome showed up about an hour later. I was pissed off for having to wait so long. As we walked into his office, I couldn't resist.

"Looks like you have a new fan club outside."

He swung his head around and his eyes narrowed. "Those people are breaking the law. They have painted graffiti on my building and are squatting on my property! It's not something to joke about."

I sat down in the middle of his big leather couch. "It'll blow over, Jerome. No need to worry."

"I have told you before. Call me Mr. Attwood."

"And I told you not to keep me waiting again. I've been sitting out there for over an hour!"

"I pay you well enough that you can wait as long as necessary." He actually snarled at me. "Now, for the past two days I have tried to get a hold of you and my calls all went straight to voicemail. That is unacceptable!"

"Stop right there," I said. "I've already been through this with Brent. I was sick, goddammit. And to be honest, I'm still not feeling well, so, frankly, I'm tired of hearing the two of you whine about it. Get over it. People get sick."

"I never get sick. I haven't called in sick once in over twenty years."

"Somebody please give Mr. Attwood here an attaboy badge for reliability. Really Jerome, fuck you!" I stood up. "Now... if you want to discuss something with me, you better get to it right away. Otherwise, I'm leaving. I told you before. My time is just as important as yours."

I don't think he even heard me. He was standing at his window looking down at the parking lot. "These people, these protesters and the graffiti artists...they're coming from Bio-Sport. Quint has stepped up her game. I want to know her schedule. I want to know when and where she is at all times."

"Then you'll need a better spy than me. Someone on the inside. Try to bribe one of her employees."

"Wake up, Hope! I swear, you are one of the dumbest people I know. Of course I have people on the inside. But they don't know her social calendar, they don't know what she does when she's not at work. I want you to get into her *social* calendar. Find out what she does on her weekends and vacations. That sort of thing. Make a lunch date with her, and when she goes to the bathroom get her smart phone, hard calendar, whatever. Get dates and times."

"Sure," I said. "No problem. But she and I aren't exactly best friends, so I doubt she'll meet me over the weekend."

"Do your best." He pulled out his checkbook and wrote me a check. "This should be adequate, based on our agreement. It's half for now. You'll get the other half when I get a social calendar."

"Is that all? I asked.

"For now. You may go." He pointed at the door.

"Jerome, you are such an asshole." I was out the door before he had a chance to respond.

Phase Two is set in motion.

...

It was so nice to be home on a Friday night and have Colt there. Since he's not with the band right now, he has a lot more time to spend with me. I felt a bit better when I got home tonight, so I suggested that we go see Nina. We took her dinner.

Nina brings a special kind of happiness to Colt. I can't really describe it, only that he shines when he sees her. I've often thought that he has the perfect life. He is always healthy and strong. But sitting there, watching him tend to his sister's needs, I realized that we all put so much pressure on him. He is healthy because we are not. He makes up for our shortfalls with all that he is. My illness has put a terrible strain on him, yet he shows few signs of stress. Nina's condition takes its toll on him, too, but he almost never lets on that it bothers him. Lately I've noticed some new wrinkles on his face and I know it's from worry. I think he internalizes his concern to the point that one day it may have a serious affect on him.

While we were sitting there with Nina, I prayed to the Being of Light. I prayed with gratitude for having been blessed to have my husband in my life. I prayed that Colt would be blessed after I pass on.

Please give him someone to love," I prayed in my heart. *And may she be healthy so he can know life without disease. He is such a good man. He deserves some relief in this life.*

I hope my prayer was heard. I hope it gets answered. I have faith that it will.

JANUARY 19TH

I woke up in the middle of the night with a new realization that something inside of me is consuming me. It's eating me alive. It was the middle of the night, so I just lay there and gave it more thought than I would during the day. During the day, I have distractions. At night, I think more about my illness. I don't want to, but I can't help it.

I didn't console myself or feel sorry for myself. I just lay there and thought, *So here I am, on the far edge of my existence. Here I am, preparing for the unimaginable....*

Most nights, if I wake up, I remember the tenderness of the Being of Light. I perceive that Being as a male most of the time, but sometimes as a female. Last night I put my hand over my heart and now my heart seemed to be part of both the Being of Light and myself. Then I slowly massaged my scar. I rubbed the area and felt my heart beating inside me. *It's going to be all right,* I told myself. *It's going to be all right. Just keep your faith strong.* I said that to myself over and over, trying to reduce the anxiety that was building in my mind.

Even after my time with the Being of Light, even after acknowledging my soul, even knowing that the Being is with me, I am still afraid. In some sense I don't really understand, I actually felt some relief at being diagnosed with a progressive and terminal disease. All the symptoms point to death, but at times I wonder if I'd turned into a hypochondriac prior to the confirmation of the cancer from Dr. Bach.

Under my hand, the beating of my heart seemed simple. It was beating fast, but it was a regular beat. The pace of the beating told me I was anxious, but what eventually calmed me was the thought that my heartbeat is nothing short of divine. It's a gift from the Being of Light. I have this simple heartbeat with its huge and complex meaning that calmed my anxiety. I understood what the Being of Light meant by saying that I'm never alone. The Being of Light is in my heartbeat. It's as much a part of my physical body as my spiritual body. My heart beats to a rhythm, not a rhythm I have chosen. My heart beats without me telling it to. My heart beats just like everyone else's because the Being of Light has set it in motion. What a wonderful gift.

This morning, I got up and got dressed and had breakfast with Colt. After we ate, I told him I wanted to go for a walk to think about things. I needed some alone time. He understood and didn't offer to come along. I bundled up and drove over to Washington Park.

As I walked, I looked around. The snow has gotten dirty because it hasn't been warm enough to melt away and no fresh new snow has fallen. The sky was blue and partly cloudy. I am alive. *I'm alive, and for this moment and the physical moments ahead, that is what is important.*

When I arrived at the cathedral yard, I prayed under the tree of prayer (that's the name I've given it). "But what happens next?" I asked. "I mean, what happens when I return to the Being of Light? What happens when my light recedes and shadows grow where I once stood? What happens then? What happens? Am I forgotten when my family and friends return to the routines of their lives and are taken up by the stresses of normal life?"

"What would you have happen, Chief?"

To my delight, it was Mr. Goldsole walking up the path. He stopped beside me. It had been such a long time since I had seen him that I grabbed him in a big hug, maybe a little too forcefully, and pulled him closer. Somewhere inside me, I loved this man in ways I'm not exactly sure of, but my love for him is rich and strong.

He loosened my grip (gently) and smoothed down his coat. "Now tell me," he said. "Hope, what is all of this about what happens after your death?"

I didn't know what to say. "I don't know. I suppose I feel like I'll be forgotten after I'm gone. It's a stupid, selfish thing to think, but I can't seem to help myself."

He nodded. "Yes, but it's a natural question, don't you think? I imagine that people want to feel like they will leave a strong memory, an impression on the world. They want to think they have touched the physical world in such a way that they will not be forgotten."

"I thought I was done with death," I said. "Once the breast cancer went away. I thought it was a miracle that I was in remission."

"It was." he said. "Please, don't overlook the actual miracle of your remission."

"Do you really think it was a miracle?" I asked him. "Or was it a terrible taunt? A way of teasing me with life and then taking it back again."

"You were granted an extension, Hope. An extension," he repeated, "because you, with the gift of free will, on some level felt that your earthly tasks were unfinished at that time."

"But, Mr. Goldsole, how would you know that? I don't believe I was given a choice to live or die. Believe me, I was there. You weren't."

But then he put his hand on my shoulder, and a new vision flashed through my mind. There I was, sick in the hospital. I had been there for almost a month. My body still hurt. That was because of the chemo, because of the radiation. It hurt because my body was struggling to stay alive. I couldn't do anything. Dr. Bach and I set goals every day, and every day I would somehow get out of bed and drag my IV pole around while I shuffled up and down the halls to rebuild my strength. I also had a lengthy schedule of medications to take at certain times, a schedule that Colt and I learned all too well.

Then I saw Colt sitting in my room, worry written all over his face. He was worried about me, but he also had other concerns on top of that. Medical bills were the enemy in those days. The various hospital and doctor bills were more than we could afford, even with our insurance. Colt didn't want to tell me how much we owed. He didn't want to tell me how the nasty collection agencies were calling and harassing him at home. These were ugly days. Just seeing them again almost made me cry.

But what I had forgotten until Mr. Goldsole touched me was when Colt and I were talking and I told him, "I don't care how sick I get, I am determined to live. I will not leave you this way. I refuse to die until we have our lives straightened out with no threats from collection agencies! We may have to file for bankruptcy, but we'll do that together. I promise you, I won't leave you alone to pick up all the broken pieces. We vowed to marry *in sickness and in health,* right? Well, I'm sick, but that doesn't give me an out. I'm still here, and we will get through this together. Through everything."

I looked at Mr. Goldsole. "I remember now! I made a declaration that I wouldn't leave Colt until things were better. Well...I guess things are better now."

"You were given a gift," he said. "You may think your life hasn't been smooth since your remission, but it's important to remember you have kept your promise to Colt."

"Wait a minute! How did you do that?"

"Do what? I didn't do anything."

"But the memory...how did you know?"

He smiled. "It was merely suggestive hypnosis. Nothing special."

I was still perplexed. "But how did you even know my history well enough to pull that memory forward?"

He didn't answer my question, but put his arm around my shoulders. "How do you feel about crossing over now?" he asked. "Is your life in order?"

The sound of his question made me recoil. Talking about death made me uncomfortable, but he said it in such a matter-of-fact tone. "Well," I finally said, "I'm getting things in order the best I can. I'm still a bit troubled, though, by a situation I'm in." And I went into detail about Jerome and his goons and Back-2-Back. I told Mr. Goldsole about Phase Two. I told him how I had planned, with Mack's help, to kidnap Jerome and whisk him away to Mack's ranch. Then the plan was to beat him into submission. I wanted nothing more than to bully the bully.

Mr. Goldsole listened without interrupting me and was quiet for a minute. "Oh, Hope," he said after a minute, "I hear what you're saying. I can understand your temptation to harm this evil man…but you don't want to become evil yourself, do you? When the time comes for you to leave this plane of existence, you will want to go without regret. If you bring physical harm to this man, I'm afraid you'll have large regrets. Those regrets will make your transition to the other side very difficult."

"But Jerome is evil," I said, "and the only things he understands are power and money. I don't have the kind of money he respects, but I know Mack and I can beat him into submission. Jerome has threatened my friend and her husband. He's threatening my family. I have to do something before I'm too weak! Before I die, I need to protect my family and friends!"

I was frustrated because I knew Mr. Goldsole was right. I felt in my heart that Phase Two was wrong, that I was wrong for asking Mack to help me carry out such a task. But what else could I do? I had actually planned to permanently damage Jerome to the point where he could never harm anyone again. But, well, deep down, I know I'm not capable of such harm.

Mr. Goldsole nodded like he was reading my mind. "Yes. But I can see that you might harm Jerome because of things he is not responsible for. He is evil, there's no doubt of that. But you also want to take your frustration with the cancer out on him. He has nothing to do with that. Also, you have overlooked something very important."

"What might that be?"

"You have *goodness* supporting you. The goodness of… what words do you use? Oh, yes, the Being of Light. When I found you in the parking lot, you described the Being of Light and a promise that you would never be alone again. You also have the support of your friends and family. All of them are striving for goodness in their lives. Take Jerome to task with *goodness*."

"How? What do you suggest?"

"Well, let's think for a moment…what would make a difference in Jerome's life? What would be a non-violent approach to bring about the change you desire?"

We talked a long time about options and approaches. Mr. Goldsole's voice vibrated on a frequency that warmed me. Even though we were standing in the winter's cold, I was warm and comfortable in his presence.

He liked the fact that Phase One was non-violent and thought that I should expand on it. "Let the evil in Jerome be his own downfall," he suggested. "Evil's weaknesses are usually pride and ego. Use those things to find your resolution. I'm certain in the end your friends and family will be safe."

With every word he uttered, I knew he was right. I had to let go of the anger, the frustration, the desire to harm Jerome. Instead, I needed to embrace goodness and work toward a righteous resolution.

When I got home I phoned Mack and told him there was a change in the plan. I was wrong to exploit my friendship with Mack. I was wrong to manipulate him into doing a dirty deed like kidnapping and thrashing Jerome.

So then I sat in my room and wondered what to do next. I drew a hot bath and prayed. Then it came to me. My thumb drive! When I had been at Jerome's office earlier this month, I'd stopped at his receptionist's desk, told her that he wanted to see her, and made a copy of his files. I filled up that thumb drive before she returned. I'd never looked at the contents of the drive. Now I plugged it into my computer and looked at the files. The answer was there. Data!

Thank you, Mr. Goldsole. Thank you for saving me from making a big mistake.

Data is the answer. New Phase Two.

JANUARY 21ST

Mondays. I resent Mondays. It's the start of the workweek and the beginning of my loss of freedom. It's when my time and efforts belong to someone else. But this morning? This morning I knew change was coming!

After work, I went to see Becky and her mother, who were protesting in front of Back-2-Back. I took a thermos of hot chocolate and enough sandwiches and pizza for everyone. (All that food filled the whole cargo area of my car.) After my talk with Mr. Goldsole, our original Phase Two was out the window, but I had an alternative plan.

Becky, her mother, and some other members of the Guy Fawkes Raiders welcomed me. Some of them were wearing the Guy Fawkes mask, that very cool white face with a mustache and a pointed beard. The use of the mask and the name of the group, in honor of Guy Fawkes (the English Catholic who, as a result of religious persecution, planned the famous Gunpowder Plot, which was to have blown up the Parliament buildings on November 5, 1605), was borrowed from the Occupy Wall Street movement, but we added the Raiders part to differentiate our movement from Occupy. I liked the sound of it.

"I have something for you," Becky said, and she handed me a mask.

"Way cool!" I put it on. "I've always wanted one of these."

"What do you think of the stack up?" she asked.

I looked around. "I can't believe so many people showed up for this."

She laughed. "Shit, the dead presidents you're handing out for this gig, you snap the whip and they'll make the trip."

I laughed, too, then said, "Yo, Becky—it's me. Speak English."

"Do your brains need dusting? I was speaking English."

Becky's mother gestured for me to sit down. She wanted us to stop bickering. It was time for a good chant. Back in the late Sixties, she said, she learned that chanting was an effective morale builder for protesters involved in any demonstration. Although she wasn't our elected leader, or even our appointed leader, she has always been full of positive energy and had a subtle influence about her. It's more fluid and less commanding than what we usually think of when it comes to leadership. The people there believed that she had a good plan and looked at her to lead. We were willing to follow her, but she instructed us to make sure we weren't giving up our power. In other words, she made sure we maintained our power of free will. Our chanting had to come, she said, from our own hearts and souls.

As we chanted and marched around Jerome's building, the Being of Light blessed me with a vision in which I could see that our past is rich with people who took the non-violent road to stop a tyrant. The Being of Light allowed me to see what underlay my struggle with Jerome and to understand conflict itself on a deeper level. In my struggle with Jerome, a very nasty man with the potential to be a true villain, I could see that deeper than the appearance of power is the need to change the *source* of power in our society. Jerome was building his power by influencing our young people with his immoral video games. He wants to change how society sees itself.

My vision showed me how we *define* our reality is how we *shape* our reality. If our children grow up watching and taking part in simulated rapes and murders, then sexual assault and thuggery will be the accepted reality.

Reality.

Reality with *toxic pedagogy.* That's a phrase I made up, but I think it works here. *Toxic pedagogy: Toxic = poison. Pedagogy = education.* Thus we have poisoned education. In my opinion, the virtual realities of some video games are the catalyst for poisoning our children's education. Right?

Right!

Toxic pedagogy is the kind of teaching Jerome is giving our children. What he's doing is poisonous to our children and to society. He's masking damaging teachings as "coolness." Our children are being conditioned by his video games to accept something as harmful as Rape Play as "cool" and commonplace. They learn that they have to be skilled at thievery, rape, and murder to be accepted by their peers. Jerome has carefully constructed an effective vehicle that delivers his corrupt message to impressionable minds that are still under construction. Kids' brains are still developing when they learn to play his games. What they learn is that rape and murder are good.

But what pushes my buttons the most is that kids are rewarded for getting more and more proficient at it. It's sickening to think about. When someone is blamed for the damage the game inflicts on children, however, it's their parents—not Jerome and Back-2-Back. Parents more or less raise their children. They direct and protect them. But who gets blamed when their son or daughter generalizes the skills learned in the videogames like Rape Play 1 and 2 and applies them to reality? Jerome's business is to make sure his victims will never find out later in life that they were influenced and manipulated by him. He teaches them—and us—to think it was the parents' fault when young people commit crimes and are arrested.

We live in a society of embedded systems of influence. We are indoctrinated at a young age by powers that influence us. They're nearly all-encompassing. They're basic to our politics, our corporations, even our entertainment. I can see that the violence of Rape Play is already manifesting in youthful minds. As the kids who play this awful video game grow up, the violence they've learned from it makes its way into our work places and universities, where the violence further manifests as rage, criminal behavior, controlling behavior, domination, and the inability to feel compassion. Empathy is negated and disappears.

But as I was marching and chanting with my friends and allies, I could also see there are people who are aware of criminals like Jerome, people who are fighting for our safety. Becky's mom has been an activist all her life. Becky's an activist, too. She learned a lot from her parents, and now she's a woman who stands up when someone like Jerome wants to seize power. I could see that my friends use a different and more ethical standard of power. The root of their power comes from their willingness to act. It comes from their free will.

Free will.

Free will is something that grows from within, something deeper arising from the human connection. It gains its strength from our bond with the earth and other people. Although there are powerful influences that seem to rule the systems we live in, it's our free will that sustains our lives. The Being of Light revealed to me that we can know the true value of free will when we direct our intentions toward good things like healing, helping others, planting, and loving and making love.

I watched Becky's mother as she chanted. When the chant ended, I hugged her and told her how much I loved her, not only for being here and for being the peaceful leader of the Guy Fawkes Raiders, but for all the causes she has been a part of. And of course I also hugged Becky and told her how much I loved her.

"Time for a new Phase Two," I told her.

JANUARY 22ND

We gathered at the condo again tonight, just Becky, Quint, and me this time. Mack wasn't specifically excluded. I still needed him, but not right now. Becky wanted us to get together so she could request a blessing for us before we set out on the *new* Phase Two, which will be non-violent. She wasn't sure that Mack would "dig it." So he was coming later.

When Becky asked Quint about Jerome and what he was doing to her and her husband, we already had some idea about what was going on, but we hadn't heard the details yet. What Quint told us was that a black SUV was parked in front of her house by eleven o'clock every night. It had been there every night for at least a week. She said it was still there when she got up in the morning and it stayed there until she went to work, then it followed her to work. While she was at work, it left, but it was returning to her house every night.

Having the SUV parked outside was so troubling that if her husband didn't have to be at work that day, Quint would call in to work and make arrangements to stay home with him. "Safety in numbers," she told us.

But what that means is that she and her husband are prisoners in their own home. They're as afraid to leave as they are to stay. They don't know what the men in the SUV are planning to do, but she's sure they intend to bring harm to her husband. They know that if they have her husband, she will do anything to get him back safe and sound.

She phoned the police, she told us, but when she did, the SUV always left before a patrol car arrived and returned shortly after the police left. Sometimes when she looked out the window, one of the men in the SUV would point a gun at her and act like he was shooting her. The terror was reinforced when Jerome phoned her every once in a while to ask if she knew where her husband was. Then he would say, "Wouldn't you hate it if the police found him in some shallow grave somewhere?"

It is time to stop this intimidation.

. . .

I am so proud of Becky. She respected what we were about to do so much that she used language we could understand.

"Magic," she began, "is more than candlesticks, cauldrons, and wands. Magic is an attitude. It's how we aim our intentions. How did this situation with Jerome arise? And will our chosen solution bring about the best result for everyone involved?"

Quint and I let her take the lead here. We turned to her because of her experience as an eco-warrior and her wisdom and experience in standing up for the defenseless.

"We come together this night," she said, "to liberate Quint and her husband and Hope and her family from the intimidation of Jerome and his thugs. Jerome's web is wide, complex, and materialistic. That is, his power lies in the materialistic world. He has given the two of you grief because he has the money and influence that enable him to do so. Unfortunately, you both have allowed him to get into your heads."

She paused, and Quint and I both had to nod. She was right.

"So," she said, "we will use the magic of the mind to liberate you. Yes, we will have to act on a physical level so you can defend yourselves, but if you don't have the right attitude, the aim of your intentions will not be successful."

She turned off the electric lights and lit two candles, one white, one black. Then she sat on the floor. "These two candles are symbols of balance," she said. "We want to bring about not only liberation, but we also want to bring balance and harmony into our lives. That is our greatest intention. Harmony."

Quint and I also sat on the floor near the coffee table where Becky had lit the candles. We three formed a triangle.

"Our approach will involve both resistance and renewal," she said. "Close your eyes. I want you to visualize the word NO. We make our stand by saying *no* to Jerome's bullying. We say *no* to his power. We reject his power on a soul level. With our eyes still closed and using the powers of our imagination, let us reshape our reality to exclude Jerome and his power and his actions. We sit here as individuals expressing our support for one another, and as we do this we become a small community. Our community is creating resistance by refusing to accept things as they appear."

To my surprise Becky was using language much like the Being of Light and Mr. Goldsole used, words like *visualize*, *reality*, *free will*, *soul level*, and *renewal*. The word that stood out the strongest to me was *harmony*.

Becky was correct. I wanted harmony more than anything else. She sure had my attention. I was totally focused on her words.

"The power of magic," she said, "is mysterious. How the power of an aimed free will works is a mystery. What I can tell you is that it operates at a depth of our soul that cannot be wholly known or controlled, but when we speak from our core and direct the force of it, we can drive the energy to create a desired outcome.

"When we embrace our connection and take note of the value of mystery, we invite clarity. Open your mind and make it possible for you to encounter the mystery and view our world through the lens of clarity. Once we have looked through the lens of clarity, we may see how the old systems and structures of our perception reveal distortions.

"Jerome's power," she continued, "is only perceived power. It's not *real* power. He is merely a ripple in reality. But if everyone is convinced he has more money, more power, and more strength than they do, more than we three have, then we give him even more power, more money, and more strength.

"At the core of each of us is the capability to understand the truth. That truth is always there. It may be hidden by the distortions, but it's always there. To change the lens of reality and look at a fuller spectrum can be frightening. It is natural to fear change. But if we want to be liberated, it is necessary to bring about change. And we need to be liberated!"

In my imagination, I could see our objective: liberation from fear for Quint and her family and for me and my family. Becky was not speaking in her usual slang, and because it was so strange to hear her speaking correct, standard English, I felt as if maybe someone else—Someone Else—was communicating through her. Her words brought visions into my mind that reinforced what she was saying. I could see the recent past, when I was pedaling through a city filled with unsmiling faces as I commuted to work. The lens of truth brought me clarity about working for corporations, which are nonhuman entities that control masses of human beings. The truth is that we surrender ourselves at the door of our employment at the start of every workweek because it is our perception that working to make some company or person wealthy is the correct thing to do. The truth is that people like Jerome are created by our perceptions, but Jerome and those like him have no power if we don't acknowledge it or believe in it. If we're not afraid of him, he holds no threat.

"Here in our triangle," Becky was saying, "I aim my free will toward the heavens, and I ask that we be blessed in what we are about to do. I ask to reclaim from the Universe our ability to be connected with the organic reality of our natural world. I ask that our small community be flexible and open to the changes we intend to create. I also ask that our small community recognize its limits as we each strive to reach the true reality. We understand that in order to counter the control of forces like Jerome, we begin by reclaiming our individual power. We ask that our aimed intentions bring balance to the natural world. With our free will we ask the Universe for this with harm to none. Amen."

. . .

Our modest ritual completed, we chatted for a little while about our plans, and then Quint got in her big Cadillac and drove home. Becky and I waited for Mack to show up, and then the three of us drove to Quint's neighborhood. Before we got there, she called my cell and reported that, as expected, the black SUV was parked in front of her house. I told her to hold on and stay in the house.

I have a Subaru WRX STI wagon, and it has plenty of power. When I got close to Quint's house, I said, "Hang on to something!" Mack and Becky hung on. I passed the black SUV, came to a stop, and then shifted into reverse, hit the gas, and rammed the SUV so hard that its air bags were activated. Within seconds, fluids from its radiator (and other things) were pouring out all over the street.

The three of us scrambled out of my vehicle and Becky put one hand in her pocket, as if she were holding a gun. "Don't move!" she yelled at the black SUV.

The men didn't move. I could see they were trying to evaluate the situation. I think they were pretty shaken up by being rear-ended from the front.

I had already dialed 911 and reported that there had been an accident.

The SUV's driver calculated pretty quickly that the only threat was the three of us, but then he had to fight with the airbag before he could reach for his gun. That's when Mack motioned for Becky and me to move back. Jerome's goon found his pistol, pointed it at the airbag, and fired. The noise from the gun going off and the airbag exploding was horrendous. Every porch light on both sides of the street came on. The airbag deflated instantly, the driver's side door swung open, the driver turned and pointed his gun at Mack.

"Mack," I yelled, "don't do anything crazy! He's not going to shoot. There are too many witnesses. Look around."

People up and down the street were outside, all of them staring at us.

We brought Mack along just in case something happened and we needed his muscle and fists, but I sure didn't want him to get shot. Nor did I want him to kill the men with the guns. I firmly believe Mack is powerful enough to overcome men with guns. The thug in the passenger seat jumped out and joined the driver. Within seconds, they were both pointing their guns at Mack, but just then I saw the passenger look up and down the street. He could see all the witnesses.

Then we all heard the sounds of sirens. Multiple sirens.

I recognized the two men. These goons came from Jerome's office. They were his big, buff intimidators. I was happy to see we had Jerome's top guys, and not just some other hired, part-time brutes.

A minute later, a fire engine, an ambulance, and two police cars arrived. I ran up to the first police car and told the officers that we had been parked in front of Quint's house and were waiting for her. We were all going to have a late night dessert at the Tummy Tickler over on Poplar Path Road, when all of a sudden this SUV came up behind us and rammed us. At the same time, Becky was acting out major neck pain and was already being tended by the ambulance crew. She moaned so convincingly that some of the neighbors swore they'd seen the black SUV ram us. Then another neighbor said he hadn't seen a thing, but had come out when he heard the gunfire and the explosion of the air bag.

"Gunfire?" the sergeant repeated.

"Yes, sir. Gunfire. I know my firearms. It sounded like a nine mill to me…well, muffled, but still a nine millimeter. It was followed by this big explosion. I don't know what that was."

The police looked at the SUV's driver and asked him if he had a gun. Both of them had holstered their weapons before the police arrived. They evaluated the situation—they were surrounded by police and fire fighters—and nodded.

The sergeant, who looked surprised at the lack of resistance, took the driver's gun and smelled the barrel. "This has been recently fired," he said, gesturing for his fellow officers to put the cuffs on the two men. Then he reached into his car and called for backup. "Why would you ram this nice lady's car and then start shooting?" he asked Jerome's thugs. The men didn't say anything. I could tell they were leaving their defense to their attorneys.

More police showed up, and soon it looked like they were shooting an action-adventure movie on Quint's block. Becky was acting it up really good. She started shouting from the ambulance, "Get those boys' fingers on some fly paper. Those halfwits tried to give me a dirt nap. This neighborhood is going to hell in a hand basket!" She was yelling so loud, everyone turned to look at her. "Those two suits were flashing their gats at my good gal," she yelled. "She was about to come apart like a two-piece biscuit. Why would they want to let the air out of us? Who are those gangsters? Oh, shit—my heart! I feel chest pain…oh, my heart…oh, the pain, the pain, it's going down my arm. Help me, I don't want to die, not here, not now. Oh, please, help me!"

I had to turn away to hide my laughter. That damn Becky can be so funny when she's trying to be serious. And suddenly I understood that her request for blessing was working. Other than some superficial bruising, no one got hurt tonight. And the neighbors were talking and telling the police that they saw the accident just like I had described it—a deliberate ram.

The cops had cuffed and stuffed both driver and passenger and were now investigating the SUV. When Quint came out, she told the police that this was the SUV she had reported several times before and that they probably rammed my car thinking she was in it. When her neighbors heard her story, they all chimed in and reported that they, too, had observed the SUV parked in front of her house at all hours of the day and night for weeks. Maybe longer! The poor sergeant was writing as fast as he could in his little notebook, turning filled page after page, but he couldn't keep up with all the things Quint's neighbors were reporting.

"Those rat finks are giving me a heart attack!" Becky bellowed from the ambulance. "Fire up this meat wagon and get me to the ICU. Can't you see I'm dying here?"

"Ma'am," one of the younger officers asked me, "are you all right?" I was shaking, but it was from laughter, not fear. But he didn't know that, so I buried my face in my hands and acted like I was crying. Which I was, but my tears were coming from the act my BFF was putting on in the ambulance.

"I'll be all right," I told him. "It's just all so upsetting."

"Lie still!" I heard one of the paramedics say to Becky.

"Gomer," she yelled at him, "don't let your mouth start something your head can't stand."

"My name isn't Gomer," he said. I could tell he was trying to humor her. "It's Rick. Now let me strap this neck brace on you. I can't do that with you moving all over."

"I'm having a heart attack, Gomer! Fire up this curb scraper and let's get out of this wheat field!"

By now I was laughing so hard watching the paramedics struggling with Becky in the back of the ambulance that I had to turn and walk toward my car, where Mack and Quint were still standing. When I looked at Quint, I saw her laughing, too. She had her hand over her mouth. Mack was oddly calm but he put his arm around me. "I think your plan's working," he muttered in my ear. "Good job!"

The police finally asked Quint to come to the station to be interviewed. They were now very interested in the threats from the men in the SUV and their boss. Quint's husband, who had also come out, drove her to the station while Mack and I waited for the tow truck to pick up my car. Then we got in Mack's pickup and went to the hospital to pick Becky up after it was determined that she was more of a pain in the ass than an injured witness.

Phase Two complete!

One more to go.

JANUARY 24TH

This morning, after going to the body shop to sign forms for the repairs and picking up a rental car, I went straight to Brent's office. When I walked in, he was on the phone. I closed the door behind me and locked it. His eyes came up and settled on me. He was still listening to whoever was on the phone—Jerome? Already?—but he was also paying close attention to me.

He ended the call when he saw me lock his door. "Hope, what are you doing?"

"I want a meeting with you," I said, "and I don't want any interruptions."

"I'm very busy this morning," he said. "How about we meet this afternoon? No, wait." He was looking at his computer monitor. "No. I'm busy all day today. How about tomorrow morning, say, seven-thirty? That should give us plenty of time."

"Brent, stop it! I am meeting with you *right now*, so call your secretary and tell her to hold your calls and put a hold on anyone else that may want your time."

He frowned but did what I told him. "This better be good," he said. "What's so damn important that it can't wait?"

"Today is my last day as your employee," I said. "I quit. And I want you to know the reasons why I quit because they're important." His eyes widened in surprise. "I should have quit when Juan punched you in the face," I continued. "You have no idea what you're doing to this company. You're driving it into the ground. The layoffs right before Christmas? That's a good sign that you're on the wrong path."

He put both hands flat on his blotter and looked up at me. "We all have an opinion, Hope, and the opinion of the board of directors is that I'm doing a good job. They even gave me a bonus for Christmas."

I walked right up to his desk. "Wake up! You're feeding the corporate machine! And the people under the wheels of the machine are suffering from your poor management! You used the layoffs to get rid of people like Blythe just because you didn't like them. It had nothing to with performance. It was a popularity contest."

Now he stood up, but he didn't raise his voice. Not yet. "Quit if you want to," he said, "but I will not have you in my office scolding me like I'm a child. I did the right thing. Now get out!"

"Yeah, right!" I wasn't about to back down. "Call Security if you want, but I'm not going anywhere yet. I've got more to say." I leaned over his desk until our faces were about three inches apart.

"Look at me, Brent. Take a good look. I'm probably the last person who will take the time to tell you the truth. And, believe it or not, I'm trying to *help* you. Getting in bed with Jerome was a huge mistake. That man has threatened me, my family, the CEO of Bio-Sport, and God knows who else." I already knew it, but I could see by his reaction that Jerome was threatening him, too. I moved around to the side of his desk and sat on the edge. "I'm drawing the line with Jerome," I said. "And when I'm done with you, I'm going to see him and make sure he knows never to mess with me, my family, or any of my friends again. That includes you, too."

Brent took a step back "What are you going to do?"

"Don't worry about it. What you need to do is protect yourself from Jerome and anyone associated with him. Brent, I don't dislike you. You may be a fine human being when you get out of the building. I have friends here, and it pains me to leave them. But I know in my heart that it's time for me to go." I handed him an envelope. Inside were documents that I had copied from Jerome's secretary's PC. Turns out, in my haste to copy what I could before getting caught, I had stumbled on to some very interesting data. "I want you to have this," I told him. "It's your key to protection."

"What is this?"

"Data. That's worth more than money." What I had given Brent was straightforward data clearly showing that Back-2-Back had a hit list. Jerome had made a spreadsheet with a list of companies and people that could be manipulated by coercion or payoffs. In the last column of the spreadsheet was the method to be used. Brent had his own column. Next to his name was no monetary reward, but only a terse note that said *daughter leverage*. Next to Quint's name was another note: *Unable to negotiate with. Resolution by other means.*

"If Jerome contacts you," I said as Brent looked at the spreadsheet, then looked back at me, "tell him I gave you the essential data to put him away. After I leave here, wait two hours, then phone the police and explain what Jerome has done to you. By the time you call the police, I will already have had Jerome in a very compromising position and he won't be able to hurt anyone again for a long time."

"But how did you—"

"You see, Brent, Jerome's weakness is ego. He is so confident that no one will try to harm him that he keeps records of his evil doings. He didn't take measures to protect himself in his own office."

Brent slapped one hand to his forehead. "Holy shit!"

I couldn't help but smile. "I'm leaving now. I've given you a second chance. Please treat the people that work here like human beings. Convince them that you actually care about them."

He was reading the spreadsheet again as I stood up. He looked at me. "Thank you, Hope. And you have my word on it. I'll do my best to be a better leader of this company. Ever since Juan punched me, I've realized I'm not the man I used to be. I've drifted away from what I was." He held the spreadsheet up. "Now, my daughter's safe. I'm glad to see the nightmare of dealing with Jerome will soon be over." He gave a weak smile. "Yeah. I need to get back to who I was."

I could see that worrying about his daughter had taken its toll on him, so I nodded and accepted his apology, then unlocked the door.

I turned. "Uh, Brent? There is one more thing."

"What might that be?"

"I would appreciate it if you gave Devin my position. He really is the best replacement for me. In the short time he's been here, he's picked up all the ins and outs of the job. If Blythe were still here, I would have suggested him, but since he's not, well…go with Devin."

"You know, Hope, I believe you're right about that. I'll call down to HR and make the arrangements right now. Good bye." He did not try to shake hands with me. Instead, he came around his desk and actually hugged me. "I wish you the best of luck with the rest of your life."

When I arrived at Back-2-Back again, the Guy Fawkes Raiders were still sitting in front of the entrance with their signs. I nodded at them, walked through the glass doors, and went right up to Jerome's office, where I told the bimbo in attendance to tell Jerome I wanted to see him. Using one long, fake fingernail, she dialed his direct line, then looked up at me. "He will see you in a few minutes. Please have a seat over there."

"Tell you what," I said back at her. "Pick up that phone and try again. I've told him never to keep me waiting. Tell him if he doesn't see me right now, I'm walking."

She shook her head and gave me a look that pissed me off. Then she very slowly picked up the phone. Too late. I was good and pissed by then, so I walked right past her and slammed into Jerome's office. My suspicions were confirmed when I caught Jerome on his big leather couch with the other bimbo's head in his lap.

"Time to take a break, sweetie!" I pointed at the door. "Out." She quickly fixed herself and looked at Jerome for permission to leave. "You don't need his permission, Sweetie," I said. "Just go!" She still didn't move.

Jerome got up and zipped himself up.

I watched him. "Sit down, Jerome. We have a few things to discuss."

"Who the hell do you think you are busting in here shouting orders at my employees?"

"Jerome, I'm a finger on a trigger. I'm the fuse to your dynamite. I'm about to ruin your day. Sit down so I can give you the ugly details."

He motioned for the bimbo to leave, which she did. He kicked the door closed behind her, then turned back to me.

"Hope," he began, "do you think I will actually let you get away with talking to me that way in my own office? You're going to pay dearly for your disrespect."

"You see right there, Jerome? You don't get it. You think you're in control. But you're not. You are at my mercy. Not the other way around."

"What are you talking about?"

I handed him an envelope similar to the one I'd given Brent. He opened it. "Those are copies," I said. "There are more copies filed with the U.S. Attorney's Office. It appears that you have incriminated yourself, starting with embezzlement of Back-2-Back funds, not to mention an ongoing scheme to take over Bio-Sport, which included terrorizing Quint. Terrorizing Brent, too. And several others. It's all right there. Just read it. I'm no lawyer, but I bet it's fair to say that you've been a bad man for a long time."

He didn't say anything. He glanced at the contents and hurled them into his waste paper can. Then he looked at me with eyes that I will never forget. They shone with pure wickedness. He squeezed his fists until his hands were white.

I managed to smile and keep my voice light, though I admit it was a struggle. I deserve an Oscar for that performance. "Nothing lasts forever, Jerome. You are now in jeopardy. Even though you can afford the best lawyers, you're still in trouble. Big trouble. Look outside."

He walked around his desk and looked out the window. News trucks were pulling up and reporters were piling out of them. Technicians were extending satellite dishes, stringing cables for microphones, and checking equipment. Field reporters had people splashing makeup on them in preparation for the camera.

I joined him at the window. "Uh oh! Look, Jerome. You know when you're watching something on TV and someone says, *Breaking News?* That's about to be you."

"What have you done? Who are you, *really?*"

"I'm still the same ol' Hope," I told him, "but like I told you, I have friends. Meet the Guy Fawkes Raiders. You've been Fawked!" I pointed at them.

"Why are the news teams here?" he asked through gritted teeth.

"Oh, that. Well, it seems that you've been threatening a sixty-two-year-old woman by the name of Quint. And—oops, I forgot to tell you, she's my friend. And we had the men parked in front of her home arrested last night. Evidently, during questioning they coughed up the fact that they had clear orders from you to bring harm to her and her husband. This town is still small, and the citizens don't like trash here. So the news teams jumped on this breaking story. They're going to want to have a word with you, too."

Now he turned to face me. "What an idiot you are! I could have paid you plenty of money. I could have made you rich. But now I'll bring you down with me. I wrote you checks. You have been paid by me. They'll send you to jail right alongside me."

"Oh, Jerome, I'm not stupid. But you? You're a real idiot. First, you kept documentation of your evil doings on company computers. How stupid is that? Even I would know not to do that. But in your investigation of me and my family, you overlooked an important detail."

"Enlighten me!"

"This whole experience is to enlighten you," I said. "I'm doing you a favor. I'm saving you from doing more harm to others and in the long run harming yourself. Recently, I've come to learn some very important mortal information. You see, in the end, we all die, and when we die, we should minimize our trespasses and we shouldn't have regrets. Regrets make it difficult for us to cross over, or so I've been told. So I've fixed it so that you will pay for your earthly trespasses before you die. And when your time comes, your transition to the afterlife will be easier. You will thank me for this one day."

"What bullshit! You self-righteous bitch!"

"You never had your men check *everything* out," I said. "Well, I've got terminal cancer and I don't have much longer to live. So even if you persuade the police that I was instrumental in your evil doings, I won't live long enough to serve time."

His mouth dropped open. "Oh, that's good. That's rich. But it's a lie. Right? I mean…come on, you don't even look ill."

"No, it's the truth. And I'm the one who orchestrated the

Guy Fawkes Raiders action outside your door to bring public awareness to your company. In fact, it was my best friend and me who painted the side of your building the other morning. And the news trucks and soon the U.S. Attorney's Office? All me."

"How—but, but—but you don't have anything on me."

"The Guy Fawkes Raiders. Emphasis on *raiders*. I raided your computer and got the documentation that's going to allow the Attorney General's Office to take the wind out of your sails."

Now he actually looked puzzled. "Why? What did I do so wrong? I didn't do anything harmful to you."

"*Why?* Jerome, my friend, you are truly a stupid man. I did it because you are a *bully*. I despise bullies. Quint and I became good friends, and when I found out what you were doing to her, what you had me helping you do to her, I couldn't stand by and let it continue. So I started feeding you useless information and used your money to organize your downfall. Those protesters down there are all getting paid by you. Via me."

The intercom buzzed and a bimbo voice came on "Mr. Attwood, some people with the U.S. Attorney's Office are on their way—"

And at that exact moment, the door burst open and the room was filled with police officers and agents wearing jackets with big, bright, yellow words printed on them. U.S. Marshal.

"Mr. Attwood," one of them barked out, "you are under arrest! You have the right…" *Blah, Blah, Blah.*

An agent approached me. "Are you Mrs. O'Dwyer?"

"I am."

"We'd like to thank you for your outstanding data collection," he said. "We wouldn't have a case without it."

Jerome began yelling some very profane but very juvenile insults at me as they took him away in cuffs.

All three phases are complete. It's over.

JANUARY 26TH

It's Saturday, and what a relief! I'm free from work, free from Jerome, and free to be me. I spent all day yesterday (Friday) with the U.S. Marshals at the Department of Justice giving a statement. In fact, Quint and her husband were being interviewed in one room, Brent in another, and me in yet another. Colt and Becky waited for me in the waiting area. He didn't have any idea what was happening, so Becky filled him in while I told my story to the agents. No charges were filed against me because I hadn't really done anything illegal. However, they made certain that I paid the proper taxes (a hefty sum!) on the checks that Jerome wrote to me.

So this morning, I woke up to a whole new me. My bright ceiling made me feel like I was in a cocoon, safe from the winter weather outside. It wasn't really cold, not snowing, either, just cloudy and windy. I didn't feel very good, so I asked Colt if he wouldn't mind just lounging around today, being lazy together. So he and I lay in bed for quite a long while, just talking and cuddling with Sahchi's big body draped across the foot of the bed. Colt told me that he doesn't sleep so well anymore, not since he learned about my condition.

"Here's the thing," he said. "I believe in God, and generally I believe that life is good. But now? Well, I don't think I like God anymore. I love you, Hope, and God is taking you away from me. The thought of that scares me. I'm afraid to sleep. I'm afraid to miss one moment with you."

"You've said that before," I replied, snuggling closer to him, "and I don't believe you've ever said anything that has touched me more deeply. But it's important for you to get a good, healthy night's sleep because as time goes on and my strength dwindles, I'm going to need to rely on your strength." I made myself more comfortable against him. "I love lying next to you."

"I love being next to you, too," he said. "It fills me with a feeling of peacefulness. These are the sweet mornings that I enjoy with the whole of my being. All of which makes me all the more afraid of the future. When I'm alone, I won't feel moments like these ever again. It's moments like these, I feel like I'm complete. I feel so connected to your soul here and now, like life is more than just the usual, routine crap. It's in these moments lying here with you that I can't help but acknowledge that we have something special."

I put my head against his chest and listened to his heart beating for a minute. "We are blessed, aren't we?"

"Yes." He was quiet for a minute, then he said, "If we have such a good thing, a special thing, why would God ruin such a good thing by doing something so unfair? Like making you ill?"

"I think God feels pretty shitty about our situation," I said.

"Really?" He let out a snicker that made Sahchi twitch her ears. "The man who's responsible for everything, the man who could stop your illness and won't—you think he feels shitty about it?"

"Well, I don't really think life works that way. I think life is set in motion and we have choices. You know, free will. And then there are circumstances we don't have any control over. God doesn't create the problem, nor does he have responsibility for it. But what God can do is help us along our life's path."

"Wow, I didn't expect that! You act as if you forgive him for the cancer. In fact, you act as if you talk to him."

"Uhhh," I said, "he is more of an *it*."

"An *it*?" Colt asked.

"Yeah. God isn't a he or she, but sometimes he is a she and sometimes she is he."

"What? That makes no sense. What does, uh, *it* look like?"

"Like light! Pure, beautiful light."

I laid my head back on my pillow, and Colt propped his head on one elbow and looked down on me.

"Are you playing with me?" he asked. "Or have you seen God?"

"Yes. Well, I think so, anyway. I see a Being of Light from time to time, and it lets me know that everything will work out, even though I'm dying of cancer. The Being of Light has even reassured me that you and the kids will go on to live good and healthy lives."

He frowned. "I'm sorry, but I doubt that I'll go on to have the kind of life I had with you."

"Don't look at it that way!" I told him. "No, you won't have the kind of life you had with me. No one expects you to. It can't happen if I'm not there. But you must keep an open mind in the future and go on living. Live your life as it is meant to be lived. Your life is not all about me. It was never intended to be about me. You have your own purpose here on earth." I looked him in the eye. "Promise me you won't get hung up with grief or be angry at God forever for this."

He looked away. We were having a conversation two people rarely have, but I was glad we were talking about the inevitable instead of avoiding it. I needed, he needed, we both needed to talk about it. I felt the more honestly we addressed the issue of my death, the better we would understand each other. The more we understood, the better we could support each other.

"I won't get hung up," he said, "but don't tell me how long I should grieve for you." A minute later, he added, "So you think life has a purpose?"

I nodded. "When I consider the finite limits that we place on ourselves…when I see how all of our life's energies are wasted in working for companies to make money that buys us both simple provisions and luxuries, I realize that all these material things have no greater soulful meaning than just being stuff. And we may or may not be satisfied in our work. Was all the time and effort worth it in the end? I see now that when it comes to working for a company, all the time and devotion we give that company, well…I see it as nothing better than submission, as resignation of the soul. We convince ourselves that we're doing something worthwhile, something important. But all we're really doing is adding pretty paint to our prison walls. Right?"

He was listening carefully.

"When I consider my lifetime," I went on, "all the time I was away from you and the kids to make a dollar, I feel almost ashamed. Of late, I've been able to examine my whole being. You know what I've found? There's a person here in me who is more than evaluations for promotion, raises in pay, more than the worker who punched a time-clock for the company. And yet...when I look back over the years, I see that I invested the majority of my time in a corporation, not in the people I love. I see that what I valued and where I put my time were at the opposite end from where I wanted to live my lifetime." I paused for a minute and thought about how to present this philosophy to my husband.

"I've had time to reflect," I went on. "And when I reflect, I don't remember work. I remember your face, the presence of my children, Becky's laughter. Things like that. And when I see and hear these things, I smile. That's where our lives should be spent—loving and touching each other. Laughing.

"Most people will agree that young children don't understand the scope of their wishes. They go about their lives, not knowing or caring where they come from or where they need to go. As they grow up, they're only guided by what feels good. What's entertaining. I suggest that that is what we all should be doing more of. Going about like children. Exploring the world and laughing."

"That doesn't sound much like a purpose," Colt said. "That sounds very hedonistic."

I gave him a playful slap. "You know what I mean. We should live more of our life with the ones we love doing the things we enjoy doing. Hedonism is a little extreme for what I'm trying to describe."

"I'm just trying to understand."

"What I mean is, I wish I had lightened up more. Relaxed into living instead of being so uptight about everything. Honestly, I don't know how you put up with my being so serious about everything."

"Well," he said, "you certainly have changed lately. I mean, Becky told me how you and she were hanging over the side of the Back-2-Back building painting your protest slogan. That was a cold morning. Things like that…you're living more now than you ever have before."

"I have," I said proudly. "And it feels great! You know, I think Junior is the most like I used to be. Not so much the hate, but the refusal to live life with positive energy. I want so much for him to live his life differently. I wrote him a letter and revealed my condition. I said I want us to be friendlier before my time is up. I asked him to let go of the anger. It would mean so much to me if he could just relax once in a while and find the joy in life."

Colt just laughed. "That's a big wish! Junior was born angry. I doubt he'll ever enjoy life. I think he spends too much time enjoying being angry."

"Well, I can still wish."

JANUARY 30TH

Becky drove me to see Dr. Bach this morning. I've been feeling increasingly shitty lately. He examined me, prescribed more pills. I think I've got more pills than the pharmacy. We also talked about the future and hospice. While he was talking, however, my mind drifted away and I remembered a dream I've already written about – the one where my granddad was dying. And in that dream, the doctor was my granddad's best friend. He was telling me that my granddad was in pain and that I could relieve him of the pain by ending his life.

As this dream replayed in my head, I looked at Becky, my best friend. After Dr. Bach left the exam room, I said to her, "Have you ever killed anyone?"

She laughed. "Lil Sis, that's a steep question. What gives?"

"When the time comes," I said, "and I decide I can't take it anymore, I want you to give me a hug, then hand me enough pills to do the job and a Mountain Dew to wash them down with. Then hold my hand until I go."

"Sis, I'm not the one to ask to do this," she said. "I love you too much."

"I thought I could handle it all the way to the end," I told her, "but now I'm not so sure. I think about the pain, the indignity of the Foley catheter and a nurse changing my diapers, and... well, ugh! I don't think I want to go all the way. While my mind is still working, I'm asking you as my best friend to please put an end to it so I won't suffer too much."

Dr. Bach came back in the room with some prescriptions and paperwork.

"Can you draw me up a DNR and a living will?" I asked him.

"I can help you set up a *do not resuscitate* order and you can get a living will from your lawyer," he said. "Then, yes, we can get those into your chart if you like."

After the appointment, Becky and I walked to my car, which we had just picked up from the body shop.

"I'm not going to be the one who puts you six feet under!" she said.

"I'm not asking you to do anything wrong," I said. "All I'm asking is for you to help me when I can no longer do for myself. There will come a time when all the medicine, the IV's, the machines, and the lifesaving devices won't help anymore. They'll only be delaying the inevitable."

"You better tune me in and get my signal," she argued. "I'll do anything for you, Sis, anything at all, but what you're asking is the most. It's the end-all. How can I do that?"

"Sure, it's hard," I said, "but can I count on you to do it?"

Becky patted my hand. "If need be, Sis." She sighed. "I'll be there for you. If need be...."

On our way home, I drove by Washington Park, where I spotted Mr. Goldsole on the sidewalk. "Oh, look, Becky," I said. "There's Mr. Goldsole. I've told you about him."

He looked at me and waved, and I waved back.

"Who?" She turned her head to look where I was pointing. "Who?" she repeated in a puzzled voice.

"That old guy dressed in that funny old brown suit."

"I don't see anybody."

"But he's right there. Standing on the sidewalk."

"I don't see him."

"Well, you have to meet this man," I said. "He is something very special." I turned on Linden Street and made my way back around the block. "He's over there, walking toward the bus stop," I told her. But now I didn't see him either. He must have caught the bus before I got back around. Damn, I really wanted Becky to meet him. Oh, well, maybe tomorrow or the next day.

When I got home and opened the door, hanging on the wall was a framed newspaper article about Back-2-Back. It had a photo of the building, where Becky and I had painted *Back-2-Back rapes the minds of our children. Down with Rape Play 1&2* on the windows. The article reported how the Guy Fawkes Raiders and I were taking action against Back-2-Back.

"I'm so proud of you that I just had to frame that and hang it on the wall," Colt said, greeting me with kiss. "But even though I'm proud of you for taking action, I sure don't want you doing anything else crazy like that again. I made one for Becky too."

I don't like to think of myself as an egotistical person, but it sure did feel good to know I was part of something that made a real difference. It's also good to know we accomplished it all in a nonviolent way. No regrets!

FEBRUARY 3RD

Colt and I spent the weekend in the town of McCall, celebrating my birthday. My birthday is actually February 7th but Colt wanted to celebrate over the weekend.

He told me he had a surprise for me and wouldn't say what or where it was. He did all the packing and made all the arrangements. I didn't have to do a thing. So we drove up Friday morning. Sahchi and I just climbed up into his pickup headed to the unknown destination. We had no idea where we were going or how long we would be there.

McCall is a resort area about a two-hour drive from our home. Colt had rented three cabins—one for him and me, one for Cleo and Ward, and a large four-bedroom cabin for Junior and Conrad, Becky, and Quint and her husband. The large cabin had a full kitchen. That was where we ate our meals.

What a wonderful weekend it was! The lake was frozen over and covered with rich fluffy new snow. We cross-country skied over it and, because there was almost a full moon, we got in a midnight ski escapade, too. I did my best to hide how ill I was feeling, and for the most part I was able to participate. There were times when I should have stayed in bed, I'm sure, but I just couldn't resist being with my family and friends. This illness seems to come at me in waves. Sometimes I feel like I'm as healthy as can be (well, a bit of an exaggeration here), and then out of nowhere—*slam*! I'm deathly ill.

Tammy Jo and Garrett came up on Sunday and we had a feast. Tammy Jo, Becky, and Quint made dinner and dessert was the best homemade German chocolate cake ever made on the planet. I was so happy to be with my family and closest friends. I cherish their love. Whatever my fate may be, at least I will be able to say that I couldn't have been a happier woman on my last birthday. And McCall is so beautiful, it must be really close to heaven.

I must say that although my illness often dictates how active I can be, the scenery at McCall was so uplifting that I was able to rise above my poor health. I found strength in the lovely, snow-covered valley. I felt empowered by the scene around me, the trees pointing toward heaven, the ice and snow-covered lake. My family and friends and I went skiing under a moon so bright that I found myself lost in its beauty. As we skied, however, I began to feel a subtle distance from my family and friends, as if I were already getting ready for the future. The bright vastness spread out before me, and I fell—or rose—into a vision in which I surrendered my soul so that it might be filled with complete and perfect joy. Out there on the lake at midnight, my soul was filled with heavenly elation, and within that celestial moment my mind was reassured that life is good. More than that, the reassurance that life doesn't end when we die. I'm going on from here. Knowing that fact, I was able to bring my mind back down to enjoy the happiness I was sharing with my family and friends. Happiness for me is knowing that my heart is capable of feeling simple love and innocent delight with those I have a connection with, whether it's earthly or heavenly.

I'm going to be fifty-one in four days. I can say for certain that in my earlier years I wouldn't have been as happy as I am today. Once I had an issue with my age, but thanks to Quint, Becky, and her mother, I see that aging is something to be celebrated. This weekend I celebrated and embraced my age. And on Sunday night, as we were skiing under the moon, I celebrated within myself. I let go of the scared little girl that looked for her granddad to save her from the world. I accepted the wonderful person I've grown up to be. What a child I have been, to be so uneasy about age, so vain about my appearance. What a child I have been!

But what is life if we don't seem foolish once in a while?

I will be fifty-one. Dr. Bach tells me that due to my prognosis or diagnosis, I forget which is the best term here, this will be my last birthday. I'm not sure how I should feel about that. I will not deceive myself into thinking there will be more birthdays. I'm a realist. Death is not to be avoided.

. . .

But enough about death. This weekend was wonderful on other levels, too.

Quint and her husband told Colt about riding their bikes over the Golden Gate Bridge. Thanks to Quint, Colt and I are going to San Francisco for Valentines Day. She's set everything up. All we have to do is show up and enjoy. I'm so excited. As Quint's husband sat talking to Colt, I could see that he was getting excited, too.

Cleo is seven months along now. Her belly is growing bigger. Ward is such a proud father. He brightens up when anyone asks about the baby. And to add a special treat, on Sunday night on the lake under the bright moon, he knelt down and asked her to marry him. Of course she said yes. It was just one more experience that I was thankful to be around for. I've told most everyone about my cancer except ... well, I'm so glad that we haven't told Cleo or Ward about my situation. They would have let my illness influence their plans. The baby is due April 22nd. Ward suggested that their wedding should be June 1st.

I think Colt was actually happier about the engagement than Cleo was. He threw his strong arms around Ward and hugged him. "Welcome to being my son-in-law!" he exclaimed. Then he grabbed Cleo and hugged her and kissed the top of her head. We all congratulated them. Well, everyone but Junior. He kept his distance. I know I've said a hundred times, but it saddens me to see his isolation from happiness and love.

When Ward asked Conrad to be his best man, Conrad looked as if he had just won the lottery. "I'm your man!" he told Ward. "Don't you worry about a thing. I'll take care of everything."

"And what he can't take care of," Colt said, "I'll help with."

I was reassured (again) that Cleo's baby and upcoming nuptials will be a healthy distraction for Colt and the kids. I looked up at the night sky and prayed a prayer of gratitude.

A few weeks ago, I had a conversation with Becky and Quint about what was left of the money Jerome gave me. We were all in agreement as to what should be done with it. That made me glad. When we returned to the cabin that night, I handed each of my children a check that covered their outstanding student loans, plus a little more. It seemed appropriate to help my kids on my last birthday. I want them to start fresh and not be hindered by the debt of an education.

What a wonderful weekend.

Thank you, Being of Light, for your blessings. Thank you, Mr. Goldsole, for showing me life from a whole new perspective.

FEBRUARY 7TH.
MY BIRTHDAY

I'm glad we went out for the weekend to celebrate my birthday. I've been sick for three days, and today I never even got out of bed. Colt has played nursemaid to me the whole time, barely leaving my side. I'm afraid now that I'm never going to get well.

Colt is such a good man. He takes such good care of me. But I can see that the stress of this is reaching him on some level. When he doesn't know I'm looking at him I can see his state of constant worry.

Illness can put so much stress on a relationship. My previous episode with cancer drove a wedge between us. Between my resentment and his fear of hurting me, we lost so much. I don't want my illness to do that again. That's why I do my best to tell Colt how much I appreciate him. I don't want to take him for granted this time.

I've got a headache.

I feel like I have no energy.

I'm not going to write anymore today, I feel like shit.

FEBRUARY 13TH

Colt and I drove to San Francisco today to enjoy the gift Quint gave me. It was a long drive, eleven hours from home, but Colt broke it up because I'm still not feeling too good. We left yesterday and made it to Reno late. We stayed the night in Reno and drove across California the rest of the way today. It was a nice trip. Colt and I were able to talk without interruption. We talked about the future. I'm surprised that he's made a conscious choice not to be bitter or negative while I'm still here. He told me he wants every moment to be good for the both of us. I agree. Our time is limited, so why spend it worrying or feeling frustrated? I told him I'm all about *living*.

Reno was like a honeymoon. I don't dare write about what we did in that hotel. Well, yes, I can say it was the best love we have made. Oh, yeah, and we made time to renew our vows at one of those cheap chapels. I said *I do!* again and, boy, it felt good to have a ceremony celebrating our love again.

What a beautiful trip we've had. The weather was friendly, too. I was worried that we would run into snow and ice that might prevent us from making it to San Francisco, but that didn't happen.

We stopped on the Donner Pass to stretch our legs. The road was clear, but the snow was piled high all around. And the mountains! The mountains were majestic! The Teton and Big Hole mountain ranges will always be my favorite places, but the view from Donner Pass is another way to see how beautiful this world really is.

We brought my car because Quint said Colt's pickup wouldn't fit in any parking spaces in San Francisco. She was right. San Francisco has such small parking spaces. I've always liked sports cars, and this neat, little, but fast as hell Subaru is very practical. Colt put our bikes on the racks on the roof, and inside we had plenty of room for our gear. Colt loves driving my car. He loves the throttle response. In fact, I was afraid he was going to get a ticket. His foot was a little heavy, but that made him happy, and if he's happy, then so am I.

It took us a little while to find the boutique hotel Quint set us up in, and when we did, we had to dismount the bikes because the car wouldn't fit into the parking garage. (They have such low ceilings as well as small parking spaces in the city.)

I can't wait until tomorrow so we can go on a walk-about in the city. I'm hoping and praying that I will be well enough to climb the hills of San Francisco. From what I remember, San Francisco is a fun and friendly place. Tomorrow is Valentines Day. Quint bought us tickets to see *Beach Blanket Babylon*. We don't know much about that, but I'm sure it will be fun.

Life is good.

FEBRUARY 14TH

Happy Valentines' Day! It's actually the fifteenth as I'm writing this, but since it's so early in the morning, this entry will be going down as Valentines' Day.

Beach Blanket Babylon was a riot! Colt and I laughed so hard our sides hurt. The night started with Colt and me approaching the theater. In his western clothes and cowboy hat, he stood out like a sore thumb. We stood in line to go in, and there was a bunch of gay guys in line, and, boy, did they like what they saw in Colt.

"I never knew sexy wore a cowboy hat like that," one of the men said. "Honey, you can hang your hat on my bedpost anytime."

Well, that certainly got our attention. I looked at Colt and laughed. I've been with him for a long time, but I don't think I've ever heard a man hit on him before. "Keep it cool, honey," I said to him. "They're complimenting you."

Colt smiled wide and said to me, "At my age, I do take it as a compliment. If anyone wants to call this old duffer sexy, that's a good thing."

I was relieved. I wasn't sure how Colt would take these guys' comments. They were obviously a little drunk and loud, but not horribly obnoxious.

He turned to the guy and said, "This hat only hangs on one bed post." Then he put his arm around me.

"You might want to give me a try," the man said back. "You'd have it made with me."

"That's a real good offer," Colt said, "but I just renewed my vows to my beautiful wife. I've already got it made."

It was obvious to me that these guys were testing Colt to see how he would react to their flirting. The more he talked to them, the friendlier they became, and before long, we were all laughing together. They explained how Colt would fit right in with the show, which is a musical revue, because it's partly about hats. After Colt and I got seated, the guys sent a bottle of champagne to our table. And, boy, were they right about the hats! The show was outrageous in comedy and hats. It was a wonderful night with new friends that were so much fun and very kind to us. I love San Francisco. I like it for a vacation spot, though I doubt I could ever live here, and I know Colt couldn't live there for sure. He's just not a big city dude.

Now it's late (or very early) and Colt is sleeping. I'm glad to see him sleeping because he doesn't sleep enough. I feel like hell, but I refuse to let my illness stop me from having a good time. And I damn sure won't let anyone know that I feel ill. I don't need anyone worrying over me or playing caretaker to me unless it's absolutely necessary. I'm not a charity case.

And now that it's so late, I can admit the pain to myself, I can admit the aches, the fever, and whatever else is making me feel this way. I hate to say it, but at least when my time comes, I won't feel any more pain than I already do.

FEBRUARY 15TH

Today was the day! Even though I wasn't feeling the greatest, I made myself get up this morning. I wanted so bad to do this ride. I put on my shorts and stuffed GORP into my pockets. I also filled my hydration system with ice water, put a cold bottle of Mountain Dew in the bottle cage on my bike. When I was ready, I went downstairs and stood in front of the hotel, waiting for Colt to come out. I so truly love my husband and today is one example why. He was wearing real cycling shorts (the black ones that look like a second skin) and a cycling jersey that advertised the U.S. Postal Service, plus sunglasses…and his cowboy boots and his cowboy hat! Oh, my God, I laughed so hard at the sight of him that I almost peed myself! He looked like a hot mess. After I took a few snapshots with my smart phone, he went back up to the room and changed into cargo shorts, a Batman T-shirt, sport shoes, and the same sunglasses. What a prankster.

Our hotel sits near Union Square. Quint suggested a route that would take us away from the Golden Gate Bridge toward the North Waterfront so we could ride down the world's crookedest (is that even a word? How about windiest?) road, Lombard street. What a crazy experience that was.

Cars were lined up to go down the street, bumper to bumper. No exaggeration, that's literally bumper touching bumper. Colt and I had to find our place in line with our bikes then ride down the hill sandwiched between two cars. Boy, was that freaky! The people in the cars were of all nationalities, and the police officer directing traffic down the famous road was having trouble communicating the order of things because of the various language barriers.

We started our descent in the cue assigned to us by the officer. The bumper of the car in front of us was eight inches away, and the car behind us was no more than twelve inches away. Colt and I were on our rear brakes the whole time. At the bottom of the switchbacks is Leavenworth Street. There was another officer there directing traffic, plus a crowd of people snapping photos. I looked up at the crowd and I swear I saw Mr. Goldsole. That took my attention away from where I was, and I ran into the bumper of the car in front of us before I could hit the brake. When I looked up again, Mr. Goldsole was gone.

"What's wrong?" Colt asked.

"Oh, nothing," I said. "I just got distracted by the crowd." I didn't hit the car hard enough for the driver to notice, and no

harm came to my bike or the car. But it was just so strange to have seen/imagined Mr. Goldsole.

What fun it was to ride through the traffic and the cable cars. Classic San Francisco! One thing I will say that I didn't like about San Francisco, though, is their lack of public restrooms! I had to pee and we looked and looked for a public restroom, but nothing. Oh, correction. We found one, but it was locked up! So we pedaled into an alley, where I squatted behind a parked car and did my business. What the hell! That's no way for a lady to act, but I was forced to. Anyway, we rode down to Bay Street and cut over to Mason Street, where the views from Golden Gate Park and Crissy Field would have been amazing if it hadn't been so foggy.

The climb up from Fort Point is strenuous. It was especially hard for me, feeling ill as I did. When we started onto the bridge, it was shrouded in mist. I knew Sausalito was somewhere across the Bay in the fog that lay like a dream at the foot of the bridge. Even with the haze, I could still see the water and numerous fishing boats moving between the sunlight and the fog beneath that bright, international orange bridge.

Colt and I pedaled through throngs of people from every corner of the world walking and pedaling across the bridge. I don't know about Colt, but I was experiencing great joy and smiling at the sight of so many people who were just as happy as I was to be on the bridge. About the time we were halfway across the bridge, the fog lifted and the true vision of the Golden Gate Bridge suddenly appeared. We were awestruck and had to stop and dismount and just stand there and stare. Nowhere else in all of the United States is there such an exquisite view of the sun and that brilliant orange suspension bridge.

Looking back from the midpoint, we had a panoramic view of the city. Like other great cities, this view can be deceptive. The city has a face that gives little indication of its soul. Along the shoreline lie wide piers, and behind those piers sit cheerful, expensive houses, solidly built homes with all the modern convinces, yet with the large, old-fashioned windows looking out on the Bay. All along the walkway near the edge of the Bay we could see the multitudes of joyous tourists and their children, all walking along, some of them shopping. Woven in a messy, unsystematic fashion are the streets that wind through one part of the city and then straighten out in a grid in another area. And there at the piers are the brightly colored boats tied up and waiting for sightseers. When I saw those boats, I felt something within me come to life, something reminiscent of the boat in my dreams. I could feel something pulling at me, something I didn't exactly understand.

The Golden Gate Bridge has a unique charm. The Bay below stretches inland as far as the eye can see, yet I felt like I was looking down at a beautiful blue lake. And what a stunning lake it could be on a cloudless winter day! I can only say that I had a day of ecstasy at the Golden Gate.

Colt and I pedaled on toward the Sausalito end of the bridge, where we stopped and took more pictures of the harbor and the lighthouse. Then the real excitement began! I'm a fixed gear rider. My bike has one speed, no gears to fool with, and a set of brakes. That's the way I like it, simple. Leaving the bridge, we approached the steep grade Quint told us about. Side by side, Colt and I practically flew down the grade. We must have been doing every bit of thirty miles per hour (though I had no way of measuring our speed). Colt could only laugh as I screamed with pure excitement. We had a sense of freedom, a sense of flight. I was reminded of my dream of the flight on the back of the Pegasus.

The boats, the Pegasus, Mr. Goldsole...what was happening to me?

The sun was warm for a February day, and the wind was almost nonexistent, so we were comfortable when we arrived at the Aurora Restaurant (named after Goddess of Dawn in Roman times) in Sausalito. It was a welcome lunch break. And it was just as Quint had described it to me, as if the cycling gods had set it there to refresh us after our trip over the bridge. I ordered a fresh Mountain Dew, Colt went for ice water. We ordered two kinds of specialty pizza and ate like champions.

Sausalito is a busy, but happily busy, town with that air of half hustle-and-bustle and half carefree contentment. Pedaling through it, I could see how this little town is amazingly different from its bigger brother across the shining water. The air is fresher, brighter under the sun, and the water is more of a rich green color. Pedaling toward the Bay, I could see more closely the blue and yellow boats waiting at the docks in the city for tourists.

When we found a café packed with tourists, the lines to the restrooms went all the way around the building. After locking our bikes up, Colt and I took our places in the proper lines. Incredibly, the women's line moved faster than the men's. I know, that never happens, but it did there. I was looking at Colt as I moved toward the bathroom, and he was still standing in the same place. After taking care of business and washing my hands, I was outside again and wiping my hands (no more paper towels inside) on my well-worn Georgia O'Keeffe T-shirt. Colt wasn't even in the door yet.

Then I was standing by our bikes again when I noticed Mr. Goldsole standing right next to me.

"Hello, Chief," he said.

I was astonished to see him. "What are you doing here?"

"Oh," he said, "just visiting. I saw you and thought I would stop and chat."

"I thought I saw you earlier," I said, "standing on Lombard Street. That was you, wasn't it?"

"Yes, that was me."

"I've come to ask you something," he said. "I want you to think carefully before you answer."

I looked around bewildered. Where did he come from? How did he know I would be in San Francisco? "Wait. How did you…Why…"

"Do you trust me?"

"Go ahead," I said. "You know I trust you."

"Have you gotten everything taken care of in your life that you wanted to do before you make the transition?"

I looked around and saw people going about every which way, shopping, cycling, walking, jogging, but then, just then,

I saw it—that familiar dream scene of people boarding a ship and other people waving. I had seen that before. Everyone was smiling. It wasn't exactly the same as in my dreams, though, for I didn't see a railway station.

What I saw was enough for me to finally understand that Mr. Goldsole was not a mortal man at all. "Who are you, *really?*" I asked him.

He smiled. "I'm what many people call a guardian angel."

Now it all makes sense! Whenever Mr. Goldsole is in my presence, I don't feel ill. In fact, I feel whole and healthy when he's around.

"Yes," I said. "I believe I have taken care of everything I needed to do. My friends and family are safe. Only I was hoping I had more time."

"Time?" he asked. "Time is a manmade construct. More time, less time. It's all a matter of perspective. I've come to know you over the years, and I've come to love you as any good man would love a daughter. I see that you are happy now and free from the stresses of material living."

I had to agree with him. "Yes, I think I am." I gave it another thought. "Yes, I finally am. It has taken me a lifetime to understand how to be free, but I've done it...."

"But you're tired," he said in a gentle voice. "And you should rest soon. Don't you think?"

I had to agree again. "Yes, I could use some rest."

"Today you have crossed a bridge of steel and ridden under the natural sun. Soon I will come to escort you across an ethereal, eternal bridge. You will find rest on the other side of the Golden Gate."

Everything around me was in motion, but I wasn't on the same plane with all that. Only Mr. Goldsole could see me, really see me. And no one on that crowded street could see him. Colt came back from the restroom and found me, but he didn't see Mr. Goldsole or hear my conversation with him. To Colt, I was just staring off in the distance looking at the people getting on the boats in the Bay. I suppose I was looking for my grandparents.

Then my mind returned to the present, to here and now. "I'm sorry," I said to Mr. Goldsole. "When will you escort me to the other side?"

"Hope, we're standing on the other side of the Golden Gate. Are you ready?"

"What? Right now?"

He shook his head and indicated the crowds of people. "Not now, but soon. You had one more request to fulfill. I want your transition to be easy on you, so after that last wish has come true, I'll come for you. Besides," here he chuckled, "I don't want to make you the center of attention here on a busy street."

"My last wish," I said. "What might that be? Oh, never mind about wishes now, I feel I've done all I wanted to. Other than last-minute goodbyes, I'm ready."

"Then, Chief, I will see you soon."

"Yes. Soon."

I know this must sound strange, but I *am* ready. You might think I should try to cheat death, that I should try to spend more time with my family. I thought of several things I should—*should* stick around for, but I know my time is up. My time *is* up. I've done what I was intended to do on earth. Whatever is left of my time is up to the Being of Light. In the presence of Mr. Goldsole, I felt like my life was complete and nothing would keep me from going with him. Call it instinct, call it soulful knowledge, call it what you will. I'm fine.

"Well, then," I said to Mr. Goldsole, "I will expect to see you soon." But not knowing exactly when made me nervous.

"Don't worry, Chief. You're not alone in this." He smiled at me and laid one hand on my shoulder. "Leave with love, forgiveness, and no regrets."

"Yep, that's what I've learned. I don't have any regrets. I love and I have forgiven. I can only hope that in my last days I, too, am forgiven."

"All you have to do is ask, Chief. Just ask."

That's when Colt mounted his bike. I looked at him for, like, half a second, and Mr. Goldsole was gone. That quick.

"Are you ready?" Colt asked.

"Gee, that seems to be a popular question today."

"What?"

"Oh, nothing. Yes, yes, indeed. I'm ready."

APRIL 28TH. POST SCRIPT

For a minute on that sunny spring afternoon, after Cleo and Ward parked their car, bundled up their baby, and entered the house, Colt still stood in the doorway, holding the door open. In the distance he saw an older, well-dressed gentleman walking up the street. Colt had no idea why an old man should capture his attention, but he hesitated and stood there watching the man walk up the opposite side of the street. A month ago, he might not have noticed the old man.

As the spring wore on, Hope's condition was becoming increasingly worse. They both knew she was headed toward the great unknown. She had always been near him, Colt reminded himself, but now she was heading to a place where he could not follow her, and the idea that he would be alone for the rest of his life was defeating him. How could he go on? Hope was too closely knitted into his existence. How could they be separated and he still survive?

Today he was exhausted, and in his exhaustion he just stood there watching the old man walk up the street. That was all the man was doing, walking, but as Colt watched him, he began to feel a strange, sort of mystical, assurance that some day he would feel good again.

But he also knew that Hope would never feel good again, at least not in this life. The end for Hope was near. He was certain about that. The love they shared had passed through its earthly stages, and now little was left of their physical love. His soul was telling him to let her go. He had almost ceased to think of himself as coupled to her. Now, even though his family was gathering around him, he knew he would soon be alone.

In his deepest private agony, he felt that the best part of him would die with her, leaving him only an illusion of himself. He was sure that a life without her would be no true life at all. He had ceased to desire anything, to have any ambition. Of his life's work, which had once seemed so important back when life seemed so big, so full of options, he saw nothing, only that he was smaller in the world without her. The future was empty. All he would have after she was gone would be her diary. He carried the little volume almost everywhere with him, almost afraid to set it down, as if it, too, might go away. It was a painfully honest record of her last months, and in it he had read her words of love and sorrow, her accounts of their relationship, of his mistakes, of her mistakes, of her recent good deeds.

Still standing there in the doorway, he watched the old man draw nearer. Now he could see that he wore a hat, a brown, old-fashioned suit, and well-polished, well-worn, leather shoes that seemed to make no sound on the sidewalk. Colt smiled at him, and the man's answering smile came across the street like an embrace of fellowship.

Could he be a widower? Colt wondered. *Does he somehow understand my loss? Has this man survived the grief I'm about to face? And if so, what could he say to me that would ease my heartache?*

"Nice day isn't it?" The old man's voice came across the street.

"Yeah, sure is," Colt managed to reply. "Pure sunshine."

"The Grand Artist is kind to us this day," the old man said with a tip of his hat. "I wish you well and bid you a good day." And he walked on.

And now something new flowed into Colt's heart. Perhaps, he thought, it was the same feeling of ecstasy that Hope had felt on the Golden Gate Bridge and described to him. Ecstasy. It was a bright burst of light that seemed to offer him hope in a hopeless situation. The desolation was still there, but it seemed less daunting than it had been only seconds earlier. The light that touched him was bright with warmth, rest, and empathy. The light could not be seen by physical eyes, yet Colt still felt it, and its brightness illuminated not only his soul but also his recent dull, dreary attitude towards the rest of his life without Hope.

Colt stood there, still holding the door, as Cleo and Ward looked back at him from the living room. Cleo was holding the baby, wrapped in a snowy white blanket that glistened in the sunshine coming through the window.

Seeing his shining grandson, Colt suddenly recognized the possibility of healing. The light was planting a sacred, healing seed in Colt that would ease his pain and help him move forward in life. The seed would grow and blossom into a healing that would allow him to become a more mature man who could see the possibility of loving again, of being satisfied in his life's work again.

Colt finally closed the front door and joined his daughter, soon-to-be son-in-law, and grandson in the living room.

"Dad, Conrad and Sam will be here pretty soon. Junior, too, I suppose."

Colt stood there, looking like he wished he had somewhere to go, anywhere but back upstairs to the room where the hospice nurse was fussing over his dying wife. "I don't think I've ever been so tired in my life," he finally said.

"I know, Dad," she said, her voice a bit shaky. "But you know you can lean on me. I'll hold you up. I know it's hard, but we have to face it."

Was the old man still out there? Colt looked out the window, but he didn't see him on the street anymore. With a sigh, he sank down on the couch and took Cleo's hand and began thinking again about the night Hope had crumpled to the floor. He had carried her up the stairs and laid her in their bed in the bedroom she had painted to look like a sunny day. He had laid his dying wife in the bed where they had so often made love. But now, though, he'd forgotten his memories of making love.

Exhausted as he was, he still felt restless. He stood up again and walked to the window and looked up and down the street. *Where did that old man go?* he asked himself. He knew that if he started thinking about making love to Hope, he would probably collapse.

During the past few weeks, Colt's routine had been centered around almost daily visits by his children, the only exception being the last few days while Cleo was in the hospital giving birth to her son. The family had spent hours sitting at Hope's bedside. Sometimes she was able to carry on a conversation with them, but most of the time she drifted away and left her family to talk amongst themselves. They didn't know where her mind was taking her, but it was clear it often took her somewhere else.

Dr. Bach had made two or three house calls, and Becky and her family were frequent visitors, too, as were Quint and her husband as well as Mack and Jenifer. Some people from work had also come to pay their respects, like Brent, who had brought along a coworker named Devin, who seemed to take Hope's condition very hard. He knew why the young man took it so hard, but he kept the secret. Colt's mother and father came every day to visit and prepare meals, run errands, do anything that would support their son and daughter-in-law. Hope thus had so many visitors that it seemed to Colt he was never alone.

Nevertheless, the past month had taken its toll on him. He refused to sleep until he fell on the bed beside Hope. Most of the time, when she was present and conscious, he sat near her and they talked about their lives. He also tried to busy himself with being a good host to the visitors who came in and out. But once, in the kitchen with his mother, he just hadn't been able to hold it together. His strength had failed and he crumbled to the floor and wept. Tammy Jo pulled him up and wrapped her arms around him. Words were of no use, so she didn't even try to speak, but just held him like she had when he was a boy. She couldn't remember the last time she had seen her son weep this hard. When he collected himself, she still didn't say anything. He kissed her and went back upstairs to Hope.

After he left the kitchen, Tammy Jo had broken down.

Now Colt turned away from the window again and followed Cleo and Ward up the stairs. Troy, the hospice nurse, was sitting across the room reading. He was a hard-working, compassionate man who made sure that Hope was comfortable and clean. As the family entered, he stood up, quietly excused himself, and went downstairs.

Hope's eyes were closed. Colt looked down at her and gave thanks, as he did every day, for all the good years they had shared. But something about her eyes bothered him. He could hardly bear to watch them shifting this way and that, the lids fluttering as she struggled for consciousness. She was closer to death.

Barely opening her eyes, she suddenly spoke. "Mr. Goldsole, is that you?"

Something came over Colt. His mind worked to understand his wife's question. *Who? Oh, yeah*, he thought, *a name from her diary.* And then he suddenly identified the old man in the brown suit. He felt a bit of something good peeking out from behind all the sadness. Working as a vet, it was something he had seen so many times before as he watched an animal struggling in death, its soul finally, peacefully, leaving its body. He believed that death came shortly after the soul left, and he believed that on several occasions he had witnessed this departure himself. The thought sent a strange, almost divine message to his heart.

Is it possible this isn't goodbye? he asked himself. *Can it be the will of God that we might be together again? Is it possible, in spite of all this heartache and despair, that perhaps this isn't the end?*

In the weeks that Hope had lain in bed, and after a week and a half of frequent episodes of unconsciousness, her body now seemed to be too exhausted for even the slightest activity. Her soul was searching for an exit. Unbeknownst to her family, however, Hope had been hanging on for something specific and today that particular detail had arrived. Her last wish answered.

Cleo walked closer to her mother's bed and held the baby out. "Mom, it's me. Cleo. We're all here. Conrad and Sam are here, and Junior has just arrived, too."

Hope's eyes opened, but she didn't seem to recognize anyone in the room.

Cleo sat on the edge of the bed. "And this is your grandson," she said. "We've named him Theo. He was born two days ago."

Hope lifted one hand and touched this fresh new life. *Her grandson.*

"He looks like you," Colt said in the most cheerful voice he could summon up. "He's got your eyes."

To everyone's delight, Hope smiled. Baby Theo brought cheer almost anywhere he was taken. Cleo looked radiant, Ward beamed with pride, and Conrad, the proud uncle, gave the biggest smile he could manage. Colt was equally ecstatic about the birth of the baby, but by now he was just too exhausted to show it. The only person who was not smiling was Junior, who stood alone near the door, looking unmoved by either his mother's impending death or his nephew's birth.

A few minutes later, Becky came into the room. They could all see how swollen her eyes were from the many tears she had shed.

Hope looked up at her. "Oh, Becky," she murmured, "I've been waiting for you. I really want that Mountain Dew to take with my pills. A bit later today."

Everyone looked at Becky, wondering how Hope could be so responsive to her but not to them.

Becky shrugged her shoulders and looked at Colt. "I made a promise to her a long time ago that I'd make sure she had her Dew," she told him. "Maybe she remembers that." She put one hand on his shoulder. "Will you come with me to get it?"

"Sure."

Once they were outside the room and away from the family, Becky told Colt about her promise to Hope, that when things became intolerable, she would give Hope a handful of pills with her Mountain Dew. "But I can't do this, Colt! I promised her, but I don't think I can do it." She paused and wiped away another tear. "Will you help me?"

Colt studied Becky. He knew his wife, and he knew this was exactly what she wanted. Hope had always wanted to die with dignity. He knew it was disrespectful to keep her alive against her wishes.

"Becky, I'm so tired," he said, his voice cracking. "If I'm this tired, I'm sure Hope's exhausted, too. She just wants to rest. We should respect her wishes. Yes, of course," he whispered, "of course I'll help you. What do you want me to do?"

"When the time comes, can you just ask everyone to step out of the room? Tell 'em you want to be alone for a minute, something like that. And then...then I need you to just be in the room with us."

Hope spent most of the day awake with her new grandson, looking at him, talking to him, loving him. Late that afternoon, Colt asked his children to step outside with him. In the hallway, he told them that he doubted that Hope would last the day.

"Make sure that you say everything you want to say to her now," he told them. "Pay your final respects." He looked Junior in the eye. "Make sure you tell her everything you've ever wanted to say."

Junior looked away in silence.

Next, Colt called Becky out of the room to allow the children individual time alone with their mother. One by one, they went in and sat next to her and shared memories and loving moments. Hope was unexpectedly lucid. Her voice was composed. She had banished to the back of her mind any thought that she would never be in this world again. And when she spoke, she stretched out her hand to touch her children. She looked Cleo and Conrad in the eye and told them that she loved them.

Junior, the last one in, was reluctant. Standing several feet from the bed, he listened to her last words to him.

"All I ever wanted was to love you," she said quietly. "It's a pity that you allow yourself to enjoy anger the way most people enjoy happiness. It's a pity, but I suppose you can't help it. But you might try, because life is long without happiness or love."

"Hush!" he said as he finally moved closer. "Hush, Mom. In your condition, you shouldn't spare one moment worrying about me."

"That's true," she said. "I don't have long to live. But you, Colt Junior, you are young, and you have a long road to travel. I want nothing more for you than a road that leads to love, happiness, and the soulful understanding of mankind."

"I think I understand," he said, and it appeared to her that he finally recognized and accepted that he had been wrong. But when he spoke, she could still hear the dead bitterness in which he lived. "There is no use telling me that," he said. "I'm not going to say I'm sorry for who I am."

Hearing his words, she seemed to lose her remaining strength. He looked away from her, knowing that his words had cut her more deeply than if he had used a sharp knife.

"Listen to me, son, listen while I can still talk with you. Promise me you'll try to learn another way of life. Alcohol, anger, and conflict—they're a dreadful way to live. Promise me?"

"Do you really think it's me who stands in my way?" he asked. "Is the outcome in my hands? Isn't it possible that it might be something more than me?"

To him, it seemed as if the salvation his mother wanted for him depended on whether or not he had the courage to stand between evil and the desire that invents evil. He saw that the same struggle lay everywhere, the same illusion of the happiness of which he had no part. He thought of his sister and brother shining in the radiance of their new loves and of himself without anyone to love. He felt naked. He stared at his own emptiness and saw his attitude where no light exists, and he felt cold. He didn't want to feel cold. The chill of emptiness, where a soulless man stares at the abyss and is afraid to fall was where Junior's soul was. And then, quietly, sweetly, a tiny light began to shine from the idea that light could exist for him, from the idea that happiness might have a place for him, from the idea that his mother was right. He looked at her and felt something very different within his being and said, "I promise you, Mom."

It was time for him to go. He paused and looked back at the figure on the bed. Then, answering the unspoken question in his mother's eyes, he said, "I love you, Mom."

Down in the kitchen, Colt and Becky put ice in Hope's favorite glass and filled it with Mountain Dew. Leaving Becky crying at the kitchen table, Colt slowly climbed the stairs, walked into the bedroom, and sat beside his dying wife.

"Hey, Babe."

"It's okay," she said in a surprisingly strong voice. "You'll see. Everything will turn out for the good."

"Becky told me what she promised you," he said. "She doesn't have the strength to do it, though, so I told her I'd help." He paused and studied her face. "Are you sure this is what you want?"

"I'm sure. Honey, it's time. I'm so tired.... So tired. Colt, do you trust my love for you?"

"Yes. I trust you. I trust the love you have for me."

"That's all I ask."

She rested one hand on his arm and looked up at him and he saw the almost childlike faith in her eyes. Did he have the strength to do what she needed him to do? Not for a moment since he had entered the room this last time had he doubted either his task or his ability to help her meet her end. Her life had come down to this hour. He understood that now. This was what she needed, what she wanted.

Becky finally came in and stood across the bed from Colt. She gave him a look and a wink, and looked down at Hope. "Colt," she said, "I'm so glad she's had you in her life."

Hope nodded. "Becky, you've been my best friend. Except for Colt." She smiled up at him. "Colt, you're a good man."

His eyes blinked rapidly, and he tried to turn away. He had no idea where the courage to do this was going to come from, but now it was time to hand the love of his life the pills that would end her life. He bit the inside of his cheek, and the pain told him this wasn't a nightmare.

"Let me have my pills now, please."

And with that, her voice faded away. She looked up at her husband and her friend. She worked hard to think up some comforting words that she might say to them, but there were no words. What would words mean now? What word among all other words might offer them any understanding of how much relief they were giving her?

Partly because she was a woman, she understood the wisdom of love, and partly because of her recent experiences, she understood that this agony and her love were the two things still anchoring her to this earthly plane. Neither religion nor philosophy was a matter of concern now, for now she was hearing her grandmother's old song. *Where the souls never die...* Was the singing coming from some other plane? It didn't matter. She knew her soul was ready to take flight. With great effort, she lifted her head and kissed Colt, who bent down, crying, and speaking to her in the intimate language that needs no speech.

He handed her the pills, and then Becky handed her her favorite beverage. Becky leaned in and hugged and kissed her on the forehead. "I'll miss you for the rest of my life."

"And I'll miss you until I see you again. Hey! You know what? I'll tell Jim Morrison you said hello."

"Yeah...do that for me."

Hope looked up at Colt again. "I love you, most of all I thank you for a wonderful life. Do you forgive me of all the wrongs I've done?"

"Forgive? There's nothing to forgive. We're clear. I love you and thank you."

"Remember. No regrets."

"No regrets."

"No regrets."

Swallowing the pills and washing them down with her Mountain Dew, Hope gradually let go of all of her personal connection to this world. She was aware that she was slipping away. Her body slowed down, her eyes went out of focus, her senses went quiet. Then a warm feeling came over her, and Mr. Goldsole, who had been in the room most of the day, unseen by everyone but Hope, stepped forward and stood at the foot of her bed. He was holding his hat in his hands.

"Mr. Goldsole," she shouted, startling Colt and Becky. They looked around the room and then at each other. There was no one else in the room, whom on earth was she talking to?

"You've come for me!"

In Hope's eyes, the room began to glow, and Mr. Goldsole was showered with wonderful beams of light. From the light came the Being of Light, holding out a hand.

Mr. Goldsole reached out too. "Come with us, Hope," he said. "Come with us. Let us show you what's on the other side of the Golden Gate."

AUTHOR'S NOTE

*C*ancer. The C-word is probably one of the most terrifying words we can ever hear in terms of our health or the health of our loved ones. Cancer is a force that is hard for most of us to comprehend. It's devious. It strikes at random. Some of us survive it. The process of its energy in our bodies can be mind-boggling.

Earlier in my life, when I was a respiratory therapist and pulmonary technician, I worked with cancer patients. For years, I saw firsthand how cancer doesn't just disrupt the victim's life, but seems to reach out and touch every person who is involved with the person who has the cancer. Once someone is diagnosed with cancer, chaos enters his or her life, and everyone involved feels vulnerable. I've witnessed many patients whose loved ones were in pain because their feelings were suddenly exposed.

Our human mind has no resource to understand what should be done or how it should be done or, worse, when it's time to not do anything. The unpredictability of the illness is the most difficult thing to grasp. Physicians can only go by experience and recommendations from the medical community on how to treat each individual. At the same time, relatives, friends, and lovers of the patient get online and become pseudo-experts and begin doing their best to influence the patient in hopes of saving his or her life. Often, the information overload escalates the chaos.

I've seen patients arguing with their loved ones about what they want and don't want to the point that words are said in anger instead of love. This is sad because what everyone wants is the same—a good outcome. Survival. We fear the death of our loved one, and we fear our own death, too, and sometimes we allow the fear of death to take over to the point that we get angry about simple, silly things. Anger is not the emotion anyone wants or needs when the C-word is claiming a loved one.

Writing this book was a very sentimental experience for me. Hope is a combination of friends I've lost to cancer. When I was seventeen, I met Sara. She was several years older than I was, married, with three children, and full of energy, laughter, and a wonderful positive attitude. When I met her, she had already had a mastectomy that left her feeling unwanted and ugly. Searching for an unobtainable feeling or connection, she had some extramarital affairs. Her husband was a good man, but, unfortunately, her cancer created such fear in him that he was afraid of hurting her physically. Their physical relationship suffered because of it. Who knows where he got that idea? She wasn't fragile, but in his mind he was loving her more by pampering her than anything else he could do. If she wanted anything, he was the first to jump and get it for her. Echoes of their lives are in this story.

Sara and her sisters were remarkable. The cancer was there, and they recognized it, but they approached life in a positive way. They kept having fun. Her sisters made sure that Sara enjoyed every one of her last days, to the point that they even set up some of her affairs. Their intentions were not to hurt Sara's husband or family, but to give Sara a good time and help her feel attractive before the end. Right or wrong, they did it, and I saw Sara smile, laugh, and have fun in her last days.

I therefore dedicate this book to Sara, who I hope lives again today, somewhere under a sunny sky.

I also dedicate this book to my close friend for many years, Mike. Like Sara, he was always smiling and laughing. He had this loud laugh that made everyone near and far take notice. I still miss hearing that laugh. Mike was diagnosed with cancer of the liver and bile duct. I remember that the doctors gave him a year or less to live. I couldn't believe it. Mike didn't look, act, or seem sick in any way. In my experience, cancer patients were ill, very ill, but Mike wasn't. He was still doing everything he wanted to do. As time went on, however, Mike became tired more often and had less energy.

I also remember a young cancer patient I had treated a few years before Mike got cancer. Oddly enough, this patient lived in the same small town as Mike. I asked the patient if he knew my friend Mike. Since it was a small town, I figured it was possible. The patient sat back in his wheelchair and smiled real wide. "He's the guy who owns the sporting goods store, right?"

"Yep," I said. "That would be him. He's one of my very best friends."

The patient laughed. "Sure, I know Mike! You know, when I get depressed about my condition, I mean on my worst days, I'll have someone take me down to his store and I'll park my wheelchair toward the back, so I won't be in anybody's way, and I'll just sit there and listen to Mike talking to people. I tell you, there's no medicine in this world better than laughter. Mike has me laughing all the time."

Mike was like that. I don't remember a time when he was angry or down on life.

"You know," said my patient, "your friend Mike caught on to what I was doing in his store, and you know what he told me?"

"What?" It was hard to imagine or predict anything Mike might do or say.

"He told me that if I wasn't going to buy anything in his shop, he might as well give me a job. So the next time I went back, he grabbed my chair and wheeled me to the counter so I had a front row seat to the daily chitchat. He referred to me as the supervisor."

Another story I like to tell about Mike took place in Las Vegas. Mike had a great fear of heights. He didn't like to get on ladders or anything else that took his feet off the ground. Every year he went to Las Vegas for the Shot Show, which is where the owners of sporting goods stores see the latest and greatest sporting goods. Mike didn't like to gamble much, so he always sought out some unconventional entertainment, like wondering through the pawnshops or whatever the sin city offered. On one occasion Mike looked at the Stratosphere.

"Can you imagine standing on top of that tall-ass building?" he asked out loud.

"You can do more than stand on up there," a passerby said. "They have an amusement park up there, and a ride they call the Big Shot. It's the highest amusement ride in the world."

"Well," said Mike, "I can't think of a better way to get rid of my fear of heights."

And he went to find the Big Shot. He took the elevator to the rooftop, where he found a long line people waiting to board the Big Shot. He got in the line, looking wild-eyed with fear and excitement, but then he saw a sign that read something like, *If you have a heart condition, or are pregnant or have a nervous disorder, step out of line here.* Mike was doing all right until he read that sign. Then he started asking himself what in the hell he was doing way the hell up there. But for whatever reason, he stayed in line.

If you don't know what the Big Shot is, it's a carriage with a seat for two people. The attendants strap the passengers in real tight, and then they launch this carriage up over a hundred feet, sending it a total of 1,081 feet above the ground. The launch is fast, and the passengers shoot up with the impact of four G's on their chests. This is done out in the open so the passengers can see the city below. Someone snapped a picture of Mike just as the carriage launched. It's the perfect picture of fear on a human face. The look on my friend's face is priceless. But the best part of the experience for us watching Mike was after the launch, when he was way up in the air and everyone could hear his loud, boisterous laughter. He laughed all the way back down, too. His laugh was infectious, and everyone waiting in line was laughing, too.

The doctors weren't wrong. He passed away a week short of a year. His funeral was held twice to accommodate all the friends he'd made over the years, also an ex-wife, ex-girlfriends, and his current wife. One thing about Mike is that he never let a day go by that he didn't tell his wife and friends how much they meant to him. He told his wife how much he loved her every day. I was there to hear it sometimes, and it was always nice to hear it said out loud.

His widow is a wonderful woman who was a great balance in his life. She didn't deserve to lose him so early. Some might say they had a long life together, but if you ask her if the eighteen years they were married were long, she would tell you they were way too short. Mike was fifty-one when he passed away, and I can say that he lived several lifetimes in those fifty-one years. For those of us left behind, having had Mike in our lives, we now live with a piece gone from our lives.

You will find bits and pieces of Mike, Sara, and patients I came very close to in this book. I wrote it to try to describe the special moments that exist within dreadful times.

May this book be a positive force in your life as you read it. What is written here comes from my experiences and should in no way influence anyone who is diagnosed with cancer. Nothing in this book should not be considered as medical advice and should not be construed to be a recommendation regarding how to approach treatment.

May the universe bless you and help you to find solace during difficult times.

Let Your Spirit Grow

Ra Lynn

ACKNOWLEDGEMENTS

For this project I would like to SHOUT OUT my gratitude (because "thanks" just isn't enough) to the following: Barbara Ardinger, Ph.D., for her advice and expertise. Jamie Albright for her fun suggestions and talent. Sara McCormick for her humor and, most of all, her amazing cover art. Sherry Wachter for her connection to my work and expression in designing this book. Steve Markle for his artistic approach to rebuilding my website. Pam Grund, fly with the angels, Kathy Rohlfing, Niki Gladys, and Candace Powell at *Reno Magazine* (RGJ) for their innovative help with promotional ideas. Cheri Levenson for her aptitude, spiritual psychology, and soulful love. Doctors Sekhon and Rembetski for their meticulous surgical skills and their ability to repair my spine. I can't thank you enough...I can walk! Jennifer, Kasey, Derek, Sandy, and all my friends at Galena Rehabilitation for their persistence, knowledge of my injury, and ability to work beyond my stubbornness. (I can walk pain free!) The staff at Dr. Sekhon's office, you are so awesome! Also my parents for not discouraging me in my youth from seeing ghosts, talking to angels, and playing with my ancestors. Of course to Kathy, my girlfriend, for her on-going encouragement, support, and love. (As with my other books, this one would not have come to fruition without her.) Patty Thomas for her assistance and advice. Beth and Les for their ongoing friendship and counsel. And last, but not least, many thanks to Christopher and Matthew for cycling with me through the streets of San Francisco and over the Golden Gate.

A B O U T   T H E   A U T H O R

Ra Lynn LoneWalker is also the author of *Shades Of Gray*. He is an eclectic mix of European and Shoshone from The Wind River Reservation in Wyoming. "I'm a storyteller," he explains when asked how he decided to become an author. "I listen to the ancestors, the elders, and the living spirits of nature to help tell my stories. I have white skin, a red soul, and an open mind. It's in this juxtaposition of cultures where the fundamental ideas for my writing are based. Beyond my cultural makeup, my work trickles down from the serendipitous experiences that life seems to consistently bring me. The experiences are gifts that should be shared. The Great Sprit has requested it of me, so it must be."

LoneWalker currently lives in Reno, Nevada. If you would like to learn more about his writing, please visit www.Ralynnlonewalker.com